The Traveling Triple-C

INCORPOREAL CIRCUS

DISCARD

JUL 2 6 2019

Community Library of DeWitt & Jamesville
5110 Jamesville Road
DeWitt, NY 13078

The Traveling Triple-C

INCORPOREAL

CIRCUS

Alanna McFall

Detroit, Michigan

Community Library of DeWitt & Jamesville

The Traveling Triple-C Incorporeal Circus

Text copyright ©2019 by Alanna McFall

This is a work of fiction. Any names, characters, places, events, or incidents are either the product of the author's imagination or are used fictitiously. Any similarities or resemblance to actual persons, living or dead, events, or places, is entirely coincidental.

Cover Art by Estee Chan

Editorial Services by:
Tanya Oemig
Cat Rambo
E.D.E. Bell

Cover Layout and Interior Design by G.C. Bell

All rights reserved. Except as permitted under the US Copyright Act of 1976, no part of this publication may be reproduced, stored in a retrieval system, or transmitted in any form or by any means electronic, mechanical, photocopying, recording, or otherwise, without written permission of the author.

Published by Atthis Arts, LLC
Detroit, Michigan
www.atthisarts.com

ISBN 978-1-945009-34-1

Library of Congress Control Number: 2019932206

To Andrea, Emily, and Dev,
the members of my own personal circus.

Prologue

"I love the gold trim. I'm so glad they went with gold trim instead of that floral stuff. Or that lacy thing Mom was pushing for."

Careful not to slip on the icy sidewalk and fumbling with her phone, Chelsea Shu turned over the card in her other hand. It was heavy stock paper, with elaborate raised type and a metallic sheen on the border that her sister Phoebe was so enamored with. "I didn't think Osric was ever going to let her get away with that. But they really do look perfect." It was the most formal and refined thing she had ever seen her brother produce. She had to assume that it was entirely his fiancée Tamika's doing. "Is it sad that I want to put it on my fridge like it's a drawing from third grade?"

Phoebe snorted. "Do it. And take a picture and send it to him. We need to give him so much shit over how long this took."

"Are you planning on making the entire wedding process a nightmare for them?"

"Only until I get bored or Tamika asks me to stop. We're doing our pestering long distance, so we have to make up for it in quantity."

Chelsea shook her head as she approached the subway station, dodging a few patches of ice as she went. She couldn't wait to get down into the tunnel and strip off her jacket; she'd be sweating into her blouse within minutes. She was convinced there was no way to get through the subways in winter looking good, not in New York. Even if her coworkers kept proving her wrong. "Okay. Well I can help you on Operation Annoying Sisters later. I need to head to work now."

"Fine, fine, though we need something good for Christmas. I'm thinking banners and confetti."

"Whatever, dork. Later." She ended the call and scurried down into the shelter of the tunnel entrance, just as a blast of wind threatened to yank the invitation out of her hands. July in San Francisco was certainly sounding a lot better than December in New York, and she needed to hold onto the reminder.

People packed into Union Square in a seething mass, everyone trying to make their connections as quickly as possible, trailing ice and water on the tiled floors and brushing past the pillars in big whooshing coats. Her high heels clicked and scratched over the salt as she weaved her way towards the Q train, and she had to hope that her boots were still in the office where she had forgotten them on Friday night, before the major snow had hit. There was no way she wanted to get home in these heels.

On the platform, Chelsea pulled the card back out of her pocket as she walked along, dodging past commuters and a homeless woman huddled on a bench. Her heel snagged on an edge of the woman's blanket, but she shook it free and kept walking without taking her eyes off of the paper.

YOU ARE CORDIALLY INVITED TO THE JOINING OF
TAMIKA JEFFERS AND OSRIC SHU
IN MATRIMONY.

THE CEREMONY WILL BE HELD ON
JULY 31ST IN SAN FRANCISCO CITY HALL.

Further details and instructions were written in smaller type at the bottom, the usual matters of times and what dinner you wanted and how many people you were going to bring with you. Chelsea would have to call over lunch and see if Heather had gotten her own invitation or not; she had been friends with Osric before she and Chelsea started dating, over five years ago now. She probably had her own invitation, all things considered, and it wasn't like there was much risk of Chelsea bringing someone else as her plus-one. Maybe another friend who wanted to score a trip to California.

She knew that Phoebe had her big plans to tease Osric, but Chelsea was honestly more proud than anything. Her goofy little brother was growing up. With an equally goofy woman, yes, but one who brought out the best in him. And he brought out the best in her. Chelsea had never seen her brother so— It was not that he was the happiest he had ever been when he was with Tamika. It was that he seemed the most *together*, the most whole.

Like everything fell into place when she was by his side. And to declare that to the world, in a big ceremony, for the whole family to see? Chelsea couldn't be happier for him if she tried. She skipped her way around a pack of tourists, barely glancing up from the flowing typeface. She could hear the rumbling of the Q coming down the express track, going slowly to take heed of the over-packed platform.

She had to get them a good present. Not just something utilitarian or bland. She could ask Heather for ideas later, or they could do a big gift from the two of them. Tamika would be more thrilled to get a new set of wireless controllers for their consoles than a set of good china. Chelsea could subtly ask them what their favorite games were when they visited for Christmas. Or just ask Osric directly, and count on him forgetting she had said anything by the time the wedding rolled around. The train lights illuminated the tinsel on a particularly exuberant Santa's hat next to her.

Chelsea was halfway to planning nerdy baby-themed gifts to wind Osric up, when she stepped onto the yellow warning strip in order to avoid a group of carolers trudging down the middle of the platform (at rush hour, for god's sake). She was too busy trying to avoid getting hit in the face with sheet music to notice the patch of ice on the textured pavement. And Chelsea Shu had never really been good in her high heels. The train lumbered into the station.

They always seemed slow when she was waiting for them, but it was suddenly clear that the trains moved pretty fast from this perspective, when the lights were shining directly in her face. Her legs were kicked out towards the platform, as if she could find purchase mid-fall if she just reached hard enough. Her arms swung out for balance, and she was still holding the card in her right hand. Her last thought was that she did not want to drop it into the muddy water pooled on the bottom of the tracks.

She could perhaps be forgiven for having her priorities out of order. It was her little brother's wedding, after all.

And then she was gone.

1.

Two Years Later

"They set another date. I . . . for the wedding. They set another date for the wedding. It's finally happening. Osric and Tamika." Phoebe wiped at the stream running down her face and cleared her throat. "I just thought someone should tell you. It's finally happening."

The headstone did not respond. Phoebe shifted her weight and toyed with the petals of the roses in her hands. One bruised and smeared across her gloves and she stopped abruptly.

"August 5th, this time. They wanted close to the original, but not . . . you know. Some bad stigma to the first one they had . . ."

She looked around the cold expanses of the cemetery. The grey stones rose out of the snow like chains of islands, connected but distinct. "They're going to be up here for Christmas. They wanted to come for today, but work got in the way. I'm sure you understand . . . would have understood."

The graves were silent and still around her. There were not many mourners two weeks before Christmas. She took a deep breath of the bracing air and continued her solitary monologue.

"You know, if anyone ever doubted that they were serious—and you remember Aunt Hua, saying they were just dumb kids—well, they've all shut up now. No one could watch what they've been for each other these two years and not know that they're in it for the long haul. Without her, I don't think Osric . . ." Phoebe took a deep breath. "There were a lot of times he wasn't really holding it together. At all. Tamika got him through it. They deserve . . . they need some time to be happy."

Her words choked off into muffled sobs into the sleeve of her plush black winter coat. The roses hung at an angle, spilling a few petals to the ground. She took a deep gulp of air and looked back at the stone in front of her.

Here lies Chelsea Da-Xia Shu,
beloved sister, daughter, friend and loved one.

APRIL 19, 1985 – DECEMBER 11, 2012

Loving memories last forever.

"I miss you, Chelsea." She broke off again, face buried back in her coat. She didn't confront the cold air again until she was composed. She laid the flowers next to the headstone, beside the fresh ones left by others over the course of the day. Next to them she placed a card, gold trim along the borders. "I love you, sis. And I miss you."

She turned and walked out of the graveyard without another word.

Sitting on top of the headstone, Chelsea Shu watched her sister go.

"Love you too, Phoebe. I miss you."

Phoebe did not pause.

2.

Chelsea sat and watched the graveyard as light snow began to fall.

Her parents had really chosen a beautiful location to bury her, even if it was all the way out in Brooklyn. But she didn't have anywhere urgent to be for the rest of the day, so there was no harm in a leisurely walk back over the bridge, rather than over the water. She was not fond of having waves splash through her, and the afternoon wind was picking up. She could stroll back across the bridge, perhaps catch a few movies, then visit Central Park before it got too dark.

All in all, not a terrible way to spend an anniversary. She didn't know why other ghosts panicked so much about them.

She stood up from her headstone, or rather went from hovering in a sitting position to hovering in an upright position. She stretched her arms above her head out of habit and let them flop back to her sides, right arm hanging as bent and smashed as ever. Her head began to list to one side and she pushed it back into its original position.

Others kept telling her that she would stop caring about it soon, about being the poster child for closed casket funerals, but perhaps it was one of those things you couldn't really wait for; it would happen the moment you stopped waiting. Her fingers grazed over the pulpy meat of the right side of her head, the shards of bone and the spots where her short spiky hair clung to the wound. She shivered at the tingles it shot through her. She had moved past revulsion a few months back, at least, and now just enjoyed being able to feel something.

She took off across the fields, skimming on top of the snow and passing through the stones. It was easier than walking through buildings or people; at hip height, she could almost pretend she was walking around or stepping over them, rather than letting her legs melt through the marble and granite. Her high heels hovered just over the snow, leaving no footprints or traces. She avoided the marks of Phoebe's boots, which mingled with the trail carved out by her parents in the morning, deepened by Grandma and her cane later in the day. Heather had come later, alone. She and Phoebe might have crossed paths as they were leaving.

Chelsea stepped past a large stone angel and a big grey tomcat yowled and took a swipe at her, its paw passing through her ankle. She stopped and knelt down to smile at the bundle of hissing fur and fury. For all that the cat was angry, it was nice to be noticed by something living. She knew almost every kennel and vet's office in the city had at least one ghost that haunted it for the sake of the cats, and she couldn't blame them. The tom's fur flattened as it calmed down, but it still glared.

There was a reason she had never been a cat person in life. But until a big friendly Labrador managed to tap into the ether and see between worlds too, she would make do. She bid the cat farewell and continued with her walk.

As she followed the path of city streets, she kept off to the side so that cars whipped past her instead of through. Usually the receptive only shuddered when they walked through a ghost, momentarily aware that something was amiss, before brushing it off and going about their daily lives. But she had seen particularly attuned people stop walking in the street when a spirit passed through them, as if they had been lightly shocked. The last thing she wanted was to cause a car crash because a receptive driver passed through her at the wrong moment.

Walking the Brooklyn Bridge was boring when one took away the parts that made it interesting: the feel of the wind, the smell of the sea, the taste of the salt. She wished she could slip into a cab and let it carry her back to Manhattan, but it didn't work like that. She could climb into as many cars as she wanted, but when they started moving, there would be nothing to keep her inside. The back of the car would pass right through and leave her where she was in the slush.

Nothing to do but walk. Chelsea let her mind drift as she sailed over the dirty mountain ranges of salt and snow.

It was about time that Tamika and Osric got married. They'd put it off for far too long on her account. Under any other circumstances, Osric would have been giving her the guilt trip of a lifetime, in a hypothetical world where she still had a lifetime. But these were the actual circumstances, and she didn't have any say in it. She was not the one living it, the one having to make decisions about what was best for herself and her loved ones. She was an observer in her own family. And she had heard all of the horror stories and warnings during her afterlife. Being so close, but so very, very far away, could drive a spirit mad.

Chelsea shook her head on her wobbling, snapped neck and kept moving forward, towards the sweeping skyline of Manhattan before her. She had that to be happy about. For a city to haunt, it was still one of the best options out there.

👣 👣 👣

"I told you not to go. Going to your grave on an anniversary cannot lead to anything good. An anniversary is just another day on the calendar, and you have to start seeing it that way."

Chelsea resisted the urge to groan at Carmen. She knew she shouldn't have mentioned it. "Come on, it's only my second. I think I deserve a little leeway."

Carmen's lips pursed and she flicked her dark braid over her shoulder. A stocky Latina woman with a hard face, she had not been too far into her thirties when she died more than forty years ago now. In the theater's darkness, her outline glowed to Chelsea's eyes, distorting the image of the teenage couple visible through her. "It is a slippery slope. It is so easy to start obsessing when you give special weight to certain dates. Let them all ease by, day after day, one after another. Do not tie yourself to any one space or time."

Chelsea drummed her fingers on her lap and watched the screen lighting up with the opening credits of the action movie.

She chanced a glance at Carmen out of the corner of her eye. "Like getting to a movie theater on opening day?" she wheedled.

Carmen shoved her hand through Chelsea's head, making her squirm and shudder. Being touched by another ghost caused sensations far stronger than interacting with the living.

"Hey!"

"Do not be cute. Seeing your family is different and you know it. Unless you were related to Vin Diesel and never told me." Carmen pulled her hand back out and crossed her arms. They just covered the cluster of bullet holes centered in her chest. "Now shush, I want to see this. Plenty of others are playing here if you are bored."

Chelsea closed her mouth and watched the explosions lighting up the screen. They could talk as loud as they wanted, of course; it wasn't like they would be bothering any paying customers. But Carmen had a thing about movies. And concerts, and plays, and operas, and TV shows, and poetry readings, and anything where someone was performing for long periods of time with no need for audience participation or interaction. Video games were never going to take off with the ghost community.

Apparently languages had been Carmen's thing for her first two decades, then college lectures last decade, and movies for the last eight years or so. Chelsea wondered how long it would take her to develop trends for how she filled her days and nights. Not that any other ghost in the city seemed to have them. Carmen was just weird.

They floated in silence in the back row, next to the teenagers, who were far more involved in each other than in the film. The only time Carmen made a noise was to click her tongue and shake her head at the knot of limbs and mouths that had started as two people. For all that she spoke about forgetting family, Chelsea didn't think Carmen would ever grow out of being a mother type. She had probably been a mother as a kid, and having her own children just formalized the inevitable. But she watched the flashy car chases and gun fights with rapt attention, her dark eyes wide open as she took it all in. There were real advantages to not having to blink.

The movie finally came to a close, and they drifted out through the walls as everyone else shuffled and trudged their way out of the theater. Good night-vision and not getting stiff from sitting still: two more perks of being dead. Carmen continued straight into the next theater for a showing of a new romantic comedy, but one movie was more than enough for Chelsea. She could not do the twenty-four hour (or on occasion, week-long) marathons that the older ones were able to pull off. She still had a more or less human mindset, and the attention span that came with it.

The oldest ghosts in the city took pride in not being tied to human limitations. They forgot about gravity, about walking, about boundaries, and would soar through buildings and people without a care, moving faster than they ever could have when alive. Chelsea was a baby in their eyes, still going through the motions of walking and staying at ground level when she didn't have to.

In Chelsea's own mind, she was still a human, so she acted like it, for better or worse. She was looking forward to being able to zip around at superhuman speeds someday. Assuming she stuck around that long.

She headed back into the streets, watching shoppers carrying big bags of holiday gifts, and commuters grumbling as they tried to get around them. A little girl with a reindeer headband skipped through Chelsea and paused, looking confused. But the mother tugged her receptive daughter through the crowded sidewalks and they were gone. One more sliver of a family going about their lives, unaware of the whole other reality they danced through every day and ignored completely.

Carmen had been onto something about anniversaries: Chelsea was not usually half this introspective. She needed to be noticed, to be looked at and seen by someone other than another ghost or a feral cat. She needed assurance that she still existed, in whatever form it might be. She pointed herself towards Central Park and started walking.

3.

The closer Chelsea got to the park, the more of her fellow ghosts were mixed in with the crowd. Some walked on the street like her, others zipped above people's heads like plastic bags caught in the wind. But Chelsea walked, and didn't get a view of the performance until she was almost right on top of it, emerging into the circle with one person in the center. One person and a handful of ghosts.

A young black woman jumped around on the pavilion, entertaining the crowd. An oval of stark white paint stood out on the performer's dark face. Little black triangles above and below her eyes emphasized even the smallest expressions, though her face was plenty flexible on its own. Fistfuls of shoulder-length dreadlocks were tied into pigtails, high above the collar of her striped black and white shirt. Her motions were energetic and emphatic, from the top of her head, down her chubby body, and to the tips of her toes. Black paint over her lips contorted as she grinned, groaned, yelped and sobbed, all in total silence.

Two years ago, Chelsea had no idea that there were any real mimes still out there. She'd seen them in movies and comedies plenty of times, but portrayed as ridiculous figures, relics of performance styles long since dead. Chelsea had no idea where this woman in her twenties had picked up such an old style, when she would have only ever seen parodies. But when Cyndricka performed, there was no irony, no self-consciousness. Every twisted face, every flailing limb, every epic tumble was put on with the utmost sincerity and artistry.

Chelsea watched as she flailed her arms and chased some

imaginary thing running away from her at approximately hip height. If the balloon dogs being clutched by the small children at the edge of the circle were anything to go by, this was her dog walker performance, a little story about her taking care of a rich woman's dog and having to chase it through the streets when it escaped.

The balloon animals at her feet weren't really the only clue. The ghost on its hands and knees, crawling away and laughing hysterically, was also a hint. The man's head was bald and his eyes deep and hollowed, and the only thing wrapped around his unearthly body was a hospital robe. But the laugh that echoed out of his empty lungs was deep and booming while Cyndricka chased him.

A teenage ghost with a knife wound in his gut stood at the edge of the circle, arms crossed over his chest and a mean scowl on his face. When the "dog" ran past him, the teenager held out a hand, and Cyndricka skidded to a stop, eyes wide and shocked. People in the crowd chuckled at her huge gestures, the way she pointed with her whole body after the dog, trying to dodge around her play-pretend foe. The teenage ghost pointed to something on his chest: an imaginary badge, and his hand rested on his belt in a mimic of a cop tapping his baton. The ghosts in the audience laughed a beat before the humans did, getting the invisible joke before Cyndricka had time to react to it, raising her hands in front of her and backing away slowly.

She shoved her hands in her pockets as she turned and walked away, shoulders rounded and face twisted downward in a picture of sadness and disappointment. She kicked at an imaginary rock and took a swing at the empty air. But when she jammed her hands back, her eyes went wide and she stood bolt upright, thrilled at a discovery in the depths of her pockets. Pulling it out, she held her empty hand in front of her face. Both living and dead audiences watched, waiting for the reveal, as she held the item close to her ear. A quick squeeze of her fingers and the elation in her painted face made it clear that a squeaky toy was going to be her ticket out of the mess she had found herself in.

Children giggled and waved their balloon dogs, adults laughed softly, and the ghosts broke out in cheers and screams, wild hoots and hollers that went unheard by the rest of the crowd. Chelsea was right along with them: she had seen this performance plenty of times, but it was easy to get caught up in the fun all over again. And to give Cyndricka the encouragement that the humans were too dignified to allow.

Armed with her squeaky toy, Cyndricka traveled around the circle in hot pursuit of the dog. She bent down and held the toy before her in a plea, squeezing it to bring in the wayward animal. Chelsea watched as she tried to attract the dog, ended up with a lot of additional dogs played by yipping ghosts on their hands and knees, and ended up swarmed by the otherworldly pack. The audience of the living ebbed and changed over the course of the show, and plenty of people glanced on their way past and kept walking, but the ghosts were there to stay. Cyndricka was a celebrity to the dead residents of New York.

The story came to its conclusion as she led the original dog back to its owner, played by a little girl ghost with an eternal black eye and a ring of bruises around her neck, trying her best to look stuffy and haughty when she took the offered leash from Cyndricka, who looked over the top of her head to maintain the illusion of speaking to an adult.

The girl looked scandalized when Cyndricka kept trying to offer her more and more dogs, handing over a fist full of leashes, one after the other, while grinning at the girl with earnest desperation. She grabbed for them wildly when the girl shoved them back at her chest, and Cyndricka sighed and let the pack of dogs pull her in the other direction. She reached out a desperate hand to retrieve the reward for her hard work, then scrambled to catch it when the girl tossed it into the air. One final leap let her grab the imaginary money before it hit the ground, and she held up her prize triumphantly. It transitioned smoothly when she grabbed her battered bowler hat from the edge of the stage area, and circled around the gathered crowd, still pulled by her imaginary dog as she held out her hat for donations.

The assembled ghosts cheered their hearts out as the humans tossed in a few handfuls of spare change and wandered away. Her meager earnings collected, Cyndricka came back to the center of the circle to take a bow, and to let her ghostly assistants take their bows. She held hands, as well as beings who can't touch each other can, with the chemo patient on one side, who held on to the stabbing victim in turn, and the strangled child on the other, with all of the additional dog actors next to her. They all raised and dropped their arms in one giant bow.

And all that the humans saw was one human woman, bowing by herself, all alone, after finishing a single, solitary performance.

4.

Chelsea hung behind as the human crowds dispersed and Cyndricka packed away her things. The sun was setting over Central Park. Several of the ghosts clapped her on the back as she wiped away her makeup with a dirty cloth, and pulled a heavy winter coat over her black and white shirt. In the summer, Chelsea knew, she just ducked behind bushes to change after performances, trying to keep her miming clothes as clean as possible, but in the winter, she needed to stay bundled up. Even for someone who bounced around and worked as hard as she did, the winter wind could cut through the thin layer in an instant.

Cyndricka glanced up and smiled as Chelsea got close, waving to her excitedly. Her performing cast meandered away to go about the rest of their nights, haunting wherever they saw fit, or just taking in the Christmas lights twinkling in the growing darkness. A few wandered off into the trees, seeking some solitude after so much interaction in one day. Chelsea said hello to a few of them, but Cyndricka was who she really wanted to see.

She hovered next to the young woman. Without her makeup, Cyndricka looked much younger, the wide-eyed, round-cheeked twenty-something suddenly visible past the confident performer. She grinned with wild abandon, showing off her crooked teeth, and a passerby hurried to walk past the strange woman beaming at the empty air.

"That was a great show, Cyndricka," Chelsea gushed. "I swear, the tumbles in that one were some of the best I've seen yet. And when Maggie did that big leap on you, and you dropped like a rock? I can't believe the humans didn't clap harder."

Cyndricka looked away and waved her hand at Chelsea to brush away the compliment, but a happy smile twisted her mouth. She pulled on her gloves, thin enough to sign through, and nodded her head at Chelsea, a question in her eyes and raised eyebrows.

"Oh, I'm doing well," Chelsea said. "Bit of a slow day. I . . . well, you see—"

She considered her words for a moment, debating whether or not to share. Whether to make a big deal about it, marking the day on the calendar, as Carmen said. "Today is actually my second anniversary. My death anniversary. Deathversary, I guess."

She was glad that she had told her, by the way that Cyndricka's eyes lit up. Turning to face Chelsea completely, she mimed pulling a birthday cake out of her bag. She carefully lit two invisible candles and held the platter out to Chelsea. Chelsea laughed and leaned forward, blowing nonexistent breath at imaginary candles sticking out of invisible cake. Cyndricka clapped her hands, after setting the cake safely out of the way.

"Thank you, Cyndricka. Not that I could really do much with cake these days."

Not like I have cake to give, she signed with a wry smile. She moved her hands slowly, giving Chelsea time to pick up each word and phrase as she made it before moving onto the next. Chelsea's grasp on American Sign Language was still shaky. *Did you do anything for the day?*

"I went to visit my grave. Saw my family while I was there, and a couple friends. It was nice."

Cyndricka gave her a thumbs-up, one of the only signs Chelsea would have been able to get before her death. She didn't think she was ever going to pick up languages as quickly or voraciously as Carmen did, but there was something to be said for the strides in ASL she had gained in the year and a half since she had met Cyndricka. Not having to sleep or eat or take breaks made full-immersion learning more literal; she had spent plenty of days lurking in the back of language classes when Cyndricka wasn't available to help her out.

"Oh, and my sister came by. You'll never guess what I found out."

Cyndricka tapped a finger on her chin for a moment, face

scrunched up in exaggerated thought. She swooped her hand out in front of her belly to illustrate a big curve.

"No, no one's pregnant."

Cyndricka stuck out her tongue in concentration, then perked up and drew an imaginary veil down over her eyes and held her clasped hands in front of her with a bouquet.

"Yeah, my little brother's getting married! He and his fiancée were supposed to do it almost a year and a half ago, but they put it off for my—well, you know. But now it's finally happening!"

Cyndricka jumped up and clapped her hands, frightening the hell out of a couple pushing a stroller past her. She made as if she was grabbing Chelsea's hands and mimed spinning her around in a circle. Chelsea gladly went along with it, her hands tingling just the slightest bit at the points where Cyndricka touched them. Not as much as they would with another ghost, but just strong enough to feel. This result was far more satisfying than Carmen's reaction; Chelsea wanted to celebrate. She wanted to have a reason to celebrate, not something to fill her days and tick off time.

"Thank you. I'm really happy for him too. I just wish I could go see it." Cyndricka quirked an eyebrow, and Chelsea elaborated. "They live in San Francisco. He went out there for college, met Tamika, and never ended up moving back. They'll be here for Christmas, though, so it won't be a complete loss."

Cyndricka nodded and went back to packing up her things. She would need to find somewhere warm to stay for the night.

"Are you going to a shelter?" Chelsea asked. When the nights got especially bitter, Cyndricka spent her time in one of the city's women's shelters, usually with a ghost or two along to guard her things and wake her up if someone else tried to steal them. But Cyndricka shook her head and fished a battered Metrocard out of her pocket. Chelsea sighed.

"Fair enough. Did you find it, or did someone toss it in your hat?"

Cyndricka tipped an invisible hat and watched Chelsea's expression. She shoved the card back in her pocket to have full use of both hands. *Do you want me to stay above ground tonight? Celebrate your anniversary, and your brother's wedding?*

Chelsea shook her head. "No, I wouldn't ask you to do that, not when it looks this cold." And Chelsea wouldn't go down into those subways. Not again. "Find a nice bench down in the tunnels, stay warm, try to get something to eat. I'll talk to you tomorrow."

Cyndricka reached out to mimic the act of gripping Chelsea's arm, but of course it didn't connect. It never really would. Cyndricka was alive and Chelsea was dead.

Good night, Coat, she signed. *Be well.*

Chelsea had to smile at her nickname. Rather than having to sign full names, to fingerspell out C-H-E-L-S-E-A, Cyndricka gave people nicknames, usually starting with the same letter as their actual names and having something to do with them. She had been so entertained by Chelsea's big winter coat when they met in the middle of June that the nickname had stuck.

At this time of year, it was Carmen in her 70's sundress and sandals that looked out of place, with the gaudy floral pattern that had earned her the name Curtains. While she didn't get hot in the summer and her feet never got sore, she would've liked to switch out the winter coat, pencil skirt, and high heels for jeans and sneakers: the sort of things she wore when she was comfortable at home. Death had caught her at her most formal and left her that way.

Cyndricka waved her goodbye, and bid a good evening to a few more ghosts as she walked towards the nearest subway stop. She would be relatively safe in the tunnels for the night, even if Chelsea was eternal proof of just how dangerous they could be. She couldn't bring herself to go down there these days, but she was glad that Cyndricka would be warm.

She watched the knitted cap's top, patched and dirty, disappear down the stairs. Chelsea could only think of how many times she'd brushed past women like Cyndricka, a million times in all the years she had lived in the city.

Her parents had moved to New York when she was thirteen, and she had started out shocked by the homeless population, decorating the streets and subways, trying to find some peace anywhere, begging for money in the trains. She had been horrified by how everyone brushed past them, and had fished out her bright pink wallet whenever she had any change in it.

But the years had gone on, and she had stopped noticing, losing some empathy as she got older. If there was someone looking particularly desperate, she would fish out a dollar, but even then, she didn't know anyone. She didn't speak to anyone. She just pitied them. For all that she had thought she was a good person, the homeless were one more part of the landscape of the city to her, as constant and unremarkable as the pigeons or the rats. Now she had the time to see them, to witness them going about their lives and trying to make their ways in a world that didn't care.

And one, a strange, mute mime in the middle of Central Park, was among the most unique people in New York—in the entire world, perhaps. Because no one else Chelsea had ever met or talked to, no ghost of any age or from any era, had ever met another human who could see them. Cyndricka Danvers was, from all evidence, the only human out there that could see ghosts. She was a pariah in one world and a celebrity in another, and, Chelsea liked to think, a friend. A friend that Chelsea never would have noticed in a million years if it hadn't been for the patch of ice and that train exactly two years ago.

She kept moving. Her anniversary wouldn't be done for another six hours, and that was a lot of night to fill. She could go back to the theater and find Carmen, join her for another movie. She could drift to any of the various Christmas shows and concerts going on across the city. She could find a particularly interesting group of humans and follow them, using them as a living soap opera, as so many ghosts did. She could sit in on a college course, or a family dinner, or float above a neighborhood and try to pick up a new language by listening to conversations. Her Mandarin was getting rusty; she could go haunt Chinatown for a bit, or try to start in on Spanish, Japanese, Italian, Arabic, Farsi, Korean, any language that was being spoken by a group of New Yorkers at any given moment. She could watch a television in someone's home, listen to the radio in a parked car, follow carolers on their way as they bid welcome to a Christmas that she would never really celebrate again. The city was huge and at her disposal, for as long as she wanted. Chelsea Shu had all the time in the world now. Just no desire to use it.

Her mind was already in San Francisco.

Chelsea didn't dream at night. She did not sleep, so there was no time when her mind was really that rested and relaxed, no physical brain to throw together images and memories when she wasn't looking. But sometimes at night, when everything was absolutely still and calm, her mind would drift enough to let her be immersed in her thoughts, to take her back to people and places so strongly that it felt like she was almost there. She would find quiet places, occasionally, nooks and crannies of the bustling city. And she would let her mind go.

Her family was always the first destination for her mind at times like this. She remembered everyone so vividly that it was almost like she was there again. Phoebe bouncing around, bold and proud, and bringing her little sister and brother along every step of the way. Phoebe had been different after the funeral, finally hit by something hard enough to leave a dent, but everything before that had washed off her back. She had been inspiring to Chelsea, something for her to want to grow into, even if she was only two years behind. But by the time she was there, Phoebe was two more years ahead, so she always had a new goal to keep her moving.

And Osric, caught as the only boy, but no more prized or respected for that. They were all so close in age that gender barely divided them, just a side note like how Chelsea was the shortest and Phoebe had the biggest feet. Nothing real could have come between them. College sent them in different directions in quick succession, but a phone call or an email wasn't too large a distance. Through Osric, Chelsea had known about Heather years before she met her, the friend of her little brother that was there to keep him in line when the big sisters were away. And visits home were always included in their lives, to bring them back to the arms of Mom and Dad: Mom at her tailoring business, Dad at his lectures, but both of them there when she needed them.

Nothing smaller than death could have separated the Shu

family. So it did. Her thoughts would always bring her back there, to the funeral, to the sights of her loved ones in tears, her siblings in shambles, her mother crying like her arm had been cut off. So much suffering from her loved ones, all because she didn't know how to walk in high heels.

Chelsea didn't let herself fall into this dreamlike state often, because she knew it would always find her back here. But the good memories almost made it worth it. Or so she told herself.

Until her mind dipped even darker, the more recent memories that filled the hazy days immediately after her death. When she had wandered the streets of the city, alone and confused, crying out for anyone to notice her, to listen. When she had raged at the commuters ignoring her as they went about their days, screaming into unhearing ears with lungs that no longer needed air. *Why was she here,* she demanded to know, *what was the point of this?* Not even the other ghosts seemed to have answers. Not everyone who died lingered on, or New York would have been filled to the brim with ancient spirits, but there was no rhyme or reason for those left behind. Only rumors and gossip about how some "moved on."

Through all these hazy and distorted memories, one stood out clearly. The night she had seen the beast lurking over the water underneath the Brooklyn Bridge.

She had looked out at it from the shore, the pale, distorted figure standing on top of the waves without a boat. But as light and weightless as it seemed on top of the water, it looked solid when the waves splashed into it, scattering around its long legs. It had turned burning eyes to her, gazing from one hundred yards away to look straight into her eyes on the shore. Its glance felt like it shot sparks of electricity through her and she'd fled back into the comfort of buildings and living humans. She had been so caught up in her own grief, buried in her own tears, that later she had doubted that she had ever actually seen it.

It was only the similar stories from her undead peers that convinced her she wasn't mad. They all knew there was at least one poltergeist in the city, one of those distorted beasts that used to be a human soul. And as far as they were concerned, one was more than enough.

When her thoughts arrived back at the poltergeist, she knew that there wouldn't be any more good dreams for the rest of the night, just a slow spiral down into thoughts that clawed at the inside of her head and left her feeling hollow by the time the daylight hit.

She had to find something to fill her mind, fill her eyes, to provide a distraction. For all that she was overzealous, Carmen knew what to do. She always had. They had met that night, when Chelsea had run away from the shore at the sight of the beast. Carmen had taken the time to slowly and deliberately coax her back into reason, and they had been together ever since. She had acquaintances among the other ghosts, spirits that she saw around, but Carmen was probably her only real undead friend.

Chelsea exited her alleyway while a clock outside a bank shone two in the morning. Carmen would be in a club, probably, or a late-running concert. And as always, Chelsea had more than enough time to check them all.

5.

Four months passed in the city, and New York thawed into a drippy April. In that time, Chelsea came to a decision.

"I think I need to go."

"Where?" Carmen narrowed her eyes at Chelsea. She was already in a surly mood because the band playing on the stage, with its thumping beat and heavy bass, was nowhere near her tastes. Of course, never mind mentioning to her that they could just leave. No, Carmen would sit through anything that took up her time, no matter how obnoxious she found it.

"I think I need to go to San Francisco for my brother's wedding." She had to shout over the music, but Carmen clearly heard her.

Carmen was full-out glaring at her now, and not just because there was a twenty-something moshing in the middle of her torso. "You know what I'm going to say to that."

"Yeah, but I just feel like—"

"It is a stupid idea, and you are going to drive yourself mad."

"Okay, yes, that's what I thought you were going to say. But Carmen, this is important to—"

"Do you realize how close you were to becoming a wailer when I found you? When I first stumbled across you, I thought you already were one. But no, you've managed to keep in your own head all this time. I'm proud of you, but I am not going to wish you well as you throw all of your hard work away. Not to mention mine."

Chelsea sighed and turned back to the band. She had known this was going to be the course of the conversation, but she still wasn't prepared. "I'm not a wailer."

"You aren't *now*. But after two weeks wandering alone, in a cornfield in the middle of Kansas in the summer sun, thinking about nothing except how much you miss your family? You're not going to give up and start screaming at the sky then?"

Carmen planted her hands on her hips and gave her an incredibly stern look, the sort that convinced Chelsea that there was no way that their living ages had only been five years apart. Carmen had four decades of death on her, but it was still baffling. A man spilled a glass of beer through her torso, but Carmen didn't break her gaze.

"I'll have a goal in mind," Chelsea argued. "I'll be going towards something, with a definite deadline and endpoint. It's not like I'm going to be wandering aimlessly across the length of the country, haunting little towns for the fun of it."

"No, you will be obsessing about a family milestone that you cannot really participate in. Even if you are at your brother's wedding, you will not be a part of the wedding. And that is going to hurt. You are not doing a great job at convincing me."

"You make it sound like I need to convince you."

Carmen pursed her lips and scowled. In the strobing lights of the concert going on around them, Chelsea thought she noticed something strange about her eyes, a flash in the circles of darkness, the hazy color that she assumed had once been dark brown. But in a moment, the flash was gone, replaced only by maternal judgment and disappointment.

"Are you really not going to take my feelings and advice into any consideration, after all that I have done for you?"

Chelsea looked away at those words.

"I'm grateful to you, Carmen," she said, watching the dirty floor, garbage illuminated in the flashing lights. "I really am. You didn't need to help me out and give me as much as advice as you did. But I . . . he's my little brother. We're . . . we were a very close family. They all still are. And I can't know that I missed a big day in his life, when there was nothing stopping me from being there."

She glanced up at the dead woman who had done so much for her since she had first found herself wandering New York, newly dead and afraid. "You have to understand that. Don't you?"

Not saying a word, Carmen held her gaze. She drummed her fingers against her sides and watched Chelsea with critical eyes.

The way she stood made her bullet holes more prominent. Five shots, all in between her breasts, with perfect grouping. The blood had run all the way down the front of her sundress before she died, and stayed with her over all of the years. She was a terrifying sight, to be sure. She was also one of the best friends that Chelsea had.

Carmen jerked her head and motioned towards the exit. "This place is terrible. Let's talk where there is some actual peace and quiet."

"You don't want to stay for the band?"

"I need my full attention for this."

They walked into the night air, followed by the thumping of drums and the squeal of an over-eager guitar. It still astounded Chelsea how different a concert felt when you couldn't feel the thumping of the music in your chest, when you only had the aural and not the physical to work off of.

The night was light and breezy, with the outfits on the humans indicating that the weather was warm for April. Carmen made her way away from the concert, down an alley, and ambled through the dark streets.

"I do not think it is a wise idea," she said after some time, her voice soft. Her Mexican accent, preserved over all of the years and all the different languages she had learned, lilted in the quieting air. "There's a lot of empty land between the coasts, some places with only a few ghosts, if any at all. When I left Boston to come to New York forty years ago, the trip was nearly unbearable, and that was a fraction of what you are talking about. That much solitude is not good for anyone."

"If I walk there in a straight line, never stopping, it should only take me about a month and a half. I can power through it, and then San Francisco has to have a decent-sized population of the dead. Any big city, really."

"You would be surprised," she said. "Some places are more at peace than others. Not everywhere in the world is as busy as the city, and the dead group together. And what will you do afterwards? Will you stay there and haunt your brother?"

Chelsea shook her head. "No. I don't haunt my family here, and I wouldn't do that to Osric. Even if he wouldn't know, he . . . he and Tamika deserve their privacy. And their time away from me. It sounds like they've been under my shadow for a while."

"So why is it okay to be at their wedding?"

Chelsea winced and wrapped her arms around herself. Or her one good arm, at least. "I . . ." She choked back a sob and tears that would never come. "Weddings are for family. Right?"

Carmen gestured Chelsea into her arms without another word. The surface of Chelsea's body lit up with tingles, but she leaned into the embrace all the same, the outline of her body phasing slightly into Carmen's. Carmen petted a hand over her short spiky hair, the haircut she had hated but was now stuck with for all time. "Shh, shh. Yes, they are, Chelsea. It is a celebration of life, and of two families becoming one. My wedding is one of my most precious memories, with my Manuel." She held Chelsea to her bloody chest and shushed her quiet, tear-less crying. "I'm sorry. You are right. But I still think you are going about it wrong."

Chelsea pulled back to look into Carmen's eyes. She glowed in the dark of the alleyway; Chelsea knew they both did. "What am I supposed to do differently?"

Carmen gave her a wry little smile. "You will not go alone. If you are going to take this foolish trip, then I am going with you."

It was not the most dignified moment of her life or her death, but when Chelsea curled forward and let herself sob, she was glad that there was someone there to hear her.

6.

They could have set out that very night, but even in death, Chelsea could not forget her mother's pre-vacation organizational sprees. "Shouldn't we, you know, prepare something?" she asked the next morning. "Isn't that what you do before a trip?"

"Like what? Do you have bags to pack? Reservations to double-check? A book to bring with you on the airplane?" Carmen clicked her tongue at Chelsea's foolishness. "The only possible thing you could do would be to learn to fly very quickly, and I have never seen a ghost younger than a decade master that. So we are going to start running, and not stop, day or night, until we are there. There is literally nothing else to it. What on earth would you prepare?"

Chelsea gave a lopsided shrug that swayed her head to the side. "I don't know. Let people know where we are, when we'll be back. Say goodbye."

Carmen paused, but nodded in spite of herself. "Yes, true. Take the day. I should find Beatriz and Rosa. They will need to tell me what happens in the episodes of *Corona de Lágrimas* that I will miss." She turned and went off to find her friends.

Of course Carmen would criticize her suggestion and then realize she had things to do. As thrilled as she was to have company, and as emotional as the last night had been, the clear light of morning was making it obvious just how grating traveling with Carmen might be. Chelsea had stuck by her side the first few months after her death, but she had soon branched out, met other ghosts, started visiting things that didn't interest Carmen, spent time with people that Carmen could not stand.

Cyndricka didn't fall into that category; in fact, it had been Carmen who brought Chelsea to her first performance. But Carmen saw the human woman as just one more distracting performance in the city, with an added bonus of ghost involvement, rather than as a source of interaction and friendship. If Chelsea was going to say goodbye, best that she did it on her own.

She caught Cyndricka just as she was putting on her makeup for the morning. Her things were spread out on the bench that she had slept on, along with her sleeping bag, damp from the last of the snow-melt in the park. Tyler, the ghost of the cancer patient in the hospital gown, who had sat watch the previous night, hovered next to her, making idle chatter. Cyndricka glanced up from painting on her eyebrow triangles to wave at Chelsea, then went back to her hand mirror with single-minded concentration. Tyler moved over on the bench so that Chelsea could sit, as if it still mattered to either of them.

"Morning, Chelsea. How was the concert?"

"I think it might be more your style of music than mine. Definitely not Carmen's."

Tyler laughed and leaned back on the bench, shaking his head. "Why did she even think it would be? She's a weird one."

Cyndricka glanced up from her makeup just enough to raise a snarky eyebrow and wave a hand at the present company and at herself. It was perhaps the wrong crowd to be calling anyone else strange. Tyler patted an affectionate hand on Cyndricka's shoulder. "You're a unique one, hon, not weird. There's a difference."

She elbowed through him and stuck her tongue out past half-painted lips.

"So what can we do for you, Chelsea?" Tyler asked. "Finally decided to run away and join our circus?"

"I don't think you guys want me," said Chelsea. "Unless someone wants to start doing a stand-up routine about a ghost with stage fright and use me as a big wooden prop."

"I keep saying we need to start doing a ghosts-only show, in the dead of night, with just us spirits as an audience!" Tyler exclaimed. "Cyndricka, come on, it would be awesome. Chelsea, tell her it would be amazing."

Cyndricka rubbed her fingers and thumb together to illustrate just why ghost-only shows were a poor idea, and Tyler conceded. "Okay, so maybe they're not the most lucrative. But it would be a lot of fun. Maybe I'll just put one together. Chelsea, you could be a set piece."

"Maybe once I get back. I came by to tell you guys that I'm going on a trip tomorrow and I probably won't be back for a couple months."

Cyndricka looked completely up from her makeup for the first time, lowering her paint and mirror to her lap. She tilted her head to the side in question.

"I've decided. I'm going to make it out to San Francisco for my brother's wedding. And Carmen is going to come with me." She spread her arms wide, even with the right bent at its strange angle. "Road trip!"

"Man, that's awesome!" Tyler clapped for her and gave a little cheer. "Bon voyage, you two. God, I haven't been out of this damn city for years. Though . . . I mean, is Carmen really going to be the best traveling companion?"

"What do you mean?"

Tyler nodded his head back and forth a bit. "Ah, I shouldn't talk shit, she's your friend. I just know some other spirits think Carmen is a little . . . I don't know, unstable or something."

Chelsea frowned; she had never thought of Carmen in those terms, exactly. "I'd say she's more tightly wound than anything. Unstable, really?"

"I think it's just gossip from when she first came to New York, and she's probably taken care of it by now. Dead and buried, even by our standards. Hey, don't let me drag down your plans. Have a good trip and bring back postcards, alright?"

"Yeah, sure, I'll just pack them in my bag." Chelsea considered Tyler for a moment. "Would you like to come with us?" She didn't think Carmen minded Tyler, even if she didn't spend much time with Cyndricka's performance crowd.

But he shook his head. "Nah, sorry. That's a lot of walking through flyover country when I've got plenty on my plate these days. Summer's coming up, you know." He bounced his eyebrows at her, and Chelsea snorted at him.

"Ogling women in bikinis does not count as plans."

"And here I thought you were barking up that tree. But no, it's not just that. Jy-hun and I are talking about getting back together, and she's got a lot of friends here she wants to stay close with."

Chelsea nodded and decided not to comment. From the undead gossip, Tyler and Jy-hun had been dating and not dating in turns for the last decade. As ghost relationships tended to be fairly long-lasting, they were a bit of an anomaly, or a salacious scandal, to hear him talk about it. "Well, I'll have to hang out with you when I'm next back in town." She turned to Cyndricka, who still had her mirror clutched in her lap. "I'm going to miss your shows while I'm gone. I'll have to haunt you for a few days straight when I get back, to catch up."

Cyndricka didn't join in her laugh, not even a mimed one, not even a smile. She fiddled with her paintbrush, twirling it in her fingers, and chewed on her lip. A smear of black paint got on her teeth, but she didn't seem to notice. Tyler rubbed his hand back and forth on her shoulder. "You okay there, Dricka?" he asked.

Yes, I'm fine, Tattoo. Tyler had been named after the ink peeking out past the sleeves of his hospital gown.

"We had a bit of trouble last night," he explained to Chelsea, still rubbing Cyndricka's shoulder. "Some jerks roughed up our gal and stole her show money." Cyndricka looked up, and upon closer inspection, Chelsea could see the swelling around her left eye, covered by the white paint, but still puffy and sensitive looking. "What I would've given to have had some poltergeist powers then," Tyler said with a scowl. "Sorry I couldn't help you out more than to sound the alarm."

Cyndricka nodded to him and brushed off his concern, but her eyes didn't leave Chelsea. She took a deep breath, shoulders rising and falling theatrically, and signed her question. *Can I come with you?*

Chelsea opened her mouth to respond. Then closed it. Opened it again. She let the words hang.

Tyler cleared his throat.

"Umm, Cyndricka, I'm not sure if that's really the best . . . you know, for a gal who's still got her flesh on her, that's a hell of a long . . . long, long walk."

Cyndricka nodded. *Yes, I know. But I want to go. My grand-parents are in R-E-N-O. It has been a very long time since I have visited them. If Coat and Curtains are going, it would be a good time to make the trip. In company, with friends.*

"It would take a lot longer," Chelsea said slowly, her mind working fast over all the possible outcomes. "You need to sleep, eat, rest. Can you pay for food and shelter?"

The glance Cyndricka gave her was more than a little pitying. *I make my way. Shows, scavenging, or stealing here and there, I make my way.*

"Well, yes, but you still—I mean, the wedding's not until August, we have plenty of time, but—" She spread her hands wide, not able to adequately put her general feeling of *no* into words. "I mean, is there any other way to get there, to see your family?"

You can't shoplift an airplane ticket. And hitchhiking is dangerous. Traveling with ghosts is safer.

"Um . . ." Chelsea shared a skeptical glance with Tyler. "Let me ask Carmen."

"Why the hell would she want to do that? I do not mean to swear, but why? Why would you not tell her no right then?"

Chelsea sighed. That seemed to be an increasingly common reaction to conversations with Carmen. "She wants to see her family. I can't really blame her, when that's the exact same reason I'm going."

"So you are prepared for the journey to go from a month and a half, to the entire time leading up to the wedding? Bringing a human with us and starting tomorrow, there is a good chance we will not make it in time."

"We can try. She'll only be with us until Reno, and if it looks like we're cutting it close, you and I can run on ahead and come back for her later. Or she can hitchhike. Or something, we'll find a way to make it work."

"You pity her."

"I—well, kind of, yes. I like her too, but yeah, I feel sorry for her." Chelsea shifted under Carmen's gaze, looking away. "What, I have to let go of all sympathy for the living? Is this another thing that I shouldn't tie myself down with?"

Carmen kept walking through Times Square, phasing through tourists and buildings with an equal lack of interest. She didn't look away from Chelsea as she walked; no one can glare as effectively as a ghost.

But Chelsea could hold her ground on this one. Having Carmen oppose her made her resolve so much stronger than it had been before.

"If you're so against the idea, she and I can go alone. She can provide me with company, and you don't need to inconvenience yourself walking across the country. She gets to go, you don't have to, and I have a friend to talk to. Everyone wins."

"No. The last thing I need is you turning into a wailer because she gets hit by a car in the middle of Nevada and does not come back. It would be a waste of all the time and work I have put into keeping you in your right mind. The human oddity is not enough. I can tolerate her presence, but you need someone else. You need me. I'm coming too."

"Alright." She tried not to smirk too openly at how quickly Carmen could change her tune when someone opposed her.

7.

It really shouldn't have been a surprise that issues came up even before they left.

The realities of being a human with both basic necessities and personal desires meant that Cyndricka actually did have to prepare for the journey. She spent the day going through her collection of things and trimming it down to what she could carry on her back. Leaving things tucked away in hidey-holes around the park could work for a day during performances, but not for the months on end that she would be gone. Chelsea and Tyler hovered over her, figuratively and literally, as she saved plastic bottles for water and set aside plastic toys and stuffed animals that had made their way into her belongings to add homey touches to wherever she spent any given night. The only apparent luxuries that she held on to were her miming supplies: the paint and makeup, the costume, the bag of long twistable balloons.

They don't add much weight and I can make money along the way. It is worth it, she said in response to Chelsea's questioning look.

Chelsea couldn't say that she was looking forward to Carmen's reaction when their journey took pit stops in order to put on mime shows. But Cyndricka was right; she knew how to live on the streets, whereas by the time Chelsea had started, she had had nothing to worry about and no risk whatsoever.

What Cyndricka didn't seem to be as good at was interacting with other living, flesh and blood people. When she didn't have a layer of makeup and performance between her and another human, she kept interactions to a bare minimum. She wrote her questions on a notebook and held it out at arm's length while she tried to trade supplies with the other homeless people in the park, some that she had lived around for years.

The people in the homeless camps tried to help her out where they could, trading her winter scarves for a sturdier shoulder bag and her current sleeping bag for a more compact one. Some of the older people smiled at Cyndricka and shook their heads fondly when she signed to Chelsea and Tyler. "Stay safe, girl," one older woman said as she pulled on Cyndricka's spare sweater over her shivering frame. "You're a good kid, just get your head right and stay safe." Cyndricka gave her a fleeting smile before she scurried off to return to the company of ghosts.

She elected to spend the afternoon conversing with her performance group, the ever-changing collection of ghosts that played along with her during her shows. With the exception of Tyler, Chelsea didn't know them that well. She decided that she had her own goodbyes to say, even if they would be a bit one-sided.

👣 👣 👣

The apartment was not how she had remembered it. Every time she came to visit, there was something subtracted, a few things added, and a great deal reorganized. Even though Heather had stayed put after the accident, it felt like a different apartment by that point. No longer the place that they had shared. The apartment they had lived in together and made a home.

She wasn't home when Chelsea floated through the front door. Being on-call gave her long, strange hours, though not nearly as bad as during her internship. In the months before Chelsea's death, they'd had to take advantage of every moment they both had free. It had been more than a little frustrating at the time, but Chelsea was glad of it in retrospect. It was like they had been unknowingly preparing, making everything count before it was gone.

Chelsea skimmed through the kitchen table, scattered with a mix of video game magazines and medical journals. The gardening magazines had all disappeared, no one interested enough to renew their subscriptions. The window boxes were still there and amazingly still holding on, even if Heather needed to stop over-watering the mint. The flowers were gone, but Heather enjoyed cooking enough to justify keeping the herbs.

The only truly sentimental parts left were the pictures. The ones that had once been held on the fridge with magnets, then framed for the funeral. Now they decorated the shelf in the living room, with a candle that had been lit for the entirety of the first year, and just on special occasions after that, or days when Heather seemed lonely. It had been out since Christmas, at least in the times that Chelsea had been by.

The first picture was a group shot: Heather on one end with her arm around young Osric's shoulders, a few old college friends in the middle, and Chelsea at the other end, holding a red plastic cup and a pasted-on smile. She hadn't wanted to go to the party where the only person she knew was her little brother, but he had all but dragged her out of her apartment, saying she needed to do something other than job applications all day. And he had a cute friend who just so happened to be into women, and he might have talked up his lesbian sister just a bit, so she kind of had to come.

The friend in question was next to Chelsea in the picture, leaning in far too close and letting her hand slip far too low on picture-Chelsea's waist. Chelsea had fled to the bathroom not five minutes after the flash had gone off, and run into another one of Osric's friends. A much better one, who had known him for years, but liked pancakes at a midnight diner far better than cheap beer at a party.

Osric had given her crap about leaving the party for months, usually a playful tease when he saw her and Heather holding hands, until he jetted off across the country after his own love.

The next picture was a classic: the two of them at the beach. Leaning against each other in their swimsuits, Heather's skin tanned a rich gold from the sun while Chelsea's showed the beginnings of a burn. Both of them had their wet hair long and down to their waists, falling together between them, shiny black mingling with chestnut brown. Chelsea wished her hair still looked like that. She wished everything still looked like that.

The last picture probably should not have been shown at the

funeral. Some of the more conservative Shu relatives had turned their gazes away when they saw it. But it was the best. Fuzzy camera phone picture, looking amateur even when printed on glossy photo paper, taken at arm's length by Heather. She beamed out from the frame, dark eyes dancing above her sharp nose and wide grin. Chelsea's eyes were closed, because she had been innocently sleeping and drooling on her girlfriend's pajama top, not posing for a photo. Heather's other arm had the comforter from their bed pulled over the two of them, though the shoulder of Chelsea's favorite t-shirt was still just visible.

Heather looked happy. Chelsea looked peaceful. They looked comfortable, together and warm in the bed they shared.

Even without physical sensation now, Chelsea felt cold.

The apartment's front door opened. Chelsea pulled away from the pictures slowly, her broken arm swinging with the motion. After all this time, it made her smile to see Heather enter their apartment, her arms weighed down with carry-out food. Chelsea bet it smelled delicious. She was so happy to see her, even if she was no longer the second woman through the door.

"Heather, can I put the cider straight in the fridge?" Roxanne asked. Heather nodded, setting down the bag of Indian food on top of several journals.

"Toss me one first, okay? And grab some plates?"

Roxanne hesitated with the plates, but found the correct cabinet on the second try. She was slowly but surely getting the hang of the apartment, and practice did make perfect. Both times Chelsea had visited since February, she had been there, eating dinner with Heather. Or eating breakfast.

Heather shucked off her cap as she grabbed two forks out of the same old drawer and a handful of serving spoons. She ran her hands through the spiky hair that barely grazed her eyebrows when it fell back down. People had raised their eyebrows when she cut it right after the funeral, but she had been wearing it that way for almost two years now. Roxanne scurried out of the kitchen to the bathroom and Chelsea had a moment with just Heather. Her Heather, who had stopped being hers a long time ago.

"Hey, Heath," Chelsea said with a little smile. Heather dished out rice and curry onto the plates. "I just wanted to drop in and say hello. And goodbye for a bit. I'm going to be away for a while."

She glanced at the fridge as Heather opened her cider and took a drink. A little rainbow flag magnet held up the gold-trimmed card. "Same place that you're going, actually. It's just going to take me a lot longer." She shook her head and chuckled. "There's no airline for ghosts. If I stand in a plane, when it takes off it would move right through me, leave me hovering on the tarmac . . . anyway . . ."

Heather tucked into the food with the single-minded dedication of a young doctor after a long shift. The sink turned on and off in the bathroom down the hall. ". . . Roxanne seems nice . . . You two seem nice together."

Chelsea scrubbed her hand over her scalp, through the hair that Heather had copied so closely and across the fragments of her skull that stuck through the transparent flesh. "I don't know why I came. This means nothing to you. And it shouldn't mean anything to me. But, you know . . . I like to see you. I miss you."

Roxanne came back into the kitchen and Heather smiled at her. Not the comfortable one that Chelsea had grown so used to, but a fresh, new look. A love that was not lived-in yet, but still being discovered. Growing. As living things are wont to do.

"I'll see you in San Francisco." Chelsea mimicked a kiss to the top of Heather's head and left the couple to their dinner.

8.

Two days later, after Cyndricka had finished all of her errands and goodbyes, and Carmen had asked what seemed like every ghost in the city to keep up on her shows and movies and fill her in later, the trio set out on the beginning of their journey.

Chelsea and Carmen walked a foot or so above the sidewalks. Cyndricka bounced on the pavement between them, large bag hung on her shoulders and coat hanging loose and open. The sunlight, while still weak and thin in the spring, was warm and the air was fresh. Flowers and grass in sidewalks and window boxes were just starting to get some color, and Chelsea wished for the world that she could smell it. They were leaving a city just waking up from winter, and it was a bit sad to think that it would be sleeping again by the time they got back.

Then they started walking along the shoulder of a highway and all poetry was gone. Screw the dirty rat warren, they were getting out.

Cyndricka kept up a smile as cars honked at her and one or two even tried to give her a scare by driving up close. But worry lines ringed her eyes after the fourth SUV laid on its horn. She waved a hand at Chelsea and mouthed a few words, exaggerated speaking.

"You want me to talk?"

Me signing will make them honk more. Take my mind off it? A college boy chose that moment to yell out of the window of his daddy's truck as he whizzed by, illustrating her point. Carmen pursed her lips and looked straight ahead.

"What do you want to talk about?" Chelsea asked. Cyndricka

shrugged as well as she could around the backpack and just avoided going off balance into a drainage ditch.

Chelsea thought for a moment.

"Are you a fan of music? Carmen and I went to a concert the other night."

Cyndricka nodded and waved for her to continue.

"Well, it was a little too much thrashing for me. My older sister went through a metal phase, but it skipped over me, and only lasted a few months for my younger brother. But Phoebe's music drove our dad crazy. I swear I could hear an argument over the breakfast table in every note."

Cyndricka gave her an encouraging nod, but Carmen was watching her out of the corner of her eye. Probably best to change approach.

"But I thought their guitarist was good, at least. What did you think, Carmen?"

Carmen was silent, and Chelsea wasn't sure for a moment that she was going to end up taking the bait, and that the entire walk was going to be like this. But she gave a mighty sniff and raised her head in a haughty expression. "I am amazed that you thought that guitar work was anything more than passable. The bassist was the only one out of the lot of them who deserved to be doing more than playing at children's birthday parties, and not by a wide margin. If you really wanted to listen to good thrasher metal, there was a band called Suffocation that went through New York in the nineties scene that was actually worth their salt. Everything I have seen since pales in comparison, because the musicians today know that they can get away with it by playing to audiences with less discerning musical palates and—"

Cyndricka glanced up at Chelsea, met her gaze, and turned away with a fit of barely concealed giggles. Carmen had too many motherly tendencies to not notice, so she smacked her hand through Cyndricka's head, but continued talking unabated. Somewhere in the first five minutes, she transitioned to talking about both mariachi and opera, and Chelsea couldn't have told you where the seam was if you paid her a million dollars. What was far more valuable was the way Cyndricka started copying Carmen's gait and facial expressions, miming exaggerated condescension and dodging the soda bottle that someone threw out of their car window with a quick skip that didn't interrupt her impression at all. The weeks and months ahead suddenly looked less like a solemn trek and more like something that could potentially be called fun. And to think Chelsea had been about to take the trip alone.

They walked for several hours before Cyndricka started faltering and her steps slowed. She kept herself plenty fit with the shows, but Chelsea couldn't imagine her diet was that good, nor her sleep that restful, when she got it. They had moved off of the highway and into neighborhood streets around midday, and the three of them kept their eyes open for parks with benches or doorways that could provide some shelter.

A small local park was nothing more than a jungle gym and a swing set, but it had benches and a drinking fountain, which Cyndricka leapt at. She had filled up old soda bottles in the drinking fountains in Central Park, but had only sipped lightly on the first one during the day, not knowing when she would get a chance to refill it. The same approach had made a half-filled bag of Doritos serve as lunch. There was a vending machine in a sheltered spot by the edge of the park, and Cyndricka carefully considered what would be easiest to grab out of it, while Chelsea and Carmen faced away from her and kept watch.

"I am telling you, Lucille Ball is one of the greats."

"Of her time."

"Of all times!"

Cyndricka waved at them to show that she had something to say, but one of her hands was too busy trying to grab the short-bread cookies on the lowest rung of the machine. Chelsea shook her head at her.

"Yeah yeah, you'll get your chance. But I need to make sure that Carmen knows how wrong she is. Lucy had the physical comedy that worked in that era, but there are comedians today that have the wordplay to match."

"Which they learned from watching generations of comedians who blazed the way," Carmen insisted.

"I never said they didn't! But wouldn't you rather have the

culmination of old and new, rather than just the original building blocks?"

That was apparently too much for Cyndricka to ignore, and she temporarily abandoned the pursuit of cookies to sit up on the block of pavement and have full use of her hands. *But the early comedians had to figure things out on their own. C-H-A-R-L-I-E C-H-A-P-L-I-N will always be the best, because of what he added to the art form.*

Chelsea groaned and let her head loll back on her neck: a particularly exaggerated motion, considering how loosely her head was held in place to begin with. "You were raised by your grandparents, weren't you? Because there's no way that someone my age just said that."

Cyndricka smiled and shrugged, then turned back to the vending machine's challenge. Chelsea put her head back into its place to keep watch. While no one else in the vicinity would hear any of this conversation, someone could still see Cyndricka, and it would be a shame for her to lose out on both food and a place to sleep because they had to run. Carmen turned back from her own direction briefly to smirk at Chelsea. A real, full smirk this time.

"It looks like you cannot blame your poor taste on your age, if your fellows do not even agree with you."

"I'll take Margaret Cho's standup over a clown any day. No offense, Cyndricka."

Cyndricka didn't even bother to pull her hands out this time, just kicked through Chelsea's feet from her position on the ground.

"Maybe it's just the queer Asian thing," Chelsea conceded. "Maybe I just feel subconsciously compelled to like her. Cyndricka, you don't talk and you like the silent comedians, while I like Margaret Cho."

Chelsea was keeping her eye on a dog walker going down the other street, so she didn't notice at first that both of them were silent. When the woman took her springer spaniel around the corner, Chelsea turned back to them and saw Cyndricka sitting up, a bag of cookies in hand and her head tilted in question.

"Hmm? I didn't mention it before?" Chelsea wondered. "I

didn't think it was really an issue. Out of this group, being a lesbian is the least weird thing we have going on."

"I don't believe anything is going to top the mime," Carmen said, looking resolutely the other way, presumably keeping watch on the curtain being pulled aside in one of the houses across the street. "If you have what you need, we should move."

Cyndricka shoved a few cookies in her mouth as she walked and crammed the rest of her haul into various pockets and pouches in her bag. She looked thoughtful when they approached the most sheltered bench in the park, tucked away under some trees. Chelsea watched her.

"Does it really bother you, Cyndricka? If you want to turn back, now's probably the best time, with us only a day's walk away." Carmen floated next to her, and she felt more than a little glad for the silent support. Chelsea had been out to her family since midway through college, but there was always someone new to tell and to deal with the reactions from, even after death, apparently.

But Cyndricka shook her head quickly. *I've tried dating women before. If you could make it work with someone, anyone, more luck to you. If I met a human who was willing to overlook the 'crazy mute mime' thing, it wouldn't matter what gender they were. There just don't happen to be any humans like that around.*

"And as much as you think me old-fashioned," Carmen sniffed, "I know that the young people today are far more open about that sort of thing. My Manuel and I were very happy together and I would not begrudge that to anyone else. As we've discussed, you may spare me any gory details." As if Chelsea was about to start vividly describing her sex life in the middle of the park. But she thought that that sounded good enough to get on with.

The night was clear, and if the way Cyndricka's sleeping bag was loose and partially open around her was any indication, it wasn't too cool or windy. None of that mattered to Chelsea at this point, but it was nice to see Cyndricka looking comfortable.

"Get some sleep. You're the only one who actually has to walk in the morning. We'll keep watch here."

Cyndricka nodded, eyes already drifting closed. She held her hands above her chest just long enough to sign *Good night, Coat. Good night, Curtains.* Then she let them fall back on top of her, and she was out for the night. Carmen watched her as she fell asleep, and then looked up at Chelsea.

"Do you whisper for the whole night, when you and the others do this watch duty?" she asked, keeping her voice low. Cyndricka's breath stayed steady.

"Sometimes. A lot of the time it's just one of us. But she lives outside in Central Park; it's not like she needs perfect silence to sleep."

"Fair enough." Carmen glanced around the park, through the trees, up at the stars, back to Chelsea. "I cannot remember the last time I waited for a human to sleep. Such a terrible waste of time."

"If you want to go watch TV in someone's house, I can keep watch," Chelsea said with a shrug. It would be boring, but she owed Carmen some time to go do her own thing, after she had agreed to come all this way with her.

"No, I am fine. There is plenty of time to do that later, when my well of patience has had time to run dry."

Chelsea stretched her leg over and kicked through the hem of Carmen's dress. Carmen batted her back, sending pins and needles shooting through Chelsea's shin. They both sat in the dark of the little park, so much calmer and quieter than the city they had just left, but feeling uneasy. Not like home.

". . . How about a game of Twenty Questions?" Chelsea asked.

". . . all right, go on."

"Okay, I'm thinking of someone."

"Alive, dead, or in between?"

It surprised Chelsea how quickly they got out of New York's hustle and bustle. The city seemed to cast a far bigger shadow than its actual dimensions allowed. The next day of walking dragged on longer and longer. The road was crowded enough that Cyndricka had to focus on hugging the curb and avoiding any car or truck that looked like it was getting too close, when not actively dodging out of the way of kicked up dust and debris.

Chelsea tried to keep the chatter alive, but she ended up having to shout over the sound of honking, which didn't leave anyone in the best of spirits. Carmen was keeping her mouth stubbornly closed, raising an eyebrow at Chelsea as if trying to wordlessly point out how much easier this would have been without a human in tow. Not about to take the bait, Chelsea kept up her steady stream of upbeat banter. But even she managed to run out of things to chat about eventually. So she resorted to drastic measures.

"Okay, Cyndricka, what kind of music do you like? Because I am just gonna start singing, okay? Anything to pass the time."

Cyndricka looked incredulous at the prospect, but it was Carmen who stared at her with outright dismay. But Chelsea was going to prove that this road trip idea was not cursed from the start, even if it did mean subjecting everyone to her singing voice.

Cyndricka did her best not to wince too openly when Chelsea started making her way through the pop charts, but she couldn't entirely hide it. Chelsea was sure that it had to at least sound better than the car horns, but by the way Cyndricka's hands were clutching the straps of her bag, she may have been wrong. Phoebe and her mother had always been the singers in the Shu family, with Osric and Chelsea inheriting their dad's scratchiness and borderline tone deafness. But since she didn't have any good knock-knock jokes on hand, it would have to be singing.

It was a blessing when Carmen jumped in and cut her off right in the middle of Chelsea's attempt to remember the words to "Bohemian Rhapsody," which had always been a favorite of her dad's.

Carmen did not say a word about interrupting her, she just started singing over her until Chelsea got the message and stopped. Her song was a great deal more dignified than Chelsea's, some classical aria in Italian. Her voice was low and smooth, and she took full advantage of not having to breathe, letting her notes stretch out and her transitions move smoothly without any breaks for air.

Chelsea let herself feel petulant for only a moment at being interrupted, because the change was truly for the better. Cyndricka was smiling from ear to ear, though she shot Chelsea a guilty look and a shrug.

"Yeah, yeah, I know, hers is better. No need to rub it in."

Carmen smirked around a tricky trill up and down the scale and did some warbling thing with her voice that was definitely rubbing it in. But Chelsea did have to admit, the day went faster with Carmen singing.

"Do Free Bird!" she shouted with cupped hands around her mouth, just to see Carmen's expression. Cyndricka covered her mouth to hide her giggles, and on they went into the rest of their suddenly more musical journey.

$$\text{👣 👣 👣}$$

"So yeah, no idea how my parents ended up with three queer kids. They were remarkably good about it when we were teenagers, though. Phoebe kind of eased the way for Osric and me, since she was so gung-ho about it from the start."

Carmen seemed honestly dumbfounded as she looked at Chelsea. "Your sister began dating women from a very young age?"

"Well, not super young, not creepy young or anything. But she knew she liked men and women from right at the start and wasn't about to limit herself to one gender just because anyone wanted her to."

"And your brother? I thought we were going to his wedding to a woman?"

"Yeah, we are, but he's had boyfriends in the past. His longest relationship before Tamika was with this guy named Michael, and they were actually really great together. Didn't work out in the end, and I think Osric is happier with Tamika than he would have been with Mike, but it could have gone any way."

Carmen shook her head at the apparent madness of it all, the thought of all these queer young people dating any gender they pleased. It was only moments like this that reminded Chelsea what era Carmen had grown up and lived in.

"So your children are on the straight and narrow, emphasis on straight?" she asked, with only a bit of wheedling, mostly genuine curiosity.

"Yes, Miguel and Rosa are both married and have children of their own."

"That doesn't necessarily mean straight these days, but I follow you. And would you and Manuel have been okay if they had been interested in the same gender?"

Carmen's jaw clenched and Chelsea wondered if she had crossed a line, bringing up her family in that context. But Carmen tilted her head and spoke with some consideration in her voice.

"I would not have been thrilled. The thought of Miguel with a man is . . . well. I would have been scared for them and their futures."

"Just scared?" Chelsea pressed. "Not uncomfortable—"

"I love my children more than anything," Carmen intercut sharply. "Nothing could possibly have stopped that." She flexed her hands in her lap, as if looking for something to do to organize her thoughts. "I assume they have done things in their lives that I would not have agreed with. I make it a point not to see them often, I left Boston just to avoid the temptation. As I—as I have told you many times, obsessing about the living does no one any good. But I have never stopped loving them."

Chelsea nodded. "Yeah, I . . . I understand. I didn't mean it to sound like I thought . . . sorry."

Carmen shook her head slightly, still looking at her hands. "You did nothing wrong."

Perhaps Cyndricka subconsciously chose that moment to shuffle in her sleep, turning over in the partially sheltered shop doorway that she was using as a resting spot that night. Both ghosts went quiet, looking out and keeping a closer watch on the dimly lit street with its handful of passersby that all, thankfully, ignored the homeless woman. It was when people stopped ignoring her that they had to worry.

9.

"I wonder why there aren't more ghosts out here."

Chelsea was trying to make conversation during a long stretch of empty country road; an old cemetery off to the side provided as good of a topic as any.

You're not still hovering around your grave, Cyndricka pointed out. *Why would other ghosts be spending their time here?*

"Not just here specifically, but here like the whole state. Does Pennsylvania just not have a lot of ghosts?"

Carmen shot her a sideways glance from where she was ambling down the center of the road. "You do realize that there are not that many ghosts in the world, right?"

Cyndricka nodded along at that, but Chelsea paused.

". . . wait, what?"

"Big, old cities like New York are exceptional in how many ghosts they have, but the overwhelming majority of people who die do not remain as ghosts."

If every dead person in history was floating around all the time, you wouldn't be able to see through them all, it would be so many, Cyndricka pointed out with a sage nod.

"I mean, yeah, I realize that." Chelsea felt bristly at how matter of fact they were being. "So if you both know so much, where do the rest of them go?"

Cyndricka shrugged, like Chelsea had asked what she wanted to have for lunch. *No idea.*

"You never wonder? You don't think about whether they all go to heaven or hell or just poof out of existence? You've been able to see ghosts your whole life and you don't think about this?"

Cyndricka shrugged again. *Why bother? I don't know why I can speak to ghosts, why others can't, or what any of it means, and the rest of the world already thinks I'm insane. It's just my life; I don't worry about the other parts of it.*

"The 'other parts' being the afterlife and people's immortal souls."

You're the dead woman; you tell me.

Chelsea didn't have any good answer for that. She fell into silence. She'd wondered, in some of her quieter, more reflective nights, what was beyond this world, if any of them had any chance to "move on." Some ghosts spent their days haunting churches, hoping for some truth to the whole heaven concept and trying to fit it into the reality they were currently stuck in.

But even experienced and self-assured ghosts like Carmen spoke of "moving on" in vague terms, an aimless goal to somehow still work towards. *Don't get too sad or you'll become a wailer, don't get too angry or you'll become a poltergeist. Do everything perfectly right and you'll somehow, at some point, go somewhere else.*

The only problem was the only ones left to give advice were those who didn't know how to do it. Carmen knew how not to go mad, but if she knew any more, she would not have been wandering New York to begin with. Maybe Cyndricka was right to find the whole debate futile.

What was your favorite pet when you were alive?

Chelsea grabbed onto the new topic. "I was always a real dog person, though my brother had a pet parrot that was really cute."

I always wanted a cat. As soon as I realized that they could see ghosts too, they became my favorite animal in the world.

"A pretty good reason. I just always hated the shedding."

🐾 👣 👣

Over the next few days, they walked through residential neighborhoods, stretches of highway, and even occasional patches of woods. Later in their journey they would have to worry more about their direction, but for now, they could just take a straight line west. A pocket in Cyndricka's backpack was crammed full of wrinkled and water-stained maps, gathered from library give-aways and gas station corkboards. But as long as they walked away from the sunrise every morning, they would be fine for at least a while.

Cyndricka settled down in parks in the evenings, or on the steps of large buildings, or even in patches of trees and tall grass alongside roads, but she walked steadily and without complaint during the days. Food was fished out of garbage cans, found left-over in the streets, and only occasionally stolen out of shops. The last thing Cyndricka wanted to do was be found guilty of going on a cross-country crime spree from border to border, but cold French fries could only fill her belly so much.

They had passed two women's shelters that offered a cot and a meal, but Cyndricka shook her head at the prospect of that much human contact. They all kept moving forward. Chelsea and Carmen kept their watches every night, waking Cyndricka up when she needed to relocate and avoid a security guard or a disgruntled business owner. She would slink away to another resting spot or try to take a few more hours of walking, then start the process all over again.

They chatted on the road, trading opinions about movies and television and music. They passed the occasional ghost lingering around a home or business, but only went by with a wave and greeting. They had avoided speaking to anyone else for a good four days when they saw the lightly glowing figure, zipping down a county road in the middle of Pennsylvania.

"Hello hello hello, ladies!" the ghost called out as he sailed by them, flying headfirst and far faster than either Chelsea or Carmen could have ever run. "What brings you both to this part of the country? Doing a very personalized haunting there, are we?"

He flew a quick circle around the trio and came to a halt in front of them, floating upright and hooking his thumbs through his suspenders. A white man with a sharp, grinning face, he was dressed like an old-style gangster. His buttoned shirt was dotted with cuts and stained with blood, but his fedora tilted back at a jaunty angle, showing off his bushy beard and wide smile. He looked like an actor in a period piece, too composed to be real.

Chelsea had met a few ghosts from the Prohibition while living in New York, but for the most part they had felt like everyday people. "I don't think I've ever seen two of our type following a fleshy this closely. This gal here do something really bad to you? She looks like the thieving type, did she steal something from you, maybe rob a memorial at your grave? Need me to throw in my weight to try and get a scare?" He gave Chelsea a big wink and cackled. "I may not be a poltergeist yet, but I still think I'm plenty scary. Wouldn't you two agree?"

Chelsea didn't know how to respond to the very sudden intrusion, and Carmen just rolled her eyes at the antics unfolding in front of them. But Cyndricka covered her mouth with her hands to stifle her giggles. She met Chelsea's gaze and signed *He reminds me of my grandfather. Same hat, even.*

"Not all of us have the fortune to have been buried in the latest trends," Carmen said with a sniff. "Or we were, and time and fashion both were rude enough to move on without us." Cyndricka gave a sideways nod, conceding the point.

The man went stock still in front of them, no longer looking quite so sure of himself. He bent at the waist. He glanced up at Chelsea and Carmen, then slowly extended his hand in front of Cyndricka's face. He wiggled his fingers an inch from her, and she pulled back with a wrinkled nose.

"Dear lord," the man whispered. "This one can see us?" Cyndricka nodded, and the man pulled his arm back to his chest. "And she can hear you too?" Cyndricka nodded again, exaggerated this time, probably in response to being spoken about in the third person.

"Meet Cyndricka, our resident miracle," Carmen said with a wry smile. "She can see and hear you, but does not speak in response. Though if you are fluent in American Sign Language or willing to watch a brief mime show, she is quite conversational, I assure you."

"And you two are—" He looked between Chelsea and Carmen, still completely dumbfounded. "You two are traveling with her? All of you together?"

"It would seem that way."

"Yep. Though we should probably keep moving if we want to get somewhere safe for the night." Cyndricka nodded at Chelsea's suggestion and kept walking down the empty road.

The man followed them, barely picking his jaw off of his chest—thankfully metaphorically, given some of the facial damage Chelsea had seen on fellow spirits in the last two years.

"I—damn. I've been around for almost a hundred damn years, and this is the first time I have ever, *ever* met a human that receptive. You always been able to do that, love?" he asked Cyndricka. She nodded in response and mimed rocking a baby in her arms. He nodded. "I imagine it would be the sort of madness you're born with. Unless you almost died once or something, fell halfway in between the worlds for a bit."

"That would just not be possible," Carmen was quick to interject. The man snorted and jerked his head back.

"This is the most impossible thing I have ever seen, so I am more than ready to believe a bit more silliness." He held his hand down to Cyndricka, who turned enough to take it as she kept walking. "Henry St. John, at your service. Whoa!" he yelped when her skin went through his hand. "That's a strong spark you got there! Sure you're not a ghost in a mask or something?" She shook her head and poked her cheek with one finger, showing just how solid she was. "Ah well, it would make as much sense as anything else about this. You are a seriously unique young lady, Miss Cyndricka. I had no idea anything like you existed."

She had been squirming and smiling at Henry's words up until that point, but her expression fell and her face went still. She readjusted her backpack and strode forward, looking straight ahead at the road. Henry rose a few feet to whisper to Chelsea.

"I say something wrong to your gal?"

Chelsea watched Cyndricka walk, trying to think of how best to say what she was thinking. "I think she's . . . I don't know, it's got to be strange knowing you're the only one of something. I know when I died, having others around who were in the same predicament . . . it meant a lot. My name is Chelsea, by the way," she said with a wave. "And that's Carmen." Carmen nodded and sped up to walk level with Cyndricka.

Henry nodded slowly. "I suppose that makes sense to me. It's been forever since I've cared, but you lot seem like babies still. No offense meant, darling."

Her jaw clenched at being called darling, but she did have to nod at his assessment. "Carmen's been dead for a bit over forty years, but I'm just about two and a half."

"When you get near a century, everything gets easier. Thinking, feeling, relaxing and having fun. Even flying I got the hang of, just by forgetting what it is to be tied down. But then again, I thought I knew everything there was to know, and here I am being knocked on my ass by the most goddamn receptive human I've ever heard of, much less seen. You all are traveling with someone really special, you know that, right?"

Chelsea nodded. Carmen and Cyndricka were deep in conversation a few yards ahead, and if Chelsea was reading the signs correctly on Cyndricka's flashing hands, it was something about comedy and cats. Cyndricka let herself speak so much faster when she wasn't worrying about Chelsea keeping up, and American Sign Language was just another of the languages Carmen had collected like baseball cards decades ago.

"I don't think I really . . . I met her so soon after I died," Chelsea said softly. Henry leaned in to listen. "Carmen introduced me when she thought I was losing touch. She's always been worried that I . . ."

Chelsea trailed off, but Henry nodded. Someone of his age had to have seen more than his fair share of wailers over the years. Chelsea cleared her throat and continued. "She was important because of that, but I don't think I ever realized just how unique what she does is. Not when there were only six months between me learning that ghosts exist and learning that someone who can see ghosts exists."

"Suppose that makes sense," Henry said, hovering around in a slow circle while he moved forward, so Chelsea was talking to his feet as often as his head. He could not have cared less about gravity or how normal humans moved, and Chelsea could get some sense of why Carmen scoffed when she talked about old ghosts. But he seemed nice enough. Harmless, at the very least. Not that any of them could really be harmed. "I might like to stay with you lot for a bit. See what something different actually looks like."

"You'll have to ask Cyndricka." She seemed to be the one who was bothered by Henry, after all.

He looked at Chelsea out of the corner of his eye, while hovering upside down, his chin only a few inches off the ground and his head bent up at an unnatural angle.

"So whose trip is this? Are you two guards for her? She going somewhere important? Walking through the heart of god's land, performing the best damn exorcisms Uncle Sam has ever seen?"

"I don't think she knows how to do exorcisms."

"Have you ever asked?" He turned himself upright and met Chelsea's gaze squarely. "I know I—a few of my friends would be interested in a good exorcist. They don't come around often, and you have to take advantage when you can. I found that out back in '33." He fell silent, looking out into the woods they were still meandering through. A car zipped past them and honked, making Cyndricka hop further onto the side of the road and Carmen shake her fist at the retreating bumper.

"We're walking to San Francisco," Chelsea said. "Well, she's walking to Reno. She's going back to her family. And whatever else she wants to do."

"That's a lot of road to cover. I think I'll stay around," Henry said with a smile. Never mind what she had just said about asking Cyndricka.

Henry stayed with them for four days and spent a good chunk of each asking Cyndricka as many questions as he could get her to answer. When she had first known she could see ghosts, how many she had seen, if there were any differences, if she had ever met a wailer or a poltergeist, if she had ever met another person even half as receptive as she was.

Cyndricka signed her answers and either Carmen or Chelsea translated for her, or if they were feeling impatient or were too busy keeping watch, Cyndricka pulled out her notebook and wrote down what she needed to say. The pages were quickly filling up with answers to the detailed questions Henry asked. More than once, one of the other two had had to yell for Cyndricka's attention when she was about to trip or walk into something because her eyes were buried in her paper.

"Do you figure it's some sort of African voodoo thing?" Henry asked baldly, ignoring sharp looks from Carmen and uncomfortable silence from Chelsea. "I've never met another colored girl who could see ghosts, but maybe there's some sorta ethnic magic in you."

Great news, in this century being black doesn't make me a witch doctor, Cyndricka scrawled with a few pointed stabs at the paper, but Henry was already off onto another topic.

After the constant barrage of questions and badgering, Cyndricka's mood was faltering. Worry-lines ringed her eyes, even when they settled down for the evening for her to scavenge food and sleep, and Chelsea would have to convince Henry to finally let her sleep each night, and he would do the floating equivalent of sitting on his hands until morning, barely talking to either of the others, which put an awkward spin on Chelsea and Carmen's time spent together as well.

I'm used to having ghosts around and it usually doesn't bother me, Cyndricka confided to Chelsea in one of their now-rare moments alone. *I don't need a lot of privacy. But some quiet—*

It had only taken a handful of days for the three of them to establish a routine, and an even shorter amount of time for Henry to come in and disrupt it all. When Cyndricka woke up one morning, caught Chelsea's eye, glanced at Henry, and burrowed back into her sleeping bag to pretend she was still sleeping, Chelsea knew that something had to change.

"Hey Henry, could we talk for a minute?" she asked when they were getting ready to leave later in the day. Cyndricka was washing up in a park bathroom and it seemed like a good excuse to draw the one man in their party away.

"All right, but I need to ask her about something when she's done. I've been thinking about any unfinished business I have keeping me here, and if your girl would mind a detour to Atlantic

City." He followed Chelsea over to the jungle gym and made a show of walking along the top of the swing set.

"Okay, maybe cut it with all the 'girl' thing. Her name is Cyndricka. And actually, that was what I wanted to talk to you about. All of the questions are getting to be a bit much, you know?" Henry raised an eyebrow and watched her flatly. "She has a really tiring time as it is, with all the walking and, you know, being alive. Maybe just stop with the third degree and let her relax sometimes. And she definitely doesn't have the time or energy for detours."

"You want me to stop talking to this gal," he said after a moment, not so much a question as a statement.

"I'm not saying that you have to stop talking to her. Just maybe . . . you know, more of a conversation, less of an interrogation."

Henry moved closer to Chelsea. The streetlamp at the edge of the park threw the silvery blood on his chest into sharp relief. He leaned in and Chelsea instinctively leaned back.

"You stumbled onto a miracle," Henry said, low and slow, looking into Chelsea's eyes as he did. "No, you didn't stumble onto it, you were *handed* a miracle. And you want to keep it all to your damn self."

"She's not a miracle, she's a person." Henry floated closer, but Chelsea kept herself in place. "She's certainly not an 'it'."

"You and that other bitch have the most special human in the goddamn world going on a stroll with you and you treat it like it's nothing. You're playing catch with the Hope Diamond. I realize how much that girl is worth, and I'm not about to ignore it."

"That's not your decision to make." Chelsea listened hard for any hint of Cyndricka coming back; she didn't want her to have to listen to this crap. "What value does she even have to you, what are you hoping to get out of all this? Or do you just get off on annoying women?"

"See, you don't even know what you're doing!" Henry said with an exasperated jerk of his hands. "I've been out there, traveling and talking to spirits longer than you've been alive or dead. There are ghosts who would try anything in the world to pass over, move on, whatever, and you have a girl who is straddling realities just going about her daily life. Get her talking to ghosts, get her talking to humans, get her trying exorcisms, get her set up somewhere with a goddamn crystal ball, and people will listen to her. Ghosts and humans alike will listen to her and to whoever she's with. She's creeping down back roads when she should be out in the spotlight!"

"Easy for you to say. You'd get all of the attention and none of the consequences." Chelsea was not about to see her friend paraded around like a carnival animal just because some old ghost said so. "Cyndricka is an adult goddamn woman, and she doesn't tell humans what she can do, so we have to respect that."

She could hear Cyndricka's footsteps and Carmen's voice coming out of the bathroom behind her, but she could not break her gaze from Henry's hard eyes. Any pretense of joy or charm was gone from his face, leaving only cold determination. She hoped she looked half as stern as that. "I think you need to leave us alone. We have a lot of walking to do and you're just getting in the way."

"Oh yeah?" He jerked back for the first time and spread his arms wide, suspenders stretching across his bloody chest. "Tell me, girl, how exactly are you going to get me to leave? No, no, the world brought me to this little treasure of yours. Something brought me to her path, and I'm not leaving. People are going to pay attention to her. People are going to pay attention to *me*. No matter what a couple of just-dead bitches have to say about it." And with no pause for Chelsea to respond, even to get her bearings, he turned towards the approaching Cyndricka and was all smiles, all flashing teeth and old-timey suaveness. "Hey there, little gal, how're you feeling? You get all tucked in for the night; I've got a few things I want to ask you."

He followed Cyndricka as she unrolled her sleeping bag on a bench. She didn't look happy, but he was not a bug she could brush away. Getting rid of Henry would not be nearly so easy.

"What can we do about it?" she asked Carmen later as they walked a few feet behind Henry's constant chatter. She had switched to speaking Chinese for an extra layer of security, even though she didn't believe that either Henry or Cyndricka could hear them. Cyndricka only knew English and ASL, and Henry didn't seem like the type to pick up extra languages for fun. Carmen's Mandarin was adequate, but her accent was muddled and occasionally difficult to decipher; it made Chelsea more than a little happy that there was at least one thing she knew better than Carmen.

"He wanted her to come with him to Atlantic City?" Carmen asked again. "He knows other ghosts there?"

"It was like he just wanted to show her off, no matter where it was. Like he's a spoiled kid that needs someone to pay attention to him."

Carmen looked off into the field of just-sprouted soybeans that they were walking through, seeming to consider her options before she spoke. "I may have a solution to our issue."

"But how? It's not like we can really threaten him with anything. He'll follow Cyndricka as much as he likes, and god knows he's faster than us, much less her."

"I have an idea. You do not need to worry about the details." Her tone, even filtered through a different language, was clear enough to shut off any and all questions. Chelsea watched her as they floated, but her expression didn't betray anything more.

That night, Cyndricka and Chelsea peeled away for Cyndricka's trip to use the restroom. Chelsea faced away and kept watch as she hid behind a bush along the roadside and did her business. Carmen took the opportunity to drape an arm around Henry's shoulders, or at least a few inches above, and lead him away, apparently deep in conversation. Henry's posture was casual, his usual swagger. Carmen glanced back at Chelsea once and nodded before the two of them disappeared into the patch of dark forests that Cyndricka would be spending the night at the edge of.

Cyndricka finished what she needed to, tossing a menstrual pad wrapper into the long grass and using a bottle of hand sanitizer to get as clean as she could. The two of them wandered over back to the flattest and most sheltered place they had seen in the last hour. Cyndricka settled down into her sleeping bag, cushioned by some long grass and dry leaves, and looked straight up with wide eyes, clearly waiting for the barrage of questions that had become routine. But they did not come.

"You can probably rest for a while," Chelsea said eventually, something to break the silence. "Get some sleep, if you want to."

Cyndricka nodded, and closed her eyes, but they were open within the minute, staring up at the stars. Chelsea turned away, back to her watch that was feeling more and more like a vigil with every second.

They were going for a walk? she signed up at the darkness the next time Chelsea glanced down at her.

"I believe so. I think so."

Okay.

Cyndricka didn't have a watch, so there was no real way to keep track of the time, away from the hustle and bustle of the cities where they had spent the last several nights. The occasional car passed down the country road, headlights passing over Cyndricka's dark form in the bushes and bleaching Chelsea's incorporeal frame in a momentary shine. But they were so infrequent it was impossible to use them as any sort of clock. Chelsea didn't even have the passage of her own heartbeat to measure out moments. She listened for Cyndricka's breath, just to know that the world was still moving, even if they felt like they were on the edge of it.

They both jerked at the sound of a shout, sharp and clear in the night air. At first a short yelp in a man's voice, it carried on into a longer scream: someone surprised and then terrified. Cyndricka sat upright and clutched her sleeping bag around her. Chelsea stood alert, as if she could do anything about oncoming danger.

As quickly as the scream had started, it cut off. None of the murmurs and chirps of nighttime wildlife had even paused.

". . . Maybe it was nothing?" Chelsea ventured quietly. "It sounded pretty far off." Cyndricka nodded and the two of them sat in silence for several more minutes, listening hard.

The waiting stretched on and on and on, with Chelsea feeling more uncomfortable by the second. She had never been that good at waiting while she was alive, had always wanted to be moving or doing something. A whole eternity of wandering and waiting was ahead of her, and this one night was unbearable.

"I'm going to look for her." Her voice sounded loud and sharp in the nighttime air and Cyndricka jerked. Her eyes went wide, and she shook her head, hands still caught up in the sleeping bag.

"I'll be right back," Chelsea said, trying to be soothing, for herself or for Cyndricka. "I just want to see where the two of them got off to. I'll be right back."

What if something comes here while you're gone? Cyndricka signed, letting the sleeping bag fall down around her waist.

"It's not like I'd be able to really help if something dangerous did come here."

That's not as comforting as you think it is.

"Cyndricka, I'll be right back. You can lie down and go to sleep; Carmen and I will just be a few minutes."

I'll keep watch here. But you better hurry back, or yell if you need me.

"I will." Chelsea didn't pause before heading off for the grove of trees, knowing her courage wouldn't last that long if she dawdled. She glanced back once to see Cyndricka watching her go.

The sleepy evening seemed to grow tense as she approached the forest. Nothing on the surface was different; crickets still chirped, the breeze still brushed lightly through the grass, squirrels still rustled in the leaves. But with each foot closer, the air around Chelsea filled with a tension, a sort of electricity. If the hairs on the back of her neck could have been moved by the physical world, they would have been standing on end. She considered going back to get Cyndricka, to see if she would feel it too, but the thought of returning and then taking the walk again felt like far too much. She continued into the woods, straight through bushes and trees.

At first it sounded like crying was coming from deeper in the grove, short, broken-off sobs that drew Chelsea towards them. But with each step they became clearer, and rougher around the edges. Like grunts or growls, the noises held more energy and fire than a cry. One low rumble was interrupted by a sharp crack of laughter, a cackle like the splintering of a tree branch. The noises rose and fell and rose again, muffled and clear in turns, and Chelsea kept moving forward, holding breath she didn't have.

"Carmen?" she called softly into the darkness. "Henry? Are

you guys out here? Cyndricka and I are getting kind of . . . a bit worried, you know?" At least she had the comfort of knowing that only a fellow ghost would hear her calling, that no living serial killers or anything would be tipped off to her approach. No one responded, but the grunting did grow quieter.

The crackling feeling in the air started to diminish and Chelsea felt bolder as she continued forward. "Carmen? Carmen, where are you at, you're worrying Cyndricka," she yelled. "Henry, I'm sure you want to ask her a dozen questions before she can sleep, so come on."

She passed through a large oak tree with a scratch in its trunk, and the sparking in the air crackled as she brushed the damaged bark, then calmed back down. A few of the surrounding trees had similar scratches, or broken branches with fresh leaves sticking out at odd angles. She didn't imagine that some broken plants could have anything to do with a discussion between two ghosts, but her attention lingered nonetheless. This was all very strange.

"Carmen?" she called again, and this one was answered.

A voice she could barely make out even in the silent night whispered, "Chelsea?"

"Carmen, where're you at? Come on out. Henry, you too, we need to get back to Cyndricka."

Passing through a few more scratched trees, Chelsea could finally see the silvery blue form of a ghost, facing away and hunched over a clump of bushes. The garish floral sundress was familiar enough to make Chelsea smile, but another call stopped short in her throat.

Carmen's whole frame was bent over, her shoulders tight around her chest and tension written into every line of her body. Chelsea could see one of her hands clenching and releasing in a quick rhythm, fingers tight and claw-like. It might have been a trick of her posture, but Carmen's dress seemed tighter and tauter than usual across her back, as if a body that hadn't changed in more than forty years had grown bigger. It was Carmen, it was clearly Carmen, but off, just slightly wrong.

". . . Carmen?"

The figure shuddered in the moonlight, a ripple rolling through her whole body. "Chelsea," she murmured, not as a question but a statement.

"Yeah, it's me. What's going on? Cyndricka and I got worried and . . . Carmen, where's Henry?"

Carmen's back rose and fell with what looked like a deep breath, though it couldn't have been. She slowly rose to an upright position. Her shoulders slid back down to a relaxed pose and corrected the optical illusion of the tightened dress, as it fell back to where it usually hung. She continued to face away when she croaked out, "Is Cyndricka okay?"

"We're both fine, just kinda freaked out. What happened here?"

When she finally turned around, Carmen's face was wan and tired, but it was still a relief to Chelsea to see it. Carmen looked lost gazing around at the trees and Chelsea, but she put on a weak smile.

"I am fine. Henry will not be bothering us and I am fine."

"Carmen—"

"I am fine. I promise."

The two of them returned to Cyndricka's camping spot in silence. They drifted through trees and bushes, feet skimming through tall grass, and Carmen watched the ground while she went. Cyndricka sat up on her sleeping bag at their approach, signing questions as soon as they were close enough to see them. Carmen raised a hand to halt her.

"Henry will not be following us anymore. Cyndricka, Chelsea, neither of you have to be concerned about him."

But how did you—

"We had a calm discussion between two people who have each been on this earth long enough to be mature and reasonable. I made it clear that he was no longer welcome to travel with us, and he saw reason. And I do not believe any more needs to be said on the topic." She looked up to meet Chelsea's gaze squarely. "He will no longer be with us and that is that." She glanced at Cyndricka. "You should get some sleep. You have plenty of walking to do in the morning, and I do not want our journey further delayed by you having to take rest breaks."

Cyndricka slowly lowered herself back to the ground, still looking up at Carmen. Their gazes briefly locked as if in silent conversation, before Cyndricka closed her eyes and did a better job of pretending to be asleep.

"Chelsea, you should face one way and I will face the other. We can at least resolve to be reasonable watchdogs for the evening."

"Is there a chance that he might—"

"No."

Chelsea wanted to say more, to dig through the walls that Carmen was throwing up, even just to wheedle her into giving some details of what she had said to him but she caught something in Carmen's eyes that she had not expected to see. Not anger, not defensiveness, not even sadness. In that moment, the slightest trace of fear lurked in the transparent depths of Carmen's eyes.

"All right," Chelsea said, and she turned back to watch the road. A sixteen-wheeler passed by, shining big lights straight through Chelsea and Carmen, over Cyndricka, and across nothing of any importance to anyone.

◊ ◊ ◊ ◊

The next morning started off stilted and uncomfortable, all of them pointedly not talking over what had happened or not happened. In the span of less than a week, silence had become strange and uncommon, seemingly empty of the chatter that had filled their walking time before.

It was nice to be quiet and serene while Cyndricka went about her morning routine, packed up her bags, and tried to clean herself up as well as could be expected. The questions had been wearing on her, and Henry's weightless weight was now lifted from her shoulders. But there was still a definite strangeness shared between them as they got back onto the road, with Cyndricka munching away on a loaf of plain white bread that she had snuck out of a convenience store one town back.

But despite how little noise they made between the three of

them, at least to the ears of outsiders, they were still a chatty bunch, and conversational lapses didn't suit them.

So what's your favorite movie? Or your favorite movie of the last ten years, Curtains? Since I pretty much have to narrow it down for you.

And Carmen smacked her hand through Cyndricka's head for her insolence, and Chelsea laughed and started listing all of the good dramas she had loved as a teenager, and it turned out all of Cyndricka's favorite movies were older than ten years and she didn't know the recent releases anyway, so who was she to criticize, and it all slowly went back to normal as they put more and more miles between them and the city, and inched closer and closer to the coast.

10.

The rain started up in the middle of the morning the next day, in a gradual little drizzle that dripped into Cyndricka's eyes and wormed its way down into her pack. She draped her poncho over the top of it, or rather the piece of plastic sheeting she was using as a poncho, but Chelsea could see where the fabric of the bags was darkening and she could only hope that they found somewhere warm and dry to spend the night. The water didn't feel like anything when it fell through her, and if she closed her eyes it was exactly the same as strolling through the park on a spring day, except for the way that Cyndricka's sniffles punctuated the sound of rain against the pavement and blacktop.

"Reno is going to be warm when we get there," Chelsea would mention every now and then.

So will S-F, Cyndricka signed with dripping hands.

"A big, warm sunny coast is waiting for us." The sentiments did not do much good, but Chelsea kept saying them. It was all she really had to say.

They finally moved out of fields and into a gradual series of towns at the edge of Pennsylvania as the storm started to really let loose. Cars and trucks splashed up torrents of water as they whipped past, and Cyndricka danced out of the way of the first few waves, before eventually realizing she couldn't avoid them all, and just trudged on through as the water washed over her coat. They passed occasional ghosts wandering down lonely streets and through fields. Carmen and Chelsea waved to them in their rainy solitude, but for Cyndricka to wave would mean a stop for an explanation and conversation. She didn't have it in her, so they kept walking.

It was around noon before Chelsea stopped listing the best indie rockers of the last fifty years and suggested they find some place to spend the day and for Cyndricka to warm up. Chelsea couldn't remember what town they were in exactly, but a commercial highway exit looked the same no matter where you went in the US. Fast food and gas station signs competed for space in the skyline, inviting in everyone who needed a break from hours of driving. These were transitional places, stops between actual stops, but they were more than good enough for Cyndricka's purposes.

The manager of the fast food place at the next exit looked Cyndricka up and down slowly as she came in the door and gestured her towards the front counter, with an unspoken but very clearly stated, "Buy something or get out." Cyndricka stood before the big illuminated menu, water from her dreadlocks dripping freely down her face and onto the floor.

She fished around in her pockets while she looked at the menu, and Chelsea glanced at Carmen over her head. Carmen's expression was just as wary as hers; they knew that Cyndricka had some money on her, saved up from the various shows in the park, but the actual amount was vague. Her hand emerged from the deep coat pocket with a fistful of coins and her little spiral notebook and pen, prepared to communicate with people who hadn't spent the last year trying to learn sign language.

The young woman at the front counter had looked bored when they came in, absently wiping trays with a wet cloth and surveying the empty restaurant, but her eyes had gone wide and wary when Cyndricka came in and started dripping on everything. Cyndricka tried to smile up at her, but it was lost in the shivering and the lines around her eyes that had settled in a few miles further up the road. Cyndricka tried to write on her notebook, to communicate as best she could with another human being.

Her pen bled. The paper was soaked through, and the ink of the cheap pen spread out in a tiny bloom, completely illegible. She tried again, and the wet paper tore under even the lightest pressure. She let her hands fall down by her waist, and for a moment, Chelsea was sure she was going to cry there in the booth.

"It's okay, take your time," Chelsea tried to comfort. Carmen placed her hand carefully over Cyndricka's shoulder.

The woman at the register pushed forward the little plastic placemat on the counter, the one with pictures and descriptions of their dollar menu items. She still looked a little unsure, but she gave Cyndricka a shaky bit of a smile. "Is what you want on here?"

Cyndricka plopped her hand down on the picture for coffee, leaving a wet train from her sleeve on the plastic mat.

"Small, medium or large?" the woman asked, and Cyndricka held her fingers close together, a very small amount of coffee indicated. "That'll be one dollar . . . just so you know, all the sizes are the same price," she said.

Cyndricka nodded and held her hands far apart to indicate a lot of coffee, and the teenager busied herself getting a cup while Cyndricka counted out coins. "Cream or sugar?" was a bit trickier to articulate with simple hand gestures, but soon enough Cyndricka had her stiff hands wrapped around a paper cup of very sweet black coffee and the woman was trying to subtly dry off the handful of nickels before she dumped them into the register. Cyndricka nodded her thanks before shuffling off to a seat, with her ghostly entourage trailing behind her.

Cyndricka tucked herself into a booth, pressed close against the wall and held her coffee near her chest, apparently trying to take in as much heat by osmosis as by actually drinking the stuff. Chelsea couldn't really blame her; before it had stopped mattering, she hadn't been able to stand the cold at all. Carmen looked out of place in her summery dress and sandals, like she had been out for a stroll along the beach on a sunny day, but she watched Cyndricka with just as much concern as Chelsea did.

"Feel free to stay here as long as you need to," Carmen murmured. There was no real reason to be quiet, but it seemed like the right sort of thing to do when Cyndricka looked so small and young in her big coat, dwarfed by the bag on the seat next to her, the one that had been slung over her shoulders for weeks by this point. "Warm up and go when you need to."

Or when they kick me out, Cyndricka signed, keeping her hands low to the table to not draw much attention to herself. She knew the necessary tricks and techniques very well by this point. Chelsea didn't want to speculate on just how early she had learned them.

She curled in further when an angry voice tore apart the silence in the restaurant, a man that Chelsea could see at the front, pale face turning red as he yelled at the teenagers lining the counter.

"I don't know where you people get off giving this kind of service! Are you just making it up as you go along? You little shits just don't give a damn, do you? Get your manager here right now; this is the way you regularly treat paying customers?"

The manager with the mop scurried over from a back corner of the dining area to intervene before the man was able to build up too much of a head of steam, or before the teenage fry cook shot back with the retort clearly just on the tip of his tongue. The man, the *paying customer*, went on a rant to the manager about the temperature of French fries and pickles on a burger, while the employees rolled their eyes and found other things to do. Carmen tutted to herself and Chelsea shook her head at the stupid things people could find to get angry about.

See? Cyndricka signed to them, nodding her head to the argument that was building large enough to fill the restaurant. *Humans are still concerned with petty things like that. Ghosts don't have to worry about things like food and warmth and shelter, and they're better people because of it. You two are both better people.*

"I would not say that. I would not say that in the slightest." It was actually Carmen who spoke then, to Chelsea's surprise. She had been all set to have to come to the defense of humanity as a whole. "We are exceptionally petty beings," she continued. "We have too much time not to be petty. We dwell and we stew and we obsess over things that happened when we were alive, and that is literally the only reason we go on. I would have thought you would know that by now."

Still better than humans, Cyndricka asserted, scowling down into her coffee. *You keep your things inside. You don't act mean or cruel to others, just yourselves.*

"Yes, Henry was exceptionally kind and considerate of the feelings of others. As are poltergeists."

Cyndricka actually did look up at Carmen at that point. She

stared, and Chelsea was beginning to feel like a third wheel in the midst of their debate. *You have met poltergeists?* she asked.

"I have had the misfortune," Carmen said with a grim expression. "And believe me, once you have met a ghost that consumed with anger and hate, you will not rush to defend the inherent goodness of our kind. We are both good and bad, just as much as anyone who is still in possession of a heartbeat."

Carmen broke off when someone approached their table. She and Chelsea both instinctively drifted back to form a barrier between the visitor and Cyndricka, as ineffective as it would have been.

The young woman from the counter held the full tray clutched in her hands: the unacceptably cold French fries and the large burger that had been picked apart in search of pickles were spread across the top of the paper mat. The woman looked over her shoulder to the front counter, then back to Cyndricka, hesitant but determined.

"That douche didn't want—I don't mean to give you some guy's leftovers, but if we're—we're gonna throw it out otherwise–" She set the tray carefully on the edge of the booth's table and nudged it towards Cyndricka. "You just looked kinda hungry, you know?"

Cyndricka reached for it slowly, as if expecting the food to be snatched away or the tray to be thrown at her face. She pulled it towards her and picked up the burger with a slow nod. The woman giggled and leaned in closer to whisper.

"And don't worry, no one's spit in this one. Not like his *new* food." She clapped her hands over her mouth to stifle any noise, and Cyndricka had to chuckle too, silently but clearly, as she grabbed a few fries off of the tray. The woman nodded.

"Okay, well, enjoy. You know where ketchup and stuff are. Holler if you need more coffee. If you—uh, if you holler, that is." With a last smile and a shrug, she returned to the front counter, back to chatting with her co-workers, punching one of them in the arm at a joke.

With the audience gone, Cyndricka fell on the food, reassembling and tucking into the burger like it was the best thing she had ever eaten.

Carmen floated over to sit on the other side of the booth, hands folded together in her lap. "What was that you were saying about the inherent badness of humanity?" she asked.

And Chelsea had thought that she was the snarky one in the group.

Cyndricka rolled her eyes and kept eating, but the corners of her mouth were turned up in a smile, even as they were smeared with a trace of mustard. They stayed at the booth for an hour, finishing off the food and a second cup of coffee, and drying off her coat and socks under the bathroom hand dryer. Then with renewed spring in her step and the slightest trace of a smile on her face, Cyndricka pulled her bags onto her shoulders and went out to brave the rain again.

👣 👣 👣

The next several days passed in relative peace. Cyndricka did her hard walking when she could, strolling through suburban neighborhoods, backcountry roads, and busy highways, sometimes all within the span of the same day, and took her rest wherever she could find it, occasionally during the day so that she could travel in the safety of night.

They all talked and chatted and joked, discovering each other's preferences and favorite topics and the things that were probably best to avoid. More and more often, as the days went on, they fell into comfortable silence as they walked, enjoying one another's company and putting miles between dawn and dusk however they could. During those stretches, Chelsea's mind often drifted to their journey's end.

What would it be like for her to see Osric and Tamika at a time like this? Would it give her the same pangs that she felt when she saw them and everyone else at holidays or anniversaries? Or would she be able to get caught up in the inherent romance of the wedding? Or would she always feel the hurt of knowing that it was a chance that she would never get?

Not to mention, a chance that she had been so close to getting. She would have Carmen at her side, but would that make it any easier to see Phoebe? Her mother and father, arrived from across the country to see the first of their children wed, after they had already buried another one? Would Chelsea cry as they all danced, together as a family but unable to see her?

Would Heather dance with Roxanne? Would Roxanne come at all? Heather had known Osric long before she had met Chelsea, she was a friend who deserved to be able to bring a date to the wedding. And two and a half years was a long time to grieve before moving on. Chelsea was happy for her, she truly was, but seeing another woman dance in the place she should have been, another woman clapping for the toast at her little brother's wedding? Could anyone survive that?

Carmen had been right. Carmen was always right. Chelsea was never more than a few steps away from being a wailer, a ghost so trapped in her own mourning and sorrow that she wouldn't be able to find any way out. She could see a future where she ended up trapped by her grief for all time without any sort of escape or relief.

Cyndricka tapped her fingers into the edge of Chelsea's foot and she jerked. The road had dipped down low underneath them, but Chelsea had kept walking in a straight line, oblivious. Cyndricka grinned up at her and crossed her eyes, mimicking how crazy Chelsea must have looked just then. Chelsea nudged her back with the tip of her foot and Cyndricka squirmed.

At least she had that going for her: the two of them going with her down this long road.

11.

They stopped at midday for Cyndricka to rest her feet at a bus stop and retrieve a drink of water from one of her precious bottles. When she set her bag on the ground and rolled her shoulders back, her joints audibly cracked. She fished out a map and Chelsea and Carmen surveyed it while Cyndricka ate truck stop chips and an ear of corn that she had plucked right off the plant a few miles back and rinsed off with water from one of her bottles. It probably wouldn't do much against industrial pesticide, but it couldn't hurt. Her face scrunched up in displeasure as she gnawed on the tough kernels, and Carmen looked up from the map long enough to say, "I told you that would not be sweet corn."

Field corn isn't going to kill me . . . is it?

"City kids."

"Oh yeah, like you grew up milking cows in Boston."

Carmen rolled her eyes and went back to the map but Cyndricka just shrugged and kept eating.

"All right, if we keep going through this way, we should make it through Akron tomorrow," Chelsea said, squinting at the dots and lines on the wrinkled paper. "I'm ready to be done looking at corn as soon as possible, so let's just keep going through and hope for the best. Should we try to dip low enough to avoid the Chicago area altogether, or does anyone have reason to stop there?"

I should stop and put on a show somewhere, Cyndricka signed, momentarily holding the corn clenched in her teeth to free up both of her hands. *I'm running low on money. If I can put on a show, I should be able to get a bit more to stretch out.*

Chelsea squirmed. She knew that Cyndricka hadn't been able to steal everything that she needed, even with the two of them keeping watch down store aisles as she crammed absolute necessities in her bag. But putting on her mime makeup in a random city that she didn't know well seemed like an invitation for disaster.

Carmen had the same take on the idea. "Are you sure, Cyndricka? Might there be an easier way? Could you just put out your hat and beg for a bit? That might be a bit less . . . ostentatious." Chelsea had no idea how she kept managing to use big fancy words, no matter what language she was speaking in.

Cyndricka gave her a look of sheer incredulity, and signed with an extra level of exaggerated slowness, so that even someone translating sign by sign out of a book would have gotten the gist of what she was saying.

I. Do. Not. Beg.

Carmen gathered that she had crossed a line, but she wasn't about to apologize for a suggestion. "I know that you may have issues of pride, but—"

I don't beg because it doesn't work. People only give you money if you give them something in return, even if it's just a laugh. So I will make them laugh.

"If you absolutely insist," Carmen said with a sniff. "Heaven forbid that anyone on this crazy trip take my advice." Chelsea took her turned back as an opportunity to roll her eyes, but she schooled her expression to stone when Carmen turned back around.

"Well, if you've got a show to put on, we should get moving," Chelsea said with a clap of her hands that didn't make any noise. "You should find somewhere to get some rest before trying to make comedy magic."

Before we make comedy magic. Cyndricka hesitated at the blank expressions on both ghosts' faces. *I mean, if you would like.*

"No."

"No."

Coat, not even you?

"Cyndricka, I'll do just about anything to help you on this trip, but I am not putting on a performance. That's just not happening."

But no one will be able to see you.

Carmen smiled sardonically and raised her eyebrows at her,

and Chelsea knew she would have at least one spectator. "I'm sorry, Cyndricka, but this one's on you."

It was not one of Cyndricka's exaggerated performance mopes, but she did sag. She was probably wishing that Tyler or one of her other ghostly co-stars had come along for the ride with her. But if death itself had done nothing to dim Chelsea's stage fright, she didn't think anything would. They repacked their gear and made their way into town with a definite cloud over their tiny caravan.

After a half hour of walking, Cyndricka started signing. *If we were all performers, we could be a traveling circus.*

". . . Yeah?"

"I suppose."

The Triple-C Circus. Since all of our names start with "C".

Carmen's sigh would have been suited to a much younger person, more of a moody teenager's and less someone who had been on the planet for over seventy years. "Well, at some point you will have to find two more people whose names start with C, and fulfill that particular dream."

I'm just saying that it would be catchy.

"Sorry, Cyndricka," Chelsea said with a shrug. "Guess the circus dreams will have to be put on hold."

"What an absolute shame," Carmen drawled. "How will the world go on without the Triple-C Circus, made up of a mime and two ghosts?"

The Traveling Triple-C Circus, Cyndricka corrected, and at least annoying Carmen had pulled her out from under her rain-cloud. *The traveling part is important. I already had a ghost circus back in the park, but I have never had a traveling one.*

"Keep dreaming, clown."

Ooh, another C.

"Shut up and keep walking."

I am shut up. I am not talking at all. Absolutely silent.

Chelsea hadn't meant to laugh so hard, but it caught her off guard.

They moved onto other topics for the rest of the day, and Chelsea didn't think about the conversation until Cyndricka brought it up again that evening when she was settling in to sleep. A chill had

taken over as the sun had set, and Cyndricka had spotted an industrial building out in a field, probably some sort of processing way
station. The single door was locked, but the generator against the
back wall provided heat, if not shelter. Carmen was camped out
by the road, ready to call out if the first workers of the morning
appeared and they had to scurry off on short notice. Chelsea had
thought Cyndricka was asleep until she had felt the fingers brush
down through her foot.

Are there any other C names in your family?

She tried to not look too surprised or dismayed by the sudden
topic. "No, my siblings are Osric and Phoebe, and my parents are
John and Ashley. No one's Chinese names start with C either. Why
do you ask?" She tried gamely to lighten the mood. "Going to wait
for my sister to die so you can get her into the circus?"

Just curious. I never had a sister.

"Well, she's older, so I've never not had a sister," Chelsea
pointed out. "I don't know any different. And my brother is only
two years younger than me, so I don't remember what it's like to
not have a brother either."

He's the same age now that you were when you crossed?

"I . . . huh. Yeah, I guess so. He's twenty-seven and getting
married." It felt like something was catching in her throat, even if
the physical sensation didn't actually exist. "But he's always going
to be my little brother. Even when he's sixty and I'm still twenty-
seven . . . and thirty-five years dead."

I know that. My brother will always be a baby in my mind.

Chelsea looked between Cyndricka's hands and her face, unsure
if she had understood the signs correctly. It was not like the darkness impeded her vision at all, but Cyndricka might have gotten
vaguer with her signing as she got tired. "Your brother?"

She nodded, head rustling in the grasses and weeds that
surrounded the tiny building. *Yes, my little brother. Six years
younger than me. He should be twenty now.* Her hands slowed and
paused before she made her next round of signs. *I have not seen
him for a very long time.*

"Does he . . . is he in Reno too?"

I don't know. Maybe. She looked away and curled onto her

side, almost spooning the whirring generator, but careful not to touch the hot metal. *I should sleep now. Good night, Coat.*

"Cyndricka, I—" There was no way Cyndricka was asleep that fast, but talking past her closed eyes, when Chelsea didn't even know what she wanted to say, seemed a step too far. The past few weeks had been a bonding experience, that was sure, but she still knew so little about this woman, whose path never would have crossed with hers without her special powers and a serious twist of fate. "Good night, Cyndricka."

If there was a rustle and sniffling from the figure beneath her, she pretended not to notice it.

👣 ❗❗ 👣

What were your funerals like?

"Why on earth would you want to know that?" Carmen asked, fixing her with a cold look.

Cyndricka shrugged, resettling her bag on her shoulders as she walked. Cars rushed by in both directions down the highway, but she seemed to have stopped worrying about signing to them in front of other humans. *I don't know. I just think it's interesting. And I like to hear what ghosts thought of their funerals. It's like your birthday, but you didn't get any input.*

"Mine was closed casket," answered Chelsea, hoping that a quick reply would cut off the discussion about anniversaries that Carmen was sure to have brewing. "I mean, obviously." She gestured down at herself with her good arm, indicating the broken side and the smashed part of her face. "No one really wants to look at this. I was an organ donor, so they took anything salvageable out of my body after I died, then closed up the box and sealed it tight."

They took your organs? So parts of you are still alive somewhere?

"I . . . huh. Never really thought of it that way." She laughed at the idea. "Let me think, I . . . yeah, if I remember correctly, they were able to get my heart, my liver, one of my kidneys, and one cornea," she said with a gesture to her good eye, the one that had been scooped out for parts, but not until after her death, when it no longer mattered to her. "That's what, four people helped?"

"I believe they can divide the liver into smaller parts," Carmen pointed out. "I sat in on a few biology lectures about five years ago, I seem to recall that."

"So yeah, who even knows how many. My lungs mostly ended up with bits of rib through them, but they took as much as they could. It's . . . it's kind of nice knowing that my parts got a home somewhere else." She shook her head and cleared her throat. "Though, you know, it's not like I'm going to go track them down or anything. Go haunt some poor guy because he happens to have one of my corneas or go hang around the dialysis center trying to figure out which of them has my spare kidney."

Why would someone who got a new kidney still need dialysis?

"Shut up, you know what I meant. Too bad they would never have a matched pair, but I think my other one got smeared over the tracks."

"All right, that is quite enough of that," Carmen said, holding up her hands in a plea for a return to peace. "My funeral was open-casket, in fact, and a lovely ceremony." She paused for a moment. When she continued, her voice was heavy and thick. "I believe it offered a great amount of solace to my son and daughter."

Cyndricka and Chelsea nodded at the sudden change of tone, glancing at each other with discomfort. Carmen had those sensitive spots, like most people in general did, and ghosts especially, but it was hard to tell when they would come out or what would set her off.

When Chelsea had been newly dead, she had assumed that Carmen had everything sorted out, compared to the sobbing mess that Chelsea had been those days. But as she got to know her better, it had become clear: Carmen had sorted through most of her big issues, but anything that had not been addressed had been left to fester for over forty years. It was less raw than anything that Chelsea was going through, but almost bigger and deeper for having been buried.

Are any of your organs still out there? Cyndricka asked, moving her hands in smaller motions as if to try and whisper without the variability of actual volume. Carmen sighed softly.

"No. My body was held in evidence for too long." Her fingers traced over the middle of her chest, across the bullet wounds, but by the way she was looking off into the woods again, Chelsea didn't know if she realized she was doing it.

If she had been a better friend, Chelsea might have pushed further and asked for details. But Carmen had always been a better friend to her than she had in return . . . though perhaps "friend" was not the best term for what they had. A mentor, a teacher, a guide, but not really someone that she would turn to for fun or conversation. If Chelsea had had a real choice for people to come with her on this trip—well, she would have chosen Phoebe, Heather, and Osric. But even barring the obvious, Carmen wouldn't have been the first to come to mind, even though it was turning out better than she had hoped. Well, there was still a long road ahead to San Francisco. She was glad she didn't have to walk it alone.

12.

"So I have a question, Cyndricka. And you don't have to answer if you don't want to, but I am really curious."

Okay, shoot. Carmen coughed pointedly at the choice of words and Cyndricka quickly corrected. *Go.*

The walk had been more than a little boring that day, with convoluted roads tracing through woods and dense trees, scenery that was indeed lovely and peaceful, but not punctuated by much to make the day go faster.

"Have you ever had a job that wasn't miming? Did you have other jobs before this and just decided that miming was the best way for you to go, or did you come straight to New York and start putting on the face paint?"

Hey, what I do takes a lot of effort and work. Have some respect for my craft.

"Sorry. But you can't pretend it's not weird."

Nothing wrong with being a little weird.

Chelsea walked backwards down the road to keep the best view of Cyndricka's signs. Carmen was taking her role as lookout more seriously, keeping an eye on the woods for animals and humans alike. Cyndricka had emphasized that humans were the ones to worry about, but Carmen was still convinced that she was going to be eaten by a bear because she didn't tie her food up in a tree every night.

"Okay, but non-miming jobs."

Cyndricka scrunched up her face in exaggerated memory, then relaxed to shoot Chelsea a snarky look.

Do you really think there are a lot of people looking to hire a mute black female high-school dropout?

"Well, I . . . I mean, you never know, there are programs and—" Chelsea stumbled out.

Cyndricka snorted and shook her head at Chelsea's verbal fumbling. *I have worked in a few places, mostly manual labor. Did housekeeping in a hotel for a while, in M-N.* She finger-spelled the state initials, and Chelsea's eyebrow quirked up.

"Why were you in Minnesota? I thought you went straight from Reno to New York?"

There are a lot of places between the two. This is not my first long trip across the U-S, even if I have never walked it before.

"Okay, but once you got to New York? Straight into miming?"

She paused before answering, looking off into the woods. *I tried a few things. Again, hotels, janitor work, stuff like that. And I would put on shows before or after my shifts in the park, just to have something that made me happy. But soon I was not making enough money to pay rent, even sharing an apartment with a ton of people. If I was going to be homeless anyway—* She shrugged. *I was already going to be in the park all the time. I had to do something to make me happy. And it pays better than hotels.*

"Wow, I . . . wow." Like so many of her stories, Chelsea had no real response. Cyndricka smiled slyly.

You have never worked in a hotel or as a janitor. Your skirt is way too fancy. Chelsea hadn't realized that Carmen was paying attention until she snorted and turned away. Chelsea nodded, feeling regret that she had brought the topic up. She looked down at her outfit, the skirt and winter coat, the high heels. Her blouse was hidden underneath the coat, had been ever since she died, but everything visible looked nice, even while partially destroyed and blood-splattered. Chelsea would wear ripped jeans and old t-shirts around the house, but her father had always instilled in all of his children how important it was to look professional on the job.

Were you a secretary? Is that why you're dressed like that? Cyndricka asked, looking more curious than teasing now. *I never asked before. A lot of ghosts seem to find their old jobs irrelevant. I cannot blame them, when they are too busy missing everything else.*

"I was in IT, network maintenance. Asian but female, kind of a clashing of the stereotypes. I enjoyed it well enough, and I was good at it, but it's not like I pine to fiddle around with a computer again. Yeah, I guess you put it right, I'm too busy missing everything else." She glanced at Carmen. "What did you do, job-wise? I came right out of college and straight into internships and jobs, so aside from fast food when I was in school, I haven't done a ton else. What about you?"

Carmen did not respond for a moment, perhaps deciding whether she was going to admit that she was part of the ongoing conversation or not. But she finally turned back from her scan of the woods for bears or other threats, and raised her hands to count off on her fingers.

"I worked in my parent's bodega in Boston from when I was six to when I was fifteen. The bodega burned down, so I worked at a series of restaurants to help contribute to my family. I held several shifts at different stores and shops over the years. When I married Manuel, I took shifts as a receptionist at the factory he worked in. And I spent most of the rest of my time raising my children, as much as I had the chance to." She fixed Chelsea with a solid look. "I have never had a 'career' or whatever it is you would call it. Not one vocation for all of my life, but many jobs to pay the bills for myself and my family." She chuckled to herself. "That was a relief after I died. I had time to relax and pursue my own interests, not just the things that would put food on the table. It was not a fair or worthwhile trade-off by any stretch of the imagination, but one must take the positive aspects of one's condition with all of the insurmountable negatives."

The three of them walked in silence, the sounds of the woods and the steady beat of footfalls punctuated only by Cyndricka slapping away mosquitoes.

I got lucky, Cyndricka signed after a while. *I always wanted to be a clown when I was little. Though I assumed that I would tell more jokes.*

"You did not plan on a mute vocation?" Carmen asked archly.

I didn't plan on a mute life. But you guys know better than me, plans do not always go right. And at least I get to do something I like. She shot a sly look at Chelsea, a smirk tugging at the corner of her mouth. *And I never had to wear high heels.*

"Yeah, well, my feet don't hurt after weeks of walking, so I think we're even for the time being." That got another laugh out of Carmen, one that she couldn't really cover that time.

Chelsea had always been close to her siblings; with Phoebe being a few years older, she had literally never lacked at least one playmate in her life. She had made friends at school, dated plenty of different women, and been closer to Heather than she could have imagined being with another person. But something about the dynamic she had with her two traveling companions was different. Grudging tolerance had turned into affection on all of their parts (if Chelsea was reading the situation correctly and not just projecting her own feelings onto Carmen and Cyndricka), and they did truly feel like a unit. Three women tackling the width of the United States on their own, even if these states were only ever going to see one.

👣 ‼ 👣

They reached Akron the next day, and Cyndricka's eyes were open for a performance space from the moment they were inside the city limits. She surveyed sidewalks, storefronts, even parking lots, looking for somewhere with a large, flat expanse of hard material where she would flail and tumble and mug for crowds without getting in the way or accidentally smacking anyone.

Carmen and Chelsea kept their eyes open as well, but every place they pointed out had some feature that made it unacceptable for high-quality miming. They would have to take Cyndricka at her word there. In all honesty, neither were trying that hard. As they passed more and more people trying to go about their days and not be disturbed, Chelsea's feelings about the day got more and more conflicted. But she could put on a nice smile if it was what Cyndricka needed, so she kept her eyes open for anything that could work.

It was ultimately a park that Cyndricka decided on, of course. Having a public restroom was a big contributing factor, as doing her makeup in a hand mirror was always going to be a more difficult task than doing it in an actual bathroom. She rinsed out her traveling clothes under glares from mothers, who came into the bathroom and left just as quickly, and draped the wet clothes over dryers as she changed into her white and black shirt. With every item of clothing or makeup she put on, Cyndricka's whole posture seemed to change, her shoulders becoming loose and relaxed, the lines in her face smoothing down even as she twisted her mouth and eyebrows. Apparently the face needed just as much exercise before hard work as anything else: one more thing about miming that Chelsea had not bothered to think about before she was traveling with one.

The sun had come out bright and blazing after the cold night and a large assortment of people were out in the park, walking, playing, and otherwise enjoying the sunshine and warmth. A violinist was set up on a corner by a playground, but Cyndricka established herself fairly far away from him, trying to make it clear that she was not purposely infringing on his territory. If the glare he shot her across the corner of the playground was any indication, he still saw it that way, and there wasn't much Cyndricka could do other than leaving that instant that would make him any happier. She did a few preliminary stretches, cracking her back from the many, many long hours with a backpack hung off of it, and got into character.

She had her crowd-pleasing familiar pieces ready to go: the Dog Walker story, the Clumsy Tourist, the Ice Cream Thief. She went through the motions with big expressions, wild leaps and bounds, clarity of story and character, and Chelsea and Carmen clapped and laughed at all the right moments, perhaps a little too eagerly.

Because no one else was paying attention.

Oh, people glanced at her, all right, saw her doing what she was doing and briefly acknowledged that yes, there was a person there doing something strange. But no one stopped, no one watched, no one even smiled. A few ghosts wandered through the park and cast them sideways glances, but they continued to float past, not noticing how special this human was. Even the violinist stopped paying attention when it became clear that the little mime over on the sidewalk was not posing any sort of threat. He wasn't doing much better, but there were a few handfuls of coins scattered across the bottom of his open case. Her hat was conspicuously empty.

But by god did she try. She pulled out her best routines, her biggest spectacles, and made her most fantastic balloon animals in a last-ditch attempt to at least grab the attention of some of the children. But all she got were glares from parents on the benches, wondering who the hell she was and why she was looking at them so earnestly. She was very quickly going from charming to creepy. And everyone could tell.

At the beginning of the day, Carmen had maintained a sort of "I told you so" look. But as more and more people passed Cyndricka by, averting their gaze and keeping their hands in their pockets, her eyes had softened. The two of them felt exposed and uncomfortable, which had to be a fraction of what Cyndricka was going through. At almost five in the afternoon, hours after she had started and with paint beginning to smear with sweat, Cyndricka sat down next to her bags on the pavement and stopped. Her sum total for a day of work was two dollars and nineteen cents and half a pack of cigarettes.

Better than nothing, she signed, right before she wrapped her arms around her legs on a park bench and didn't move for almost an hour. Carmen and Chelsea sat by her sides, offering what very little assistance they could.

Carmen got their attention when a couple of police officers started to approach, strides purposeful and stern and their hands resting oh-so-casually on their batons. Her voice was short and clipped and she watched them with an unwavering gaze while Cyndricka hurried to gather up her things. Although there were only a few hours left until sunset, at most, she started walking out of town. Chelsea couldn't really blame her. There was nothing for them there.

13.

As if the weather were keyed into Cyndricka's mood, rain started falling just as the sun went down. She had gotten most of the makeup off of her face in a convenience store bathroom, but the remaining smears of white trickled down Cyndricka's cheeks and forehead. She looked like she could have been a ghost herself, the colors evening out into a dusty gray in the dying light. They made a strange little funeral march, the three of them walking in silence through the rain.

If it had been clear out, they would have heard her earlier. But while their senses were warped in a lot of ways, the sound of the rain and Cyndricka's footsteps still covered up a great deal of other noise. They were walking down a small county road, a hilly stretch punctuated by stoplights and the occasional passing car, when they saw a transparent figure down on its hands and knees, looking into a storm drain.

"Looks like we have company ahead," said Chelsea, trying to keep her voice casual. The memory of Henry was not too faded, but at least this person, in tattered blue jeans and a baggy t-shirt, didn't look like another old-timey bigot. "Do you guys want to say hello? Or just kind of . . . detour?" They seemed to be on the only road going in their direction, but it was an idea at least worth mentioning.

Cyndricka shrugged and kept trudging forward. But as they got closer, she looked up with a bit of interest. Through the rain, they could just hear a low female voice entreating something in the storm drain, "Come on, climb out, right there, you can do it."

When Cyndricka's foot came down on a fallen branch, it was

still firm enough to make a solid snap, and the woman jerked and looked up from the drain. She turned to them, and even after everything Chelsea had seen in the last two years, she still had to gasp.

If Chelsea had been asked to picture a headless ghost, she would have come up with a guillotine victim or someone else with a single clean cut. Whereas the woman before them, with blood and bone fragments spilled down the front of her Ramones t-shirt, had clearly been on the wrong end of something messy. If Chelsea absolutely had to guess, she would have said a shotgun, at very close range. A single ridge of bone and tattered tissue was all that remained of a jaw, and a few stray teeth were scattered across the shoulders. Nothing else of her head remained. How she managed to see them, much less call out, Chelsea would never know. The jaw ridge jerked futilely, but the voice that came out was clear.

"Hey, you two, help me out here. I'm trying to lure this kitten out before it drowns, and you two both look less scary than me . . . well, you do." She pointed to Carmen, and Chelsea thought that was rich, when she outnumbered the woman on recognizable facial features by a large margin. The three of them approached the storm drain cautiously.

"Come on kitty, meow loud enough for this human to hear you," the headless woman murmured. "Come on, kitty kitty kitty. You two can help too, you know. If you're not too busy staring down my goddamn neck hole."

Before either Chelsea or Carmen had a chance to properly respond, Cyndricka had lowered herself down onto her hands and knees, splashing in the water running down the hilly street. She glanced back at the headless ghost and tilted her head in a questioning look.

"She wants you to tell her where it is," Chelsea translated. "Her vision isn't as good as ours in the dark."

There was no real way to tell if the ghost was surprised or not by expression, or lack thereof, but her voice was hushed and slow when she spoke. "You can—she can . . ." A tiny mew drifted out of the drain, and the ghost shook her neck stump and spoke with a determination born of urgency. "It's far back there, on a little ledge sort of thing on the left. Put your hand right in over here."

She pointed and guided Cyndricka's hand and yelped when she brushed against her. "Jesus, and sparky too! God, I have a million questions, once you save this little idiot."

Chelsea lay down against the ground to get a better view. She could just see Cyndricka's dark hand wrapping around a minute black and white form, fur plastered flat to its body from all the water pouring in around it. The kitten squealed and cried out of fear and cold and carved a tiny row of red lines into Cyndricka's hand before she could get a good grip on it.

"Okay, now you have to be careful about this next part," the headless ghost cautioned. "If it gets out of your hand, it'll go straight down the drain. Careful. Put those solid muscles and bones to work, girl."

Chelsea held the breath she didn't have as she watched Cyndricka pull the cat slowly off the jagged ledge and over the wider opening of the drain. The kitten kicked at her wrist with its back legs, and Chelsea could hear a hiss of air escape between Cyndricka's teeth, but she held on around the kitten's tiny round belly until she was able to ease it up out of the opening, on top of the metal grate, and finally into her arms. She quickly unbuttoned her coat, heedless of the rain coming down around her and the filthy state of the animal she had just pulled out of a sewer, and tucked the kitten in next to her chest. It mewled as she buttoned the coat over it, still holding it close to her body with one arm, and the headless ghost stared at her as well as someone with no eyes could stare. Cyndricka gave a shaky smile, and Carmen cleared her throat behind the group.

"I am sure we all have a lot of questions," she said with a surprising level of gentleness in her voice. "But for the sake of the now two members of our group with body temperature concerns, I suggest we find shelter before we discuss anything." Cyndricka nodded with chattering teeth, and they took off at a much quicker pace towards the nearest town. Being on her hands and knees in the gutter had soaked her completely through, far beyond what the lightly falling rain could have done.

The best shelter turned out to be a big warehouse store with building supplies, set off of the road and far enough away from the nearest town that people could feel like they had accomplished something just by going. Cyndricka had to practically wade her way across the parking lot, which was set in a bit of a dip in the surrounding area, but she audibly sighed with relief when she got under the awning out front by the shopping carts. She set down her bags, which landed on the cement with a heavy splat, and set about carefully extracting the kitten from her coat while the headless ghost watched her, and Carmen and Chelsea made sure that all of the employees had left for the evening.

"I don't think I've ever seen someone who—" started the ghost, but she seemed to catch herself mid-sentence, just as Cyndricka was starting to look wary. She waved a hand at Cyndricka, who nodded with her own hands full of kitten, and said "Hi. My name's Jamie. Thanks for stopping, though you didn't have to. I didn't expect that you could see me, so thanks for saving that cat even with this staring you right in the face." She gestured to her eviscerated neck. "It freaks out the dead enough, I can't imagine what it's like for the living."

Cyndricka tucked the kitten into her lap just long enough to sign *I've seen worse*, before grabbing the little creature just before it tried to escape. Jamie paused, and Chelsea realized the reason for the delay.

"She says she's seen worse," Chelsea supplied, trying to bring herself to look straight at Jamie, to meet where her gaze probably would have been on a full face. "This is Cyndricka. She can see and hear us, but she doesn't speak. Sort of a trade-off, I guess."

Jamie turned between Cyndricka and Chelsea, impossible to read, and somehow managed to whistle, or make something resembling a whistling noise. "Wow. You guys are—you guys are one hell of a traveling party."

Circus, Cyndricka managed to sign just before the cat jumped out of her arms, and Chelsea had to chuckle. Appropriately enough, that joke was not going to die.

After Cyndricka fed the kitten some torn up cheese slices, it decided that she was maybe not so bad. The two of them had a fairly peaceful sleep under the store awning. The three ghosts sat further off, having a full set of introductions and keeping a watch out over the flooded parking lot. Jamie took in the explanation of Cyndricka, or as much of an explanation as any of them had, in silence, as well as the story of where they were going. Chelsea ended her part of the story with a plea to not pester Cyndricka about it too much, and she could practically feel Carmen go stiff by her side, though neither mentioned their earlier traveling companion. Jamie waited until they were completely done to make another long whistle, which caused the ridge of her jaw to quiver.

"Yeah, I can . . . I guess I can see why she wouldn't want everyone up in her business about it. But she could be the most important person in the world. You guys get that, right? You're traveling with someone who can talk to the dead. How many scam artists and con-men say they can do that, and it's some mime chick wandering around New York who has the gift? You could make a whole new religion out of stuff like this."

"I do not believe Cyndricka is looking for disciples," Carmen said. "And this is a trip to San Francisco, not Mecca."

Jamie shrugged, a strange-looking gesture with only a neck above her shoulders. "Hey, might as well be the new promised land. I always liked it when I was there."

"Not an Ohio girl originally?" Chelsea asked.

"Fuck no. Came up here to live with my girlfriend and I think you can see how well that turned out for me."

Chelsea hissed sharply. "I'm glad my ex-girlfriend is still living back in New York, then."

Jamie reached out for a fist bump and Chelsea returned it with a smile as their knuckles slid through each other's. Carmen rolled her eyes by her side, at these silly dead queer girls and their rituals.

Jamie chuckled and let her hand fall back by her side. "So should we try to find an animal shelter around here? I didn't see any other cats around and no sign of a collar, so I figure the little thing's alone. I think there's a vet's office a few miles up, if you don't mind a detour."

"We will have to see how Cyndricka feels about it," Carmen said, glancing over at the sleeping bundle of cloth and fur. "As the only one with the capacity for any real impact in the animal's life, I would think that she has the first and last call."

"It'd be nice to have a pet along for the trip," Chelsea pointed out. "Increase the number of living things that can see us by a hundred percent."

"You two are going to come away from this spoiled," Jamie said with a laugh. "Fancy big city ghosts, used to having a miracle human at their beck and call."

"I existed quite well on my own for my first several decades," Carmen said.

"Can't say that she hasn't made things more fun," Chelsea wheedled and Carmen looked away. "I know it's been an easier time for me, at least."

"But I get what Carmen here is saying," Jamie said, gesturing to Carmen as she spoke. She seemed to overcompensate for her lack of facial expressions with big hand and arm movements, and Chelsea was glad for the extra information, even if she did keep getting elbows swinging through her side. "Ghosts are good company. The best we're ever going to have, present company excluded, so why not get used to it? I'd rather spend my days with some spooky folks than lurking over the people I knew when I was alive."

Chelsea's mouth snapped shut. They had not included the precise reason and end goal for their trip in the summation of their journeys thus far, and she couldn't really blame Jamie for her views, not when they were held by most ghosts. Those that didn't want to become wailers, that was.

It was Carmen who cleared her throat and spoke, looking at Jamie without glancing over at Chelsea at any point. "It is true that you do not want to dwell. But I do believe that there is something worthwhile in trying to find closure through your connections to the living. Seeing your loved ones move on and grow as people can be a balm to your soul. Perhaps even the one that ends up giving you some rest."

"I guess so," Jamie conceded. "And I lurked around my girl for a while after I went. But once she got with someone else . . . well, last time I saw her, their kids were cute. Adopted babies that we would never have been able to get away with, back when she and I were going together. But the times have changed, and I'm glad that she's survived to see it all."

"You are very lucky in that," Carmen said slowly. "I often wish that my husband had remarried. My children needed a mother, and he just—" She trailed off while looking out over the parking lot, just as the sun started to rise over the surrounding fields. "I believe that it would be best for Cyndricka to wake up and start moving. She would not want to be caught here for long."

Cyndricka's plan, actually, was to get up and walk for a while through the fields and roads, taking care of her business and eating some breakfast, then loop back to the store once it had opened, to appear to be a normal customer coming in for some morning shopping. Given that she was already breaking one rule, with the kitten tucked down into one of her deep pockets, she elected to actually pay for a bag of cheap cat food, counting out nickels and pennies to a cashier that was still half asleep. A couple of paper cups fished out of the garbage served as food and water dishes, and she petted the kitten gently as it gobbled down what was probably more food than it had ever seen in its life.

Once it was dried out, the kitten was a puffball of long fur standing on end, a twitching cloud of black and white. It made an earnest attempt of cleaning itself after it ate, but Cyndricka still rubbed her sleeve over its muzzle to wipe away crumbs. The cat squirmed and protested against the indignity but didn't seem prone to clawing any more now that the panic of the previous night had passed. With its belly full and its face clean, the cat scampered across the little stretch of empty road that they were resting on and batted a paw through Chelsea's foot.

Chelsea couldn't help cooing. She bent down to twiddle her fingers in front of the cat's face. It squirmed and swung its front legs through her skin, going so far onto its hind legs that it overbalanced and fell onto its back. Cyndricka covered her mouth in a laugh and when Jamie joined in, there was nothing quite as disconcerting as seeing and hearing a headless ghost coo.

Even Carmen crouched down on the ground to make the kitten chase her skittering fingers, dancing over the gravel and dust. Its white legs and belly were getting stained from the wet dirt, and it would probably need a bath soon, more than just a quick rinse in the rainwater. Chelsea was surprised how quickly her mind had started including the cat in their plans.

But there were still the realities of the situation to keep in mind. "So, Jamie, you said you knew where a kennel was? Should we get moving so that this little guy . . . gal, whatever it is, can get some vet attention?"

Cyndricka's face fell in an instant, and she reached out to run her hands through the little animal's fur, scratching just behind its ears and eliciting an almost inaudible purr. The kitten clambered into her lap and seemed to instantly go to sleep, despite them both having only been awake for a few hours. For a baby like that, that was a long stretch of time.

Would you mind if we kept her for a bit? Cyndricka signed, not taking her eyes off of the rise and fall of the kitten's chest while she moved her hands. *I bought all this food for her and it would be a shame for it to go to waste. I don't have to eat cat food just yet.*

"She's a girl?" Chelsea asked, to put off the actual topic for a bit. Cyndricka nodded.

I checked. I was thinking of naming her C-H-A-R-L-I-E, though. After C-H-A-P-L-I-N.

"What's she saying?" Jamie asked, and Chelsea had completely forgotten that one member of their group was not in on the conversation.

"She wants to bring the cat with us. She's already named it Charlie, so I think it might be too late to go back. Though Carmen, if you—"

But Carmen was already sitting next to Cyndricka and passing her hand over the little body. Even if it didn't touch, and the fur passed right through Carmen's hands, it was the sweetest thing she had seen in a long time.

"Well, Cyndricka, it looks like you have everyone on your side for this one. Do you think you'll be able to travel as fast, though?" Chelsea asked, to try and keep up some semblance that this journey was still her own. Cyndricka nodded and climbed back to her feet, cradling the sleeping cat carefully. She slipped it back into her pocket, and save for one displeased mewl, the cat didn't seem to mind being passed around and stored in what was probably a warm little fabric cave from its perspective. Cyndricka moved carefully when she pulled her bags back onto herself and arranged them, and she was soon ready to go again, looking happier than she had for days.

"Well, all right, let's get a move on, then." Chelsea floated back to her feet, Carmen along with her. Only Jamie stayed with her legs crossed on the ground, looking up at them with her empty stump of a neck.

"So, it was nice to meet you three. I wish you all the best on your—"

Cyndricka didn't use any actual sign language, just waved her arm in a big "come here" gesture, and it spoke more than enough volumes. Jamie jumped to her feet with a big happy whoop.

"Aw man, thanks, I didn't want to ask or nothing, but you guys are some of the coolest folks I've met in a damn long time, and this town sucks. Let's get on the road if that's what we're doing. Daylight is a wasting, gals!"

In the course of one night, their group had gone from three beings to five, but rather than feeling awkward or crowded, it felt comfortable. Homey. Chelsea grinned and clapped her hand on Carmen's shoulder; with Jamie marching proudly out front and Cyndricka walking close behind, they had drifted to the back of the pack. "And you were worried about me being alone out here."

Carmen shook her head with her eyebrows raised. "Well, how was I supposed to know that you would be a magnet for every strange ghost in the continental United States?"

"I don't think it's me that's doing it," Chelsea said, keeping an eye on the clown woman now doing a forward-moving dance with the headless ghost as they went along the road. "I don't think it's me at all."

14.

They made their way into the heart of the Midwest with renewed vigor and energy, putting long miles between sunrise and sunset with only a few stumbles and pauses along the way. The four chatted as they walked through towns and cities, and down long stretches of empty road, or worse, crowded roads. Cyndricka and Chelsea hugged the curb while Jamie and Carmen wove in and out of cars, mostly avoiding the drivers, but shrugging if they happened to pass through one or two. Cyndricka ate as she walked, the random collection of things she stole, saved, or occasionally fished out of garbage cans, but she stopped and properly set up whenever Charlie needed to be fed or watered. The rest of the time, the kitten rode either tucked away in a pocket or perched on her shoulder, needle claws dug into the straps of the backpack for balance. At least one of the ghosts could usually be persuaded to entertain her, making big exaggerated faces and fanning their fingers out for her to reach. Cyndricka would occasionally have to dance around to keep her balanced on the bag, if she went for an overly large swipe, but most of the time she was a good little traveler on the long road.

Jamie turned out to be a good companion as well, both during the days of happy-hearted banter and the evenings of hushed conversations and quiet hours of watch duty while their two charges slept. Chelsea didn't know what Carmen thought of her; it seemed especially rude to switch to Mandarin when Jamie was already put out from not knowing American Sign Language. But every now and then she would notice the two of them having discussions about a range of topics, from how the world had changed over the twenty-two years since Jamie had been killed, to what bands these days "totally sucked and are just ripping off the good stuff that came before them."

Chelsea, for her part, had gotten used to the sight of Jamie more quickly than she had thought, and found herself in long conversations as they walked. Chelsea sat back and listened to Jamie talk about what the queer scene used to be like and what had happened with her ex.

"Natalie got the hell out of Dodge after I got shot," Jamie said as they wandered through a quiet little suburb, light filtering down through the trees and sending speckled shadows through their faces to hit the smooth sidewalks. "She finally had to admit that there was no way she was going to be safe there. Packed a bag, stole the family cat, walked out and never saw her family again. It was one of her brother's buddies that pulled the trigger, so it's not like it could have ever been the same again."

"I u—" Chelsea stopped herself. She had started to say that she understood, when in fact she had absolutely no idea. It was true that she could never go back to where she had been, the life she had lived before; Heather would always be beyond her reach now, along with everyone else she had known and loved. But her death had been the result of a stupid mistake. Her own stupid mistake. If she had been looking where she was going, everything might have happened differently and she could have been celebrating Osric and Tamika's second anniversary, not the second anniversary of her death. It was bad, and she would not pretend that it was not.

But Jamie had been stolen from her world. Carmen too; Chelsea could see the five exit wounds on her back as she walked ahead and interacted with Charlie while Cyndricka's shoulders shook with laughter. People had set out to kill them and been successful at their task, and it was infinitely unfair. Chelsea could sympathize, but never really empathize, because she didn't understand. She could mourn her own death, but she could not really find it in herself to be angry, other than her frustration with her own clumsiness. How Carmen or Jamie had managed to not be eaten up by anger, to have it devolve into hate until—

Chelsea had only met one poltergeist in her afterlife, and it was more than enough. The image of that long, distorted figure lurking over the dark water under the Brooklyn Bridge was going to stay with her for the rest of however many days she had left. She could firmly say that she was glad Jamie and Carmen were both the people they were, people who were able to keep hold of themselves under any circumstances.

Her pause had gone on for a beat too long. Jamie tilted her shoulders in question, her own type of miming, miming what human expressions usually were. Chelsea shook her head. "I'm sorry. I can't— I'm sorry."

A shrug, her shoulders rising and falling around her neck. "It is what it is. Nothing to do about it now. And I was lucky. The guys who did me actually got punished for it. I think one is still in jail, which is a lot more than I can say for a lot of other spirits I've seen."

"You seem exceptionally calm about it."

"I've had a lot of time to think." Jamie paused for a beat, then continued with a grin in her voice, if not on her body. "And always gotta keep aiming to pass over, you know? Find that one bit of something that makes you let go and be gone. Maybe being calm is mine. Worth a shot."

"I guess it is." They continued to walk in silence. Then Charlie sneezed and almost fell off of Cyndricka's backpack, they all had a good laugh, and the day settled back into the slow progression of one set of feet walking down a road and three more pairs floating along behind (plus four paws on a shoulder, of course).

Cyndricka didn't bring up doing another miming show for almost a month, until they were well past the urban sprawl of Chicago, through the suburbia around Bloomington, and almost all the way to Cedar Rapids in Iowa. The afternoons were getting hotter and the days longer, as spring completely and fully gave way to summer, but the Midwest still seemed to fly by on gilded wings, or at least on a good mood. They had their patterns and their beats and the topics they favored and the ones they avoided, but the emptiness in Cyndricka's pockets did mean that something had to change eventually. There was only so much she could steal without pushing her luck, and she seemed to feel an extra push to take care of herself now that there was something more vulnerable than her that needed her protection.

The plan was the same as before, setting up for an afternoon in a busy part of the city and putting on her best acts, hoping to get at least some attention and pocket change. She draped her miming outfit over the top of her bag the day before they entered town, so that the wrinkles would be a little less egregious by show time. Charlie sniffed at it with interest before flopping over and rolling over the top of it, spreading as much fur as she possibly could onto the shirt.

Thank god we found a black and white cat, Cyndricka signed, rolling her eyes at Charlie's antics. *If she had been orange or something, she wouldn't match the color scheme at all.*

"Always nice when animals are considerate like that," said Jamie. She was getting better at deciphering Cyndricka's signs through long hours of practice, between watching Cyndricka and being tutored by the others at night. She still used a large amount of guesswork, but she could often get the gist of a conversation—if Cyndricka signed very, very slowly and used simple words. It was a process.

"So I'm looking forward to seeing this show of yours," Jamie continued, jamming her hands in her pockets and strolling along as cars whizzed past them. "I've seen your practice and all that, but I've never actually sat down and watched a real mime show. Truth be told, I didn't know they still existed."

Yes, they do, and miming has a long, noble and uninterrupted history, thank you very much.

". . . Okay, Chelsea, can you get that one for me? No idea what she was saying there."

Chelsea snickered so hard, as much as she tried to keep it in, that her broken arm flopped by her side, and Carmen shot her a strange look out of the corner of her eye. She ignored it while she translated but hung back to speak to Carmen while the others continued onwards.

"What?"

"Nothing. I find it interesting how well you and Jamie are getting along, is all," said Carmen. She slipped into Mandarin with a comfort and ease that Jamie would have been jealous of, had she not been playing with the cat. Chelsea squinted at her.

"What do you mean?" she responded, sticking to Mandarin as well, even if she didn't know what they were being so secretive about.

"You seem to have a great deal of affection for her."

"This would have been a damn long walk if I hadn't figured out how to get along with all of you."

"You know what I mean. Coyness is not as appealing of a look on you as you seem to think."

Chelsea rolled her eyes and let her head loll back on her neck until she was looking almost behind herself. "People think any time you put two lesbians in a room together, they want to start going at it. Did you want to bang every straight man you ever met? Plus all the bi ones?"

"Certainly not. I met Manuel when we were teenagers, and we were very devoted to each other over the course of our relationship."

"Oh, bringing your husband into the conversation is way too easy, you cannot dodge like that. I think she's a nice woman and she's fun. Where's the harm in that?"

Carmen looked surprised. "I do not think there is any harm. I am actually quite happy to see you bonding with her."

". . . Why?" Chelsea asked. Carmen checked that Jamie and Cyndricka were still far ahead of them, seemingly forgetting that they were talking in a language that neither of the other two understood.

"You know I came all this way out of concern for your mental health and wholeness. Having different relationships with different people will help with that. Not everyone takes the movie and concert track that I do. For many, that is not enough."

"*Is* it enough for you?" She watched Carmen's reaction closely. She had not been expecting the conversation to go this way but was intrigued now that it was there.

Carmen sighed and waited a few beats before she spoke, seemingly organizing her thoughts. "When I was first dead," she said finally, "I required a great deal of distraction to keep myself in my own head. I filled the empty hours and space with anything I could. It has become my habit over the years, and it works for me. Even if it is potentially not the healthiest means of coping."

"Do you ever consider . . . do you ever try different techniques?"

She met Chelsea's eyes. While the smile on her face was touched with a great deal of sadness lurking in the depths of her eyes, the smile itself was still there. "Sometimes I busy myself with younger ghosts. The newly deceased, who do not seem to know their way." She chuckled softly, still trying not to draw the attention of the others ahead. "If they can learn better habits than I did, so the better for us all."

Cyndricka and Jamie did notice when Chelsea and Carmen stopped in the middle of the road, if only because the sounds of their voices had abruptly silenced. They watched the two ghosts embrace for a few moments, arms melding through one another as they went through the motions, before Cyndricka cleared her throat with a devilish little grin. Chelsea slowly drew back from Carmen. Carmen clipped her fingers under her chin, and Chelsea squirmed away at the little shock it sent through her.

"Come on, you two," called Jamie jokingly. "You'll have plenty of time to hug out your feelings after we all make camp tonight. No need to do it out in the road!"

Chelsea flipped her the bird without looking but glanced over just in time to see Cyndricka cover Charlie's eyes from the rude gesture. She was still a baby, after all, and innocent eyes needed to be protected from the big mean world.

15.

"Come here, kitty! Just for the hand! Go for the fingers!" Charlie made a heroic leap across the blacktop, sailing through Chelsea's hand with all four sets of claws extended. She landed with a bit less grace than one usually sees in a cat, but at least she had the excuse of still being a kitten. Though she did seem to be particularly clumsy, even for her age, so Chelsea was not putting high bets on her future as a hunter.

Carmen clicked her tongue and shook her head, looking up from the map that Cyndricka had spread out over the patch of pavement next to the overgrown playground. "You know you are teaching her bad habits, right? She is not going to be able to differentiate when it is okay to attack people's fingers and when it is not. You two will be to blame when Cyndricka has to deal with a badly-behaved cat." She pointed her finger between Chelsea and Jamie, making sure they both got plenty of blame each. Jamie twitched her hand back and forth over the ground, making Charlie stand tense and ready, trying to figure out where it would go next and how best to attack it.

"Do you think she can tell the difference between ghosts and humans?" Jamie asked. "I mean, I imagine she can figure out which ones she can jump through and which ones she can't, but does she know we're all the same species? Or, I don't know, different phases of the same species?"

Chelsea shrugged. Her experience with cats had always been limited. She wasn't going to be the one to speculate about the boundaries of their understanding and sentience.

I just wonder if C-H-A-R-L-I-E is going to be different because of this, Cyndricka signed, easily distracted from the dull task of mapping backup routes in case of emergencies. *Most cats hiss and try to claw at ghosts, but she's already fine with you.*

"Well, don't wild cats hiss and claw at people?" Chelsea pointed out. "Is it all just a matter of what they're raised with?"

Cyndricka petted Charlie's soft black and white fur, making little kissy noises at her while she did, and pulled away just enough to sign. *She can be the first cat domesticated by both ghosts and humans.*

"Just because you are a remarkable human does not mean that everything you do is the first of something," Carmen said, her tone lighter and more teasing than her words. "I have known plenty of ghosts who haunted houses solely to interact with the cats, who were being raised by humans simultaneously."

Okay, maybe not the first, but maybe the first co-parenting arrangement? Because none of those humans knew that there was a ghost also raising their cat.

"Fair enough," Carmen conceded. Charlie bounced over to paw at the map; she had discovered the other day that it had the magical power of making crinkly noises, and she had been obsessed with it ever since. Carmen tried to look stern when she shooed her away, but her smile betrayed her.

Jamie flicked her fingers to draw the cat's attention back to her and mused. "Do you think it's just domestic cats who can see us? Like, what about a lynx or a puma? A tiger? Are there ghosts in Africa hanging out with lion packs for fun? That would be worth the trip, I think."

"Have fun walking across miles of water," Chelsea laughed. "Nothing to see but more water and more sky every day, maybe a boat every now and then, having to walk either a mile up or through waves. Our walk is really damn long, but at least the scenery is nice."

You could walk under the water, Cyndricka pointed out. *Be an underwater explorer, no need for air or worrying about pressure.*

"And no way to bring down a light. We can see pretty well in the dark, but would you like to test out what it's like a couple miles down?"

Community Library of DeWitt & Jamesville

Jamie snorted, which was more than a bit disturbing to see, as it made the ridge of bone on her neck quiver. "Maybe I'll check out the jaguars first. There's land all the way down to the Amazon, right?"

"At least some of it. And it would be okay to walk over part of the ocean, just not a million miles of it. Thousand, whatever. A lot of miles of water. I figure you can stay sane strolling across a canal."

"Or," said Carmen, and let it hang in the air for a moment, "I have heard tell of an amazing new attraction in this day and age where animals are kept in enclosures away from their native habitats. Have you ever heard of these magnificent things called zoos?"

Chelsea snorted. Jamie crossed her arms over her chest and cocked out a hip.

"If I had a tongue, I would be sticking it out at you," she said.

Oh, I can do it for you! Cyndricka signed excitedly. She stuck out her tongue as far as it would go at Carmen, who rolled her eyes. *I can even still talk like this*, she said. *Though I need my hands to do this.* She stuck her thumbs in her ears and wiggled her hands, the picture of an annoying kid. Carmen glowered down at her.

"I would have grounded my children for doing something like that. Or slapped them around the ears."

Good thing I'm not your kid, then. And that you can't slap me anyway.

Carmen swatted her hand through Cyndricka's head. Cyndricka shuddered and squirmed away.

"It works well enough, I suppose," Carmen mused, looking at her hand. "Someone should have taught you discipline before, to tell you to respect your elders."

You don't get to count dead years in your age. It's not fair.

"So says you. Although my body no longer ages, my mind matures and grows every day." She tried to take up a dignified pose, but Charlie chose that moment to leap through her lap and onto the map, only a little bit encouraged by Chelsea and Jamie. Carmen shot them a glare, even as her mouth twitched up at the edges.

"Now, if we could be serious for a moment, we should focus on our upcoming route, whether we want to get into the outskirts of Iowa City or not. Or would you like to end up in a gutter just like this little beast here was?"

Cyndricka shook her head at the over-dramatics and went back to the map with Carmen, leaving Jamie and Chelsea to snicker at their own pursuits with the excitable kitten. Chelsea looked over at Jamie, stretched out on the ground next to her. From this angle she was looking at the top of her neck stump.

She had thought she was used to seeing Jamie's head, or lack of head. But the new angle, being able to look straight down the splintered remains of her trachea, both down into the murkiness of her gaping throat and through her to the ground beneath, was almost too much to take in. Chelsea knew that her own appearance wasn't much better, but she had the luxury of not being able to see her own reflection in a mirror. She tried to hide it when she averted her gaze, to make it out like her attention was drawn back to Charlie scampering on the ground, rather than consciously away from the sight of Jamie.

Jamie noticed. Of course she did. Chelsea imagined that she noticed every single time someone did it, but she didn't say anything. She sat up straight, giving Chelsea the angle of approach that she was most accustomed to, and continued playing with Charlie, even if her movements were not quite as energetic as before.

Chelsea wondered if it was another one of those things that she would just get over in time, or one that she could pit herself against, trying to get over it until she could let herself stop noticing. She would have to ask Carmen later, because the last thing she wanted was to cause pain to someone she had come to think of as a friend.

What was your—

Cyndricka stopped signing abruptly, and Chelsea glanced up from her hands to focus on her face. Cyndricka looked uncomfortable as she thumped her bag onto the sidewalk, as if she had been caught saying a bad word as a child. Jamie turned between Cyndricka and Chelsea.

"Okay, I thought I had the beginning of that one, but did it just end abruptly?" she asked.

"What were you saying, Cyndricka?" Chelsea asked her. Cyndricka shuffled her bag around as she unpacked it in the shop doorway that was going to be her bed for the night, not looking up for a few moments. When she did turn back to them to sign, her face was twisted up in something that looked like guilt.

I was going to ask what your funeral was like, Jeans. Her eyes darted up to Jamie's shoulder, then back to the ground. *I'm sorry, I did not think. You said that your girlfriend left after you died, so . . .*

"What was that?" Jamie asked, and Chelsea tried not to stumble on her own relaying of the thought.

"She, uh, she was going to ask what your funeral was like, but then she thought better of it." Reading expressions from Jamie wasn't really a viable option, so Chelsea found herself babbling to fill the silences, when she would otherwise have been watching. "She asks it of almost every ghost, it's just a habit." Cyndricka nodded furiously even as she didn't look up. Jamie just shrugged.

"Makes sense. But I never really got a funeral, actually."

"No?" Chelsea could see Carmen's head turning just a bit back towards them, away from her perch on the sidewalk, keeping a lookout for anyone coming down the street.

Jamie gave a little shrugging jerk of her shoulders. Chelsea wondered how long it had taken her to get used to not being able to nod or shrug when she needed to. "My body was dumped at first, and the cops kinda had a hard time identifying me. Can't imagine why," she said with the sarcasm laid on thick. "So I was a Jane Doe burial in a county graveyard for a few months. The cops put it together eventually and they changed my headstone, it actually has my name on it now, but there was no reason to dig me back up and put me somewhere else." She waved her hand dismissively. "I'd been separate from my family for years by that point. So yeah, about as lowkey as you can get, altogether."

Cyndricka nodded slowly as she dished out food into Charlie's little paper bowl. Chelsea was fighting the urge to let her jaw drop at just how casually Jamie could tell the story. Carmen seemed to be the one taking it in the best.

"Chelsea, if you are just going to stare, be useful and keep watch while I talk to Jamie." She moved over to sit next to Jamie, whose raised shoulders seemed to indicate surprise or uneasiness. Chelsea moved over like she had been told, looking out onto the street while Cyndricka laid down on the pavement, with her bag between her back and the wall, a safety precaution even when she had three sleepless companions to help her out.

"I understand the difficulty of coming back to consciousness in the midst of your own homicide investigation," Carmen said matter-of-factly. "But I cannot imagine not having your death recognized or acknowledged by your loved ones. I am frankly amazed that you did not lose hold of yourself and succumb to being a wailer."

Jamie crossed her arms over her chest, leaning back above the pavement as she spoke. "You're pretty direct about that, aren't you? But yeah, there were times I felt like I was going. Never met a wailer before, only heard about 'em, but I could feel that something different was happening. And I don't know, I just didn't let it happen. Fought hard to keep hold of myself, like I knew I was supposed to do." She paused, and Chelsea glanced back to see her tapping her foot silently through the ground. "But I don't blame those who can't, who let it take them over. It was damn hard, and I was lucky . . . The Eagles were in the playoffs that year," she said with a laugh. "Wanting to see if they could win the Super Bowl kept me connected to my own head through the worst of the times. And after that, it got easier, a bit at a time. Having someone else would have been useful, but I did it by myself."

Chelsea had turned back around towards the street, but she could hear Carmen's murmured noise of agreement. "That is very admirable," she heard her say.

". . . Thanks. I don't know if it really is, in the grand scheme of things, if it matters at all. But thanks."

Cyndricka's breathing was slowing and steadying with the onset of sleep, as well as the little breathy noises coming from the kitten tucked under her hand. The ghosts dropped their conversations down to a whisper. They moved past the topic of caskets and funerals, thankfully, and let themselves drift into silence for most of the night. Save, that was, for the occasional joke that Jamie would whisper into Chelsea's ear to make her giggle and earn a glare from Carmen.

"What's the worst thing about being a bisexual ghost?" she murmured right behind Chelsea, who tried to keep her shoulders from shaking, and to keep her voice steady.

"What?"

"Nobody thinks you exist . . . and you're a ghost."

Cyndricka expressed her opinion about the disruptive giggling by tossing a drying t-shirt through the two of them and rolling back over in her sleep. Chelsea held her finger up to her lips to beg Jamie for quiet, and Jamie held her finger to the empty void on top of her neck in apparent agreement.

Chelsea wondered what she had looked like when she was alive. She had some vague ideas, a woman that she had constructed in her mind based off of Jamie's voice and mannerisms and everything about her. The specifics changed constantly, and they were probably all far off the mark, but it was entertaining to think about.

All of these potential faces were very attractive, and exactly her type.

16.

The rain had started coming down heavily early in the morning and showed no sign of letting up through the afternoon, or even as it moved into evening. The rain gutters and sewers in these outskirt towns around Des Moines were flooded by two o'clock, and the streets were mostly filled by three. Weather forecasts read in convenience store televisions said nothing but more rain for the towns ahead. The howling wind, gathering speed across miles of flat land, whipped the rain nearly sideways. They knew that Cyndricka would need to find somewhere to spend the night indoors. *I might float away otherwise,* she had pointed out, and Chelsea had to agree with her, given the circumstances. The three ghosts had split up to find a place for her to spend the night, and Jamie had come running back a half hour later, saying that she found a shelter, but it was closing the doors soon. Cyndricka sprinted there and arrived just as they were locking up for the night.

By some divine miracle, the woman at the front entrance had been sympathetic about the issue of Charlie. She wasn't going to be allowed inside the sleeping area itself, out of health code and allergy concerns, but the woman was enough of a cat lover that she offered to take the kitten home for the night and bring her back in the morning. Cyndricka had scribbled her profuse thanks on her notepad at the rule-bending, if not explicit breaking, and gone into the shelter as happy as she could possibly have been at the prospect of spending the night in a room full of humans.

The meal they served was small but serviceable, a sandwich and a little bag of carrots, and Cyndricka tucked into it without reaching for any of the food in her bag, lest anyone try to swipe it in the course of the night. A few other people tried to strike up conversation, both among the staff and those staying at the shelter, but most were thrown off by the notebook, combined with her hesitation and wide-eyed stares. While the other residents gathered around a television in the corner, mostly women and children watching cartoons, Cyndricka settled in early, sliding her bag underneath a cot and climbing underneath a set of thin, over-washed sheets.

If anyone tries to take my things during the night, wake me up. You know the drill. She turned away from the other humans in the room while she signed, trying to keep herself somewhat sane-looking, but there was still a raised eyebrow from a teenage girl two beds away. Chelsea nodded and floated against the wall.

"One of us is always going to be here and watching. Sleep well."

Have a good night. She pulled the blankets over her shoulder and was asleep, or at least pretending to be asleep, almost instantly. Chelsea knew she was going to be itching to get out of there as soon as they had Charlie back in the morning, and it would have been the same no matter how nice or cruel the other people had been.

Carmen was gathered in front of the TV with everyone else, but Jamie wandered around the large hall and the cots, taking in the sights, however limited they were. Chelsea watched her pace back and forth, saw her lean over the shoulders of people reading books or skimming through newspapers. She loomed over an older woman for a few minutes, standing half-inside her shoulder to read from the woman's worn paperback. She looked up and saw Chelsea watching her and waved.

"Doesn't anyone in this damn place read mystery novels?" she called out. Cyndricka turned in her sleep and Chelsea held her finger to her mouth to hush Jamie. Jamie cringed at her mistake, but Chelsea understood. For the vast majority of their existences, ghosts could speak as loudly or as quietly as they wanted without worrying about disturbing anyone. She strolled closer to Chelsea and whispered.

"Sorry, I didn't mean to wake her."

"It's okay, you didn't think about it," Chelsea said, not quite as quietly as Jamie, but still keeping her voice down. Jamie put her hands on her hips and looked around.

"Do you want me to keep watch over her for a bit? No one's really reading anything good."

"I'd say take your time now, since the books will probably all get put away and the TV turned off when people head to bed. I'm fine here for now." She grinned up at Jamie. "It's a long night, you'll get plenty of shifts. And Carmen likes to wander, so we'll be switching more than enough times."

Jamie gave one of her short, aborted nods while resting her hands on her hips, and Chelsea found herself feeling a little silly about it, musing how it was almost cute, once you got over how absolutely horrifying she looked at all times. If she had had any blood, she felt like she almost could have blushed. Jamie tilted her head, which read as a sort of quizzical look with the tilted stump of blood and bone.

"Mind if I just sit here for a bit? Though I'd get it if you want the alone time, traveling all around with your lot."

Chelsea patted the air beside her. "I don't mind at all. It can get lonely when Cyndricka sleeps. You never realize how much people do it until you watch it from the outside."

"I get that," Jamie said. "I used to hang around with some friends of mine . . . well, not with, next to, you know what I mean." Chelsea laughed and Jamie continued. "And I swear, after they went to sleep, I would end up wandering through town looking for anyone who was either awake or had left their TV on. Anything to hear another voice. I found some insomniac dude the next town over, and I think I lived in his house for three months straight before I got bored of watching him play video games. Boredom and loneliness will lead us to some crazy things."

"I was very lucky, being in New York when I died," Chelsea commented, though she would never have thought that she would be happy about recounting where she had been hit by a train. "It's a big city, so not only are there a lot of ghosts, but a lot of things that just never shut down. There's always a midnight showing of a movie, or a secret concert at the crack of dawn, or just clubs with loud music and drunks hanging around outside them. It used to annoy the hell out of me when I was alive, never getting a moment's peace, but now . . . well, I have an eternity of peace on my hands, so a little noise is nice. It's why Carmen came all the way there. Picking up new languages alone has filled probably a decade of her afterlife."

"Anything to stop yourself from going nuts out here is important," Jamie said. Chelsea raised an eyebrow at her.

"Out here? Were you ever in Iowa before, or—"

"Out, like out of life. Outside of the normal order of things." She shrugged and looked away, as much as she could look. "Just out, you know? It's kind of easier than just thinking of it as being dead. Like you're in a different location that you're just passing through. Like your road trip. This is just one more stop before you get where you're going."

Chelsea just nodded to that, not altogether sure if she agreed with it. For her, death did not so much feel like a place she had to push through, as a state of being that she had to accept, no matter how difficult it would be. Or maybe that was the problem, that it felt difficult, that she *let* it feel difficult. Perhaps if she let it feel easy, for even a moment . . . she didn't know.

Their conversation moved onto lighter topics as they kept watch. At one point, a woman made a motion towards Cyndricka's bag, but a quick shout from Jamie brought her around just in time to shoot the would-be thief a glare and leave the woman to scuttle off to targets that didn't have supernatural help.

The shelter calmed to stillness, broken up only by a handful of people whispering to one another from adjacent cots, and the staff wandering through every now and then to make sure that peace was kept. Chelsea broke away from Jamie and Carmen to take her own stroll, get a bit of the privacy that Jamie had mentioned earlier. She had been right, most of the books were stored away and the television was off, but newspapers and magazines had been left open on some of the tables. She had to either read short articles or resign herself to only having two pages worth of the content of a longer story, but it was a nice chance to get back in touch with the world, even though she had spent the last several weeks trudging through a solid chunk of it.

One paper was laid open in the classified section, a few postings circled in different colors of pen, different people all looking at the same paper in the hope of something to get them through the days. Chelsea hovered over the wrinkled sheet, idly wondering if there was any place that wouldn't mind having Cyndricka for one day of work, so she could coat her pockets with more than a handful of change from another mime show. She was skimming over the postings for different entertainment jobs and thinking about what a bad time Cyndricka would have at being a clown in a family restaurant, when she noticed it.

"Madam Valentina Speaks to the Dead," it read in a swooping, flowery font that someone had clearly paid extra for. The rest of the announcement was in smaller, more sedate type underneath. "Madam Valentina is a world-renowned medium who can bring peace and harmony to the wandering spirits of your loved ones. Contact her for séances, communions with the deceased, and exorcisms. See past the veil with her help." A phone number was written underneath and at least it wasn't a 1-800 number, but a real extension, a 515.

Chelsea snorted and shook her head. How many of those sort of things had she seen when she was alive, people claiming to have supernatural abilities and knowledge? And in her two-plus years of being dead, every ghost that she had spoken to had expressed the same surprise and admiration for Cyndricka, the same assertion that they had never seen or heard of anyone else who could do what she did. People handed out money to these mediums, big ones on TV or small ones in local newspapers, when the real deal was living on a park bench in Midtown, putting on mime shows to feed herself and talking to the dead every day. It would be funny, if it was not most likely the grief-stricken and those in mourning who were handing over their cash to con artists.

She shook her head and moved on in her wandering, forgetting about it in the wait for the night to be over and for them to be back on the road.

They gathered up their goods and their cat the next morning, with a great deal of cooing over Charlie from the shelter coordinator. She looked better groomed, certainly, and the bit of ribbon tied around her neck was cute, but she was still happy to see her mother and her ghostly playmates. And the ribbon was shredded in a matter of minutes anyway.

They were almost all of the way out of town when Jamie pointed out the sign by the side of an off-road, a printed bit of plasterboard advertising Madam Valentina's services in the same curlicue font as the newspaper ad. Chelsea laughed and told them about the posting she had seen the previous night. Cyndricka giggled while Carmen just rolled her eyes, but Jamie was entranced by the sign.

"Do you think she really can?" Jamie asked. "Speak to the dead? Another medium here?"

"You have clearly never lived on the east coast," Carmen scoffed. "Or, apparently, watched late night television. Those scam artists are a dime a dozen, and none of them have any genuine ability. The only real medium is walking between us right now."

"It's a huge world," Jamie shot back. "And you're telling me that out of six billion people, there has only been one person ever who could speak to the dead? How could you possibly know that? It's not like ghosts can hop on the internet or make a phone call to share news. Everything we know is through word of mouth and gossip. Plenty of ghosts have never heard of your girl here, and maybe we've just never heard of this lady."

Carmen gave her a hard stare. "We do not have time and Cyndricka does not have funds for that sort of diversion."

"We actually have plenty of time," Chelsea pointed out, as devil's advocate. "We're ahead of schedule."

"See," Jamie countered, and Chelsea could just imagine the sort of petulant expression her face would have had to match her voice, if she had been able. "I think you just don't like when anyone disagrees with you, and you try and make it sound smarter than whatever they're saying."

"No, I am just not a fan of wasting time on dallying around. And besides, Cyndricka needs to get into the next town before nightfall if she doesn't want to be sleeping along a highway."

"No, what Cyndricka needs is to—"

Three sharp claps broke the conversation mid-sentence. Even

Charlie stopped destroying the ribbon for a moment. Cyndricka was scowling at her companions and clenching her jaw hard. *Coat, translate for me,* she signed with abrupt, short motions. *Both Curtains and Jeans need to hear this.*

"Okay," Chelsea said. Cyndricka gently lifted Charlie off of her pack, then placed both on the ground for full use of her arms. She stood taller without the weight of the bag.

Just because I cannot speak does not mean I am going to let you speak for me. She paused for a moment. *Except for what Coat is doing now. You know what I mean. You are talking about seeing another human who says she can speak to ghosts. Maybe she can, maybe she's lying her ass off, but if she can, it is a big deal to me. The biggest deal out of the group. So don't assume you know how I would feel about it and don't use me as a tool in your argument. If you want to go is your decision, but where I go is mine.*

Cyndricka let her hands fall by her sides and waited for Chelsea to finish translating. When she finished, Carmen was looking at her sandals and Jamie was kicking through the rocks alongside the pavement. Chelsea looked between the three of them.

"I sincerely apologize," Carmen was the first to say, slowly. "I did not intend to disregard your feelings on the matter. You may—you know that I can tend towards bluntness. I am sorry that it crossed into insensitivity."

"Yeah, I'm sorry, Cyndricka," Jamie said. "Your body, your feet hitting the pavement. I guess it's Chelsea's trip, but this is your part of it. If you want it to be."

Cyndricka looked between the two for a moment, then nodded at Chelsea. *Okay. That's all I've got to say. Thanks for the help, Coat.*

"No problem."

Cyndricka picked her bag back up and popped Charlie back onto her position on top. She took a long look at the curlicue sign.

Worth a shot, I guess. It might be fun.

A few blocks down from the turn-off, Cyndricka set Charlie down to play in the grass in Madam Valentina's front lawn. It did look like this was just her home, a small brick house with lacey curtains, instead of some more mystical location, but Chelsea supposed everyone had to start somewhere.

I guess I just go up and knock, Cyndricka signed, looking at the house appraisingly. *You all should join me, so if she can see you, you can explain. If not, I'll just leave.*

"Whatever you think is the wisest course of action," Carmen said primly. Jamie murmured her agreement and the four of them made their way up the front drive without another word. Cyndricka gripped the straps of her backpack and set her jaw.

An intricate web of beads hung over the front door, framing a cardboard sign in the same curlicue font: "Welcome to the Den of Madam Valentina." Charlie, who had followed them up to the front porch, pawed at a tasseled shawl draped over white plastic patio furniture. When Cyndricka took a breath and pushed the doorbell, the tinkling sound of windchimes rang out and then cut off abruptly in a burst of static.

"Very refined," Carmen said with a raised eyebrow. Cyndricka didn't sign anything back, just gestured to herself with a frank expression of *Really?*

"Fair enough, my apologies."

A few moments passed and Chelsea's impatience got the better of her. She leaned forward and poked her head deliberately through the front door to see if anyone was coming and got her first glance at the supposed mystical den.

The front room was decorated with a dozen shawls and other sorts of lacy hangings, draped over doorways and mirrors, or just tacked to the walls. The lights were dimmed and tinged with red to give a mystical feel to what otherwise looked like a normal front hallway. Just inside, Chelsea could see a stick of incense burning, so she assumed the house was fragrant; she wondered what scent it was.

Cyndricka rang the staticky wind chime bell again and a middle-aged white woman came sweeping out of a parlor in a swish of skirts, beads, and bangles. Her big mass of curly blonde hair was tied back with a scarf and on her way to the door she paused to grab a bottle of perfume and give herself a quick spray. It was a complete, if a little cliché, picture of what a fortuneteller or mystic should look like.

"Um, hello?" Chelsea tested awkwardly, her head still stuck through the door. "Can you see me? Or hear me?"

Madam Valentina stopped a foot away from the door. She furrowed her brow and looked around the front room.

"Right in front of you," Chelsea added. "I'm partway through the door. I take it you can't see me, but—"

Valentina slowly reached a hand out and skimmed it through Chelsea's face and all the way to touch the wood of the door. She closed her eyes and took a deep breath in and out, seemingly concentrating on something.

"Um, say something if you can hear me. Say 'hello' or 'yes' or, I don't know, 'lemon.'" Chelsea got no response, but something in the woman's face held a lot of concentration, and Chelsea could feel a slight tingle where her arm was pressing through her head. Unsure, she pulled her head back through the door and looked at Cyndricka with a shrug.

"So the woman in there can maybe sense something, but—"

She was interrupted by the door swinging open and Madam Valentina sweeping her arms wide to spread her many shawls.

"Welcome to the den of the Madam Valentina, where I shall reach past the ether and pierce the veil to speak to—to speak to . . . um, can I help you?"

A homeless woman with a big backpack and a cat were evidently not what she had expected to be waiting on the other side of the door. Cyndricka smiled and gave a little wave, then looked to Jamie.

"Madam Valentina, we would like to speak with you. And Cyndricka would like to speak with you, one medium to another." Jamie said it very directly, like she had no doubt that she would be heard and understood. And Valentina did turn her gaze away from Cyndricka and to the "empty" space next to her when Jamie spoke. But she looked back to Cyndricka after a moment.

"Pardon me, but I'm very busy today and—"

While she had been looking in the direction of Jamie, Cyndricka had been preparing her notebook. She held it up with the question, *Can you see the ghosts traveling with me?*

Valentina jerked back and her eyes darted back and forth across the porch. Her gaze rested briefly on each of the three spirits and Chelsea did get the sense that she was being looked at, if not entirely seen. It was like being looked at by someone just waking up or squinting through a dense fog. Valentina looked squarely back at Cyndricka and stretched her arm to beckon her into the sitting room.

"I think you ought to come in and have a cup of tea."

The four entered and Charlie bounced in after them. Cyndricka glanced at Valentina and nodded towards Charlie in question, but Valentina waved her hand vaguely.

"Yes, yes, the cat is fine, though my boy Lucius might growl at him. What is your name, dear? How did you find this place?"

Cyndricka sat down at a small table with a gauzy magenta cover and took her time writing out her answer. Valentina hovered for a moment, then bustled off to start a kettle going when it was clear that Cyndricka was writing a longer answer. She finally sat down across from her with two cups of tea and took the offered notebook.

My name is Cyndricka and I saw an ad in the paper. Or actually, my friends did. We've been walking from New York and noticed your ad about speaking to the dead. I've never met another person who could do what I do. Can you really see them? Or talk to them?

"My dear, you make it sound so easy," Valentina said with a soft smile. "You must be very attuned to the spirit world to perceive the messages of the deceased as clear words. Or are you perhaps saying that you can put words to the energies that they send you?" She spoke clearly, as if she thought Cyndricka slow or like a child. Cyndricka slid her notebook back towards her and hurried to write an answer.

No, I can have conversations with them. I've been able to all my life. Your ad said you speak to the dead, I thought maybe you could too.

"I think you might be confused, my dear. The dead do not speak like you or me—or I suppose just like myself. I can perceive their messages with a great deal of concentration and openness to the powers of the universe, but our abilities are not like calling the afterlife on a telephone. Have you often heard voices, dear?" She said the last part especially gently, complete with a careful hand placed on Cyndricka's forearm.

Cyndricka's expression went hard and she busied herself taking a sip of her tea, shaking off Valentina's touch. She glanced at the ghosts and raised her eyebrows, asking for their input.

Carmen decisively walked out of the room and towards a staircase. Jamie leaned over the table and put her jaw right in front of Valentina's eyes. Chelsea drifted off to the side, looking at the spirit and woman in profile.

"HELLO," Jamie said loudly and firmly. "MY NAME IS JAMIE AND I AM SPEAKING TO YOU."

Valentina's eyes closed in some quiet rapture and she smiled and nodded. "Yes, yes, the spirits are drawn to your energy, miss, and they greet me as a fellow living person who may sense beyond the veil. You are truly blessed in your abilities." She opened her eyes again and reached through Jamie to take one of Cyndricka's hands in both of her own. "Be proud of what you have and do not try to reach for things beyond the mortal ken. You would only make yourself look foolish in the eyes of the living and the dead."

Cyndricka took her hand back.

Chelsea huffed and went over to stand by her side. "Who does this lady think looks foolish here?"

That got a small smile out of Cyndricka and she nodded into her tea. Jamie leaned back away from Valentina and shrugged.

"Well, it's kind of impressive, but I'm sorry I brought us all out of our way for this. If she's gonna condescend to you, wanna see if she'll offer you lunch to go with the tea?"

Cyndricka nodded and wrote some rambling message about food for the soul and the body. While Valentina bustled back into the kitchen to grab a plate of cookies, Cyndricka signed to Jamie and Chelsea with a sad little smile.

She's the most receptive person that I've met before, by a fair margin. But even with another miracle person, I'm still the freak. Or just crazy and hallucinating all of you, walking across the country alone.

Chelsea and Jamie were cut off from their protests by Carmen walking decisively back into the room. "You are no more insane than any of us. Tell this Madam Valentina that her bed has a blue and purple quilt, that she has five crystals on her bathroom counter and that she needs to do her laundry, the hamper is overflowing. Oh, and there are two frisbees on her roof."

Cyndricka and Chelsea grinned and Jamie cackled out loud. Valentina returned a moment later with cookies and a look of confusion. "Is something funny, my dear?"

Cyndricka was quick to write down the details from Carmen and slide the notepad across the table. Valentina read over it slowly, eyes getting wider and wider. She looked up with her mouth slightly ajar.

"How did . . . did you go up . . . but I didn't hear you . . . how?"

This response was a lot quicker to write out.

A little ghost told me.

Fifteen minutes of awkward denial and a few cookies later, Valentina ushered Cyndricka and Charlie out the door, the snickering ghosts trailing behind.

"At least she didn't charge you for a séance."

I should be charging her. Cyndricka paused to munch her cookie as they walked back towards the main city thoroughfare. She shoved the end of it in her mouth to free up her hands. *I considered trying it, once. Talking to the dead for money. But it's the living I can't stand talking to.*

"Good thing you've got plenty of dead to talk to along the way."

17.

The first show that Cyndricka put on with a cat in tow was right off the downtown part of Omaha, a nice urban break from rural wandering. She found a suitable sidewalk corner where she would be eye-catching but not in the way and set up shop. It really shouldn't have been surprising, the idea that having a kitten would help them draw more attention. The ghosts tried to keep her distracted over by Cyndricka's bags while she performed, but by nature of being the only one who could distribute food and tummy rubs, Cyndricka had become Charlie's favorite, and she would not bear to be parted long enough for her to dance around. So Cyndricka had adapted on the fly, including the stray kitten into her cast of otherwise imaginary characters.

The routine quickly evolved to center around Charlie's involvement, with Cyndricka pulling big twisted faces as the cat followed her through a journey of trying to get a job. The fictional relationship developed as she came to appreciate the tiny co-star more and more, even as her troubles grew, and the audience cooed and giggled over the heartwarming antics.

And what an audience they had: a big crowd that gathered around and laughed at all the appropriate beats, and even clapped at the end of scenes. Coins and dollar bills trickled into Cyndricka's upturned top hat, and a few phones came out to record the animal and human miming duo. Though Charlie didn't seem to grasp the silence aspect of miming; she meowed every time Cyndricka walked away from her, drawing a guaranteed "aww" out of the audience. The "aww-dience," as Jamie whispered to Chelsea, before she guffawed and clapped at a particularly heroic leap of

Cyndricka's, where she twisted in mid-air to avoid tripping over Charlie. Sometimes it seemed like she was part cat as well, between her flexibility and the seeing the dead.

Jamie was just as caught up in the show as the humans, whooping and cheering at every twisted face and big sweeping arm. It might have just been the novelty, whereas Carmen and Chelsea had each seen some version of the performances a dozen times. But there was a sincere joy in the way she clapped and laughed. She leaned her arm against Chelsea's, sending sparks shooting through both of them as they melded together, but not unpleasant ones. Never unpleasant. It would always be strange to look into eyes that weren't there, a mass of viscera where a head should be, but at the same time, Chelsea felt that it was nice to be looked at. To be noticed.

Cyndricka's performance ended for the day and she took a mighty bow. Then she held up Charlie, to mimic a bow, and the crowd lost their minds from the sheer adorableness. It had not been her most refined or polished piece, adapting on the fly to having a tangible, solid figure alongside her, but it was certainly the most financially successful Chelsea had ever seen, with big handfuls of change clinking as people emptied their pockets into the hat before walking away. Jamie pulled away from Chelsea's side to go congratulate Cyndricka, and Chelsea tried not to rub her arm at the points where they had drifted into and through one another.

Carmen caught her eye and smirked. Chelsea stuck out her tongue, like the mature individual she was.

The sheer thrill of the good show, the positive response, and the refilled pockets sent Cyndricka on a spending spree. Chelsea's previous idea of a spending spree had usually involved shopping for games and books, a nice night out at a restaurant, and a movie with popcorn and candy. But she still got caught up in the relative luxury of Cyndricka buying a box of her favorite cereal, an extra blanket that looked warm but still folded down very small, and a little collar for Charlie, who was learning how to keep at her heel fairly well, but still made them all nervous around traffic. She got stronger and more exploratory by the day.

Cyndricka beamed while she counted out dimes onto the counter in the box store, trying to use up as much of the bulky metal money as she could before she dipped into the actual bills. She even waited until Charlie was sleepy enough to be nestled into a pocket and went to a cheap diner, tucking into a plate of pancakes and drinking as many refills of coffee as the glaring waitress was willing to bring her. By the time she settled down for the night, in a very fortuitous park, in the warm-looking evening with a clear sky, it had been probably the best day of the entire trip, and she rested easily with Charlie curled into a ball on her chest.

Chelsea shook her head and gazed down at the sleeping creatures fondly. She tried to imagine an afterlife where she had never met Cyndricka, never met any of them. She still missed her old life desperately if she ever thought about it. Osric remained the point of this whole journey, and her heart ached when she thought about Heather back in their apartment.

But there were new things, new people, here that she never could have imagined before.

"God, I'm glad that I tagged along with you guys," said Jamie as she stretched out her arms. It had probably been a habit when she was alive, one that stayed long after there was any actual use for them. "I haven't had that much fun in years. Decades. That show's the sort of stuff it's worth hanging around for."

Carmen snorted and rearranged her dress over her knees. She was seated on the back of Cyndricka's bench for the night, watching out over a nearby parking lot. "I will admit that I see more of the appeal of her performances, the more that I see of them. She is a talented mime. By the standards for mimes."

"Shut up, she's great by any standards," Chelsea said with a light kick into Carmen's side. "And we need to keep quiet, or we'll wake her up. We're back on the road in the morning, and she needs her rest."

The three of them went quiet, listening only to the sounds of the park settling down for the night, distant cars driving through neighborhoods, the light snuffling of Charlie's breathing mingling with Cyndricka's gentle snores. She had never spent nearly enough nights outside when she was alive. Despite being the one to originally impose the silence, Chelsea sighed and whispered. "I can see what you mean, Jamie. This is the sort of night you stay around for."

But once the words were out of her mouth, they sounded less content and comfortable than she had intended. More wistful, more . . . sad, somehow. And that seemed to be the way that Jamie took them, by the way she turned around to watch her. She sat in silence, and Chelsea almost thought that her comment would be allowed to pass and disappear into the long night ahead of them.

"Why do you think you stay around?" Jamie asked after some time. "Why didn't you guys . . . move on, I guess? That's what I've always heard it called, anyway."

Carmen drummed her fingers on her knee and Chelsea tried to gather her thoughts enough for a coherent answer. So many people died every day, in so many different ways, with so many things left undone. But the world wasn't filled to the brim with ghosts, and not every ghost she had met had that One Thing that kept them out of eternal peace, or eternal suffering, or eternal emptiness, or whatever happened to people who didn't come back as ghosts, be it eternal or not. How could she give a reason for something she barely understood?

"I have a family," Carmen said, and continued before Chelsea could respond with whatever she was going to babble. "I mean, I have children. They are adults now, but they were quite young when I was killed. I believe that the cause of my post-life existence is them."

"Yeah, but . . ." Jamie paused, and Chelsea knew enough about her body language by now to read the hesitance in the set of her shoulders and the twist of her hands. "Lots of people die who have kids. Wouldn't the world just be filled with parent ghosts if that were the case? Be even more depressing than it is now, everyone just wandering around crying about their kids."

"I am a mother, not a wailer," Carmen said, but softly, not quite a reprimand, just a firm correction. "I cannot speak for the rest of humanity, or even the rest of the parents in the world who have died and left behind children. I was taken from my son and daughter under dire circumstances, as I am sure you can tell."

Chelsea and Jamie both looked down at her bullet holes before they could catch themselves. It wasn't like it was a new sight, anything different from what they saw every day, and by far the least gruesome out of the three of them. But they held an extra weight just then, an importance beyond the bloodstains on the garish floral pattern.

"I had a great deal of emotions to work through just then, more than one instant could bear, even if it was the last moment my heart was beating. If I had to venture a guess over why I am still here, that would have to be the one. I needed more time to feel. Afraid, sad . . . angry. Being surprised in my own home did not leave me with much of a chance."

Chelsea had never heard Carmen speak that much about her death. Though to be fair, Chelsea had never asked as much, even the sideways question of Jamie's that had gotten them there. If she were a braver person, she would have asked more, pushed for the whole story.

She was not a brave person. Or at least not that brave. She cleared her throat and spoke about herself, a far, far safer topic. "I think I just had things I still wanted to do. My brother's wedding, yeah, but little things too. Little even by those standards, before everything got a lot smaller. I had gotten a promotion the month before and my sister and I hadn't gone out to dinner to celebrate yet. My mom was going to make some of my grandpa's old recipes over the holidays, had been buying all the ingredients from Chinatown, and I hadn't had some of that stuff since I was a kid. God, I even just wanted to get through my workday so that I could get home and get out of my high heels. A pint of ice cream was waiting for me in the freezer, and the season finale of Heather's favorite show . . . I wonder if she ever got around to watching it." She did not realize how many words had spilled out of her mouth until Jamie and Carmen were both staring at her. She rubbed at the back of her neck, fingers tracing over the sharp ridges of the snapped vertebrae jutting out through her skin. "I don't know. It's silly now, but I guess I was just looking forward to a lot. A lot that I missed my chance on."

Jamie's hand slipped into hers, both in that the form of her fingers phased through Chelsea's palm, and that she curled her hand around Chelsea's, the intended gesture clear. When Chelsea squeezed, there was nothing to offer resistance, nothing to hold on to, but she appreciated the sparking sensation nonetheless.

"What about you?" she asked Jamie. "Any reason you're still here?"

"I don't know, maybe I was supposed to be here," said Jamie. She sounded embarrassed at the idea. "I mean, I didn't do much with my life. Wandered around, saw some concerts, fucked some ladies, fell in love with one of them, and got shot for it. Maybe I just needed to do something else with my life before I was done with it." She shrugged. "Notice kittens in storm drains. Cheer really hard for mime shows. Anything, really, long as it means something to someone." She still had not let go of Chelsea's hand. "I figure it's better than nothing, if I'm still here."

It would have been a touching moment, had Cyndricka not reached up and grumpily smacked her hand through Chelsea's leg just then. Chelsea jumped and yelped, and Charlie gave a displeased little mewl before turning over and going back to sleep. Cyndricka held her hand out straight above her, and Chelsea tried to remember what that sign was for. Then she realized that it was not an actual vocabulary sign, just Cyndricka miming a talking mouth, and then a talking mouth shutting. That would explain Carmen's laughter.

"Sorry, Cyndricka, we'll quiet down and let you sleep."

Good, she signed in actual words. She did not seem to have opened her eyes during any part of the interaction.

But right before she was truly asleep again, her hands moved over her chest, just dodging Charlie's sleeping form. And if Chelsea had her signs right, it was something along the lines of *I'm glad you're all here, at least.*

18.

"But, like, does it really help, having ghosts there in the show with you? It doesn't get distracting?"

"Yeah, I did always wonder that too. What if they go completely off the rails when you have something in mind?"

We rehearse. Sort of. It's not like I'm up on a stage or anything, but some shows are more prepared and polished than others. And they know if they do something wrong, I will just walk through them.

"Huh. I might jump in there with you next time, if it's not too much trouble."

I always enjoy the company. Make Coat do it too.

"Chelsea, what do you say? Me and you go into show business together? Drag Carmen along with us?"

"Do not bring me into this."

"No way, do your clowning on your own."

"Please? Please? Pretty please?"

"The puppy dog eyes don't work when you don't have eyes."

"Low blow, girl."

Coat, listen to Jeans. Join the show. Do it.

"No no no, and you're not going to make me. I will turn this road trip around and head right back to New York, young lady."

I dare you.

"Oh, you are getting so haunted tonight."

"Watch out, Cyndricka, she means business."

You are a bunch of hot air.

"Hey! No need for slurs here! Let's keep this civilized."

It had been that way for the last hour of walking, the three of them trading banter, and Carmen even getting in the occasional line, usually perfectly timed for maximum impact. Charlie perched on Cyndricka's shoulder and darted her eyes back and forth as if she was actually following the conversation.

Nebraska didn't hold many distractions, not much to break up the landscapes of swishing green grass and wide open sky, so there was nothing to it but to keep walking. So that they did, getting up early in the morning and keeping in a straight line west, with minimal breaks for foot rests and chances for Charlie to play, until sundown. Then food, a handful of hours of sleep, and onward the next morning.

The days were well and truly hot now, and Chelsea could see Cyndricka's clothes soaked through with sweat by the middle of the day. She could only imagine how she smelled. But she marched gamely onward, looking for all the world like she was not going to be stopped by anything. They were in high spirits, if Chelsea would allow herself the pun.

The sun had just started to sink towards the horizon when they saw him standing in the road. A car passed by, and the headlights shone through his transparent body, but threw the sheer strangeness into sharp and undeniable relief. He looked like an older man, maybe in his sixties, but that was only guessing from his clothes and the lines of his body. His face was—

There was no good way to say it. His face was melting. Not that it had been melted off somehow, and that was what had killed him. No, he was actively melting, as a ghost. Eyes and brows sunk down across his face, lips came unmoored from their proper spots and dripped down onto his chest, hair pooled on his shoulders and slid down the rest of him. But the features did not just stay off once they were gone; they dripped and dragged down to his feet, and he seemed to shift, turn fuzzy and distorted, then reappear with his face back where it had started, only sagging and melting all anew. The features did not all follow the same patterns, either. He would phase when his eyes were at his knees, but when they were back in place, his mouth was still around his waist, and everything was out of sync. He looked like a falling sand castle that someone was trying to keep together, scooping up bits and sticking them back on the top only to realize that another wall had collapsed in the meantime. He stood in the middle of the road, watching the pavement with eyes that seemed eager to join it under his feet.

Jamie took a step back; Chelsea wondered if it was the stark realization that she was no longer the most frightening thing around them. She heard Cyndricka's breath catch in her throat and saw her try to slip Charlie off of her shoulder and into her pocket. After the weeks of quick growth, it was a tight fit for the kitten, but even the animal seemed to realize that it was a better time for silence just then. Only Carmen seemed unmoved by the sight. Chelsea looked to her with a jerk of her head towards the melting man. Carmen only sighed and shook her head.

"No, seriously, Carmen, what is—"

But Chelsea was interrupted by the answer to her question. Because the man raised his ghostly head to look at them, opened a mouth that was still trying to retreat from his face, and let out a cry. No, that wasn't the right word, never the right word for these things that she had heard about so often but never seen before.

The ghost wailed. A wail from the very depths of his chest, his core, probably his actual soul: a warbling sob that sounded like it was ripped out of him, the very sounds themselves painful to make. It went on and on and on, far longer than any living lungs could have managed and longer than any other type of ghost would have bothered with. He wailed because he couldn't do anything else, because he did not know how to do anything else, because he was so caught in his own sorrow and pain and loss that all he could bring his immortal soul to do was wail.

Is it dangerous? Cyndricka signed. Chelsea's gaze flicked between her hands and her face, trying to gauge just how she was taking all of this. But with Charlie safely tucked into her coat, there was a sureness and determination in her face.

Carmen was not looking at Cyndricka, had not taken her eyes off of the wailer, and didn't know that she had been signing. Chelsea placed a hand through her shoulder to get her attention. She didn't jump or anything, but turned around quickly, before Chelsea pointed to Cyndricka, who repeated her question. As the only one in the know, they needed to keep Carmen with them and on their side.

"No," she said with a firmness that Chelsea didn't know anyone could feel at a time like this. "They are not dangerous. I do not recommend that we spend a great deal of time here: dangerous for your body and harmful for your mind are different things. But we are in no immediate danger."

"God, he's just standing there," said Jamie in a hushed voice. "Just letting it happen to him, over and over."

"They get caught up," Carmen pointed out. "They get so stuck in loops, mourning their past lives, that there is not much they can do on their own to pull themselves out."

"I'd always heard about them," Jamie whispered. "But they always sounded scarier, less . . . sad. So sad." She managed to move her feet forward, creeping closer to the wailer standing rooted in the middle of the road. "Hey there, mister. Can we—is there anything we can do to help you here?"

The wailer jerked his head up at her, but kept crying out, phasing and melting and existing in an in-between haze, but never pausing in his cries. Jamie came closer, laid a hand gently through his shoulder, and while he jerked, losing his nose off of his face in the movement, he didn't pull away. Jamie turned back to the group.

"You said they can't do it on their own. Is there any way we can help him?" she asked. Her body language was firm and strong, standing upright even with shoulders that were tight and tense. Having the wailer screaming that close to her could not have been pleasant.

"We need to keep moving," Chelsea pointed out. "If we don't want Cyndricka to have to spend the night out here."

"I—" Jamie looked between them and the melting man to her right. "Yeah, that makes sense. Let's keep going."

The man stayed in the middle of the road as the four of them walked past him, trying not to pull too far away as they went by. Chelsea mistook it for a sign at first, but Cyndricka actually crossed herself subtly as she walked past the ghost. One more question about how she was brought up, true, but more a question of how she saw these ghosts, all ghosts. But this wasn't the place for asking questions, not when they still had to walk far enough away that they could find some rest.

They had passed through Kimball a few hours ago and were approaching one of the smaller communities in the region, the little settlements nestled in the middle of huge stretches of interstate highway.

In all honesty, Chelsea had stopped paying attention to city names. But they had crossed an invisible line somewhere, stepped across the border into a literal ghost town, because the further into the little town they walked, the more wailing they heard, from more and more sources. Male, female, in-between and neither, young, old, some with words mixed in, others with just empty shrieks. Shops and houses lined the main drag through town, and it was bizarre to think that there were still humans going about their daily lives, unaware that their quiet little village was the loudest place in the whole afterlife.

Except that it did seem to be taking its toll on the townspeople. For all that it was set up and decorated like a perfectly normal city, the people packing up their stores and getting ready to go home moved slowly and heavily, like there was a weight on each set of shoulders. Stress lines ringed every set of eyes that Chelsea could see and even children played quietly on the sidewalks and in the front yards.

A female wailer watched a group of children playing house in front of a small ranch-style home. She reached a hand like melted wax out to touch a toddler's braided hair, and the child burst out crying for no reason. The ghost pulled her hand back as flesh and skin sloughed off bone, then went fuzzy and reformed into a grasping hand again.

As the sun set completely, doors shut and locks thudded into place with a finality unheard of to a city girl like Chelsea. Maybe it was the lack of living voices to offset the cries, but once there were no more humans in the streets the wailing seemed to grow louder, cresting and falling, but filling the night completely. The humans had their blinds closed and their noises muffled; whether they were unusually receptive or not, the whole human population seemed to know that they were living in a cursed land. A mournful land filled to the brim with tears that could never fall from the ghosts' eyes, so instead fell from their bones themselves.

I want to keep walking, Cyndricka signed with wide eyes and small hand motions that she kept close to her chest, as if she was capable of shielding herself from anything. *I can sleep during the day tomorrow. Have a few hours off.*

"We're still pretty set for time, you can take the day," said Chelsea, keeping her voice light as they passed a gathering of three wailers, moaning and crying in a trio by a bench that Cyndricka might have been able to use otherwise. "And I can't imagine trying to sleep through this, so I don't blame you."

Cyndricka nodded but did not try to communicate anymore, preferring to clutch at the quivering lump of kitten bulging out of her pocket.

They walked further and further through town, past driveways leading off between widely spaced houses, passing more and more of the wailers as they walked in silence. Anything else would have felt like an imposition, like no one had a right to make noise here but the afflicted. But Carmen did eventually venture some words, causing the others to lean in to hear her as they walked.

"I have never heard of this behavior from wailers, but it does make sense. Though usually solitary, if more than a few of them happened to be in one spot, they could form a sort of feedback loop, becoming more lost in themselves in the company of their own kind."

"And attracting more of them?" Jamie asked in hushed tones. "Or just changing ghosts that were already here?"

"I do not know," murmured Carmen softly. "In the grand scheme of things, I am still very young. Please do not forget that." Chelsea had, because Carmen always seemed so in control. But in the moonlight of the lonely streets, with only a few streetlights shining through the melted and melting horrors, Carmen looked every inch the young woman she had been when she died, and not the mature figure she had grown into in the decades since her death.

On the other hand, Jamie seemed entranced by the ghosts that they passed. She turned her shoulders and torso to watch them even as she kept moving forward, pressing through trees and sign-posts without a care. She lingered over a man with a cut throat, a pregnant woman with a stab wound in her chest, a teenager with the dark eyes and blue lips of a drug overdose, even as those lips slipped from his face. Chelsea wanted to pull her away, to cover her eyes, to block out all the wails, but none of those things were at all possible. Was this what it had been like for Carmen, when she had worried about Chelsea? She reached for Jamie's hand, and at least the touch of her fingers got Jamie to turn.

"Are you holding up okay?" Chelsea asked in a whisper. "We could—I don't know, you or both of us could run ahead and wait for Cyndricka and Carmen on the other side."

"No, I wouldn't want to do that to our girls. But I just—" Jamie waved her hands vaguely in front of her then let them fall back to her sides. "I want to help. Somehow."

"I don't know if these people can be helped."

"I want to at least try."

Chelsea couldn't blame her. She even admired it. But the things surrounding them, floating here and there, dripping over every street, every sidewalk, every lawn and parking lot and doorway, were hideous. Beyond that, they were pitiful, and Chelsea wasn't sure she had it in her. Maybe it was all an excuse to stay away, to avoid getting caught herself, to replace fear with disgust and anger, but she would take it. She would not become one of these monsters, trapped in her own grief for all time. She tried not to think about any hypocrisy on her part and wanted to just continue on her journey without any more introspection or soul-searching about it. It wasn't madness if there actually was something waiting for her at the end, right?

They could just see the far edge of town before them, off in the distance where the last buildings petered off into open stretches of road. They were so close to being out, and if it was not for consideration of Cyndricka's heavy bag and sore feet, Chelsea would have sprinted for it. They just had to keep walking and get out as soon as they could.

Perhaps it would have gone that smoothly if it hadn't been for the hole in the road. Maybe it was a way for the humans to express their feelings about what was happening around them, to let their roads and buildings subtly fall into disarray, to match the disfigured spirits around them. Maybe it was just a normal crack in the pavement, and Chelsea was getting a bit too philosophical.

But whether it was mystical or mundane, the gap caught at Cyndricka's foot, toppling her down to the ground. She twisted in midair to keep the pocket with Charlie in it pointed upright, but the twist stopped abruptly at her ankle, which crumpled underneath her when she tried to pull herself back to her feet.

The ghosts all reached forward out of instinct, trying to catch her at first, then help her up, all before realizing the folly of their instincts. Cyndricka half hobbled, half crawled over to the gravel shoulder by herself, stretching her foot out in front of her and rubbing at the muscles of her calf with gritted teeth. She flexed her foot back and forth a few times, and hissed.

Dammit. Not broken, but I don't think I can walk right now, not with the bags. I need to stay here for a minute. Maybe an hour or two, she signed. She didn't look any happier about the prospect than Carmen or Chelsea, who both hovered awkwardly beside her, shying away from wailers that drifted by.

"It's okay. They can't hurt us," Jamie pointed out. "Take the time you need."

Cyndricka pulled her bags off her back and Charlie out of her pocket, settling in for at least a bit of a stay. She sipped water from a bottle, dribbled more into her cupped hand for Charlie to lap at, and stared at the ground. If the wailers thought it was at all strange for three normal ghosts to be surrounding one human and a cat, they didn't say anything or even look at them askance. They just continued their pacing and crying and melting, as they had for god only knew how long before. Jamie watched them, and even reached out to touch one that passed close. It did not acknowledge her. In a more introspective moment, Chelsea may have questioned how quickly she had begun to think of the wailers as "it," but this was not that moment.

But even she had to pause and listen when a cry of a different timbre and tone broke through the mournful drone. This one was higher, yes, but also more specific, less of an unbroken single moan, and more of a series of sobs and keens. There was something more there, more of a mind buried in the depths of that sorrow.

Words emerged from the sound, and they knew this was something different. Jamie hurried off in the direction of the crying, Chelsea and Carmen close on her heels.

The young man was standing behind a little diner, an all-night trucker's stop with flickering neon signs. He was turned away from them, but his clothes looked mostly matched to the current year, a t-shirt and skinny jeans that hugged his body. He ran a dark hand over the cement of the restaurant's back wall, specifically over a small circular groove about five feet off of the ground. The probing fingers tightened into a claw and another sob ripped out of his throat. But also the words.

"No, no, I don't—not like—no, don't want to be—let me leave, I just—" His hand tightened into a fist and slammed through the wall. When he bent forward and rested his head against the cement, his forehead phased through, unable to support him in death.

Jamie approached first, hands raised and voice gentle. Chelsea was a few steps behind, watching the young man. At a closer range, she could see the bullet hole in the back of his head, somewhat obscured by his dense curly hair, and small and clean enough to be an entry wound. She had never known the look of them before, but she had far more experience these days. She could sense Carmen at her back. Jamie came closer and spoke to the crying figure.

"Hi there. Hey. How are you doing, buddy? If you want to turn around and say hi, I think that would be swell. Just try not to be scared of what I look like, okay? Can you do that for me?"

His shoulders shook and swayed, pushing and pulling him through the restaurant's back wall, but he gradually lurched and turned himself around. No one was going to compete with Jamie in terms of sheer gruesomeness, but the exit wound in his forehead was large and ragged, leaving a clear window directly into brain tissue. The hole stayed consistently shaped and circular, even as other parts of his face began to melt and sink, as if aging was taking hold of his young face with a sudden vengeance.

But rather than let them slide and sink uninterrupted, he tried to stem the flow. He clutched his hands to his face, pushing and readjusting with his fingertips, trying to keep his cheeks under his eyes, his jaw at the top of his neck, his lips in their proper place without twisting them into an unusable mess.

He whimpered and moaned as he struggled with his face, muttering pleas to any sort of force that might have stopped his rapid decay. It was horrible to see, more horrible than any of the others they had encountered so far, because he still felt fear. He felt fear and shock and something other than empty, raw grief. And still, he melted.

One eye widened as it came to rest on Jamie, even as he struggled to push the other one back into its socket to stop it from popping out. He saw her, acknowledged her, but his cries remained as vague as before, a stream of "no, no, no, not this, I—no" from his throat.

Carmen stepped forward, speaking just loud enough for Chelsea and Jamie to hear her. It was unclear whether the young man would have been able to hear them, or recognize the words, but there was still basic courtesy to keep in mind.

"I do not think he is all the way gone. If he is still at least partly coherent, there might be a chance to bring him back," she said. Jamie gave an aborted little jerk that might have been a nod but didn't turn away from him, even as he covered his whole face with his hands to keep his nose from escaping. Chelsea watched it distort and squish out from between his fingers. "It will be difficult, though," Carmen clarified, perhaps unnecessarily.

"Hey there, buddy," crooned Jamie, approaching him as one would a scared animal. "How are you doing there? Are you all right?"

He rocked on his feet and turned his head this way and that, shaking and trembling as he clutched his face in his hands, melting features showing through his transparent fingers. But he seemed to tilt and lean in Jamie's direction. She kept trying, looking for something more from him.

"My name is Jamie. Can you tell me your name? Do you have a name that you can tell me, buddy?"

He was definitely pointing himself in her direction now, hobbling and stumbling across the parking lot pavement. He stumbled and came down on one knee to hold himself up. To be mimicking the effects of gravity that closely, he must have had a very recent death. He slowly climbed back to his feet and peeked through his fingers at them. Jamie continued her plea.

"Do you have a name? Can you remember a name? It doesn't have to be the one from before." Her voice perked up, like this was the best thing that anyone could hope for. "It's a new day, why not pick your absolute favorite name in the whole world, and I'll call you that?"

He paused and stood stock still for so long that Chelsea wondered if he had frozen somehow, brain overcome by the effort of thinking about as complex of an issue as names. But he sucked in a big breath that he didn't need and croaked out a single word, lilting up at the end as more question than anything.

"Jim?"

Jamie burst out laughing in sheer relief. "Aww kid, that is the best damn name I have ever heard! Did you grab that off of mine, or do you just really like being a guy named Jim? Either way is perfectly fine, mind you, but I am curious."

He looked at her with blank confusion, but that was infinitely better than the blind panic had been. His chest rose and fell in quick successions and he still let out a thin, whining moan, but nothing like the others that they could hear in the distance.

Jamie stepped closer and his eyes fixed on her, focused and clear and firmly in their place. His cheekbones were slumping down, giving the impression of the fastest aging of all time, but his eyes were as solid as a ghost's could be.

"Well, Jim, you and I are meant to be friends," Jamie went on. "Jim and Jamie. Or Jimmy and Jamie, even, if I could call you Jimmy. Can I call you Jimmy?"

She paused to let him answer, and his eyes darted back and forth before he whispered "Jim" again. It could have easily been a repetition of the first time, but Jamie plowed forward as if it had been an answer.

"All right then, Jim it is. I don't mean to be one of those folks who gives nicknames all over the place without asking people. That's why my friends here are Chelsea and Carmen, not Chel and Carrie or something. I respect what people want to be called,

Jim." She turned to the other two and swept her arm out, inviting them closer. Jim's eyes went wide, but still stayed grounded in their sockets. "Come on Chelsea, come on Carmen, come meet my new friend Jim."

Carmen was more confident in her steps as she walked forward. But she had dealt with this sort of thing before and knew what to expect. Chelsea was hesitant, but she did manage to bring herself forward after a beat. Jim still had little whining keens coming out on each nonexistent breath, but more slowly, as if he was a toy winding down. His nose phased back into a wide, flat shape, presumably his original one, and kept its form, save a little drifting and melting at the edges of his nostrils.

"Hello, Jim. My name is Carmen." She reached out her hand for him, and calmly turned the shake into a wave when he jerked back. "Is there any way we can help you here?"

"She's a really good helper," Chelsea added, just to have something to say. She wasn't used to this kind of thing, she never would be, but Jamie had to go and try to be all noble and Carmen had been so good to her when she was new, it only made sense to pass it on. "Do you want to . . . I don't know, we and a friend of ours are trying to get out of this town. Would you like to walk with us for a bit?"

Jamie's body language perked up, and even with the lack of a smile, it warmed Chelsea's heart more than she would care to admit.

Her proposition seemed to be too much for Jim to take in just then, and he settled for drifting towards Jamie. He came close, hobbled up to her and leaned his head against her shoulder, letting his forehead phase through her t-shirt, disregarding the scattering of blood and viscera and teeth. Either disregarding or not noticing at all.

She raised a hand and slowly, gently laid it on the top of Jim's head. He turned into the touch, all but nestling in to her, bending down to get as close as he could, but in a truly innocent gesture, nothing predatory or creepy about it. He sniffled and huffed under his breath, but his face was the most solid one that Chelsea had seen in the whole town, her group excluded. Jamie moved her arm to wrap it around his shoulders and leaned down to murmur to him.

"Why don't you come with us, Jim?" His face didn't register any recognition of the words, but he moved when Jamie did, walking with heavy feet after them as he tried to keep his head on Jamie's shoulder. But in a very, very human gesture, he soon became frustrated trying to keep close to her while she walked, and instead trailed after her, eyes trained on the back of her neck.

Cyndricka was looking worried when they returned to the shoulder she was sitting on, and that anxiety turned into anger as soon as they were back in sight. *You three just run off without any word and come back trailing a wailer behind you?* she signed in a flurry that Chelsea could barely keep up with. *You couldn't have said anything or sent one of you back sooner, something other than leaving me to wait? I thought one of you might have turned. Maybe the others were gone too, and I was all alone! I can think of a lot in five minutes, and I do not appreciate it!*

It was the angriest Chelsea had ever seen her, certainly as angry as she had ever been at a ghost. Even when being bothered by Henry, she had tended more towards fear and sorrow than anger. Charlie was screaming her little kitten yell to match her mom's anger. Chelsea hovered over to try and offer comfort; Cyndricka turned in on herself and wrapped her arms around her legs, but not before picking up Charlie and cradling the bundle of fur to her chest.

"I'm sorry, Cyndricka. I think Jamie had to—" She tried to pick her words carefully to describe what had just happened. "We heard this guy crying, he sounded like he just turned, and Jamie really wanted to help. I'm sorry that we ran off like that."

You should be, she signed, sparing her hands out from her crossed arms just enough to sign before pulling them back in. But a few moments and deep breaths later, she pulled them back out again. *But you are back now and we should keep walking.*

"What about your ankle?"

I don't mind limping. I don't want to be here. She clambered up to her feet and unsteadily pulled her bag back onto her shoulders. Not the most inspiring beginning to another long bout of walking, but Chelsea felt comfortable in letting her make the choice. *Let's go.* She started limping her way out of the town, past more wailers lining the street, and trailing her company of four ghosts. When Chelsea glanced back, Jim was in the wake of the pack, looking confused, but following Jamie like he would be doomed if she was out of his sight for a moment. And perhaps that was the case.

19.

The sun was rising as they at long last passed the final building and looked out at the expanse of highway that would take them to a real city if they were lucky, back to some potential bastion of un-haunted civilization. Cyndricka looked ready to drop: sleep deprivation, hunger, fear, and walking on a twisted ankle could not have been pleasant in any way, shape, or form, but she smiled when they passed out of sight of the last building, finally back on the road.

The only one who didn't look like they had just climbed out of hell was Jim. He froze in his tracks on the pavement and reached out to try and grab Jamie's hand, though Jamie didn't notice until it had already passed through her.

"Come on, Jim. Let's get out of here," Jamie said, chipper and casual. Jim shook his head ever so slightly, his shoulders hunched and his eyes wide.

"Jim, we need to leave. This isn't a good place to be. And Chelsea and Cyndricka have places to go."

Maybe it was her imagination playing tricks on her, but Chelsea thought Jim's face shifted more the further Jamie walked down the road, continuing its slow melting. Jim moaned softly, a pleading note in it, and Jamie looked at him for a long, long time. Cyndricka, Chelsea, and Carmen also stopped to watch them. The early morning light shone through the ghosts, and highlighted the other wailers wandering between buildings in the town, crying their way through their deaths.

She walked back. Jamie slipped her hand through Jim's and turned to the group.

"Guys . . . I think I need to stay here."

Carmen was already nodding slowly while the words were settling into Chelsea's brain. Cyndricka's mouth twisted and tightened, but she didn't sign anything. It was apparently up to Chelsea to ask.

"Why? What do you think you—what are you going to do here? Aside from turn into a wailer yourself, probably."

Jamie shook her neck stump. "I don't think I will. Or at least I'm hoping. But I do think that my way moving forward has to be trying to help people, to make the most of this time I've got on my hands. I keep going with you all, and Cyndricka's the only one who can do anything for anyone. Not that I begrudge you; I'm lucky to have gotten the chance to know you." Cyndricka's twisted mouth curved slightly up at the edges at the compliment. Jamie continued. "But there's a town full of spirits right here that I can try to help out. Maybe just talking, just trying to get to know them, whatever I can do. Don't know if it'll help at all, but . . . like I said. I have to try."

"Your instincts are good," Carmen said, voice firm and clear. "Keep asking them questions, get them to engage with you. If there are people in the area who speak other languages, try to entice them to learn. Go to schools, lectures, readings, then quiz them afterwards. Have big, long conversations that they can easily hold onto the thread of. And do not be surprised if you cannot save all of them. Or even most of them. But I wish you all the luck in the world."

Jamie shook Carmen's hand and gave an attempt at a nod that came out looking more like a bow. "Thank you, Carmen. It's been a pleasure traveling with you. I hope I can do as much good helping them as you've done with Chelsea here."

Carmen shook her head. "Chelsea was not nearly so far gone. And she did most of the work herself. You have a harder task ahead of you. I wish you well." She turned and started to walk down the road again. Chelsea liked to think she was giving them privacy, not trying to distance herself so quickly. But either would have made sense; they all knew the dangers of dwelling a little better now.

Cyndricka perched Charlie on her shoulder so that Jamie

could more easily brush her fingers over the little animal in a facsimile of petting. Charlie mewed and batted at the hand and Jamie chuckled. "Well, Cyndricka, I know I'm not supposed to say this, but you might be one of the most unique people I've met. And not just 'cause of those fancy powers of yours. If I ever get the chance to meet a person like you again, I'll have had the luckiest afterlife a ghost could ask for. Take care of this little girl for me, okay?"

We will try to come back through here, Cyndricka signed. Her face had relaxed and resolved into an actual smile. *It's not like we have a better path to take or anything. Good luck, Jeans.*

"And good luck to you guys." She turned to Chelsea, and Cyndricka walked after Carmen with a smile, leaving just the two of them standing by the side of the road.

". . . I really don't know if you're making a good choice here," Chelsea said finally.

Jamie shrugged. "I don't either. But it's a choice, and I haven't made a ton of those in the time since I've been alive. I keep on with you guys, and I'm just still wandering. I stay here, and I'm doing something. That has to be worthwhile, even if it doesn't end up working."

Chelsea looked away. When she had met Jamie just those few weeks ago, she had looked away for very different reasons. How quickly those reactions could change, especially while traveling with someone. "It makes sense," she finally muttered, and she must have been imagining the stinging in her eyes, when there was no physical reason for it to be. "I can understand having a goal. Since that's what this whole damn walk is about."

"Have a good time at your brother's wedding," Jamie said, and she rested her hand through Chelsea's broken shoulder. "He's lucky to have a sister like you. Not many end up with one who's dedicated from beyond the grave."

"Dedicated, but not obsessed," she said. Jim hovered a few yards away, arms wrapped around himself and not looking away from Jamie. Chelsea waved her hand at him. "You get better now, Jim! When we come back through here, I want to have a real talk with you, okay?"

He did not respond, but the smallest trace of a smile, or at least an upturning of his mouth, crossed his face.

"You should probably get going. Find Cyndricka a safe place to sleep before she drops off her feet." Jamie's hands drifted down to both of Chelsea's shoulders, holding her at arms' length and tilting her neck up and down as if to take her in. "It's been a real trip, Chelsea Shu. You three keep going on yours."

Chelsea leaned forward without really thinking about it and touched her lips lightly against the ridge of bone that was all that was left of Jamie's face. She had no idea what she had looked like before, who the rest of the people in her life had known her as, even what she had been like before a couple decades of death had changed her. But Chelsea liked this Jamie, this strange, caring woman with the remnants of a head and lack of a face. Her lips tingled when she pulled away from the kiss, in a way that felt different than the usual sensations she got. A little less supernatural, a bit more like the most natural thing in the world. Jamie chuckled and gripped her hands on Chelsea's arms, sinking into the fabric of her winter coat.

"Nice . . . if you all come back through here, we can try our hand on a little more of that business."

"I would like that," Chelsea said with a smile. Jamie would never be Heather. They were very different women that Chelsea had met at very different points in her existence. But Jamie was not a replacement. She was something very different altogether that Chelsea was fortunate to have known.

And to think that if they had not been walking at Cyndricka's pace, if Carmen and Chelsea had run in a straight line from coast to coast, they never would have met. The blessings of small miracles.

Chelsea walked backwards and waved at Jamie and Jim until the road dipped down, leaving them out of sight in the brightening sun. It looked like a hot day, even if she couldn't feel it, and the plains around them seemed to sing with life in the breeze. She finally turned around and engaged with Carmen and Cyndricka as they all walked. Carmen raised an eyebrow and gave her a smirk, but didn't say anything about the kiss.

"Do you think she's going to be able to do it?" she asked

Carmen. "Do you think she can save any of them? Jim, of course, but any of the others as well?"

"I think she is going to give it her all," Carmen said with a nod and a soft smile. "And I think that will be good for her as an individual. And for the rest of them, who knows? It is a large, crazy afterlife. I certainly understand that better now than I did before this whole endeavor."

Me too, Cyndricka signed. *Not always good information to have, but I am glad we met Jeans.* She paused to scratch Charlie under her chin. *And we got a cat out of it.*

"There is that," Chelsea conceded. And, as always, they continued on their way down the road.

20.

As the weeks passed and they made their way into Wyoming, Charlie grew into more and more of a proper cat with every day. She paced along Cyndricka's shoulders and over the top of her backpack, gripping in her claws when she needed extra balance but steady for the most part. They didn't know exactly how old she had been when she became trapped in that storm drain, but it soon seemed likely that she had spent the majority of her life on the road with them She certainly behaved like it, growing more confident in being at least a few steps away from Cyndricka as they walked, or playing in the bushes and long grass when they made camp for the night.

Cyndricka was also changing. Or to be more specific, she had been changing since they set off, and it was becoming obvious now. Her miming routine had kept her athletic when she lived in New York, a layer of fat covering long, lean muscles, but the long days of walking with only minimal breaks had made her hard. The curves were fading off of her face, no matter how much food she managed to get or how cheap the food in question was. Sharp lines were growing in her face and body.

It was only Carmen and Chelsea who remained the same as they walked and spring turned unapologetically into a hot, dry summer, with Carmen looking at home in her breezy summer dress and sandals and Chelsea looking like a madwoman in a winter coat.

They were traveling through a dusty stretch of Wyoming highway, Charlie scampering in the reddish gravel and dirt while Cyndricka counted handfuls of change from her pockets. The mime shows had continued to have admirable returns, with the presence of Charlie to draw the attention of adults and children alike. Chelsea had taken to trying to teach Charlie tricks while Cyndricka took breaks or dozed through the worst heat of the day. Chelsea was hampered by only knowing how to deal with dogs, and the lack of treats to reward the cat with, but Charlie seemed to have a decent grasp on "sit," and they were making progress on "stay." Not a lot of progress; there were too many interesting bugs around for a young cat to be content staying in one place for any length of time.

Chelsea was working on just such a training session, while Cyndricka drank water and sat cross-legged in the dirt, signing back and forth with Carmen about what towns they were planning on going through next. They could no longer walk during the middle of the day because of the sun, and soon enough they would have to switch over to a nocturnal schedule. They had been at rest for a few minutes when the sound of a car started to approach from the distance. Chelsea stood up, apparently an invitation for Charlie to jump through her feet and start chewing on a tuft of grass, and looked out at the dust cloud coming down the highway towards them.

Cyndricka rose to her feet leisurely and moved back off of the road, still chatting with Carmen. Even before the trip, she had clearly been used to dodging around cars and wasn't about to be ruffled by having a single car buzz past them. She leaned down without looking and tapped the side of her leg, calling Charlie over in order to stay out of the way. But when the sound of skidding tires rang through the air, both Cyndricka and Carmen joined Chelsea in watching the pickup truck tearing down the highway.

The truck drifted back and forth across lanes, and even from their location Chelsea could hear hooting and hollering, all in the tone of young men with a great deal of alcohol in them. Cyndricka stepped further back into the dry drainage ditch beside the road and watched them coming.

Two young men were in the front seats, but the truck bed was filled with another five, cheering and tossing beer cans back and forth between them, cracking them open to take long drags. There was some sports insignia draped across the side of the truck, but Chelsea had never followed that sort of thing when she was alive and saw little reason to now that she was dead.

"Oh joy," deadpanned Carmen with a sarcasm that put Chelsea's efforts to shame. "Drunk young white men. Cyndricka, I think it would be best if you try to tuck yourself away for a bit."

Cyndricka was already climbing down into a thicket of tall gold prairie grass, but from the shift in the hollering from the truck, she had been spotted. With the truck coming closer, Chelsea could see her grip the straps of her bag tightly and sink down into a sort of squat, braced and ready to dodge or run.

"Hey, hobo bitch!" yelled one red-faced man as the car slowed enough for him to lean over the edge. His drunken buddies laughed around him, pointing at Cyndricka and Charlie, oblivious to the two ghosts traveling with them. "Have one 'a these, why don't ya!" He chucked the empty beer can from the side of the truck, but Cyndricka managed to jump out of the way of it easily. He was very drunk and his aim was very bad.

But in a split second, Chelsea realized two things. The first being that Charlie was not yet as good at dodging as Cyndricka was.

And the second being that it was a full, closed can of beer.

Charlie yowled when the metal canister slammed into her side, and a bright red blossom of blood stained the white parts of her coat. She hissed and screamed and splayed all four sets of claws out, but the perpetrators were already squealing away. One of them leaned over to cuff the beer-thrower in the head along with a shout of "Douchebag, don't hit a cat!"

Cyndricka scooped up Charlie, but then had to release her back to the ground when she clawed long stripes down both of her arms in her panic and pain. Cyndricka untied her large coat from around her waist and calculated her approach for the second attempt. Charlie's left rear paw was pulled up off the ground and her sides moved in and out with ragged effort. Her ears were pasted down to her head and her eyes were as wide as they could possibly go, with the pupils thin slits in the bright sun. Chelsea was speechless, still in shock from how quickly their nice afternoon had gone to hell, but Carmen was busy muttering a stream of advice.

"All right, you grab her from the top with the coat and wrap her up like a baby, tightly but gently. The last town was a few miles back, but we will find help. Keep pressure on the bleeding and we can find a vet there. She will be fine. Chelsea, tell Cyndricka that Charlie will be fine."

Cyndricka was shaking, shoulders quivering under the weight of her backpack and more sweat pooling in the fabric of her t-shirt. Chelsea took a moment to steady her own nerves, then placed a hand on Cyndricka's shoulder. She jerked but didn't look away from Charlie.

"Charlie's going to be okay. We just need to be quick about this and take care of her, then she'll be alright. You can do this."

Her hands were too full with the coat to sign, but she gave a jerky nod. She took a deep breath of her own, as the only human with working lungs of the group, and lunged forward to wrap the coat around Charlie's squirming form.

᠂᠂ ᠂᠂ ᠂᠂

How Cyndricka had the energy to jog after all of the walking across hard ground she had already done that day, to say nothing of the last few months, Chelsea could not be sure. She seemed to be working on sheer adrenaline and panic. The bundle in her arms screamed and yowled over every footfall, no matter how steady Cyndricka tried to keep her, and the guilt of causing Charlie any more discomfort was written all over Cyndricka's face. But a small spot of blood had seeped through the dark green coat, so speed had to be prioritized over sparing Charlie any more immediate pain.

Carmen sprinted ahead to scout out the town for a vet's office, being the fastest of the group by a fair margin. Her steps seemed to slide through the air, cruising her along with an unnatural speed that came with the decades of separation from the heavy realities of her body.

Chelsea ran alongside Cyndricka, keeping an eye out for any more danger on the horizon. Usually she would have had an advantage over Cyndricka, not being hampered by aching muscles or lack of breath or any of the other things that slowed down human runners, but Cyndricka wasn't letting herself be bothered by any of that nonsense just then. She was barely seeing what was on the ground in front of her, so focused on Charlie that she almost tripped into three potholes in quick succession. Only a short reminder about the danger of falling with Charlie in her arms got her to at least watch where she was going.

They had passed through Pine Bluffs with a decided lack of interest that morning, too busy chatting about what movies they were looking forward to seeing in the next year, what theaters in New York were best for sleeping in without being caught by the staff, and why there weren't many drive-in theaters still around. A few people out on the streets and sidewalks had given sideways looks to the homeless woman making hand gestures at the air and being followed by a cat, but none of the group were bothered by it anymore. Subtlety was honestly just too tiring to keep up at all times.

People openly stared now at the sight of Cyndricka running down the street with a yowling lump in her arms. She turned this way and that, glancing over signs and trying to find somewhere that would be able to help Charlie. She groped in a pocket for her notebook, but she hadn't expected to use it today and had tucked it into her backpack instead. It was supposed to be a long walk with no one to talk to but the people who already knew her language and knew her for what she was.

Chelsea took off in her own direction to try and find a veterinarian. She passed a couple of strip malls, a laundromat, even a doctor's office, but she assumed that it would be better to at least try and find an animal hospital before they tried to guilt their way into a human one. She cycled back to Cyndricka, to regroup and find out where she had already looked when she heard Carmen calling through the streets.

"Over here, I found one! Chelsea, Cyndricka, I found one!"

Chelsea had never run straight through so many buildings in quite that little time, but she was following the sound of Carmen's voice, obstacles be damned. Through the wall of a grocery store, straight through displays and aisles, then out the opposite wall, without a pause or a stop or any niggling thoughts in the back of her head that she would crash into something. It was running at its finest and most pure, fueled by blind panic over the life of a stray cat that they had pulled out of a sewer. A ghost's voice was not transmitted by sound but something else that none of them even pretended to understand, but it allowed Chelsea to follow without having to worry about how many things were in the way.

She passed right through Carmen when she reached her, unable to notice and stop quite in time. She backtracked a few feet to where she was standing and looked up at the sign she was staring at. Carmen kept yelling in an unbroken stream while Chelsea read.

"Pine Bluffs Local Animal Hospital," it said across the front awning in big friendly blue letters. It was tucked into a storefront, between a tattoo parlor and a bicycle shop, but it seemed legitimate and clean, not that Cyndricka would have rejected a biker with a sewing needle, if it would help Charlie. There was nothing on the sign or windows about emergencies, but it had to be better than nothing. Chelsea added her voice to Carmen's calls, and Cyndricka skidded around a corner to join them less than a minute after Chelsea had arrived by supernatural means.

She flung open the door and ran up to the front desk, eliciting startled jumps from the few people sitting in the waiting room, and a round of energetic barking out of the three dogs, pulling on their leashes to see what everyone was so excited about. Charlie hissed and spit from the depths of the fabric bundle and Cyndricka lifted her up to set her on the desk under the wide gaze and dropped jaw of the receptionist.

"What is—how did—who–" the woman stammered, looking over Cyndricka's disheveled and sweaty appearance. But Charlie gave another pained yowl, and her professional instincts took over. "What happened here?"

Cyndricka tried again to reach for her notebook, but she required at least one hand to keep Charlie still. She tried to mime the throwing of a projectile and something that was probably supposed to be a sign for broken ribs (it was not her finest perfor-mance of all time), and the woman nodded slowly, clearly confused but at least getting the gist of it. She called out for someone named

Darnell, and a black man in his thirties came bounding out from the back room, wearing a pair of scrubs with cartoon kittens on them.

Darnell took one look at the situation and reached out gloved hands to unwrap the jacket and take Charlie in a firm, professional hold at the back of her neck. He turned her gently to get a good view of her injuries, deftly dodging claws, and hissed when he looked at the blood smeared over her right half and the tense way she was holding her back leg up.

"Okay, ma'am, I'm going to take your cat back to the exam room and I can take a look at what the damage is. You stay here and tell Rebecca what happened and she can fill me in. Your cat is going to be all right." He spoke with a gentle voice, deep and drawling, and he looked in Cyndricka's eyes when he spoke. It was sad how much of a rarity that had become on the trip. "What's its name?"

A promotional notepad for heartworm medication sat on the desk, and Cyndricka grabbed for it and the receptionist's pen. She scribbled "Charlie" and showed it to him. He nodded, seemingly nonplussed.

"Okay, well ma'am, I'll see what's wrong with Charlie, then be right back." He took Charlie's back feet in his other hand and carried her into the back room; barking and meowing and even the chattering of birds emerged in a wave when the door was open, then faded back to the usual din of the office as soon as it was closed again.

Cyndricka seemed to lose all energy and slumped over on the edge of the counter all at once. Now that Charlie was in capable, professional hands, there was no more reason for her adrenaline, and the exhaustion that so often follows panic was able to set in. Carmen and Chelsea each hovered at her shoulders to offer what support they could while she scribbled at the notepad on the counter to write out the story for the now skeptical-looking woman.

There wasn't much detail she could really add, just that a bunch of men had driven by and thrown a beer can off the back of a truck. But the woman, this Rebecca, was very interested to know what they had been doing before then. Just walking down the highway?

Why? The cat had been walking too? With a bad leg? No, no, the leg had been hurt by the beer can, and yes, Charlie had been fine before then. Yes, she was being fed. Yes, she was well-cared for . . . no, she wasn't spayed. And no, she had not had her shots. Cyndricka squirmed as the questions went on, probing beyond the immediate circumstances that had led to Charlie's injury, and into the larger context of Cyndricka's time as a pet owner.

"I'm sorry, you pulled the cat out of a storm drain?" Rebecca asked with raised eyebrows. "Has she seen a vet since then?"

No, wrote Cyndricka, staring down at the notepad as her hand moved slowly. *She seems okay. Healthy.*

"Ma'am, how do you know that she's well? It sounds like this cat has never been seen by a veterinarian. We get that around here with barn cats, but this sounds like a proper stray. Has she been tested for heartworm?"

No.

"Does she have any of her vaccinations, feline leukemia or rabies?

No.

"In just a few months, she'll be old enough to breed. How are you going to make sure she doesn't get pregnant with a litter of her own?"

I don't know.

"Ma'am . . . do you have the means to take care of a pet?"

"Don't listen to her, Cyndricka," Chelsea murmured in her ear. Carmen nodded along, and Cyndricka's eyes followed her from her periphery vision. "You take good care of Charlie, we've seen it."

But Cyndricka slowly wrote out her answer, pen dragging listlessly across the paper. *I do not know. I try, but I'm not sure she's okay. Please make her better.*

Rebecca's lips tightened, but she nodded. "We take care of animals here, ma'am. We will do our very best for Charlie. You can have a seat, and I will call for you when Darnell comes back with more news. What was your name again?"

Cyndricka Danvers, she wrote even more slowly, slow enough that the ink pooled and blossomed from her pen into dots on the paper. *Tell me when she is better.*

"I will do just that. Our benches are right over there." She gestured to the benches that could not have been more than five feet away, and Cyndricka slumped her way over to fall into them with a thump. She swung her bag down to the ground just as heavily, making a dog next to her whine and paw at the tile floor. Carmen sat down on one side of her, Chelsea on the other; a cat peeked its nose out from its crate to sniff at the bafflingly scent-less Chelsea, before its owner moved seats to none-too-subtly put some distance between her and Cyndricka.

21.

Cyndricka ended up snoozing lightly, back pressed against the wall and chin resting on her chest. Chelsea watched the slow rise and fall of her breath and caught Carmen's gaze. This day was not looking good. And she wondered if Carmen was thinking what she was. She leaned across Cyndricka and whispered to Carmen in Mandarin.

"How is she going to pay for this?"

Carmen shook her head and sighed. "She will not be able to," she responded, matching Chelsea for language, just in case Cyndricka chose that moment to awaken. "She barely has enough money to take care of herself. She does not succeed in that, by the vast majority of people's standards, and she does not have anywhere near enough for surgery for a stray cat."

"So, what, they're not going to help Charlie? They're just gonna turn her away?"

"No. They will ask Cyndricka to surrender her to Animal Control. It is not even like she bought Charlie anywhere; in the eyes of everyone, this is a homeless woman being a good Samaritan and bringing in an injured stray, not a person trying to care for her hurt pet. They will not want to give Charlie back." Her eyes lingered over the top of Cyndricka's bowed head. "And after that witch's speech, I do not know if Cyndricka will want to take her back."

"She's her cat," Chelsea pushed, still trying to wrap her head around what had just been said. "She's Cyndricka's pet, our pet, not a stray. It's not her fault that some bastard threw a beer can out of his truck like a maniac. It's not fair."

Carmen gave Chelsea a sad, condescending smile and Chelsea

found herself wanting to curl up like a little kid again and wish all of the bad things away. "Chelsea, dear," Carmen said. "When, in any of this, in anything we all have been through, has fairness come into play?"

". . . I don't want to have to be the one to tell Jamie on our way back through."

"I do not think anyone does."

They drifted back into silence, letting Cyndricka sleep as all three of them sat in the tiny waiting room for their little traveling companion.

Almost an hour and a half later Darnell returned from the back room, gloves removed and hands still shiny wet from a recent cleaning. A bright red cut decorated his forearm and there were a few spots of blood on his perky cartoon scrubs, but he practically bounced into the room. Rebecca at the desk pointed to Cyndricka, who she had been sending increasingly frustrated glances at for the entire duration of his absence. He tapped her on the shoulder and leaned in to quietly wake her up.

"Ma'am. Ms. Danvers, I think Rebecca said? Ma'am, your cat Charlie is going to be fine. We've got her all patched up and she is good as new. And a strong little girl, at that."

For all that her eyes were bleary and unfocused, still caught in the haze of sleep, Cyndricka beamed up at him, and Darnell smiled right back. He ran a hand back over his neat cornrows and returned her smile with almost the same wattage, but not quite.

"We're going to want to keep her for a few nights to recover, and she's going to have to take it easy after that for a while. Cats with broken ribs, there's not a ton you can do, and keeping her quiet and calm is going to be a beast, I imagine. And while she's here, we would like to take the time to spay her and catch her up on some shots, if that's alright. Rebecca mentioned that she hasn't had a lot of professional care. But Charlie is doing fine."

Thank you, Cyndricka wrote on her notepad, and she looked about as relieved as humanly possible when she held it up to show him. *I really do owe you a million.*

His bright smile faded at that. He slowly sat down next to her on the bench; Chelsea dodged out of the way, which got a single chuckle out of Carmen for being twitchy enough to still worry about those sorts of things.

"Ms. Danvers," he started, then paused, looking her up and down with a hesitant expression. "I don't want to assume anything, but . . . are you going to be able to pay for Charlie's treatment?"

She didn't bother to write anything on her notepad; she just shook her head. For all that Chelsea and Carmen had been the ones to discuss it, it had to have been in the back of her head. Darnell nodded slowly.

"I understand how difficult this has to be. I used to work at a charity in Cheyenne that did vet work for the pets of people who couldn't care for them. But they went under 'bout a year and a half back, and nothing's popped up to fill their place in the area. I see so many people come in here, only wanting the best for the animals they love, and—" He trailed off and looked at the tile floor. He ran his hands over his hair again and sighed. "Would you be willing to surrender Charlie to the local shelter? I promise you that I will make sure she is provided with the best care possible. I can try and make sure she's adopted out, help spread the word about her. Lot of people looking for a young cat to train as a mouser." He shook his head. "I'd adopt her myself if I could. But the five I got at home would kill me if I brought in another stray to share the food bowl . . . I am so sorry, Ms. Danvers. Would you like to come and see her?"

Cyndricka nodded. It looked like a colossal effort for her to pull herself to her feet, and Darnell reached out a hand to support her elbow, hovering nearby in case she needed it. She gave the smallest glance backwards, to her invisible compatriots, and jerked her chin to invite them in with her. Carmen nodded and Chelsea whispered "Thanks. We're coming."

Charlie was still looking very woozy when they entered, ears drooped to the sides and trying to keep her upper body steady on her front legs. A neon green bandage wrapped up her right back leg from paw all the way up to her hip, and she tried to bend around to sniff at it. A shaved patch on her side made a sharp contrast, faint beige skin showing where black and white fur had been before. A bandage was taped into place, but Chelsea could just see the puckered edge of a series of sutures. She looked much smaller than she had for a while, like the tiny, half-drowned kitten that Cyndricka had pulled out of a drain. Her ears perked up slightly and she mewed when Cyndricka entered the room.

All three of them knelt down to see better into her metal crate. Cyndricka pushed her fingers through the bars and made kissy noises with her lips to the groggy cat who didn't seem able to focus her eyes perfectly yet. Darnell stepped past her and opened the crate.

"Let me get her out here on the table so you can pet her. And she should be okay to hold, if you're very gentle."

Cyndricka nodded and her hand was feather soft as she traced over Charlie's fur, freshly cleaned and still looking a bit damp. Chelsea leaned over and twiddled her fingers in front of Charlie's nose; Charlie batted at them with a frustrated little grumble, and then continued to lean into Cyndricka's touch, almost falling over on the exam table.

Cyndricka glanced up at Carmen and Chelsea while she was turned away from Darnell and looked pointedly down at the cat under her hand. She opened and closed her mouth, miming speaking words, and Carmen understood a beat before Chelsea did, by the way she nodded. But it clicked for Chelsea too, and the two ghosts leaned over and began to coo to the cat that had become a vital member of their team.

"Hey there, Charlie-baby. I know this is scary, but you're going to be fine with these nice people here. We love you very much, but this is a good place for you to be safe. Good kitty."

"You have been a good traveling companion with us, and I will be sorry to see you go." When Chelsea shot her a glare, Carmen sighed and softened her voice to continue. "You are a very good kitty. Chelsea and I love you and will miss you. And I know Cyndricka is going to miss you very much, darling girl."

Cyndricka nodded, and wove her fingers under Charlie's stomach to lift and pull her to her chest, cradling the groggy bundle of cat. The tears began to fall in earnest when she planted a kiss to the very top of Charlie's head and Charlie squirmed under the attention. Behind them, hovering in the doorway, Darnell looked away.

"Should I leave you for a minute?" he asked with a thick voice. "Give you some privacy, or—" He cut off when Cyndricka shook her head. She held Charlie close for one last moment, petted her from the tip of her black nose to the white dot on the end of her tail, then set her back on the table and left the room, trailing two ghosts behind her.

Out in the office, she filled out some paperwork, cast one last look at the door to the inner room, then left.

She made it two blocks before she ducked into an alleyway, slumped down beside a trashcan, and cried her eyes out until she fell asleep, her two ghosts besides her as sentries, as always.

22.

The night in Pine Bluffs was not any more interesting than the day in Pine Bluffs had been. It was a nondescript little town that they would have had no reason to stop in but for this accident. Once she had cried herself out, Cyndricka felt no reason to linger. The three of them took off back onto the highway, redoing the morning despite how tired Cyndricka had to be. Chelsea couldn't think of anything to say to make it better, so they walked in silence.

After an hour of walking, they passed a disturbed patch of gravel on the side of the road with a smattering of blood in the dust. The can had rolled into the weeds and split open, leaving a damp patch on the ground swarming with ants. Cyndricka stopped and looked at the sight for a long moment. Then she hoisted her bag higher on her shoulders and kept going. Chelsea and Carmen trailed behind.

They made camp not too much further down the highway, tucked into a patch of scrub grass and behind a low-to-the-ground billboard that would serve as a windbreak in the cold night. Cyndricka dug into her bag to get out her precious food storage, and froze when she pulled out a bag of dry cat food in the process.

"Oh, Cyndricka, I'm so sorry," Chelsea said, for lack of anything better. "I'm sure that Charlie is being well taken care of. She can get all fixed up, then . . . I don't know, be adopted by a really nice family . . . maybe she can surprise them with some of her circus tricks."

Cyndricka squeezed her eyes tight, her whole face seized up

while trying not to break. Carmen glanced at Chelsea out of the corner of her eye and tried her own tactic.

"This hurts now, but the pain will fade," she soothed. "You will find a way to move on. You did what was best for Charlie and that is what counts."

I left her there, she signed slowly, once her hands were empty. *I left my cat.*

"You had to," Chelsea reminded her gently. "There wasn't really any other choice."

She is the first thing I have ever had to take care of. And as soon as things got bad, I left her. Cyndricka's jaw clenched and her shoulders tensed, practically up by her ears. *I think it must run in the family, if I'm the sort to leave innocent things that trust me.*

There was no good way to respond to that, or at least none that Chelsea knew. There had been points during their journey when Cyndricka had been sad, when things had seemed rough, the road endless and the world cruel, but Chelsea had never seen such an empty look in her eyes. She looked like she was a million miles away. Or at least however many miles there were between Pine Bluffs and Reno. Charlie was just a cat, true, but this was all so much more than that, and Chelsea didn't know where to begin.

But apparently Carmen did. She stood in front of Cyndricka. Then she moved closer, sandals right underneath Cyndricka's nose until there was no way she could not notice her. Chelsea was fairly sure she would have kept creeping forward until she was standing in the middle of Cyndricka's chest, had she not looked up into Carmen's eyes.

"This will not do," Carmen declared. "You are right. Charlie is an innocent creature in our care and we cannot leave her behind."

Too late, Cyndricka signed, practically punching the words out into the air; if she had spoken them, they would have been spit into the night.

Carmen tilted her head and smirked down at the human woman. "Cyndricka, please take a moment to recognize that you, as far as we know, are unique among all humans." Cyndricka looked away and Carmen pressed on, emphasizing the words harder. "You have the power to speak to the dead. And right now you have two undead spirits at your beck and call. I believe that really does count for something in situations like this."

Cyndricka's hands moved slower, shaping over the words carefully, as if she considered each sign individually. *What are you saying we do?*

"You do not want to leave her. She does not want to be left." Carmen smiled and clapped her hands together. "So we are going to go and get her back."

Chelsea peeked around the corner, before she realized just how silly and unnecessary that was. On a mission like this, it just felt wrong to walk down the street in the open, even if no one else could see her. She surveyed the street, now empty and quiet. The tattoo parlor had been the last to close for the evening, but the heavily inked owner had left over half an hour ago. Now there was no living soul left in the street, not even any buildings high enough to have apartments above them; no people to glance out their windows and see a grand theft feline in progress.

Cyndricka had slept for a few hours back at the billboard after they had hatched their plan, and they had spent the following day returning to Pine Bluffs and moseying around, trying to grab some food and not look too suspicious. The last thing Cyndricka needed was to be harassed by police in the middle of their daring rescue. Once the sun had set, they returned to the veterinary office and the stake-out began.

"This side is empty!" Carmen called out from behind the building; the whole spirit of sneaking was lost on her. Chelsea kept her eyes peeled, refraining from the luxury of blinking as she made absolutely sure that the coast was clear. Cyndricka and Carmen were setting about breaking in through the back door, with its weaker lock and already somewhat splintered door frame. Carmen had checked through the place earlier, determined that it didn't have any security cameras, and come up with a good, easy route for Cyndricka to take, that would lead her through the smallest number of doors. She was accompanying Cyndricka inside the place, while Chelsea was guard. Or at least watchdog. Guarding implied the ability to stop someone.

She took another look around the front street, then ran through the tattoo parlor, phasing through glass and wood and a tray of inks and needles, until she arrived in the back parking lot. No cars had arrived in the sixty seconds since Carmen had called the clear. When she looked at the back door, it wasn't obviously damaged, though someone could see the scrapes along the handle if they looked. No one in their group was too familiar with breaking locks, so it had been a sloppy job.

She could just faintly hear the sounds of Cyndricka rustling inside the office, if she strained to hear. This presumably meant that she hadn't entered the kennels themselves yet. Once the dogs saw her, there was a very good chance that she would have to grab Charlie and run to avoid anyone coming to investigate why all of the animals were creating a racket in the middle of the night.

And after they stole back Charlie, perhaps making Cyndricka guilty of theft, and certainly making her guilty of breaking and entering? Well, they would figure that out when it happened and if she was ever caught. Chelsea didn't think that the police would be too invested in chasing a woman across state lines for the crime of kidnapping her own cat, but crazier things had happened. And as Carmen said, very, very little was fair in this life or death.

Her scan of the outside complete, she ran through the bike shop, letting wheels and spokes skewer through her body without leaving a trace. She wondered briefly if it would be better for Cyndricka to steal a bicycle before they left town, to dramatically reduce the long hours of walking. Though that would probably be more likely to bring the authorities down on their heads. She burst through the front window of the shop and back out onto the empty street.

There was still nothing there, nothing in the distance, no one in sight. She supposed the best option would just be to keep going in circles. She had never actually done a stakeout before, and even if a ghost stakeout required a great deal less finesse, she still worried that she wasn't doing it right. What if she was going too fast and missing something? Had she sped through the back parking lot too quickly? She sprinted back through the tattoo parlor and slid into the parking lot just as a single dog gave a sleepy bark from inside. Still no cars. Back through the bicycle shop, and she was going to drive herself mad trying to look in five different directions at once.

"Chelsea, is anyone there?" Carmen yelled out from inside. "What does it look like?"

How could she have forgotten to give updates? She really wasn't good under pressure. She dipped her head through the metal door of the office and yelled through the halls, "I don't see anyone out here, you guys are good!"

Carmen made some general noise of assent and a few cats yowled in the dark hallways. She pulled her head back out through the door and was about to run through the bicycle shop again when she saw them. The headlights.

It was only the beams stretching down the back alley, but they grew larger and closer with every second. This parking lot only had access to back doors of the three stores, so there was a one in three chance that Cyndricka was about to be caught. Why had she not thought to check down the streets too, instead of the immediate areas in sight?

"There's a car coming!" she yelled into the vet's office, and it may have been the only time she had ever heard Carmen say "shit."

Carmen came running out to check just as the battered sedan pulled around the corner. They could see Darnell sitting in the driver's seat. He pulled into a spot and turned off his engine as Carmen sprinted inside to guide Cyndricka out.

"Okay, you need to go out the front entrance," she heard Carmen say. "No, pry it—put all of your weight into it, really pull, you need to get it open fast. Hurry, Cyndricka, or this will all have been for naught!" Even in tense moments, Carmen had a flair for the poetic.

Chelsea thought as hard as she could, trying to come up with options. Darnell climbed out of his car, a set of keys in his hand, and made for the back door. It would have been too good to be true if he had just really wanted a midnight tattoo. Chelsea called out to the two inside, begging them to hurry, and then just stood in front of the door with her arms spread. Maybe if he was very receptive, and very superstitious, and didn't have a good reason to be here at all, and didn't have anything that couldn't wait until morning—

He paused as he fit his key into the lock, then bent down to peer into it. His stance changed, and he went from casually curious, going about an evening errand, to alert and tense, preparing to apprehend an intruder. He opened the door quietly and passed through Chelsea's body. He didn't even shiver.

"Guys, he's coming in now! Get out of there or hide, you have to—" she yelled, following him into the office while she pleaded, but she was interrupted by him turning on a light and shouting.

"Holy shit! Hey, you—" He cut off, then lowered his voice to a whisper. "Ms. Danvers? Cyndricka?"

Chelsea stuck her head through Darnell's chest to try and get a better view of the situation. Common courtesy had to be disregarded in extreme circumstances.

Cyndricka was frozen like a deer in headlights, still caught mid-lean trying to pull open Charlie's cage. The cat, for her part, was mewling and licking Cyndricka's fingers where they were wrapped through the bars; Carmen tried to shush and calm her, but to not much avail. Another cat in the crate next to Charlie's was reaching out and batting its paws through Carmen's braid.

"Okay, Cyndricka," said Chelsea, loud enough for Cyndricka to hear, no matter how much her instincts told her to whisper; those had proven very unhelpful tonight. "Hold your hands up and back away slowly. Try not to look like a threat at all and maybe he won't call the police." Carmen and Cyndricka both tensed at the words.

Darnell pinched the bridge of his nose and let out a long, long sigh, emptying his lungs before he took a deep breath and spoke.

"Okay, ma'am, this is really not okay. This is private property and you signed over the cat. She's not yours anymore and you can't just break in here."

His words spurred something in Cyndricka and her brow furrowed. She pressed a clutched hand to her chest and emphatically mouthed *She is mine. I love her.*

"Lots of people care about animals that they can't afford. You did what was best for Charlie, you can't go back on it—no, look, I'm not debating this with you, I'm calling the cops."

Darnell rustled through his bag looking for his cell phone and Cyndricka's eyes went wide. Carmen whispered a strained "No," and Chelsea could follow the line of Cyndricka's gaze around the room, saw how it settled in a drawer labeled "syringes," and just hoped that Darnell didn't notice.

"Okay, Cyndricka, let's not do anything extreme," Chelsea said slowly, stepping between the two of them with her hands raised. "Can you make a break for it, run while he's distracted? You can probably get far enough away before any cops come."

Cyndricka took a step out, closer to the drawer.

"Cyndricka, you can't hurt him, that'll be way more dangerous."

Darnell pulled out his phone and turned it on.

"Carmen, help me talk some sense into her!"

Cyndricka took another step forward—

"Cyndricka, no!"

—and fell to her knees. She clasped her hands in front of her chest and looked up at Darnell, while surrounded by mewling cats. She looked him in the eye and made one sign, circling her hand across her chest.

Please.

Darnell froze, looking down at Cyndricka. He gripped his phone hard and started to raise it up.

Then he put it back in his bag. "God, don't let me get fired for this."

He reached to flip the light switch and stepped further into the room. Cyndricka smashed herself back against the wall, and Darnell stopped in his tracks and held up his hands. "I'm not gonna hurt you, ma'am. No hurting here, see?" He took a slow, exaggerated step forward with his hands still up. "I'm going to get Charlie out. Is that okay?"

Cyndricka gave a quick, jerky nod. She scrambled to her feet and shimmied along the edge of the wall, disturbing a few cats as she moved away from Charlie's cage. Charlie yowled and reached a paw through the grate to beckon her closer. Carmen drifted over and put a hand on Cyndricka's shoulder, comforting, but still not taking her eyes off of Darnell.

"It's okay, we'll be out of here and with her in no time."

Darnell fiddled with the complicated latch until it clicked open and he lifted the small cat out. He held her in his arms and looked at Cyndricka for a minute before speaking.

". . . Alright, so this is what I think I'm gonna do. I was the one who closed up tonight. That's why I came back, to grab a bag I left. I'm gonna to tell my co-workers that I changed my mind and decided to adopt Charlie, bringing her right home. Not like I'm close with the people here, no one's gonna be over at my house to check. But there are some things I really need to do first, before I let you go. Do you have a few minutes? I don't know how much time you left for your . . . middle of the night cat theft." He shook his head and a bit of the bright smile from earlier came back out to shine. "Goddammit, this has to be one of the weirdest nights I've ever had."

Darnell placed Charlie down on the exam table, holding her in place with one hand, then looked to Cyndricka. She nodded and gestured for him to continue what he was doing. Chelsea and Carmen hovered alongside.

"So I can give her her shots right now and let you be on your way. The stitches on her side are dissolving so they won't need to be taken out at any point. You really should get her spayed soon, but there's a charity still running in Laramie if you have the ability to head that way. The splint on her leg should be able to come off in a week, since the bone wasn't broken. These scissors are for cutting bandages, you can take them. Then . . . I don't know. You keep doing whatever you do, I guess." He shrugged. "She's clearly well fed and you love her and it sounds like this was an accident. I can't really blame a person for wanting this girl." He laughed and shook his head. "Though maybe don't try to break into any more vets' offices. I like to think that we're good people on the whole, but very few are gonna be chill enough to make deals with a homeless lady stealing cats, all right?"

There was almost a genuine smile on Cyndricka's face when she nodded. Darnell asked her to hold Charlie in place while he got the shots ready. Charlie yelled and squealed when the injections went in, but she was able to tuck into the arms of her mama, which seemed to make everything okay.

Within the hour, they were back on the road. Charlie was supported in a careful sling around Cyndricka's neck, and her backpack was filled with simple medical supplies and some cat food that Darnell had just happened to have extra of lying around.

Carmen nodded while they walked. "Well, Cyndricka, I believe I was wrong about my assessment," she said levelly.

Both Cyndricka and Chelsea looked over, both confused, and in Chelsea's case, more than a little eager to hear Carmen admit fault for something. Cyndricka tilted her head to the side to supply the requisite *why?*

"I believed that supernatural means would be necessary for this endeavor. They were not. The world is strange like that sometimes, I suppose."

Cyndricka nodded slowly. Maybe she was considering it. Maybe she was just tired. Or maybe she was so distracted looking down into her sling and running gentle fingers over Charlie's fur that she had no space for any other thoughts. But that might have been the best, Chelsea supposed. Changes in worldview had to take time, when abrupt things like death didn't go forcing them.

They settled for the night in a back alley, with Cyndricka curled on her side on a piece of cardboard, holding Charlie to her chest to keep her warm and safe. It was a clear night, warm, and a good one to spend there before they left Pine Bluffs.

23.

Their time in Wyoming underneath wide open skies had felt endless, but they really only skimmed the state's corner before their path took them down into Colorado. Long stretches of walking took them through prairies or down highways cutting through national forests, with only a handful of towns and neighborhoods to pass through, and occasional places big enough to be called cities. The green of the Midwest had long ago turned golden around them, huge expanses of yellow plants and wide, wide blue sky. The sky had always felt so close in New York, like it was down among the buildings, but now Chelsea felt like she could float away in a light breeze. She wondered what would happen if she tried to run straight up into that horizon but held back the temptation to try. The thought of what Carmen would say if she started wandering the stratosphere was enough to stop that train of thought.

As the days got hotter and hotter, Cyndricka spent periods of time focused solely on walking, too tired to move her hands enough to chat, even when they weren't busy holding Charlie steady in her sling. Carmen and Chelsea would talk, obviously, but the general mood would occasionally send them all into silent travel. It was the comfortable silence of companions who had been together for a while. It wasn't tense or angry, but it was silence nonetheless. And it left Chelsea with time to think.

With all of the time they had spent on the road and all of the things that had happened, she had almost lost track of their goal, even though it was hers to begin with. They were coming up on three months on the road, with Osric's wedding two months away.

If she let her mind dwell on it, she would wonder if she was going to be ready for it by then. Seeing the effects of obsession and grief on a ghost firsthand had shaken her. She recalled Carmen's words from the very beginning of the whole adventure, her worry that she would turn in the middle of her trip if left unattended. Was there still a risk of that? If her mind did so much on its own due to something as simple as walking in silence, what would it have done with genuine isolation? Would she ever really be in the clear? Or was it a battle that had to be fought anew every day?

She was tempted to ask Carmen for any more details that she could offer, as if she was still newly deceased and asking for advice about how to move and whether there would really be any harm in walking through walls. But that would be a bad sign, would send Carmen into a fit of hovering and constantly checking on her. For all that she cared about her deeply, Carmen's attentions could be grating if left unchecked. So she kept her mouth shut and kept watching the horizon and highway as they walked.

To think that becoming a wailer was the least frightening option, in terms of things that could happen to a spirit. Though perhaps poltergeists were only frightening to those around them, not to themselves. Wailers turned all of their sorrow and turmoil inwards until it destroyed them; poltergeists rotted and festered with their anger and rage until they burst outwards and destroyed others. They were spoken of in hushed voices, rumors and gossip amongst the dead, and Chelsea had heard plenty of ghosts doubt that they really existed. But she had posed that question to Carmen long ago, to be greeted with a firm "yes" in a tone that didn't invite follow-up questions.

Cyndricka also seemed to be growing more antsy and fidgety, when she could find the energy to be. Her body would all but collapse by the end of the day as she flopped onto her sleeping bag and settled Charlie on her chest, but she would stay staring at the stars long after the cat's breathing had grown steady and even. Chelsea and Carmen would converse with her when she was in the mood, but when she drifted into stillness, they would leave her to her thoughts instead and stay on watch in silence.

This eventually fazed Carmen, the constant seeker of distractions and diversions. On days when the map had nothing ahead of them but more road and the occasional mountain, and Cyndricka's face was already closed off from the moment she woke up, Carmen proposed a new arrangement, which the other two would generally be okay with: Carmen would run down the highway to the nearest town and do her own business there, then rejoin them when evening fell and Cyndricka reached her limits. They had all become fairly certain in their estimations of Cyndricka's normal pace, so it wasn't difficult to figure out where sunset would find Cyndricka on a normal day. Carmen would go off in the morning in search of movies or concerts, or even just the opportunity to lurk in people's homes and watch television with them.

It was a way of getting both interaction and alone time at once, as far as Chelsea could tell, and after a few days of following the pattern, she began to be noticeably more relaxed and cheerful, engaging fully when Cyndricka was in the mood to talk. And at night, she and Chelsea would have whispered conversations about what had come into theaters in the last few months, and what Carmen had been able to gather about the skipped episodes of a sitcom, based on the two-minute recap from the beginning.

She came back from such a sojourn to find Chelsea and Cyndricka consulting a local map during a break by the side of the highway. They had snagged one (one of the relatively few free things Cyndricka had grabbed in her time thus far) in Cowdrey, and it was marked with more than the major highways and county roads. Carmen looked at them skeptically while they giggled and pointed, and Charlie batted at the unfolded corner of the page.

"What are you two snickering about?" she asked, with a pointedly maternal voice.

Cyndricka turned the page towards her and pointed at a little star on the edge of the next town. A small text bubble underneath it read "Chesterton Historical Haunted House." Cyndricka dissolved into silent giggles again and Carmen rolled her eyes.

"Yes, yes, seeing the living trying to comprehend matters of life and death is hilarious, I know. Anything else?"

"Oh come on, it's great," Chelsea said between attempts to stop laughing. "You have to read the blurb on the back, it's about as clichéd as you can get. Women in long white dresses, senses of dread, curses running down generations. If it talked about anything legitimate, yeah, they'd maybe have something, but this is just a tourist trap."

Carmen gave her a particularly lofty raise of her eyebrows, until they practically disappeared into her hairline. "And you are, after all, the greatest authority on such matters. How many years ago did you die? How many decades? How many centuries, perhaps, is the better question, as you have accumulated so much otherworldly knowledge in that time."

"Okay, I really don't think you're allowed to be that smug until you've cracked a century yourself, okay?" Carmen kicked her foot lightly through Chelsea's head, which devolved into a very mature slap fight while Cyndricka pumped her arms next to them, miming as if she was rooting them on. Chelsea could only hope she was cheering for her.

"Okay, okay, fine, stop head-butting me!" She shook herself away from Carmen's incorporeal assaults. "But we have to go that way tomorrow anyway; it's the quickest way through town."

We could stop and look at it, Cyndricka pointed out, trying to keep a straight face. *I would like to see how much they have right.*

"Are we doing nothing but detouring lately?" Carmen scoffed, throwing her hands up. "At this rate, we might not make it to San Francisco by December!"

"Well, there are worse places for Cyndricka to spend Christmas than California," Chelsea pointed out with a smirk. "But seriously, we're making really good time through the west. We're heading into Medicine Bow National Forest in a couple days, so we should take it slow now to give her a chance to gather supplies in town. The end of the day tomorrow will find us pretty close to this Chesterton place, so we can just take a look inside for fun. And you're the one always looking for entertainment, so it should be right up your alley, in a meta sort of way. Ghosts reading about ghosts with a human who speaks to ghosts, judging other humans for their beliefs about ghosts, in a house that may or may not have real ghosts in it."

"Yes, yes, I understand your point, I did witness the rise of meta-comedy first hand." But the promise of entertainment had

Carmen perked up, a considering look on her face. "I suppose if it does not take away too much of our forward momentum, it could be a refreshing break from events."

Cyndricka punched the air in a silent cheer, Chelsea whooped, and Charlie meowed because she wanted to join in making noise. Carmen grumbled about going back into town to watch a movie if everyone was going to be this silly all night, but she smiled nonetheless.

They entered Chesterton in the middle of the day and saw immediately that they had made the right choice in stopping. Tucked away in a valley between a few different creeks, existing as an offshoot of County Road 24, Chesterton had clearly built its culture around the one thing of note in their history. Every shop, every parlor of any kind, every store that wasn't a convenience store, and even some of them, had merchandise advertising the haunted house. Postcards, historical books, little bobble-head women in white with screaming faces. It was late June, and the town already looked ready for Halloween. Cyndricka had to cover her mouth and look away from several of the shops, just to stop herself from laughing too obviously.

If I did a performance here about ghosts, I could make a fortune, she signed. Chelsea had to admit that she had a point.

"Do we want to stop long enough for a show? If you add some local flavor, there would probably be a fairly big turn around." But Cyndricka shook her head, looking resolute.

I wouldn't want to make fun of ghosts.

". . . You do realize that we seem to be the only ones around to be offended, correct?" Carmen asked, looking skeptical and more than a little judgmental.

Not just you two. All ghosts. After everything that the undead have done for me over the years, it would be wrong to poke fun, especially when I'm the only human who would get most of the jokes. We can stay and laugh at the humans being wrong, but then we should leave.

Carmen met Chelsea's gaze, and Chelsea shrugged. "No one ever said that our trip had to make sense . . . I would think that a mature and experienced ghost such as yourself would—"

She broke off to dodge Carmen's slap, dancing out of the way and through a wire carousel of spooky postcards.

They reached the house in the late afternoon, and for all that the town seemed to be funded by the merchandise, the actual admission was free, part of a local historical society. A security guard sniffed and looked down his nose at Cyndricka as she entered but didn't say anything. Charlie was taking a nap on the top of the backpack and covered by a coat, and even if she did wake up or begin making noise, there was no real harm in getting kicked out of the place they were just visiting for fun.

Chelsea looked over the front room, with its informational displays about the history of Chesterton and the old family that had lived there when the city was first founded. (Carmen muttered a question about which tribe the land was stolen from, but curiously enough, none of the displays felt interested in sharing that information.) There were a lot of dry paragraphs about mining rights and local legislation, and Chelsea could see more with every word where the whole "historical society" angle came into play. But that was apparently just a ploy to get the context out of the way first, because past the first room, the walls read out all the details of a murder mystery.

A young woman, in the prime of life, engaged to the son of a local railway tycoon, but really in love with a rancher. High romance, intrigue, scandal, and murder: all of the things that made up a good ghost story. She was found strangled out in the prairie land, with no sign of who had done it. She was buried in her finest white gown, and not two weeks after her death, people started seeing flashes of white at the corners of their vision, flickering skirts disappearing around corners, the usual specs. Haunting feelings, the sense of being watched, and occasionally the sound of weeping on the wind. Chelsea paused over the description of the mournful crying, and she wondered if there had actually been a wailer here, the remaining spirit of the young woman who never got to be with the one she loved.

But Cyndricka was the one to first catch the flaws in the official story. She pointed at a grainy picture of the woman in her coffin and traced the line of her long white dress with a single finger.

As a ghost, she is wearing what she was buried in, not what she died in, she signed, far, far too happy to have noticed it before the actual ghosts did. A copy of the local sheriff's report on the wall included a description of the blue floral dress that she had been in when she died. Cyndricka was right.

An account from the rich fiancée described the alabaster beauty of the ghost that had visited him in the night, hovering above the foot of his bed when he awoke at midnight. It didn't sound like any of the strangulation victims Chelsea had met before, with their heavily bruised throats and blue-tinged faces. Cyndricka shook with laughter over the tales of doors slamming shut and vases falling off of tables untouched.

If they had seen a poltergeist, they would have known. Right, Curtains?

"Very true. It is not a being that you could easily mistake for a normal ghost," Carmen said with a sage nod. "Or a beautiful young woman." Chelsea wondered if there was any more detail coming, but Carmen was caught up in investigating what was apparently the key piece of evidence against the rancher, a bloody piece of rope with horse hairs caught in the knot.

They spent an entertaining afternoon picking their way through the various exhibits, correcting everything that was wrong and pointing out every inconsistency that led them to believe that the house was just very windy, not haunted by the spirits of the deceased. The security guard began to shadow Cyndricka as the windows grew dark, and they knew it was time for them to find a useful place to spend the night. Or, as Chelsea put it, "a place for some real ghosts to haunt, with their mime along for company."

Chesterton, for all that it apparently revolved around this one house, died fairly shortly past its doors, and soon a line of abandoned houses was the only thing still connecting them to the city, and keeping them from spending the night on the side of County Road 24 again. Cyndricka picked a place and dodged around a "Condemned" sign and through an overgrown lawn to jimmy open the house's front door, just as the sun set. For all that the days were increasingly hot around here, the nights became cool quickly with no trees to hold onto the heat. Cyndricka unrolled her sleeping bag just inside the doorway and pulled out the constantly reused paper plate and bowl to feed and water Charlie.

Garbage and building debris cluttered the house, broken beer cans and splintered pieces of plywood scattered across the floor. Cyndricka shoved trash aside to clear a space for her sleeping bag and made it seem almost cozy as she laid out her things.

But for all that they had stayed in far worse places over the past months, Chelsea found something about the house unsettling. There was a sort of sharpness to the air that seemed familiar, but she couldn't place why. Here and there across the walls were gouges in the wood with frayed scraps of wallpaper hanging off of them. Chelsea passed through one of them while looking for the kitchen and felt a vague buzz ripple up her arm. She wondered if they should pick another empty house, but Cyndricka was already unpacking her bag so she let her jitters pass.

Chelsea and Carmen ventured through the halls of the house to see if there were any useful supplies for Cyndricka to scavenge, even something as simple as a blanket to use for extra padding between her and the floor. Chelsea took the upstairs level while Carmen did a thorough investigation of the lower and the basement.

Chelsea glided up the stairs, the thin wooden type that looked like they would creak if someone with actual mass were to step on them. She paused when a scratching and shuffling broke out above her. A few squeaks drifted down to her as well; rats, most likely, though perhaps an opossum or a raccoon. She and Carmen would have to keep an eye on Cyndricka and Charlie to make sure they didn't get bit during the night. The last thing they needed to deal with was the need for rabies shots.

A window slammed in a bedroom and Chelsea jumped in spite of herself. They had seen plenty of ones hanging open and unlocked on the different houses they had passed, and wind could gather a lot of speed as it tore across the open land out here. But still, Chelsea knew she had to investigate, to make sure that nothing could hurt the two of her traveling companions that could actually get hurt.

The noise had come from the bedroom at the end of the dark hallway, with its heavy wooden door, and Chelsea found herself walking more slowly and cautiously as she approached it. She was enacting every possible cliché from a horror movie, but the awareness didn't do anything to cut through the growing sense of unease. If she had still been alive, she might have swung open the door quickly and definitively, to show herself that there was nothing to fear and that she was being silly. But in the absence of working limbs, the only thing she could do was step through the door and stand in the bedroom.

The dark bedroom with the tall figure standing in front of the window.

Except that standing was the wrong word for it. This thing did not stand, but perched on the very tips of long, clawed feet, in a way that shouldn't have been able to support it at all. Long, spindly arms clutched at drapes and dug into the threads. Its back was hunched and its head hung low, and Chelsea could have counted the protruding vertebrae exposed through the ripped remains of a t-shirt if she had wanted. But she didn't want to at all. Because of all the aspects of this horrible thing before her, from the ash gray skin to the lank hair hanging around its shoulders, to the glimpse she got of a gaping and distended jaw when it turned its twisted head, one part stole her attention and would not let it go.

The creature stood before the open window and moonlight shone through it; pearly beams landed on the dusty carpet behind and beneath it. It was obviously not a solid creature, not something of this world.

But the hand that was clawed into the drapes dragged downwards, and the drapes came with it. Long, thin rips in the real, solid, tangible fabric followed the trail left by the bony fingers. It was ripping the drapes. It was a ghost that was able to impact the physical world.

Poltergeist.

She tried to back away slowly. She tried to be calm and collected as she exited the room, to not draw its attention in any way so that she could warn the others and they could all run as fast as they could. But with even one step back, one tiny little motion towards the door, the poltergeist turned. Its face was long and horrible, with fangs far too big for a person bulging out of a normal-sized mouth and gums, propping its jaws open in a constant rictus grin. It smiled all the wider when its eyes fell on Chelsea and shot a jolt of electricity through her brain: pitch black eyes with fires burning in the center of them, like bright coals in the middle of a pile of soot.

She screamed. There was really no point in not, and perhaps it would alert Cyndricka and Carmen in time for them to get away. She screamed and jumped back through the door just as the beast extended a claw for her.

She was halfway down the hallway when it caught up with her, a sprint for her but two or three strides for the stretched, inhuman monster. She glanced back to see its claws reach for her bad arm and touch, digging in and dragging back.

Pain flared through her. Actual pain. It had been so long that she had forgotten what it felt like, how it filled her body and her mind all at once. The last pain she remembered was the instant before everything had gone black, the impact of the train before the world had stopped, but that had just been one horrible second before her neck snapped and everything ceased to matter. This continued and continued and would not stop, as the beast somehow managed to get a hold of her and pull, dragging her back towards it. She could see tears forming in her coat, the fabric that she had worn for over two years splitting under the claws and revealing ghostly flesh underneath. And even there, muscles and bones ripped and tore and pulled apart, tendons snapped, and there was no blood for her to spill, just horrible pain that shot through her intangible form.

She screamed and screamed and filled the hall with noise, but she couldn't bring herself to form words, not when the pain was knocking her senseless. She fought with all of her might to pull away from the thing. She had not used any strength since she had died, and barely knew what would work in aid of getting away, so she just pulled in the opposite direction as hard as she could, hoping and praying that something would give, that the beast would let go or her arm would tear off completely, anything to let her escape.

She heard footfalls on the stairs behind her, and a high-pitched gasp when Cyndricka saw the creature. Chelsea tried to wave her away, tried to make her leave, but when she looked back, the poor human was stuck in place, just as frozen as she had been.

The poltergeist gave another tug, and Chelsea knew that this was the end, the actual end from which there would be no return, no second chance. She had made a decent shot of her afterlife. This could be the end.

Until she took one last look back at Cyndricka, the one that would have to last her for the rest of eternity, and saw it, right behind her rigid shoulder. Another poltergeist.

"Cyndricka, behind you! Get out! Get the hell out of here!"

Her voice and her fight were back in an instant, and she thrashed against the grip of the creature. She let herself fall to her back so that she could kick with her feet, stabbing at its fire-bright eyes with her high heels and tugging back in spite of the burning in her arm.

She couldn't tell if the ability to make physical contact worked both ways, or if the beast was just surprised, but it jerked its horrible head back and made a sound that was half growl, half shriek, and entirely something that chilled her to the bone.

She seized the opportunity and dropped down. Its claws were slightly curved, like a cat's, so she needed to move towards it first to unhook herself from its grasp. Moving towards it again, throwing herself at its face, definitely surprised it, and she scrambled back to her feet, temporarily free and trying her hardest not to focus on the stabbing pain running up and down her arm.

Cyndricka was already down the stairs, running at full tilt away from the second poltergeist, Charlie clutched in her arms. The cat screamed and hissed back at the monsters that it had the misfortune of being able to see. Chelsea climbed over the railing of the stairway and dropped down to the second story, praying with all of her might that some things still made sense. And yes, when she moved her legs, she was able to run down the open air, and not all of the rules of the afterlife had abandoned her in short order.

Her joy was short-lived, though, as the poltergeists were hot on their trail, hurdling over the stairs and falling down to the floor. They reached out and tore at curtains and wallpaper as they went, digging deep grooves into wooden railings and cackling out demonic laughs as they caused as much chaos as possible.

Cyndricka sprinted back to the front room, past all of her things laid out on the floor and reached for the door. But just as she wrapped her hand around the knob, a poltergeist leapt in front of her and slammed a hand into the door, leaving a splintered mark from the impact. It leered at her, leaned in until the tattered remains of what looked like a denim jacket hung down in front of Cyndricka's face as it peered down at her from above. Cyndricka followed its movement with wide eyes, completely rimmed with white.

Chelsea only had a moment to take all of this in, still pursued by her own attacker. She followed Cyndricka as far as the door, then flew through it, hoping that perhaps she could lead them away. She dashed out into the front lawn.

And was confronted by three more poltergeists, grinning their toothy smiles at her from the moonlit grass and sidewalk.

She had barely more than an instant to turn around and dodge the swing of her pursuer. She slipped under its grasping arm, back into the house through the front window, and hoped that the others would not give chase. She hoped in vain, a glance backwards told her, but it was worth the thought, at least.

When she arrived back inside, the air had been taken over by a whirlwind of debris, as broken glass and smashed appliances and splinters of wood and plastic flew through the air. The poltergeist that had been chasing Cyndricka stood in the center, ripping new objects from the wall and floor and tossing them back and forth to a collection of other poltergeists that had come to join in on the fun. Cyndricka herself huddled in a corner, hunched over and looking away to try and shield her face and Charlie from the rubble. Chelsea could see her bent over and shaking, could faintly hear her panting and gasping. Cuts dotted her arms and shoulders, blood soaking into her t-shirt. A vase smashed against the wall over her head, showering pieces down on her back, and she squeezed herself into a tighter ball.

Chelsea didn't have to worry about the debris, but was plenty busy herself dodging out of the way of thrashing claws and snapping teeth. A half-dozen poltergeists filled the living room: hanging off of the walls, draped over the stair railing, throwing debris between them and laughing from deep in their distended throats. Tattered clothes showed the vestiges of their humanity, the only indication that they had once been people. Now they were only monsters. Chelsea ran through the tornado of casual destruction, past the main staircase, and into the room beyond it, the kitchen. For Cyndricka's sake, she could only hope they didn't go in there, with the potential for knives and forks and any other sharp things that people had left behind before fleeing this hellscape.

She bashed right into and then through Carmen at the entrance to the basement. Her eyes were just as wide and panicked as Cyndricka's had been. She looked down at the shredded mess that had been made of Chelsea's arm and gasped.

"Oh god, they're—"

"Poltergeists, it's poltergeists, they have Cyndricka and Charlie in there!" Chelsea gasped out. She would have started screaming again, except that that would only have drawn more of them in here. And who knew how many were outside, waiting for them to try and escape. She hunched back into the corner of the doorway, trying to think, to come up with some way for them all to get out of this.

Carmen's eyes were just as panicked as hers, just as terrified at the prospect of her own end . . . but then she stopped. Her mouth closed into a thin line and her expression shuttered. When she turned to run back into the front room, it was with purpose, sandaled feet braced in the air and the hem of her skirt flapping around her.

Chelsea followed. What else could she do?

"You beasts from hell!" Carmen shouted, floating in the threshold of the kitchen, looking out at all of them. A choking sob came out of Chelsea's throat when the poltergeists turned towards her, teeth flashing and mouths grinning wider than was humanly possible. Carmen stood her ground, staring out at them without a trace of visible fear. With their attention taken elsewhere, a few of the poltergeists missed their catches, letting picture frames and spare shoes fall to the floor.

In the corner, Cyndricka popped her head up from her hunched pile. Tears streaked her face and Charlie mewed from the cradle of her arms. Chelsea could see her eyes dart to the door and windows, but there were poltergeists in front of all of them, impossible to slip past, even if their attention was on Carmen.

"You terrible monsters, you filthy animals with barely a shred of humanity left, you demons from the depths of the pit!" Carmen spat the words out at them, putting as much venom as she could behind every accented syllable. "You horrible, horrible things!"

If she had a plan in mind, Chelsea wished that she would get to it fast. But Chelsea would not run until she did, until they were all free. So she watched as Carmen set her shoulders, closed her eyes for a moment, and yelled.

"Are you ready ... for the Traveling Triple-C Incorporeal Circus!?!"

24.

Had Chelsea been asked what she had expected to happen next, she never would have guessed it in a million years. And by the looks on the poltergeists' long, twisted faces, neither would they. The tornado in the center of the room fell apart as they released their objects and watched Carmen.

Carmen continued, pasting a grin on her face and throwing her arms wide. "Yes, indeed, you see before you the Traveling Triple-C Incorporeal Circus, the most fantastic, the most incredible, the most astounding cross-national circus for ghosts, where we put on shows for wandering spirits, guaranteed to thrill you and chill you to the very core! We have acrobatic feats, we have performances, we have songs, we have everything a post-death audience could possibly want to not be left feeling quite so . . ." Here Carmen gave the crowd an honest-to-god wink. "*Grave.* You all seem like a very active and receptive audience, and we can only hope that you will let us perform for you tonight! What do you say?"

They didn't say anything. Chelsea wasn't really sure whether or not they had the capability. But the claws were staying down and the debris remained on the floor and they were all looking at them expectantly.

There had never been a performer more true or dedicated than Cyndricka Danvers, because she leapt to her feet and strode over to stand next to Carmen, putting on the biggest, most stretched smile possible on a human, and sinking into a low bow with sweeping arms and pointed toes. At the bottom of the bow, she glanced up at Chelsea and nodded. Carmen watched her out of the corner of her eye, silently pleading for some movement.

Chelsea's bow was not quite so artistic as Cyndricka's. In fact, she almost flipped over backwards, from how hard she was shaking. That seemed to entertain the poltergeists even more than professionalism would have, and the growls in their rough, screeching voices were definitely colored by laughter. But the ones standing between them and the doors were still there, and the poltergeists were watching their every move. It was clear.

They were about to put on a circus.

"Get your makeup," Carmen hissed to Cyndricka out of the corner of her mouth. Cyndricka nodded and sidestepped around several poltergeists to reach her bag. They turned and licked long tongues over sharp teeth, and it was a blessing she always kept her makeup in the same pocket, otherwise there was no way she would have been able to retrieve it without looking away from the poltergeists for an instant. She stepped carefully, trying not to tread on Charlie, who was tangled between her ankles and shaking like a small, furry leaf.

Carmen turned to Chelsea and put her hands on the sides of her arms, looking into her eyes. Chelsea flinched at the way even the tingles of Carmen's touch sent fire shooting through the tear in her arm, but she kept steady. She could feel the gazes of the poltergeists on her.

"I need you to come up with something you can do," Carmen whispered.

"I— I don't—what—"

"Cyndricka is going to mime, I am going to sing, and you need to think of something to entertain them. Just being part of the group is not going to work."

"How do you—"

Carmen squeezed her hands, fingers drifting through Chelsea's arms. Chelsea winced, but did not look away.

"I know ghosts and anger," Carmen whispered, voice low and strong. "I have seen people I knew become poltergeists, good ghosts that I cared about, and I have had to stop myself from turning more than a dozen times. Distraction works. All the movies, all the concerts, all the shows, do you think it was just boredom?"

She stared straight into Chelsea's eyes. "This is our only chance.

If we do not entertain them like this, they will entertain themselves by killing us. All of us. Broken glass for Cyndricka, and those claws for you and me. So come up with something you can do, now. Sing a song, do a dance, recite a poem, anything. Do not let them become bored, or all they will have is their anger and you at their mercy."

Chelsea was shaking as much as Charlie, feeling like a small animal trapped by predators she barely understood. Carmen's hand gently cupped her chin to ground her. Tingling skin against her face, cool in contrast to the burning in her arm. "We did not come all of this way to end here. We have a wedding to get to, remember?"

Chelsea nodded. She had a place to be and this was just a speed bump. She was going to get to San Francisco.

"What should I do? I don't know anything that they'll like, that they'll—"

"Help Cyndricka with her performance and I will think of something. We will all get out of here, I promise you." She squeezed into Chelsea's face one more time before letting go and directing her to where Cyndricka was waiting by the stairs, with the most hastily done makeup job of all time smeared across her face, and blood showing through the black and white striped shirt she had pulled over her t-shirt. But a grin was firmly held in place, and she beamed out at the poltergeists waiting for their entertainment.

You know the one about the Metrocard and the cop? she signed quickly, arms held close to her chest. Chelsea nodded. *Be the cop. Look really stern and scary when I look at you. Cross your arms a lot. Make it obvious when you are going to slap me.* Chelsea nodded again and stepped to the side, as the cop did not come in until later.

Cyndricka launched into a big, sweeping rendition of one of her most autobiographical performances, the tale of a homeless woman who comes across a discarded Metrocard, only to have to deal with the opposition of a Keystone-style police officer trying to keep her out of the subways.

Some of the story's intricacies may have been lost on the crowd. There was a great deal of subtlety and pathos to the plot (as

Cyndricka would claim and defend with all her might), but what really got the crowd of poltergeists chuckling were the pratfalls. So Cyndricka gave them the biggest leaps and falls and tumbles that she had ever done. It started by pretending to slam into the subway gate when the turnstile wouldn't let her pass, then morphed into being caught in the gut by strollers, rolling bags, fellow buskers, and anything else that could possibly give her reason to make a dramatic winded face and stumble around for air, legs shaking and barely holding her up. Chelsea wondered how much of the shaking was actually part of the act.

The poltergeists were actually a good audience, against all logic. They growled and shifted back and forth on their claws, but let out their raspy, shrill laughs whenever Cyndricka did anything designed to garner a laugh. Just as Carmen had said, they were all rapt, unwilling to miss a second of the performance, save to look at their fellows with demonic grins and gesture at the dancing human as if to say, "Are you seeing this?" None of them made any further move to attack. A few along the edges of the group picked up pieces of debris and tossed them lightly between their hands, a clear reminder to the performers of what could happen at any moment, but they all seemed spellbound.

Chelsea did her best to contribute to the show that was evolving before her eyes. The normal set-ups for the cop to arrive seemed to have passed by, but with the plot unimportant, she grabbed at any opportunity to come in and glare, to cross her arms over her chest in spite of the pain that ripped through her body when she did.

Keeping a stern expression through pain was difficult, but she hoped she managed. The fear was harder to master. She brought herself to look away from the twitching claws and clattering teeth on each of the poltergeists watching her. She knew that if she became caught up in the glowing eyes, she would find herself frozen with fear, unable to move or save her skin, as incorporeal as it was, but still very, very damageable in this context.

Cyndricka drew the set to a close with a giant tumble, starting a few steps up the stairs and essentially doing a backwards somersault down them to land in a big pile of limbs at the bottom. Her chest rose and fell hard from the effort, but she kept her big comedy face on, through the sweat-smeared makeup and dreadlocks falling in her eyes where they had come free of her pigtails.

Chelsea strode over to glare down at her and tap her foot against the ground, like she had seen Tyler and the other ghosts back in New York do a dozen times, and Cyndricka gave a guilty grin up at her before slumping down and holding up her hands to presumably be cuffed. Chelsea slapped the imaginary bands around her wrists and made a big, exaggerated motion of pulling her up, trying to keep her hands from sliding through Cyndricka's wrists. Cyndricka went with the motion, pulling herself to her feet while giving the impression of being dragged, and they slumped off to the side, off the makeshift clearing that was their stage, Charlie close on their heels.

Applause would have been too much to ask for, obviously. But they were all hoping and praying for some sort of positive sign from their audience, any indication in the world that they were not about to be smashed with kitchen appliances or ripped to shreds, respectively. Chelsea's hands balled into fists, fingers passing through her palms with how tightly she held them as Cyndricka walked off of the performing area.

But as if by some miracle, some incredible combination of luck and skill, the poltergeists started yelping, calling out, but in lighter, not quite as threatening, tones that almost, almost sounded like cheering.

Carmen seized on the opportunity and bounded out to the front of the stairs, arms spread wide. "Thank you, ladies and gentlemen, poltergeists and polter-guests, that was the amazing duo of Cyndricka and Chelsea, the most talented human performer and her lovely ghost assistant! Now here to perform for you, I am the Incredible Carmen, master of music, legend of lyrics, and aficionado of arpeggios."

That one seemed to go over the heads of their audience, leaving blank looks with burning eyes, but Carmen plowed forward. "Humans think that they are the sole creators of music, with the ability to use instruments, but those delicate bodies have their limits." That one did elicit a chuckle from the poltergeists, and Cyndricka shrunk back against the wall, still trying to catch her breath. "The best human singers are the ones with breath control,"

Carmen continued. "But once one becomes a ghost, that is no longer of any concern, and real art can begin."

She set her shoulders and planted her sandals on the carpet, held her hands clasped in the center of her body, right underneath her bust and her bullet holes, in a perfect mimic of an opera singer. She opened her mouth wide, paused just enough to build anticipation and have the poltergeists lean in, and began to sing.

Whatever Chelsea had been expecting, "Modern Major General" had not been it. For all that she looked exhausted, Cyndricka beamed from against the wall at the performance.

Carmen plowed through the fast and tricky lyrics, hitting each of them with precision and diction and, true to her word, not pausing at any point. The lack of need for air really did free her up to do whatever she wanted with her voice. The poltergeists cackled and leaned in, coming in close around her as she bounced from word to word, syllable to syllable without any pauses in between, no hesitation at all before she jumped onto the next note.

When she transitioned to another song, she did it so smoothly that it took Chelsea a full line before she realized she was listening to something else, and that it wasn't in English. An Italian piece by the sounds of it, something with trills and notes soaring up and down the scale, but still holding enough diction to hear consonants. The poltergeists were bouncing on their claws, completely caught up in the show. Chelsea glanced at Cyndricka and looked until she met her gaze.

Should we try to escape after this? Chelsea signed. Her motions were slow and clumsy from limited use, so used to speaking aloud in response to Cyndricka's signs, but silence was of the utmost importance just then.

If we do, I don't know if they'll follow us or not. Curtains seems to know what she's doing. I trust her.

Chelsea nodded. She trusted Carmen too, and it was probably best to follow Carmen's knowledge above her own twitchy instincts. She watched the second transition, into another opera patter song whose language Chelsea could not even guess, and hoped that this was going to work.

For the third song, Carmen changed it up, some variety to hold the attention of the beasts hanging off of her every note. She had chosen a duet song, it seemed, and was singing both parts, skipping back and forth between a high female line and a low male's line. While it still sounded like Carmen at every moment, she was able to keep up a strong baritone. Probably another one of those matters of letting go of the limits of the human body, whether lungs or the voice box. She sang faster and faster, and revealed in an instant that the song was in fact a trio, no, a quartet, as more and more lines were added. If Chelsea listened closely, she could catch flashes of Carmen providing her own harmony in the midst of the song, soaring from high note to low note, and still hitting the middles with just as much precision and impact. If Chelsea hadn't been so terrified for her very existence, she would have loved to relax and listen to the glorious things that Carmen could do with her voice, for hours on end.

Into another song, a big, rousing piece in Spanish that involved a lot of shouting from low in the chest and bellowing out vows of something or other.

Chelsea ended up so caught in admiration for Carmen's music that she stopped thinking of her own planning, distracted by the first thing that offered her some escape from her own fear. She jumped when Cyndricka put her hand through her ankle to gather her attention.

What are you going to do? she asked, and Chelsea could feel her face drop.

"Um, I don't—" she stammered out in a whisper. "I never did anything really performance—I did some gymnastics as a kid, but—" Did she have a firm enough grip on her hazy current relationship with gravity, and enough control of her injured arm, to summon back up even the most basic moves? But what else did she have in her arsenal? A female poltergeist on the edge of the crowd was inching closer, bright eyes burning in their direction. Chelsea tried to ignore her, and the remnants of the blue floral dress hanging off of her spikey frame.

You're funny. Can you tell jokes? Cyndricka's signs were fast and sloppy, the visual equivalent of stammering, while Chelsea was busy doing the oral version.

"I'm not—god, Cyndricka, I can't—"

Try. If you freeze, look at me. Cyndricka's face was just as set as Carmen's had been. It seemed that Chelsea was the only one unable to keep her cool. *We are all getting out of here.*

Carmen watched Chelsea out of the corner of her eye as she danced through a string of high notes. The poltergeist in the blue dress edged closer, and Chelsea set her shoulders and strode out in front of the crowd of restless, hungry spirits that were all too ready to tear her to shreds. To say it could be a tough crowd was the understatement of an afterlife.

Carmen brought her song to a bombastic conclusion and took a theatrical bow as the monsters clamored for more. She threw her arms wide and beamed at the assembled crowd. "Thank you, thank you! And now, we have more of the amazing talent of . . . Ms. Chelsea Shu!"

"So . . . welcome, gals and ghouls!" She tried to keep her voice from shaking as she flipped through any and all jokes she had heard in her lifetime. "Whu-why didn't the restaurant let the ghost in?" She tried to leave a comedic pause, but she could feel that she was rushing through even as she was doing it. "Because they didn't have a license to serve spirits."

Carmen laughed loud and hard, blatantly in order to cheer Chelsea on, but the poltergeists shifted in their places. They dug their claws into the wooden flooring beneath them like overgrown cats and tossed their heads back and forth. Chelsea swallowed thickly. "Um . . . how many poltergeists does it take to screw in a light bulb?" Another too short pause. "Two. One to keep replacing them and one to break them and scare all the humans in the room." It was not a masterpiece of comedy, but the poltergeists did seem to respond to that one more. The shout-out to themselves or the prospect of humans in fear? Or both?

"Umm . . . what, what did—" But her mind was a blank, completely empty of anything that could help her. All she could see were sharp teeth and twitching, ready limbs and claws ripping hunks out of the floor, and all she could feel was the pain in her arm and the closeness of all of them, getting closer and closer, and she could only imagine what it was going to feel like when they were all ripping into her at once and—

The only reason it caught her eye was because it was solid, the only corporeal thing moving in the room, separate from all of the transparent poltergeists. She focused on Cyndricka's waving hand, trying its hardest to get her attention. She was hunched over, bent in half on her knees in front of the poltergeists, but facing Chelsea and meeting her eyes. She gestured towards Chelsea, then to herself, then back to Chelsea, inviting her to follow her lead. Then her signs were clear and intelligible, even as she moved fast. Chelsea took a moment to understand what was being said to her, then repeated it to the crowd.

"Well, folks . . . please don't make any *snap* judgments about me." And on "snap" she grabbed her hair in her hand and yanked her head to the side, showing off the inhuman angle that her neck could bend and the way the bones jutted out without breaking through the skin.

She looked at the crowd through a sideways perspective, and . . . yes, they were having fun now. They jerked and cackled and looked at one another with large, toothy grins. Chelsea pushed her head back into its proper spot balanced on top of her neck and looked to Cyndricka for the next line.

Cyndricka had to move slow to fingerspell part of the pun, but Chelsea was still able to get it fairly quickly. "I know I am still in *train*-ing, but someday I'll be a real *smash* hit." And she slapped the bad side of her face to show exactly how much of a "smash" it would be, and the poltergeists burst out into howls of laughter. It was all so stupid, such juvenile jokes about herself, but she managed to eke out a smile at the sheer absurdity of it all.

She was in the swing of things enough to almost relax into Cyndricka's next joke, another pun that needed to be fingerspelled. She nodded along as she watched the signs, and only once flicked her eyes up to the poltergeists leaning over Cyndricka and towards her in anticipation.

"What did the train say to my face?" She actually did manage to give a decent comedic pause this time, raising her eyebrows at the crowd and waiting for them to quiet down before she continued. "I find you very a-*track*-tive." She turned the pummeled meat of her face towards them on the punchline, eliciting even more laughter and howls of sadistic glee.

"What did my face say back?" She had them hanging off of her every word, and it was difficult not to get caught up in it. She shrugged and smiled at the Cyndricka-provided punchline. "Squish." She dug the fingers of her left hand into the wound, showing just how squishy it actually was, and feeling the light tingle that she was supposed to feel, instead of the actual pain that the poltergeists could get out of her. That thought was almost enough to freeze her again, but she still had a job to do.

Cyndricka's face was twisted up in concentration and her hands were still, as if she herself was having trouble coming up with a new joke. Chelsea took the chance to spare a glance over at Carmen, who was looking at them with encouragement and hope. And it really was a miracle, that a joke popped into Chelsea's mind unbidden.

"You all enjoyed the musical stylings of the beautiful Carmen Gutierrez?" she asked the crowd, and received positive growls in response. "Well, she is just wonderful, has been for our entire trip. On a road trip like this, it's nice to have someone riding *shotgun*."

The laugh this got from Carmen actually did sound sincere, not to mention surprised. When Chelsea looked back at Cyndricka, she was beaming and giving her a thumbs up.

"Give me a hand folks!" She threw both of her arms wide, gritting her teeth against the shocks this sent through her. She took a moment to gather herself, keeping the wide grin plastered on her face, and grabbed her right arm in her left. And in one big jerk, she bent it backwards, showing the initial break, the twisted flesh underneath the ripped coat, and the exposed bone from the poltergeist's attack. She choked back a scream and just managed to get out the punchline. "Since I can't use this one!"

They went wild, bouncing in their places, ripping at the walls and tossing debris into the air. Cyndricka shielded her head from anything falling on her, but grinned at Chelsea from beneath her arms. Despite her shaking and quivering like a leaf from the pain, Chelsea managed to smile at her as well.

Carmen, bless her, seemed to realize that Chelsea was at the end of what she could take, and bounded back onto the makeshift stage. "Give it up for the comedy of the amazing Chelsea!" If the growling and inhuman shrieking could be interpreted as applause, she would take it. She shifted her arm back into the way it usually hung by her side and limped off to the edge of the clearing, while Carmen launched into another aria. Cyndricka crawled over to sit next to her.

You did good, she signed. Chelsea nodded, not able to put words together just then. For all that she no longer had adrenaline or exhaustion to deal with, there was still a great deal to be said for taking a moment to oneself.

25.

The performance went on for the majority of the night, with the three swapping out whenever the one needed to regroup, come up with new material, or in Cyndricka's case, drink water, eat, and rest against a wall, looking like she would kill for a chance to sleep.

Carmen was able to keep up the performances for the longest, with forty years of musical knowledge under her belt to help her out. She eventually moved away from opera and into pop songs, making long, complex medleys of anything up-tempo and lively for the dead crowd. The poltergeists cheered and laughed and growled, and seemed to become calmer over the course of the long night, as if the performance really was soothing them.

Chelsea watched them during one of Carmen's songs, a retro number from the eighties that she thought she remembered her mom singing, and she could pick out poltergeists that seemed to be particularly affected. Their long, twisted faces seemed to smooth slightly, sharp teeth dulling at the tips and eyes dimming just the slightest bit in the dark house. It wasn't a complete transformation, by any stretch of the imagination, and they were still as hunched over and horrible looking as all the others. But when they shook their heads and turned this way and that, there was a trace more humanity to be seen in the remnants of their spirits.

Morning light began to bleed through the remaining traces of curtains hanging from the dusty windows, and Chelsea wondered, not for the first time, what their end game was. Cyndricka was definitely fading, having dashed her way through the most energetic possible renditions of her best pieces, adding in falls and tumbles wherever she could logically fit them, and several places where they didn't belong. The blood on her shirt was dried and brown now, and Chelsea could see bruises blossoming on her arms and shoulders, deep purple on her skin. Charlie was curled in a quivering ball in her lap. Cyndricka looked up at Chelsea with tired eyes sporting bags underneath them and faintly signed.

Okay, I trust Curtains, but this just keeps going on. I don't know how much more I have.

Chelsea nodded and signed back. *Keep brainstorming jokes for me, but I hope we can try to slip out soon. I don't know what her plan is.*

Carmen had to see the effect the show was having on her partners, even if she continued to go strong. Chelsea caught her glancing their way in the middle of a long note, and Chelsea tilted her head enough to make the question clear. Carmen gave the slightest of nods and finished off her song on a long-held high note that was mimicked by several of the poltergeists surrounding them.

"Alright, that was a lovely performance, if I do say so myself!" Carmen exclaimed, clasping her hands together. "But I believe that I heard some voices in the audience as well! Is there anyone among you that would care to join me in the next piece?"

The poltergeists broke out in screams that Chelsea was choosing to interpret as enthusiasm, not outrage at the idea. Carmen beamed out at the writhing mass of ghosts. "Yes, how about one that everyone will know? Something with lots of appeal for all of you terrifying monsters!" She held her chin in her hand and cocked out her hip, the picture of exaggerated concentration. She held up a hand as if to go "ah ha!" and began to sing, slower than before, but still clear and strong.

Singing about werewolves with Chinese menus.

Chelsea's jaw dropped. Out of all of the absurd things she had seen in the course of that night, seeing Carmen leading a chorus of demonic ghosts through "Werewolves of London" still had to top the list. The poltergeists didn't seem to have a firm grasp on the verses, growing restless as she sung the set-up, but she only had to launch into one round of the "aaaaoooooooooo!"s to get the rest of them hooked. The panes in the windows quivered at the cry of two dozen ghosts howling. Chelsea could hear the few remaining glasses in the kitchen shatter, and Cyndricka was shaking her head and giggling to herself. Though that might have been more from the sleep deprivation than anything else.

Carmen sped her way through the verses, putting extra emphasis only on the tales of people being ripped to shreds by wolves, so that she could rejoin the poltergeists in the choruses. They were getting more and more involved in it, howling and shrieking towards the ceiling. Carmen jerked her head once at Chelsea and Cyndricka, and they both started to creep along the walls of the living room, edging around the poltergeists getting caught up in their song. Cyndricka clutched Charlie to her chest and grabbed her bag in passing, right from under the foot of a poltergeist with shredded jeans around its long, pointed legs.

Chelsea watched Carmen begin to slip to the side as well, while Cyndricka opened the front door as quietly as possible. Carmen continued singing, goading the poltergeists to new, louder heights with her voice, inviting them to continue with the howling song, yelling along with them as the verses were entirely forgotten. She casually strolled along the wall, her voice continuing as Cyndricka scampered out the front door, through the front lawn, and to the road just as the light of morning was hitting it. The poltergeists were more focused on one another than on Carmen now, laughing and trying to sing over the top of their neighbors. They were so involved in their games that they didn't notice when Carmen's voice cut out, the two normal ghosts that had been in their company slipped through the walls of the house, and the entire traveling Triple-C Incorporeal Circus sprinted down the road and as far away from the town of Chesterton as their feet could take them, not stopping until it was almost noon.

For all they knew, the poltergeists continued to sing "Werewolves of London" for all eternity, and the citizens of Chesterton would have to create new legends to explain it.

26.

The thrill of surviving certain doom carried them for several days down the road. Often, they would find themselves recalling some aspect of the performance, a particularly heroic tumble of Cyndricka's, the highest high note any of them had ever heard from Carmen, or a punchline from Chelsea that had made the entire congregation burst out laughing, poltergeists and fellow travelers alike.

Or they would bring up the failures that had almost gotten them killed: the times that Cyndricka had tripped and rolled through a poltergeist, when Carmen had forgotten the lyrics to a song in the middle and had to make random vowel noises until she got back on track, and of course, the first few minutes of Chelsea's standup routine all together. They would laugh so hard that tears would run down Cyndricka's face and Chelsea and Carmen would end up floating upside down, doubled over in laughter, with Charlie meowing along to join in the merriment.

Other times, usually in the evenings, they would go quiet, reflecting on how far they had come, and how close they had been to having it all end at once. Chelsea had been afraid for the others before Chesterton: she had feared for Cyndricka's well-being in the face of Henry's badgering, had worried for Charlie's life in the storm drain and with the beer can, had worried and still did worry about Jamie's fate alone with the wailers. And she had worried more than was really called for about Heather and everyone back in New York.

But Chelsea had never been worried for herself. As far as she saw it, the worst thing that could have happened to her already had, and everything else had to pale in comparison to death. With every step down the road, she was on her way to completing a goal, so she had no real need to worry about anything else. Having the potential for her own destruction shoved in her face so abruptly made her think about what could have happened, if she had come this far only to be destroyed before she reached the wedding. It became too much to handle at moments like that, and she went back to chattering with the others, bringing up their victories rather than dwelling on their near-losses.

Though one immediate reality that they did have to deal with was the impact the trip was having on Cyndricka and Charlie, the two members of their group still tasked with the upkeep of living bodies. Charlie was recovered from her injuries, it seemed, but she would yowl if she twisted the wrong way, an apparent ache still lingering in her ribs. And the months of traveling were taking their toll on Cyndricka. Even with a bag that had lightened as she used supplies, the weight seemed to drag on her more every day.

And that was before one considered the heat. With the blistering sun beating down on the blacktop, it became impossible to travel during the day. Every morning as sunrise approached, Cyndricka would find a tree, a building, a billboard, anything, and curl up in its shadow with her coat and sleeping bag forming make-shift awnings however she could prop them up. She tried to take off her boots away from the gaze of the ghosts, but Chelsea had caught sight of the cracked calluses and blisters, bleeding through the thick socks that she layered on at the start of every walk. She laid out her socks and shirts in the sun to let the sweat dry and tried to get some rest in the miserable lean-tos, tossing and turning into the dust, until the sun set and she had to pack up and start walking.

She stretched every day, but her back was bending visibly and her shoulders rolling from the backpack's constant, unrelenting pressure. Chelsea and Carmen wanted more than anything to be able to take some of the load, but it was a hope that could never be. So even after the thrill of surviving Chesterton passed, they both did their best to keep the mood light and the conversation quick.

They made their way out of Colorado in this manner, and crossed through the top of Utah on their way to Nevada. They could walk for hours in the evenings without seeing a single car, just miles of empty highway stretching out in both directions and endless stars above. If Cyndricka had any feelings about being this close to seeing her family in Reno, she didn't share them, but as the days wore on, Chelsea could see her expression becoming more shuttered and closed off, the echo of family memories written all over her face.

So one night Chelsea decided to take the plunge.

"So, Cyndricka, what's your family like? I'm looking forward to getting to see them."

Carmen gave her a carefully blank look out of the corner of her eyes, but didn't say anything. Cyndricka readjusted the bag on her shoulders as they kept walking down US-40, Charlie jumping at grasshoppers in the weeds and scampering to keep up.

I grew up with my grandparents, Cyndricka signed after a while. *I lived with my parents until I was six, but after my brother was born, they got rid of me.*

"I . . . got rid of? Like—"

It was okay for me to be crazy when I was the only child in the house. Talking to people no one else could see, knowing things I couldn't possibly know, laughing in empty rooms by myself. The ghosts were my friends. I didn't know any better. She practically punched the signs into the air. *When there was another child to learn my bad habits, I had to go.*

Carmen rested a hand lightly on Cyndricka's shoulder, though she might not have noticed. Or she was too caught up in her tale to care. "Oh, mija—" Carmen murmured, the words eaten by the whizzing of a car passing by. Cyndricka continued.

My grandparents took me in. I never lived with my parents again. Her signs slowed as she began to remember, nostalgia written all over her face. *They . . . they believed me. For the first time in my life, there were people who believed me. They were skeptical. But they took me at my word when I said I saw ghosts.* She paused in her telling, watching the road under her feet. *But it took a long time for me to tell them. Even by then, I was learning to keep it secret.*

"And they . . . they helped you?" Chelsea asked, words feeling cautious on her lips. If this story had such an upbeat ending, why did Cyndricka still sound so unhappy and depressed? Not that Chelsea thought that childhood trauma could just be brushed off. She was so out of her depth in matters like these.

Yes, they did, she signed, and her expression lightened some. *Part of it was just teaching me how to act normal, how to hide it. I never learned that well*, she admitted with a little sideways smirk. *I mostly just stopped talking. Not all the way, that came later, but quiet enough. But I knew that they loved me. That was enough.*

If the look on her face was anything to go by, it hadn't been, but Chelsea was not about to press on that particular tender spot.

My grandfather loved old movies. He and I would watch C-H-A-P-L-I-N and all the classics, silent movies with big, wonderful clowns. I wished that I could do that. Communicate everything I needed to without words, no words to get me in trouble with the living who heard me talking to the dead. Of course, not using words makes you even stranger to everyone else. But it works for me. It has for many years now.

". . . Could you speak?" Carmen asked. "If you tried?"

Cyndricka shook her head firmly, without any hesitation or self-doubt. *My brain knows what speaking leads to. It doesn't like to make words anymore, and I can't blame it. I get along fine.* She flashed Carmen and Chelsea a grin. *I've made it this far with you two. So it works.*

"I suppose that is true," Carmen conceded, and Chelsea nodded.

Cyndricka was apparently done having that conversation. She pulled three rubber balls out of her pocket, ones that she had found left behind in a playground in Myton. If there was an aspect of clowning that she was genuinely bad at, it was juggling. Trying to toss the balls from hand to hand and stopping long enough to retrieve them every time they dropped occupied both her hands and her attention enough to cut off any further conversation. Charlie scrambled after each of the balls that fell, providing another light-hearted distraction from anything else going on.

They entered the city of Orem, on the eastern shore of Utah Lake, about midday. It was the first actual metropolitan area they had seen for a while and Cyndricka started charting out a good place to put on a small show for the afternoon.

"Are you really ready to put on a show again so soon after last time?" Chelsea had to ask. The tear in her arm ached as they scoped out parks for the day.

Miming wasn't what got us into trouble last time, it was what saved us. I feel ready to put on a dozen shows, she signed with a big smile. Her smile faltered when she glanced at Chelsea's arm. *Unless it would make you feel uncomfortable, Coat.*

". . . I mean, don't expect me to join in," Chelsea laughed it off. "I'm a performer on a strictly life-or-death-or-undeath basis. And besides, you could use the money. You and Carmen are free to do your own thing."

As if on cue, Carmen returned from scouting out spots and Cyndricka started getting set up on the sidewalk at the edge of a city park, trying to capture foot traffic without stepping on any businesses' toes. She pulled out a hand mirror to do her makeup on a bench, and it was just like being back in Central Park.

Even down to having a performing partner, it turned out. Carmen watched Cyndricka tracing black makeup over her lips and asked "What role would you like me to perform?" Cyndricka almost dropped her palette.

You want to be in the show?

"I do have to say that it was rather enjoyable to perform. And I feel that I better understand the bravery needed to be on a stage alone. I would be happy to accompany you, if you will have me."

". . . Cyndricka, your eye makeup's going to smear," Chelsea pointed out when the tears started to well. Cyndricka held both her hands to her chest and gave them both a watery smile.

Thank you . . . Okay, Curtains, do you want to be an enemy, a love interest, or an animal?

Chelsea wandered through the park while the two sketched out a loose outline for their first performance. It was a nice day, not too hot and yesterday's mild dust storm had calmed down. Families wandered down the street, along with young women in sundresses, and people on their lunch breaks eating out on benches. Charlie was curled up on top of the backpack for a nap in the afternoon sun. Cyndricka was already catching attention with her makeup and signing to what others saw as empty air. At least a few people watched with confusion, unsure if she was already putting on a show or not.

But Chelsea could tell the moment that Cyndricka snapped into performing mode. Her movements had a bounce and pop to them as she jumped up from the bench and carefully positioned a hat on the pavement to collect tips. Chelsea stood a few yards away as the start of their audience and couldn't help grinning when Carmen moved just as bouncily.

Finding the Perfect Flower was a quick little piece that Chelsea had seen Cyndricka perform with Tyler plenty of times, in which Cyndricka was trying to woo a picky paramour who kept turning their nose up at offered gifts. Cyndricka threw herself onto bended knee over and over in front of Carmen, who turned away in a huff and stamped her sandals in frustration. Cyndricka would sway back at the power of the rejection and slump away to find the next gift, and after a few rounds of rejections, a handful of people had gathered to watch, standing near Chelsea's post. It felt like a good sign when she had to move in order to get a better view.

A few people stuck their heads out of shops across the street in order to watch, gathered at doorways or windows. A middle-aged Filipino woman peered out the door of a convenience store and looked over wire-framed glasses with a curious expression. She glanced inside to see if any customers needed her, then leaned against the doorframe to watch. Chelsea hoped that this was a bright point in a dull shift for the woman, the sort of thing that would give her a smile to hold on to for the rest of the day.

At the front of the gathering, Cyndricka's hat was collecting scatterings of pocket change and a few dollar bills. The story came to a charming conclusion, Cyndricka finding the perfect flower (a dandelion pulled out of a crack in the pavement) and presenting it to Carmen. Carmen minced and cooed over it, and offered her cheek when Cyndricka leaned in for a peck. She kissed Cyndricka's cheek in return, and though the audience couldn't see it, the way Cyndricka's face lit up in a huge grin told the story. Some people chuckled and dug out extra dollars when she came around with a smile and the hat. The woman from the convenience store was all the way out on the sidewalk now, watching openly.

Carmen stepped forward to the center of their performing area while Cyndricka grabbed a sip of water and dumped her money into her backpack. "Ladies and gentleman, we are the Traveling Triple-C Incorporeal Circus, and that was the amazing Cyndricka! May we have a round of applause, please!" None of the living people noticed, but Chelsea gave a cheer from the back. "Thank you! Next up, we have . . . well, more of the same, as you all would not appreciate my singing. And here we go!" Cyndricka jumped back into center "stage" and gave a little bow at Carmen's introduction. *The Nervous Babysitter* was another solid piece, and Chelsea cackled when Carmen took on her bratty child role.

This one didn't go over quite as well as the first, or maybe people just had places to be. The size of the audience fluctuated over the course of the act, groups wandering on to continue their days while others paused to watch. The only person paying rapt attention was the woman outside the convenience store. Something about her caught Chelsea's eye; maybe just the way that she didn't look away through any of the routine.

Carmen was down on her knees with her arms crossed over her chest in a pout. It almost covered the bullet holes. Cyndricka shook her finger at her in reprimand for breaking a vase and when Carmen stuck her tongue out at her, she reeled back in shock and offense. It was cute. After all they had seen recently, Chelsea could appreciate cute.

The jingle of keys caught Chelsea's attention; the woman was rummaging in her purse as she left the convenience store and made her way across the small street, still in her polyester uniform shirt. Chelsea drifted towards her, wary, but she didn't look angry. Her attention was direct, taking in every moment of Cyndricka's show. She was short, had to weave around people to get a good view, but she made her way right to the front. Chelsea wandered her way directly through other people to keep this woman in her sight.

Cyndricka was busy tripping over invisible toys that the child had left around their playroom, but Chelsea managed to catch Carmen's eye when she looked out to the audience. Chelsea jerked her head in the strange woman's direction with a questioning look and Carmen immediately dropped the foolish child character and stood up straight. Chelsea walked closer to the front until she was right beside the woman, close enough to read the name tag "Imelda" on her chest. Carmen leaned over to speak softly into Cyndricka's ear, and while she didn't break her character, her eyes flickered up to Carmen and she snuck a quick nod in between actions.

Imelda sucked in a sharp breath and her eyes went wide behind her glasses. She looked at the people around her, the other happy members of the shifting crowd, and looked through Chelsea.

No. No, that wasn't correct.

This woman looked at Chelsea. Direct eye contact, gaze meeting gaze, one person looking at another person. Nothing squinting or vague about it like with Madam Valentina. She was looking at Chelsea and actually seeing her. It couldn't be true.

Chelsea leaned close. She didn't want to speak aloud in case she was wrong, couldn't stand to get Cyndricka's hopes up. She got close and whispered, "Can you see me?"

"Yes," Imelda murmured under her breath, glancing carefully at the living people around her. She tilted her head ever so slightly towards Cyndricka's show. "She sees you too?"

27.

Cyndricka sat in the convenience store's break room with a paper cup of coffee while Imelda finished her shift. She carefully counted up the money earned from the shows, though one cost was off her mind for the night: she would be eating dinner at Imelda's house. They had hashed out the arrangement quickly as soon as Cyndricka was done with her show. Imelda spoke in rapid Tagalog, too shocked and excited for English. Carmen translated while Chelsea relayed Cyndricka's American Sign Language responses.

Charlie lapped from a plastic bowl of water on the floor, the open tin of cat food already licked clean. Cyndricka shifted back and forth in her seat, reading the various signs on the walls: mostly official notices or reminders about restocking dates. She drummed her fingers on the table, the side of her cup, anything that she could drum them on.

She was really talking to you? she asked Carmen for what had to be the tenth time. *She wasn't just saying words? I know this sounds bad coming from me, but she's not just crazy?*

"If we were not having an actual conversation, it would have to be the greatest coincidence in history that our answers aligned so precisely," Carmen reassured her. "She is no more mentally ill than you are."

That is really not very reassuring, Cyndricka pointed out.

"Yes, my apologies, I realized that as I was saying it. I mean, neither of you are mentally ill."

Thanks. And she did say her son could also see them? You're sure that's what she said?

"Yes, Cyndricka, that is what she said. You can ask them all the details over dinner."

"And hey, when was the last time you had a hot meal?" Chelsea added, trying to sweeten the pot. "That one restaurant in Wyoming with all the clowns?"

If you are just going to put on makeup, do not call yourself a clown! Cyndricka signed emphatically. It had been an easy topic to distract her with ever since they had stopped there on a day when it was too hot to walk and no other restaurant with air conditioning had been as cheap. *Clowning and mime are art forms! You do not just scribble on a piece of paper and call yourself an author, do you?*

"Yeah, I know, and this place is going to be way better than that." Chelsea patted Cyndricka's shoulder. "So you've never met another human who could speak to us?"

Never. She paused and took another sip of her coffee before slowly signing, *I used to hope, but I never met anyone else.*

"It is a very large world," Carmen said gently. "It would be very unlikely for there to be absolutely no one else. It is incredible luck that you and she have found one another."

Another employee walked through the back room and raised her eyebrow at Cyndricka sitting at the table. Cyndricka glued her eyes to her coffee and waited until the woman had grabbed a lunch bag out of the fridge to answer. *I almost don't believe it,* she signed. *I cannot let myself believe it. I always wished for someone else. And her son too? To stumble onto it just seems too easy.*

"Not everything has to be hard, you know," Chelsea said.

Cyndricka gave her a petulant look. *Maybe not for you.*

". . . Fair enough."

Cyndricka went back to her coffee. Chelsea sat cross-legged on the floor and skittered her fingers across the tiles for Charlie to chase, letting the young cat get some exercise before they moved into who even knew what kind of house.

After about half an hour of waiting, a young man in a cashier's uniform swung the door of the break room wide, looking inside and beaming. His dark hair flopped over his forehead and his plastic-framed glasses took up most of his face. He looked between Chelsea, Carmen, and Cyndricka with a big smile.

"You're the one who can see them? I ran over as soon as my mom called," he asked Cyndricka in lightly accented English. "It's you?"

Cyndricka nodded and gave a small wave. Carmen extended her hand for a proper hello.

"Yes, this is Cyndricka Danvers, my name is Carmen Gutierrez, and our other ghostly friend here is Chelsea Shu. It is nice to meet you."

He seemed taken aback by the offering of a hand, but he mimed grabbing it anyway, going through the motion with their skin about an inch or so apart. Chelsea stood up and his eyes flicked to Chelsea's injured face and smashed arm, but he painted on a smile. Cyndricka covered her mouth with her sleeve to hide a small grin.

"I'm Jose Vitug, nice to meet you." He rested his hand on the back of the chair across from Cyndricka. "Do you mind if I sit here?"

It's your table, Cyndricka signed before catching her mistake and scrambling for her notebook again.

"She says it's your table, you can do what you want," Chelsea translated this time, and Cyndricka shot her a quick smile while she got her notebook out and ready. Jose looked confused, but nodded and pulled out the seat.

"My mom's only the shift manager, not the owner or anything. And I only work on weekends or after classes." Chelsea caught herself looking closely at his round face, and he laughed and pushed his bangs back. "Community college, not high school."

"Sorry."

"I know I've got a baby face," he said and shook his head. He propped his forearms on the table and looked at Cyndricka as though she was the most interesting thing he had ever seen. "So, if you don't mind me asking . . . you can't talk? Is that because of the ghost thing, do you know? I mean, I've never met anyone else aside from my mom, and I'm just wondering if I'll end up losing my voice too. Like if you get to speak to double the amount of people, but for half the time."

Caught off guard by the suggestion, Cyndricka mulled it over before she began writing. Chelsea and Carmen waited patiently, not wanting to step on her toes during her second-ever meeting with a fellow ghost-speaker.

No, I do not speak for other reasons, the notebook read when she slid it across the table to Jose. *I can hear, though, and I can write (obviously). I use sign language with ghosts who know it, or write with those who don't, and they speak back to me.*

"Wow . . . just wow." Jose nodded and looked up at the other two. "So you guys learned sign language? And Tagalog? Mom said you spoke it to her."

"We have both learned sign language through our time with Cyndricka," Carmen explained. "I just have spent decades since my death learning languages for entertainment. Tagalog is one of my newer additions, so I apologize for any errors I may make."

"I think when you're dead, no one's gonna call you out on bad grammar," Jose said with a laugh. He leaned back in his chair and laced his hands behind his neck, letting out a low whistle. "Dad is gonna go nuts, hearing about this. I mean, he'll be happy to have you over, but he's probably going to ask a million questions, so get ready."

Cyndricka slowly pulled her notebook back to herself and wrote out a new question. Her brow was furrowed and she moved her pen slowly.

Your father can hear ghosts as well? Or he is one?

"No, no, my dad's alive and well, and he can't hear them at all. He's not even one of those people who gets a funny feeling when they walk through him, like—"

"Receptive?" Chelsea supplied. "That's what I've always heard them called." Or at least, since she'd died. She'd never thought about it before then.

"He's none of that stuff. But my mom and I keep him clued into what's going on with the ghosts in the area. Oh man, I hope Lorelai comes by the store while you're here, she's a really fun spirit. Though try not to look at her stomach if she arrives. She's still sensitive about the tire treads."

He believes you? Your father believes you and your mother? Cyndricka's words were becoming sloppy on the page.

Jose nodded casually. "I mean, apparently my mom had to

explain it to him when they were first together, and she did prove it to him, like with little tests. He would write something on a piece of paper in another room, a ghost would read it and tell her, and she would know what it was without ever having seen it. By the time I was around, he was already used to it. He gets interested in keeping up with what's going on. In the dead community, he calls it, like it's a neighborhood next to ours or something." Jose chuckled. "I think you'll like him, when we go back to our house. I—oh, god, I'm sorry? Did I say something wrong? Are you okay, ma'am?"

Cyndricka nodded quickly and scrubbed at the tears running down her cheeks. She grabbed for her notebook and scribbled a few words before thrusting it back at him and busying herself with her coffee, looking pointedly away. Jose picked it up.

I am glad to hear about your dad. I just had a harder time of it, is all.

Jose nodded slowly, flicking his eyes between Cyndricka and the paper. "I guess I . . . I guess I did have it really lucky," he said after a long moment. He looked up at Carmen and Chelsea. Chelsea could see his eyes lingering over her smashed face and the bullet holes in Carmen's chest. "Guess I don't need to tell you guys that, but . . ." He shrugged, at a loss. "I always knew. And had someone else who knew, so—"

He reached out his hand flat on the table, reaching out to her without touching. "But you've met someone else now. So that should help, right?"

Cyndricka's face was still wet when she smiled at the young man, but her eyes were light as she watched him over the edge of her coffee cup. She nodded a couple of times, and Jose's face lit up again.

Chelsea had to wonder if there was something about being able to see the dead that made humans little balls of sunshine; one was a coincidence, but three was a trend. Perhaps it was just having the knowledge from an early age that it could all be over in an instant. Maybe that made them a little brighter, as a way to cope. Or as a way to deny. It was unlikely that she would ever meet another human with this ability, so she would have to settle for speculating with this very, very small sample pool.

28.

Dinner at the Vitug household was a bigger ordeal than any of the traveling group had anticipated. Jose assured them that it wasn't normal for this many ghosts to show up for a meal that they couldn't eat, but Imelda had talked to a ghostly friend of hers during the break, who had spread the news and drawn in more ghosts, who wanted to witness three ghost-speakers in one place. They hovered around the table next to Carmen and Chelsea, staring at Cyndricka and peppering her with more questions than she could write answers to, at least not while trying to eat a dish of fried rice at the same time.

And as interesting as the questions from the ghosts were, Cyndricka was focusing on talking to Imelda, seated across from her, and Jose by her side. Mr. Vitug, a solidly-built man with a soft, low voice, asked his own questions as well, but they tended more towards the conversational, rather than the deeper questions about the realities of her powers that Imelda and Jose sent her way.

"Have you always heard them? Even as a baby?" Imelda asked. Cyndricka nodded. "My mother told me that I always seemed to be caught up in things that were not there," Imelda continued, with a nostalgic smile. "And when Jose was a baby, I could tell right away that he could see them. Spirits that had been parents in life would gather around his crib to coo at him, and his eyes would focus on them."

"More than they did normally," Jose laughed. "Ooh, that reminds me, I want to check something." He pulled his glasses off his face and squinted at Cyndricka. Then he pumped his arms and gave a big whoop. His father glared at him, and Jose lowered his arm and put his glasses back on. "Sorry, Dad. Just excited." He beamed at Cyndricka. "You're in focus too, I knew it. I can see ghosts clearly no matter if my glasses are on or not. Everything and everyone else is blurry when I take them off, except for Mom, or if I'm looking at myself. And you're clear too."

Imelda peeked over the edge of her own glasses at Cyndricka and smiled at the results. "It is like we are half-ghost ourselves. In touch with the spirits."

"Sounds better than 'one foot in the grave'," Chelsea whispered to Carmen. Carmen nodded slightly. It felt very strange, being pushed to the side in favor of a conversation with another human. Usually Cyndricka made it very clear that any interactions with humans were done grudgingly, and would look up at the two of them for connection and confirmation that they had not left, often upsetting her conversation partners. But Cyndricka was enraptured by the Vitug family, answering their questions and asking plenty of her own. She was even ignoring the food on her plate in favor of conversation, unheard of for someone who saw so little of it on a day to day basis.

"I'm going to go play with Charlie," Chelsea said to Carmen, floating away from the table and accidentally backing through a handful of other dead people. "I'll be in the living room if anyone needs me." Carmen nodded and went back to being a spectator in the conversation between the living, along with the rest of the ghosts.

The Vitugs had four cats of their own, probably for the same reasons that Cyndricka had enjoyed having a cat. Charlie was huddled back in a corner behind a chair to avoid a calico that looked about her age and wanted a playmate, while the three older cats sat to the side and pretended to have more dignity. She perched on the edge of the threadbare floral couch to bend over and twiddle her fingers for the young cat to chase, and a big tortoiseshell lump of a cat immediately came over and sat in the center of her, looking very proud of himself and as though he wasn't going to move for a very long time. Chelsea sighed and moved one seat over.

They still had plenty of road ahead of them on the trip. The entire span of Nevada was not going to cross itself. But not for the first time, Chelsea thought about what Cyndricka was doing on this trip.

If Cyndricka stopped and stayed here, it wouldn't be too difficult to get to Reno, if she saved up enough money for a bus ticket. Perhaps Imelda could try to get her a job in the convenience store, or she could live with them while she got on her feet. Or once she got to Reno and saw her family, she could stay with them and visit Imelda and Jose whenever she wanted to. For all that she had built herself up there, the only thing waiting back in New York was a cold park bench and some ghosts to put on a mime show with. As much as Cyndricka liked Tyler and the others, was that worth a trek back across the entire country, in the growing winter?

Jose walked into the living room as the two young cats were jumping back and forth through Chelsea's arm. He carried two bowls of dry cat food balanced on one arm, and a large dish of water on the other.

"I put in enough for your cat," he said with a smile. "What was her name again?"

"Charlie."

"So it's Cyndricka, Chelsea, Carmen, and Charlie?" He quirked an eyebrow up at her. Chelsea snorted.

"The C thing was originally a coincidence, then became a selling point. The cat's named after Charlie Chaplin."

Jose nodded as he set down the bowls to be beset by the hungry animals, though he still looked confused. To be fair, it would have taken some time to explain the whole history of the little makeshift circus. "So you guys are going to San Francisco, right?" Chelsea nodded. "If you don't mind me asking, what's in San Fran that's so important?"

"I don't mind. My little brother is getting married. I wanted to go to the ceremony, and Carmen and Cyndricka decided to come along too."

". . . They walked all the way from New York just to go to a wedding with you?"

"I mean, we're stopping in Reno to see some of Cyndricka's family first. It's not all about me. Just . . . you know, most of it, I guess."

"You have some really good friends—"

He trailed off and sat down on the couch next to her. The big tortoiseshell finished eating and jumped into his lap. Jose petted the cat absently as he talked. "I'm curious. I don't think I've ever met a ghost who decided to travel as much as you have. Most pick one spot to haunt and stay there. Your brother's wedding is this important?"

Chelsea nodded slowly. "Yes. We were always a close family. He's only a year younger than me, and our sister is two years older, so we all as sort of grew up in one big lump. Hit most of our milestones in a close range of time. It felt like everything big we did in our lives happened around the same times, making them almost communal—" She debated her next words, then plowed on anyway. "When Osric and Tamika—"

"Osric? Really?"

"My dad was an English professor, shush. When Osric and Tamika announced their engagement—" She paused to lean down and pet her fingers over Charlie's back. "Well, my fiancée had actually just proposed to me. We had wanted to keep it to ourselves for a bit, have our own time, but Osric beat me to the punch."

Jose stared at her, but she shook her head and kept going. "I wasn't mad at him or jealous or anything. And Heather and I had been dragging our feet over it anyway, so we decided to hold off and not steal the spotlight. My brother was doing a quick engagement anyway, we wouldn't have had to put it off long . . . and then we had to put it off forever." She shrugged her good arm. The bad one was feeling better than it had right after the poltergeist attack, but still twinged every now and then. "So I guess I want to go to at least one Shu family wedding. Even if it isn't my own."

Jose exhaled long and low and rubbed a hand over his mouth. "And your friends decided to help you get there?"

"No, they don't know that I was engaged. Carmen would say I was obsessing. Turning into a—do you know what wailers are?" Jose inhaled a sharp breath and nodded. "Yeah, you know. She's always been worried that I would turn into one. And I guess she's right to be worried. But I still feel like I need this . . . I need to be there."

"I'm so sorry," said Jose. He looked the most morose Chelsea had seen him yet. She shook her head.

"It's not your fault. It's not anyone's fault. My death was an accident and those happen. There's nothing I can do about it now. And my loved ones can hopefully move on." She smiled just a bit. "And my fiancée was actually a friend of my brother's before she ever met me, so she's gonna be there. With her new girlfriend. I've been in the ground almost three years now, but I have to admit, that's gonna sting."

Jose nodded calmly for a moment. Then snorted. "Oh my god, that is just bad on top of worse on top of awful, Jesus!"

Chelsea had to laugh along. "I know, right? I'm dead, give me a freaking break already!" She rubbed her hands over her face and leaned back against the couch. "I should tell Carmen and Cyndricka. It's been way too long without telling them."

"Several months and a dozen states? Yeah, I'd say."

"Shut up, meat bag."

"Make me, Casper."

29.

Cyndricka stretched out under a pile of mismatched blankets on the Vitug's living room couch that night, head resting on a throw pillow. The couch didn't fold out and was a bit too short for her, so her knees were slightly bent as she readied herself for sleep. But after god only knew how long since she had slept in a warm house with cushions and blankets, Cyndricka nestled into the lumpy quilts like they were Egyptian cotton.

The rest of the ghosts had left after dinner, as per an arrangement Imelda had made with them years ago. The ghosts were welcome during the days, but were guests and had to act like it, respecting the family.

"But how would you stop them?" Carmen had inquired when it came up over dessert with tea and coffee. "You don't have any way to make them leave."

Imelda nodded over her ice cream and answered in Tagalog, a long answer that she punctuated by gesturing with her spoon. Carmen listened to the whole thing and nodded before translating for Cyndricka and Chelsea.

"She says that they respect their privacy most of the time," Carmen said. "And if they do not, the most powerful punishment is to ignore them. The ghosts here have become so accustomed to being seen and heard that taking the attention away abruptly is very difficult for them." She smirked at Chelsea. "I will have to use that technique when you chatter too much."

Chelsea mused on all of this as she watched Cyndricka drumming her fingers on her chest and watching the ceiling, a departure from her usual view of clouds and stars. If Cyndricka were to decide to ignore her, to cut off one of her very last connections to the human world, she didn't know what she would do. She would be losing a lifeline and a friend.

A friend that she had been hiding part of the truth from.

"I have something to tell you two," she whispered into the dark room, out of consideration for their hosts down the hall. They had all been invited to stay the night on the condition that they keep quiet and restrict themselves to the living room and bathroom. The Vitug's were putting an exceptional amount of trust in a group that they had just met.

Cyndricka lifted her head off of the pillow to glance at her. Carmen looked up from her perusal of the newspaper Mr. Vitug had left open on a coffee table. Chelsea steadied her nerves; she had been through a great deal with these two. A little revelation was nothing compared to wailers and poltergeists.

She laid it out just as she had to Jose, simple and concise. She could not always bring herself to look, stroking her fingers through the calico's fur while it slept instead, but when she glanced up, Carmen was watching her with a thoughtful expression. Cyndricka bit her lip and looked away as Chelsea finished speaking.

"And I know it's not a huge difference, but . . . I wanted you two to know what we were really walking into, for me."

Silence took over. Telling it like this, whispered in a dark living room instead of spoken openly in the night, made it seem larger than it was, a secret capable of unraveling everything. Carmen nodded, taking in what had been said. She strolled over to Chelsea, reached out, and smacked her hand through Chelsea's head.

She tried not to yelp too loudly and wake any humans up, but the calico awoke and hissed at her sudden jerk back through its body. She had honestly been expecting it, but that didn't make the sensation any less startling.

"Okay, but let me—"

"You lied to get me here. This isn't just your brother's wedding, you consider it yours too. You knew I would not have agreed to come if I had known it had the potential to send you reeling that much." She paused with her hand raised for another strike.

"I'm sorry, I know, I just . . . I mean, it would have been

important for me to go regardless." Her voice cracked. "And I am so glad you came with me. Both of you. And I wasn't sure if you would, Carmen, if you knew it was about Heather too." She gripped her left hand through her short hair and huffed out a dry sob. "I'm sorry I kept it from you. And I won't pretend it wasn't a shitty thing to do. I'm just so happy that you two have been with me. I don't know what this trip would have been like without you."

Faster, for starters. Chelsea looked up just in time to catch Cyndricka's signs. Cyndricka smiled at her, reassuring. Chelsea's smile back was shaky, but very grateful.

Carmen lowered her hand back to her side. She looked thoughtful, pursing her lips and considering her response.

"If you had told me this before, I would have begged you not to go. I believe it is too much of a risk, and your evasive behavior means that you know it too." She paused. "I might have even threatened not to come. But seeing as I am ultimately glad that I did . . . I suppose it worked out for the best." She pointed her finger right into Chelsea's face. "Do not take this as an open invitation to keep things from me in the future. I will not tolerate this a second time. If you have anything else to share, now is your opportunity."

Chelsea nodded. She held open her arms and Carmen sighed before stepping into her embrace. Aside from the normal tingling, Chelsea felt an additional warmth where their skin touched, though she might have been imagining it.

They turned when they heard the shuffling of blankets and the creaking of springs in the couch. Cyndricka sat up all the way to face them. A thin stream of tears was trickling down her face. She gave a sniff and wiped at her eyes.

"We're not really fighting, it is fine," Carmen said with a motherly little smile. "There is no need to cry."

Cyndricka shook her head and took a deep breath. *No,* she signed. *There is something I need to tell you two as well.*

The three of them sat and talked through the rest of the night, sharing their stories and secrets until Imelda padded out of her bedroom at dawn in slippers and a robe. She waved and smiled at her otherworldly guests, unaware of what had transpired in the course of their long night.

That morning was a strange one in a lot of different ways. Jose hurried through his morning routine to get to an opening shift at the convenience store, but Imelda and her husband had time to cook breakfast and make coffee. Mr. Vitug cooked eggs in their small kitchen and Imelda double-checked how Cyndricka liked her coffee before giving her a mug of black with a large load of sugar.

Even after dinner the previous night, Cyndricka moved hesitantly, sat on the edge of her chair, and looked as though she expected her plate to be pulled away from her at any second. Carmen read the newspaper over Mr. Vitug's shoulder, and after Imelda told him where Carmen was, he held the pages at an angle to let her read more easily. Carmen relayed her thanks to Imelda, and Mr. Vitug gave a small smile and nodded in her general direction.

Carmen, Chelsea, and Cyndricka were not the only guests that morning. Various ghosts floated in through the windows and the walls of the kitchen. A smiling young woman with tire treads across her stomach bounded in and began chatting with Jose as he scurried around the kitchen, shoving a piece of toast in his mouth and grabbing his keys off the table. An elderly man in a hospital gown settled in on the other side of Mr. Vitug to read the paper. And a woman with a diagonal gash cutting into her shoulder and clumps of dirt clinging to her blouse, as if she had been chopped at with a shovel, gossiped with Imelda in rapid Tagalog, though the ghost's grip on the language was more tenuous.

"Okay, see ya, bye!" Jose scurried out the door with a hasty wave and a smile at Lorelai, the ghost with the tire tracks. She twiddled her fingers at him with a sly smile. Imelda looked away from the display with pursed lips. The shovel-victim, Maritza, clicked her tongue and Lorelai shot her a glare, all of which flew over Chelsea's head. Imelda took a sip of her coffee and turned to Cyndricka.

"You can use the shower, with Jose out. Clean clothes, too."

Cyndricka paused with fork halfway to her mouth, eyes wide. She glanced at Carmen and Chelsea, as if asking if she had heard correctly. She patted her pockets, looking for a notebook.

"I think it's still on the couch," Chelsea pointed out. Cyndricka sighed and signed to Carmen.

Ask her if she's sure it's okay.

Carmen translated to Imelda and Imelda nodded vigorously. Cyndricka had cleaned up as often as she could in public restrooms and parks along the way, and neither Chelsea nor Carmen could tell anyway, but Chelsea had to assume she smelled pretty vile by that point.

"Leave your clothes in the basket and set outside the door. I am doing laundry today," Imelda said. "I can repair any rips too?"

Cyndricka paused and turned her fork over in her hands. She set it down to sign, but kept watching Imelda while her hands moved.

Why do you want to do all these nice things for me? What do you want in return?

Carmen offered the translation to Imelda, with her eyes flicking cautiously between the two living women. When she finished speaking, Imelda laughed and shook her head.

"Before Jose was born," she said in English. "I thought I was only one in the world who saw them." Mr. Vitug looked away from his paper to lay his hand over his wife's. She smiled at him and continued. "Then I knew there are two. Now I know there are three. But I was alone and I know what it is. I need to help you how I can. I know what it is to be a lonely."

"A wandering spirit in your own right, I suppose," Maritza said and the man in the hospital gown nodded. Lorelai looked away, out the window following Jose's path. Cyndricka met Imelda's gaze squarely and nodded, just once, a confirmation that she knew exactly what it was like.

Chelsea did not know Mr. Vitug or his story, but she was pretty sure the sense of being alone and detached was shared by everyone else at the table. Death had a funny way of doing that, as, apparently, did speaking to the dead.

30.

They stayed for three days before the group made plans to leave. Even with what they knew about the last chapter of their journey, everyone agreed that they'd come too far to alter their path or give up on their plans. Cyndricka took the time to eat and sleep well, to rest her back and feet, to reorganize her bags and clean and mend her clothes, but she was still ready to leave by the fourth day.

Carmen spent the time absorbing as much media and information as she could. She chatted with Imelda and the other ghosts to secure her hold on the intricacies of Tagalog, she watched television during the day, she read books off of the Vitugs' shelves while Jose did his schoolwork nearby, so he could turn the pages. Chelsea didn't remember the last time she had seen her so relaxed and content; even at her happiest on the road, Carmen was tense when she lacked some form of distraction. Now she didn't have to go out and seek it. She could take advantage of having humans with both hands and access to books and TV, a very rare luxury for a dead woman.

Chelsea was not nearly so starved for entertainment, but she did take advantage of the new conversational partners. Ever since Jamie had stayed behind, she'd had exactly two people and one cat to speak to, give or take some poltergeists. In contrast, ghosts came in and out of the Vitug home all the time, some stopping by every day, others lured by gossip about another ghost-speaker being in town.

Maritza, the shovel-victim, was one of the constant guests. She came by every morning that Imelda didn't have an opening shift, and late in the afternoon on the days she did, to talk over coffee while she got ready for her day or relaxed after work. On the second day, she got there early, before Imelda was back and while Cyndricka was taking a nap, so she stayed to chat with Chelsea (only making it a bit clear that Chelsea was her third choice).

"Yeah, they moved into town about five years ago," she told Chelsea with a conspiratorial nod, as though she was sharing some huge secret. "There were only three of us here then, me and these two other ghosts that moved on a couple years ago. Now the town's just full of us, everyone wanting to get in on the ghost-speakers. Course, most of 'em are too lazy to learn the lingo. That's why Imelda likes me best. Cause I bother to learn. A lot of the others just talk to Jose, 'cause it's easier."

Chelsea nodded, though she thought that was probably unfair to the other ghosts, and a little rude to Jose to make him out as an inferior substitute. She had been lucky that Cyndricka could still hear, and was able to still communicate, through writing or just being expressive, before Chelsea got around to learning as much sign language as she could. She couldn't even imagine how frustrating it would have been if she had had to pick up a language in its entirety before she had been able to communicate with Cyndricka, and the appeal of an easier route, another speaker with a language she already knew, would have been awfully tempting. But Maritza seemed to just enjoy gossiping about people, so she let her go unimpeded.

"You know that Jose knew Lorelai before she died, right?" she told Chelsea, watching her expression closely and gauging her reaction. "She was a classmate of his in high school. They weren't friends or anything, she didn't know he could speak to ghosts, but as soon as she died and came back, she was all over him. I really think it's just too easy like that, having a human to talk to right off the bat."

"I knew Cyndricka fairly soon after I died," Chelsea commented. "Not immediately, it was a few months before Carmen introduced us, but still pretty soon."

Maritza scanned her up and down, judging, before she went on. "I guess that's okay. But at least you didn't know her before you croaked. It's like Lorelai is cheating at death. Or the afterlife, whatever you want to call it, she's doing it wrong."

She switched topics soon after that, on a largely unbroken monologue about the different ghosts in the town, the infighting between them, and who was a creep who hung out in the women's locker room at the community college gym. Chelsea nodded along for most of it, playing with the cats and at least giving a token attempt at paying attention.

She did bring Lorelai up to Carmen later, when Carmen was taking a break from soap operas and strolling through the streets of Orem. They had invited Cyndricka, but they couldn't really blame her for turning down the prospect of more walking.

"Imelda is worried, but for different reasons," Carmen said with a knowing nod. "Apparently Jose had an infatuation with this Miss Lorelai before she died. Then she comes back, meets the real Jose, and they form a rather deep friendship. Imelda is quite concerned about it."

"She thinks they're gonna fall in love or something?"

"Perhaps. On a more general note, I believe she worries that it will cause Jose to retreat from the human world, if his closest companion is a ghost. She has tried to encourage him to interact with the living as well as the dead his entire life, to avoid—"

"Becoming like Cyndricka," Chelsea finished. Carmen nodded. Her eyes betrayed sadness.

"While our Cyndricka is a lovely woman and her situation suits us very well, it is not healthy for her. I cannot blame Imelda in the slightest for trying to stop her son from becoming an outcast or a recluse."

"Yeah. I mean, if you had met Cyndricka when you were alive, what would you have thought?"

Carmen looked off into the distance. "I would have passed her on the street. Perhaps given her a dollar. If my children were with me, I would have pulled them closer. People speaking to the air were not terribly uncommon where I lived."

Chelsea snorted. "Makes you wonder if there were even more ghost-talking folks around."

"No, I walked by them after I died," she said simply, flatly.

"There was never anyone there. And to the rest of the world, that is how Cyndricka always looks. Aside from these two people here, she will never be understood."

Chelsea looked at her as they walked. "You're worried about Reno." She didn't frame it as a question, and the twitch on Carmen's face confirmed it. "You're worried about what she'll do there, and afterwards."

"We both understand the need for closure, more than anyone," she said. "But after this goal is completed, what more does she have? A long walk back across the country to go live in a park? When we were under the impression that she would have somewhere to go, it was different."

"We can't make her decisions for her," Chelsea said slowly. "She's the only one still living her life. We can give advice, support her, but she's still gonna do what she wants. And she wants to go to Reno."

Carmen sighed and tugged at the hem of her dress, reorganizing it over her legs. "I cannot stop her. I could not stop you. One wonders why I even bother trying."

"Because you care about us," Chelsea said with a smirk. "And we care about you, and listen to you, even if we're not always gonna do what you say. I'm always glad to have your advice, Carmen. I'm just stubborn as hell."

The touch to her shoulder was halfway between a caress and a smack, and it wasn't clear if Carmen even knew what she was going for there. They walked back to the house in silence.

That night, Cyndricka decided it would be a good way to show her incredible thanks for the Vitug's generosity by putting on a show for them and the local ghosts. Cyndricka had told Jose about what she did for money, and he had been immediately intrigued, though a little confused about the fact that mimes still apparently existed (a notion which Cyndricka quickly disabused him of). Lorelai had spread the news to the rest of the undead community, and the living room was filled that final evening: Imelda, Mr. Vitug and Jose on the couch, Chelsea and Carmen on the sides of the room, and all of the other ghosts floating behind the couch to get a good view.

Cyndricka had a skip back in her step, thanks to the food and rest in her system. Her dreads were pulled up into their high pigtails and her makeup was as clean and precise as Chelsea had ever seen it. The rips and tears and threadbare edges in her costume were lovingly tended to, a co-project between her and Imelda. Despite the language difficulties, they had spent an afternoon with just the two of them, working on the mending in near silence, and the hard work paid off now as Cyndricka twisted and turned in her lovely costume.

She stepped into the middle of the living room floor, ready to begin, and Imelda was the first to clap, followed closely by Jose and Mr. Vitug, then by cheers from the ghostly crowd. For the first time since they had left Central Park, Cyndricka had a proper mixed human and ghost audience for her performance, as it was always supposed to be.

In the familiar setting, Cyndricka put on the best show Chelsea and Carmen had yet seen. And after having performed for and escaped from a pack of ravening poltergeists, Chelsea found that her stage-fright was a far smaller issue to deal with; she didn't take the center stage at any point, but she reprised her role as the scowling police officer in Cyndricka's performance about the lost Metrocard.

Laughter filled the living room, though the ghosts and ghost-speakers got more of the jokes than poor Mr. Vitug, or at least a beat faster, as they had the advantage of seeing all of the performers. Cyndricka took a brief interlude to rest and get a drink of water, and Carmen stepped into the center to sing one of her medleys. (Mr. Vitug took the break to use the restroom.) Their audience was practically bouncing in their seats or in mid-air, respectively, and Carmen beamed at the positive reaction, as well as relishing the fact that her survival did not depend on this one. When she sang her way through the thrilling conclusion, everyone applauded and she swanned her way off of the makeshift stage, nodding to Cyndricka as they passed. Cyndricka launched into her Rich Woman's Dog routine, which required so many additional actors that it worked better for her to just do it alone. Chelsea smiled at Carmen as they stood off to the side.

"We all seem pretty happy here," Chelsea muttered into Carmen's ear. "Even you seem to like it."

Carmen nodded, just a short jerk of her chin. She didn't take her eyes off of Cyndricka when she whispered back, "It is a good environment with nice company. We will have to make a return stop through here on our way back to New York."

"Or we could just . . . you know, stop here. Cyndricka stays with them until she finds a job she can actually do. Has ghosts to talk to, but humans as well. Maybe she learns how to write in Tagalog, I don't know." She watched Carmen. "It's something to think about."

Carmen turned and met her gaze. "Are you sure *I* am the one who is worried about her?"

"We both are and you know it. I just . . . I feel like this could be a good place for her. She doesn't need the big city distraction like you do."

"And she does not have anything tying her to New York City. Like you do."

It stung, but Chelsea nodded. "Yeah, like me. Hell, you and I could run back and tell the performance crew that the hot new place to be is Utah, and she wouldn't even lose them."

"And are you going to stay in New York after all of this?" Carmen was not bothering to watch Cyndricka's performance now, turning to face Chelsea straight-on. "Once we have attended the wedding, will you still need to haunt your ex-fiancée every few weeks?"

". . . I didn't think you—"

"Of course I knew about that, even if I didn't know you two were engaged. I notice things and ghosts talk. As I said: are you going back to New York after this?"

". . . I don't know."

Carmen nodded. "We still have time to figure it out. But perhaps have your own mind organized before you throw out suggestions to her."

Cyndricka did a big flying leap after the woman's imaginary dog, and it was a blessing that Charlie had learned how to stay out of the way of the pratfalls in Cyndricka's performance. She did hop

on the back of Cyndricka's head when she was on the floor and
start licking her hair, but it was well-timed to get a second laugh
from their audience. Chelsea watched her performance with the
rest of them, and cheered the hardest of the whole crowd at the
end, though Jose gave her a run for her money.

The next morning, they were off. The Vitugs offered to buy
Cyndricka a bus ticket, but that was a level of generosity she could
not accept; she knew money was tight for them with Jose in school.
But they did see her off with a backpack full of food to eat on the
road, things that did not need to be cooked and would take a long
time to spoil. She even had a spare umbrella from the back of their
closet to keep some of the sun off her when she slept.

Cyndricka received a handshake from Mr. Vitug and a quick
back-slapping hug from Jose. Maritza and Lorelai said their fare-
wells to the whole trio; Chelsea saw how closely she stood to
Jose, and she wished the young woman the best. Looking at the
two together, it was impossible to miss that she was still a teenager, while despite his self-professed "baby face," he was growing
into a man. Chelsea shook both of their hands, still a confusing
gesture to Jose, and wished them the best of luck. They were
going to need it.

Imelda and Cyndricka held each other for a long time, rocking
slightly back and forth. Cyndricka tucked her face into the curve
of the older woman's shoulder and breathed deeply. To Chelsea,
it sounded like she was fighting back sobs. They pulled back just
enough to see each other, arms still around one another's shoulders,
and Imelda planted a kiss to Cyndricka's forehead. That morning
she had tied Cyndricka's dreads back into a knot at the base of
her neck, held with a strip of black ribbon. Now with a faint
lipstick mark on her forehead, Cyndricka was heading out with
Imelda's influence written on her face. She smiled through a scattering of tears, and Imelda nodded in complete understanding. The
languages between them could not have meant less just then, gone
in the face of shared experience and shared pain.

Cyndricka, Chelsea, and Carmen looked back and waved at the Vitugs as they left. Chelsea called back until they were out of hearing range, shouting goodbyes to the dusty wind as they entered what was undoubtedly the last leg of a long, long journey.

31.

It took them the better part of three weeks to get to Reno, walking at their previous pace at night, with renewed vigor on all of their parts, and replenished health on Cyndricka's. Chelsea even noticed that her damaged arm wasn't hurting as much as it had been before, though that could perhaps be attributed to the upturn in mood. There was something nice about being back with just the three of them (four, including Charlie) on the road, after the crowded nature of the house. It was like they were in their own little world again, a capsule that traveled with them wherever they went.

The detour left some unpleasant side effects too. Being shown so much kindness and generosity by strangers had opened Cyndricka up, and the scorn and disdain she received from people directly after that, the ones who brushed her aside as crazy or openly mocked her, hurt all the more, like soft skin once calluses have faded.

Her actual calluses were doing quite well, with the active blisters on her feet healed, but none of the toughness faded away. The nights were shorter over the summer, but she could still put in miles between sunset and sunrise, with a gorgeous sky full of stars overhead. But during those scorching days, scrunched up in whatever shelter she could find or make, she would curl into a ball and let herself cry. Carmen and Chelsea offered anything they could do to help, but short of going back and abandoning the rest of the journey, there wasn't much anyone could do. At least the tears were evidence that she was not becoming dehydrated, as much as she would sweat when she walked, dirtying the clothes that had been clean for such a short period of time.

When the streetlights signaling civilization came into view, glowing on the dark horizon, Cyndricka's breath caught in her throat and she stopped dead in her tracks. Chelsea and Carmen kept walking a few steps, engrossed in a conversation about the development of punk rock, before they noticed she was no longer with them. They turned back to her and waited.

I'm fine, she signed after a moment. *I just . . . it has been a long time since I was here. I never thought I would see it again.*

She bent down and picked up Charlie from where she had been pawing at her bootlaces and playing in the dirt. The cat mewled at the indignity of being taken away from her game, but quieted when Cyndricka held her close and petted along her side. The spot where she had been shaved for her surgery had a fine growth of fur again, about half the length of the surrounding fluffy black and white, but dense and enough to cover the scar. Cyndricka held her cat to her chest, shuffled to readjust her backpack on her shoulders, and kept walking towards the city of Reno.

Charlie crawled up her shoulders to sit on the top of her backpack for the ride, freeing up Cyndricka's hands to discuss the buildings and locations they were passing. *If you go down that street for a while and turn right, you're at my old elementary school. My middle school was in the other direction down that way. I only did one year there, but I liked it. The special education teacher was stupid, but nice.*

Carmen and Chelsea nodded along to her silent monologues, walking backwards in front of her to catch the increasingly rapid signs being thrown out of her hands. Chelsea struggled to catch the trickier ones and vocabulary she hadn't come across much before.

"Wait, slow down, I never learned many of the signs for school stuff."

"Why not?" Carmen asked. "I know the course I recommended to you covered it."

"Yeah, but Cyndricka's not in school now." Chelsea shrugged. "I never thought it would come up much."

Cyndricka tried to slow down her signs, but they kept speeding up as she passed more and more sights she recognized. *I remember that grocery store. And that shop over there. The storekeepers were really nice . . . we cannot steal anything from there.*

Chelsea and Carmen nodded, though Chelsea had to bite her tongue from pointing out that a lot of stores probably had nice storekeepers.

They kept moving through the city, favoring detours and places Cyndricka remembered over main thoroughfares. A few people peeked out of their curtains at the woman walking down the road alone at night, but no one bothered them as Cyndricka enthusiastically pointed out different homes.

That one got replaced since I've been here, but it's okay, the foundation was cracking already when I left. And over there is where I fell and broke my arm. Did I tell you about that time? I was about eight and a neighborhood kid had—look, a playground! I wished there was one in this neighborhood when I was younger, and now there is!

She hopped from topic to topic with barely a pause in between and Chelsea had to laugh. Cyndricka stuck her tongue out in response, so it was probably even on both sides. They kept walking with Cyndricka providing a steady narration, past trailer parks and mobile homes with elaborate succulent gardens out front.

She moved with purpose, with a clear goal in mind, even if her words were all over and her hands in a million places at once. Chelsea had never been to Nevada before, but she could guess where they were going.

And when they saw the large sign out front, simple and clean, with "Mountain View Cemetery" written on it, Chelsea knew she had guessed correctly, as much as she hated to be right just then.

The gates were locked up tight for the evening, but the sky was just starting to lighten in the east, a pink glow creeping over the mountains in the distance.

"Should you try to get some food somewhere, find an all-night diner and come back in a few hours?" Chelsea asked. But Cyndricka had already set down her bag on the curb across the street and sat down, watching the gates. Without a word, Carmen and Chelsea sat down beside her.

They sat in still and silent vigil through the rest of the night and through dawn, until a groundskeeper unlocked the gates at eight in the morning. Cyndricka gathered up her bag and Charlie, set her shoulders, and walked inside.

Down the paved road, past small markings to commemorate the final resting places of the dead. A scattering of leaves and flower petals coated the pavement, and Cyndricka's footsteps left little marks as she walked. Neither Chelsea nor Carmen left any trace. There they were, in acres full of bodies without spirits, visited by two spirits without bodies and one human who was in-between.

Their headstones were plain stone. It didn't look as fancy as marble or anything, maybe granite, but Chelsea had never been much in the know with these types of things. The first person close to her who had died had been herself. Cyndricka set down her backpack to the side, bending down to let Charlie jump off to the ground first, and stood between the two graves.

"Marcus Danvers, 1928 to 2000, Beloved Husband and Grandfather," read one. The matching headstone next to it was just as simple and sparse: "Delilah Danvers, 1930 to 1999, Beloved Wife and Grandmother." The two stones were joined at the bottom, connected even in death, with a tiny extra inscription: "Gone is the face we loved so dear, silent the voice we long to hear" running along it.

I didn't get any say in the inscription, Cyndricka signed slowly, not taking her eyes away from the stones. *I was only twelve when he died. No one asked me. I wouldn't have . . . would not have chosen that.*

Carmen stood next to Cyndricka and wrapped her arm around her shoulders. "It sounds like they were lovely people. People who loved you very much. I'm sorry that you lost them so early."

You know, I thought I had at first. She paused for a long time before continuing, but neither of them were going to rush her. *I thought that their ghosts had gotten lost somehow. Wandered off and couldn't find their way back.* She gave a wry smile though her mouth was trembling. *I ran away from my first foster home a dozen times, just looking for them. It wasn't until the third home that I gave up.* Her shoulders shook and bent forwards, but no tears spilled out from her full eyes. Not yet.

Chelsea flanked her other side, pressing flush against Cyndricka. It sent lightning shooting through her bad arm, but she wanted to be as close to her friend as possible, to let her feel that someone was there. Cyndricka wiped her eyes and signed with wet hands.

It had never been permanent to me before. So many of my friends were dead and I assumed that they would have stayed for me. That I would have been a big enough reason. Her hands shuttered to stillness and a broken croak came out of her open mouth. It was the first time Chelsea had ever heard her voice.

She sunk down to her knees between the two graves. Tears spilled freely down her face, a full flood that clouded her eyes and turned her face puffy. Another croak out of her long-unused voicebox and a gasp of air as her whole body shuddered and shook. Chelsea and Carmen sunk down with her, wrapping their ghostly, frustratingly intangible, arms around her and letting their grip sink into her, as they could not squeeze.

Charlie climbed onto Cyndricka's lap. She stuck her nose into Cyndricka's face, whiskers brushing over wet cheeks, and meowed in demand to know what had made her mama so sad. Cyndricka pulled the cat into her arms and squeezed tight, to have something solid and warm to hold onto. Charlie, to her credit, only mewled and squirmed once before letting herself be pressed to Cyndricka's shirt, its front already soaked.

"They did not mean to leave you," Carmen murmured in her ear. "We do not choose whether to stay or go. If they could have stayed with you, they would have."

"We've got you. You're safe," Chelsea whispered into her other ear. "Take the time you need."

Cyndricka choked out a sob and nodded. She curled forward around her cat, sheltered by her ghostly family, and over the bodies of the two dead people she would have given the world to speak to, but who were very, very silent.

Cyndricka cried herself out over the course of the morning, sobs dying down to empty, dry shuddering, as if she was hollowing herself out of all the grief that had been sitting inside of her. The two ghosts stayed wrapped around her, only peeling away to investigate any noises on the nearby road. But the Danvers' graves were tucked away behind some trees and taller headstones, offering cover when cemetery staff drove by in little carts. As the sun started to rise all the way overhead and the headstones' shadows grew small, Cyndricka moved just enough to gulp from one of her water bottles like a woman who had just wandered a desert, with none of her usual conservation and care. She laid out food and water for Charlie, who gobbled it down as usual, but she didn't take any food for herself. Instead she just laid down on her side in the grass, curled in a ball between the two stones.

While she settled, Carmen began to sing softly, a warbling melody echoing out across the grass and trees and markers of the deceased. The song was in Spanish, impenetrable to both Chelsea and Cyndricka, but her voice carried enough emotion to make the content clear: love, loss, solace and peace, all woven into the soft consonants and flowing vowels. To the tune of the otherworldly, supernatural lullaby, Cyndricka's eyes slid closed. Her breathing steadied and the rise and fall of her chest smoothed out with sleep. Belly full, Charlie curled back against her and was also asleep instantly. Chelsea and Carmen waited over them in the cemetery.

There was so much to talk about, so much to address, that Chelsea barely knew what to touch on first. Both of her parents were still alive, three of her grandparents and a step-grandmother as well. She had always known that her parents loved her, and her siblings too, even if they fought like cats and dogs. They had always been around and alive.

From every other viewpoint, Chelsea was the one in the ground and her loved ones were the ones in Cyndricka's place. Except that they all had each other. And Cyndricka just had wisps on the wind that used to be people, and a cat to sleep on the grass next to her. Better than nothing, but not by much.

Though there was another possibility. She nodded to them, sitting right in between the headstones. Carmen nodded. She had probably noticed a lot sooner, but had been too busy helping Cyndricka. They both had been, but now they took the moment to acknowledge them.

"You see those, right?"

"Yes, Chelsea. They are a bit hard to miss. Even Cyndricka surely saw them, though I do not know if she has acknowledged what they mean."

The splashes of blue and purple were vibrant against the light colored stone. They looked like violets of some kind, carefully grown and tended, not the clean cut and organized flowers bought from a store and wrapped to go. Someone had cared a great deal to put those flowers by these two graves.

And they were fresh.

"We'll bring it up when she wakes up," said Chelsea. Carmen nodded, but switched to Chinese when she next spoke.

"Though I beg you not to be surprised if she decides not to pursue that line of inquiry. She came all this way to pay respects to her grandparents, not to reunite with a family that rejected her as a child."

"Carmen, she lives on the street back in New York. In a park."

"And if she chooses to go back to that, does that not say a great deal about the sort of family she is leaving behind?"

Chelsea had to nod grudgingly. Nothing here could be fixed easily. These were years upon years of hurt layered on hurt, built up and possibly twisted in the mind of a silent woman with dead companions. Whatever Cyndricka was feeling right now, it was utterly unique. And it was her weight to bear; Chelsea couldn't carry it for her any more than she could carry the backpack, no matter how hard she tried. She sat silently next to Carmen, watching birds flutter between the trees of the cemetery. Another day on guard duty, after who knew how many before it, and who knew how many to follow.

Cyndricka woke a little after noon and immediately reached for her backpack. While falling straight asleep after crying was a strong and powerful image, she did burn a huge number of calories in any given day. She fell upon her food, gobbling down handfuls of breakfast cereal and trying to unwrap a granola bar at the same time. She leaned back against her backpack while she ate, cramming enough food into her mouth to free up her hands, so she could sign while she chewed.

Anything interesting happen? she asked. Her movements were light and careless, flung off her fingers like brushing away flies. Chelsea shook her head.

"We were discussing the flowers that have been left on your grandparents' graves," Carmen said, and Chelsea shot her the most shocked and offended look she could give on such short notice. They hadn't talked about it, but Chelsea had assumed that they were going to ease into the topic, give Cyndricka a chance to get into the mood to talk about it, or at the very least wake up first. Apparently, Carmen had different opinions.

Cyndricka glanced down at the bouquet of flowers behind her on the stones. She nodded and ate another handful of cereal, this time calmer and slower, actually taking the opportunity to chew. She swallowed, wiped her hands on the grass and signed again.

Yes, I noticed those before. Maybe from a cousin. Or my parents. Or maybe my brother. I have no idea if he's the type to grow flowers. I did only see him twice, and he was in diapers both times.

"Do you . . ." Chelsea tried to go with the conversation's general tone. "Do you want to spend the time to find them? While we're here?"

Cyndricka raised her eyebrows, but kept the rest of her face expressionless while she ate another handful of cereal, chewed and swallowed, and wiped her hands off again. *Why would I want to do that?*

Chelsea looked at Carmen, hoping for some help, but her face was just as stony. "I don't know. Because they're your family? It might give you a place to stay for a while. I mean— I mean, you did say that's what this whole trip was about."

No, I said this trip was about visiting family. She patted her hands on the grass over both graves, stretched out so she touched them both at the same time. *This is the family I came to see. I couldn't care less about the others. If they are still in R-E-N-O, good for them. If not, that's fine too.*

"All right," Carmen said, before Chelsea could interject anything. "If that is your take on the situation, we respect that. So where are we off to next?"

Cyndricka crossed her legs underneath her and leaned back

against the grass, looking relaxed in the mid-day light. She signed over her chest, watching the sky above. *Still onto the wedding. Just let me relax here for a bit. It is a nice cemetery.*

"... Take as long as you need," Chelsea said again, just like the night before. She looked around her, up at the trees, across the well-maintained stones, some with flowers, some without. "It's a nice place."

I stopped here right before I left the city last time, Cyndricka signed to the sky. *A boyfriend told me he was going to take me somewhere better than this, away from my foster family. The one at the time, that is. We got as far as Omaha.*

"What happened in Omaha?" she asked in spite of herself. She really didn't want to know the answer, but if Cyndricka wanted to tell it, she was willing to listen. Or watch, as the case may be. Cyndricka snorted, what almost sounded like laughter.

He left me in a hotel room with a cracked skull. The usual. She reached out and petted Charlie, who was stretching and waking up bit by bit. *Neither of us have good luck with Nebraska, do we? We should just go around it next time. I met a girlfriend in Omaha. She was nicer. And deaf. She helped me learn sign language, which proved very helpful.* Chelsea could see her grin up at the cloud. *I saved on notebook paper with her, which was nice.*

"What happened to her?"

I was a pity case. She got bored. Again, the usual. Cyndricka stretched her arms up above her, fingers laced to pop her fingers before she kept going. *I kept to my own after that. I never had any luck with humans aside from my grandparents, so why bother keeping it up? The dead took care of me fine, and the living gave me money if I was funny enough. I was going to choose when and why they laughed at me. So it became miming and N-Y-C to get by. I've been there ever since.* She sat up and grinned at Chelsea, a big, toothy smile. *Until your brother went and got himself engaged. Then I decided it might be a nice time to see the West again. And pay respects to the only good living ones out there, even if they did fail at being ghosts.*

She patted the ground again and laid back with another little laugh under her breath. Carmen nodded down at her.

"Of course, you do recognize the irony of your little trip?"

Cyndricka nodded on the ground. *Yes, I know. I think it has to be pure luck, how many good living ones I've met out here.*

"And bad dead ones," Chelsea pointed out, only wheedling a bit. Cyndricka half-nodded, head angling across the grass, leaving blades stuck in her dreadlocks.

It's just a road trip. You're bound to meet all sorts when you go out that far. It happens, there's no bigger point or anything.

Chelsea nudged Cyndricka in the side with the toe of her high heel. She squirmed on the ground like a cat on its back. "Come on, you know better than that by now."

Whatever. Take what big messages you like. It's just my weird life. Cyndricka stuck her tongue out at Chelsea, which she returned. Cyndricka threw a handful of grass through her, Chelsea teased Charlie into jumping onto Cyndricka's head, Carmen sighed and rolled her eyes, and for now, they were back to being their own little traveling circus.

32.

Chelsea hadn't been in a proper forest for years before the trip. She remembered camping with her family upstate and one memorable vacation she took with Heather, when they both got poison ivy and spent the entire first day back home covered in calamine lotion, but she had been a city girl through and through for the majority of her life. Camping while dead probably didn't have the same impact as while alive, since she didn't have to worry about things like water or warmth.

They had already traveled through some lovely forests in their walks, but Cyndricka had done what she could to avoid them for the most part, rerouting their trip with little detours to stay in the bounds of civilization, and the running water and shelter that came with it. But the area around Lake Tahoe was breathtaking enough that even she had to admire it. With the trees for shade, they could finally go back to traveling during the day, and Cyndricka could use the nights to rest her legs from all of the mountainous terrain. They had searched army surplus stores back in Reno until they found a solid set of used hiking boots, and they were proving an essential purchase.

Charlie spent the days chasing after any and everything that moved, Cyndricka woke up to the sound of birdsong in the mornings, and if any of them ever questioned their direction, Cyndricka just took a break while a ghost ran ahead to find the next trail sign and come back with a proper heading. It was a nice set of days.

They came out on the other side near the end of the month, tired and with Cyndricka and Charlie sporting more than a few ticks, but feeling renewed, as though they had come through some baptism at the hands of nature and were emerging on the other side all the better for it. Cyndricka spent most of the next day in a public library, surreptitiously cleaning up in the bathroom on the basement level and relaxing her feet, but by the late afternoon, they were back on the road, moving through California and so, so very close to their goal. So close, Chelsea could almost taste it.

For lack of any better options, Cyndricka spent the night beneath an underpass, tucked away in the corner of cement while she ate. As a distraction from the cars whizzing past them at all hours, she asked Chelsea more and more questions about what they were going to be walking into.

What's your brother like? she asked, with no hesitation over the topic of brothers or family in general. Chelsea tried to sum up Osric.

"Um, he's a nerd-type, I guess? A gamer, but not like that's the only thing he does, you know? He does some sort of medical accounting thing, way more formal than anyone ever expected him to do, and Tamika's a hospital administrator. My parents never ended up with a good Chinese doctor in the family, but they got pretty close, I guess." She chuckled to herself. "They almost got a doctor for an in-law, but that damn train messed that up."

I forgot your girlfriend was a doctor, Cyndricka said with her own soft smile. *She likes helping people?*

"Yeah. Yeah, she does . . . Like, it's not totally altruistic, she also likes solving puzzles and working out mysteries to make people feel better . . . in fact, if I'm totally honest, helping people was probably lowest on the list of reasons to go to medical school, but it was still on there." Chelsea shook her head at the memory of the cocky friend of Osric's she had met all that time ago. "I think she mostly wanted to have everyone struggle to say her name right. Doctor Heather Vavagiakis. It has a nice, if really long, ring to it, doesn't it?"

Carmen raised a sardonic eyebrow. "You would have been Chelsea Vavakis?"

"See, even *you* didn't get it right!" she crowed, pointing at her with unbridled glee. "The language master, and you messed it up!

No, but I probably would have kept my name. Or mashed them together. Chelsea Vavagiakis-Shu? Shu-Vavagiakis? Shvagiaskis? Which sounds better?"

They all sound really bad.

"Hey, shut up, her name is fun. I would have been happy to— no, okay, it's a shitty name and I probably wouldn't have taken it, but I loved her. So maybe. If she really, really wanted me to."

Cyndricka clasped her hands together beside her face like she was swooning, which got a chuckle out of Carmen. Ganged up on, she turned to Carmen.

"Okay, I never asked, what was your maiden name? Something cool, or were you glad to give it up for Gutierrez?"

Carmen shook her head and held it high, looking very dignified for a moment. "I was Carmen Theresa Reyes. A royal name. I was very proud of it. But I was also very proud to take Manuel's name, and to wear my wedding ring. I do not understand all of the people today who do not want to share names, I was very happy with mine." She looked down at her bare hand and flexed her fingers. "I wish that I had been wearing my ring when I died. I had taken it off for cooking and left it in its little dish on the counter. It stayed in that dish for a very, very long time. Like Manuel's ring stayed on his finger . . . I was not so happy about that."

Cyndricka and Chelsea met each other's gaze in the dark of the shaded underpass. Carmen continued to move her fingers back and forth.

"All these years later, and you can still see the mark where I wore it every day. It is like I still have the impact, if not the physical." She held her hand before her face, looking at the slightest possible indentation on the ring finger. "Manuel had the same thing. The impact but not the physical. For so long after I died, him mourning and our children suffering and—"

Carmen trailed off, still looking at her ring finger. Chelsea reached out to brush a hand through her shoulder.

"We know you miss them," she said gently. Cyndricka stretched from her spot on the concrete to brush a hand through Carmen's foot as well.

Rather than be comforted, Carmen jerked at the contact and

looked sharply between the two of them. "Do not mistake this for—for grief. You cannot begin to understand."

"I wasn't trying to." Chelsea drew back carefully, as if afraid she was going to spook her friend.

"Neither of you—you can't possibly—old age and accidents, that's how you lost your loved ones. But me?" She gestured sharply to her chest, trying to beat it without being able to make contact. "I was stolen from my children. They looked at me and decided to leave my children without a— And I had to watch them grow up without being able to—"

Carmen squeezed her eyes shut and gritted her teeth, the words choking off in her throat. Chelsea had no idea where to even start addressing this.

"Carmen, I—"

Cyndricka started signing something, but cut off when Carmen jumped to her feet, abruptly enough to make the others jerk back. She looked taller than normal, somehow, strangely intimidating in her summer dress and sandals.

"I need to go into town," she said flatly.

"I don't think there's anything nearby but Ione, and that's tiny. Would you rather—"

"I will be back by morning. Stay safe here."

"Wait, Carmen, I don't—you shouldn't be alone right now, I don't think, and—" Chelsea tried to call after her, but she was off running down the county road without another word. Cyndricka actually stood up to watch her go, running down the pavement in the sliding ghostly steps that never touched the ground. She turned back to Chelsea, eyes wide.

What was that about?

"I don't know. I mean, she doesn't like to talk about her family much, but—I don't even know." It struck her how little she really knew about Carmen's life before, or immediately after, her death. So much of their relationship had focused on Chelsea's death, Chelsea's life, and Chelsea's journey, with occasional detours into Cyndricka's. "I mean, she's got a right to her privacy, if she wants it."

I guess so, Cyndricka said with an offhand nod. *I guess I just figured that we had given up on those things by now.*

"We'll see her in the morning, see if she wants to talk after she's had time to take in a movie or something. Get some rest, I'll be fine keeping watch." Cyndricka settled down into her sleeping bag, but Chelsea could see her eyes reflected in the headlights of passing cars for some time to follow.

The next morning Carmen was not back yet. If they had found a better place the night before, they might have waited, but Cyndricka had had more than enough of the slanted cement and the sharp gravel. They had been discussing their route over the past few days, so Carmen was sure to have an idea where they were headed, possibly even crossing paths as she returned later in the morning. Still, Cyndricka packed slowly and took her time eating breakfast and feeding Charlie, then cleaning herself and her cat more thoroughly than usual, packing and repacking her bag for things like proper weight distribution and density. Finally, at what had to be mid-morning, they started to walk.

Morning turned into afternoon and afternoon into late afternoon with still no sign of Carmen. They kept on their predetermined path, even going through an inconvenient construction area that hadn't been marked on any of their maps, but they took a long break in the middle of the day, hoping that she would catch up or find them or something.

The shadows were growing longer as they approached the edge of Ione, a little town dwarfed by a big prison, and Cyndricka put her backpack down on a city bench with a firm finality. They had barely walked five hours over the course of the whole day, a mere fraction of the pace they usually made. But there was no way Carmen would let a second night pass without finding them, so they settled in to wait out her return.

Their stopping location might not have been the best choice, the edge of a park that had clearly seen better days. Streetlights were dark with piles of broken glass beneath them, mingled in with the shards of bottles. People passed with hands jammed deep in their pockets and heads bent low, walking fast to whatever destinations they had in mind. Cyndricka held Charlie close in her lap until the cat squirmed at the indignity. They would have backtracked, found a better place to settle in, but the thought of missing Carmen in passing had them both on edge. Cyndricka looked tense and rigid in her seat, head turning and eyes flicking to and fro as she scanned the streets for any sign of their wayward ghost.

It was probably her insecurity that drew them in, strolling down the street with their thumbs hooked into their belts, investigating the twitchy woman sitting on the bench under the dark streetlight. Chelsea spotted them when they were still about thirty yards away.

"Hey, Cyndricka, a couple of cops are coming your way. To your left, walking slow."

Cyndricka tapped her fingers in her lap as acknowledgment that she had heard, a sign they had for when a nod was too obvious. She didn't look at the officers, didn't jerk or act like she knew they were there. She put on a perfect performance of someone who had just remembered a slightly important but not vital appointment, and casually stood up off of the bench and dusted her coat off. She swung her bag onto her back and gathered Charlie up into her arms again just as the two men came close.

They were middle-aged officers, both white men, when most of the people they had passed in the city so far had been black or Latino. One was a heavy-set man with a wide gait, while the other looked sharper, eyes slits in his thin face as he watched Cyndricka stroll away from her bench. They altered their path, angling to cross into her as she walked away, and Chelsea floated in between them to give Cyndricka updates without her having to look.

"Okay, two guys, coming at you still from the left, but walking. Turn down that street with the brighter lights, right there? Okay, definitely still following you. Speed up, but not a lot." They had encountered police before on their journey; it would have been impossible not to, with how many states they had passed through and how distinctive and strange Cyndricka looked most of the time. Some of them hadn't been so bad, asking her if she needed any help.

A few had given her trouble, but mostly given up after shouting a few things at her or telling her to get her ass out of a park, but the cop with the thin face looked different. Like a predatory animal aimed at her, a hunting dog locked onto her scent. The heavier

cop with dark hair trailed after his partner, slower and less determined in his pseudo-pursuit, but another body coming after her
nonetheless.

"Okay, Cyndricka, they're on you," Chelsea said, trying to
keep her voice calm. "They're definitely on you, and I think you
need to stop, otherwise they're going to actually chase. Slow down
to a walk and pretend to notice them."

She did just that, and Chelsea could see the shake of her shoulders as she came to a stop disguised as a pause on one of the few
well-lit corners, as if she was looking at street signs. She turned up
and down the road before "noticing" the two officers coming up on
her fast. The one with the thin face reached her first.

"What're you doing out here?"

"Do you have any ID?" the other officer spoke up. His words
weren't filled with quite as much venom, but he leaned over his
partner's shoulder into her space nonetheless. His upper arm
passed through Chelsea's body, and she saw a slight shudder ripple
through him. The thin-faced man continued to sneer.

Cyndricka gently dropped Charlie to the ground and held up
her hands in front of her. She gestured to her mouth, opened and
closed it a few times to indicate her inability to speak, then carefully,
slowly mimed writing in a notebook. The cop's eyes narrowed.

Chelsea scanned the street for any humans nearby, anyone
who could provide at least some sense of being seen. Not that that
would stop anything from happening, of course, but she could at
least hope.

Cyndricka watched the cop with wide eyes, asking permission
without asking for the right to reach into her own clothes, but
he just glared. She slowly, slowly lowered her hand into the deep
pocket.

Maybe Charlie thought that Cyndricka was reaching for a
treat, or maybe she just felt the tension as well, but the cat let out
a sharp yowl that made all of them jump. The officers jerked, but
the thin one looked angry at himself for his surprise. He kicked
Charlie away with his heavy boot, the cat flaring up into a bundle
of fur and claws.

The memory of the thrown beer can in Pine Bluffs might have

made Cyndricka more protective, or perhaps it was just instinct, the need to protect her pet. All Chelsea could see was the immediate, thoughtless reaction, the lunge forward to—to what? Comfort Charlie? Run away? Attack the officers? The man with the thin face clearly decided which one he thought it was.

The baton came out of the cop's belt and into Cyndricka's ribs in one fluid motion, with absolutely no pause for her to react or defend herself. She doubled over, winded and wheezing, and the cop stepped forward, looking down at her with a hard, cold stare in his eyes.

"Cyndricka!" Chelsea shouted, but there was no one but her to hear it.

"Get. Back. And answer me when I ask you a question." he said flatly. "I asked you, what are you doing out here?"

She gulped for air and held her arms around her middle; her backpack almost threatened to tip her over with the weight moving towards her front. Charlie yowled and put her paws on Cyndricka's leg to sniff at her. The cop brushed the cat aside again with his boot and bent down.

"Answer me," he hissed. "Speak up. Now."

Behind him, his partner rolled his eyes and looked away, but did nothing to stop him. The thin-faced man was bent over Cyndricka, coiled like a snake and ready to strike again. Cyndricka held up her hands and shook her head frantically, but couldn't bring forth any words.

"Help us! Somebody!" Chelsea screamed, and just kept screaming, but the street was empty, and what could anyone have heard anyway? She took a wild swing through the cop's head, teeth gritted against the waves of pain in her bad arm, but he didn't even flinch. For how unreceptive he was, the scratches that Charlie was leaving on the outside of his boot were doing more good. He grabbed Cyndricka's hair and pulled her head up, forcing her to meet his gaze. She was shaking, her mouth hanging open as she tried to get air and plead as well as she could without the use of words.

She held her hands up in a silent, squirming plea. He raised his baton again and Chelsea could do nothing but keep screaming . . .

and just in time to see that horrible tableau, she came around the corner at the end of the block.

Carmen.

She saw her friend freeze, illuminated softly by a remaining streetlight. When she spoke, her voice sounded distant, from much farther away than at the end of the block.

"Leave . . . leave her alone . . ."

Chelsea's cries trailed off as she watched Carmen approaching with long steps that seemed to stretch her legs out over the pavement, as if she were walking in a funhouse mirror. Her familiar floral dress, the charming tacky pattern that had earned her the title Curtains all that time ago, shifted, pulled taut and stretched across her chest, tears gaping at the seams. The air around Chelsea turned sharp and buzzy, full of an electricity that felt familiar.

Carmen paused in the middle of the street, watching them. Chelsea took a step towards her and watched the harsh line of her shoulders going tense. The baton came down on Cyndricka's back. Carmen's face twisted and her eyes slammed shut, and she stretched her back, flexing like she was unfurling wings from her shoulder blades.

Her dress ripped. The incorporeal fabric that held firm over forty years split down the middle to show the ragged skin and clotted blood of five bullet holes in between her breasts.

"Carmen," Chelsea whispered as her friend moved closer, looking very little like her friend anymore.

Charlie pulled away from her assault of the officer's boot to shrink back, spine curved and fur on end. She yowled and hissed, which drew Cyndricka's gaze away from her attacker and towards the being behind him, stretching taller with every moment and towering over them. She was caught by surprise from his next blow and fell to her hands and knees, the weight of her backpack driving her further down.

"Answer me!"

She looked up at the monstrous man, and the ghost behind him, her friend who was stretching, distorting, her eyes blazing with fire as her fingers grew out into claws, and all of them were suddenly, undeniably, in the presence of a poltergeist.

The beast that had been Carmen raised its arm over its head, reaching for the street lamp. It only had to reach a bit to wrap its clawed fingers around the large yellow bulb. Chelsea could only watch, frozen all over again. There was nothing to do but gape as Carmen crushed the bulb in her hand, raining broken glass down on the whole scene.

The two cops yelled, throwing their hands up to shield their heads. Cyndricka dropped down and curled herself into a ball, blocking an attack from someone, anyone at this point.

Chelsea found her voice as the Carmen-beast bared long teeth that seemed to tear its face apart and dragged its claws across the ground, picking up shards of fallen glass.

"Cyndricka! Grab Charlie and run! Now!"

Cyndricka didn't have to be told twice. She shot out like a snake to seize the terrified Charlie, clambered to her feet with her hands coming down in the broken glass, and took off at a dead sprint, mindless of the weight on her back or the bruises on her body.

The thin cop started to come after her. He didn't pursue her for more than five or so steps. After that, he was distracted by the pieces of glass that had just jammed themselves into his chest. Or, from a ghost's point of view, the glass that Carmen had just stabbed him with.

Both men stared down at the spreading red stains against the front of his blue uniform, spreading and soaking the stiff fabric, edging across his badge's gold. The Carmen-beast made a horrible sound, a croaking rattle that seemed like a laugh but drove a chill up Chelsea's spine. The thin man's jaw dropped to his chest when she twisted the glass, cutting wider gashes through fabric and skin. The glass was not embedded deeply in the wound, just enough to draw blood and cause pain. Poltergeists liked to have more fun with their victims, at least the human ones. Ghosts were less interesting. If she went for Chelsea, it might end far more quickly.

The thin cop screamed at the glass and fell back a few steps, barely keeping his feet underneath him. His partner watched in horror while more pieces floated off the ground to dart into his stomach, his collarbone, the side of his face, as Carmen picked up more and more pieces and jammed them into him.

"Carmen, stop it!" Chelsea screamed at the monster with its horrific grin as it scrambled for more and more shards, laughing at the screams coming from both cops now. "Cyndricka's safe now, you can stop!"

But the two humans made the mistake of running, heavy black shoes slapping against the pavement, the thin one dripping blood as he sprinted in the opposite direction from where Cyndricka had escaped. The poltergeist chuckled and gave chase, dropping down onto all fours with its long arms clawing into the ground to pull it forward with each big stride, leaping after the cops as they stumbled and skidded back towards the darkened park.

Cyndricka and Charlie were out of sight down the other end of the street, escaped into the night. With the two biggest threats off in the other direction, Chelsea had to assume that they were safe. She needed to follow Carmen. Carmen had come all this way with her to stop Chelsea from losing herself.

Now Chelsea had to return the favor.

33.

The poltergeist glowed slightly in the dark. It grabbed fresh handfuls of glass under each broken streetlight, along with fistfuls of rocks and gravel to fling at the fleeing officers of the law.

They screamed and ran, faces red and voices hoarse. The heavier cop had tears streaming down his face, though he had only a scattering of scratches across his back, spots of blood dotting his shirt. The ghost screamed in the night, a roar or a battle cry, and he barely avoided falling to his knees. His partner ran on unhindered, fully willing to leave the other man behind.

The heavy cop seemed to notice this, and suddenly they were not two men trying to outrun a monster they couldn't see, but two men trying to outrun each other. They pushed and clawed at one another, trying to push the other one back towards whatever was pursuing them. This slowed both, allowing the poltergeist to catch up, chucking more and more shards like throwing stars, some falling to the ground, others embedding deeply enough in their flesh to stand upright on their own.

Chelsea ran flat out, legs surging back and forth as she tried to keep up. A big piece caught the thin cop in the back of the thigh and he fell to his knees, chin scraping the pavement as he came down hard. His partner sprinted off and disappeared into the night.

That was all right. The poltergeist had a downed victim in its sights now. He rolled onto his back and drew his gun. The poltergeist laughed as it drew closer, reaching out one long-clawed hand to twist the barrel and yank it out of his grip, tossing it into the dark grass.

"Shhhuh—" the poltergeist rasped out around its long teeth as Chelsea caught up to the two of them, sprinting as fast as her shorter legs could take her. "Shhhuut meeee gan, huh? Gan, rhy heeere?"

Its clawed hands scrambled at the edges of the ripped dress, pulling it wide to expose the bleeding bullet holes, which gushed blood down her front as Chelsea had never seen them do before.

The cop crawled backwards, smearing a trail of blood behind him from his cut thigh. He blinked and shook his head, like he was seeing something in front of him but couldn't focus his eyes.

The poltergeist loomed over him and bent down. Intangible blood dripped from the wounds and disappeared in mid-air a few inches off of its body. It growled down into his terrified face.

"Gan? Do't gan? NO! Noh tuh meh, noh tuh hrrrr, noh tuh no-onn!"

The long, clawed hand reached out and scrambled over the ground. A long spike of metal, perhaps part of a fence at one point, rusted and jagged at the end, came to her hand from the long grass and she twirled it between her fingers, inches from the man's red and shaking face.

If Chelsea was going to do something, if Chelsea was going to stop Carmen from doing this, not for his sake but for hers, now was the time.

"Hey! Carmen!" she shouted. "Carmen Gutierrez! You— you—"

The poltergeist raised the spike over its head, clutched like a dagger, ready to plunge down and—

"You're missing the circus!"

The spike continued its backwards journey, still preparing to take the plunge, but as if in slow motion, with the poltergeist's hand trembling around the rust.

"Yeah, did you hear me?" Chelsea continued, hearing the hysteria taking over her voice, but still going. She came to a halt only a few feet behind the creature, the one thing that still had the capacity to destroy her completely and totally. "You're missing the circus! The, uh, the traveling cir—no, the amazing—"

The spike was held at the peak of its arc, the monster's arm held straight above her head, her shoulders tense and hunched and curled in like the monster it was. Chelsea set her own shoulders and screamed at the ghost, as loud as she could.

"You're missing The Incredible Traveling Triple-C Incorporeal Circus, and I won't let you walk away on closing night! Not when you're one of the goddamn stars! So just—just put the fucking spike down and GET READY FOR THE GODDAMN SHOW!"

As far as dramatic speeches went, it wasn't the strongest.

She ran around to the beast's front to see if anything had helped. And to put herself between utter destruction and a man who deserved every bit of it, but not from a woman who deserved to be better than this.

She looked up at the twisted face, at the hair pulled free of its braid, at the teeth distorting the image of one of the best friends she had ever had.

"Come on," she said firmly. "We have a show to put on . . . San Francisco won't know what hit it."

The spike hit the ground with a clatter. The cop stumbled to his feet and limped away as fast as he could.

He was a pincushion of glass and metal and rock, covered in blood from head to toe, and there was a good chance that he would bleed out before he found any help. Chelsea didn't care. She kept her eyes on the poltergeist. On Carmen.

The monster's—no, Carmen's hands came down on Chelsea's shoulders, gripping into her ghostly flesh over her collarbones. It hurt just as much as it had back in the haunted house, but Chelsea clenched her teeth and kept firm, looking up into Carmen's horrific face. The hands kept squeezing into her but did not move anywhere else as she leaned forward, braced against something that had not been solid for almost three years.

With a loud cracking sound, her jaw shifted and contorted, coming back into what looked roughly like an appropriate spot for a human. The long teeth, inch by inch, sank back into her gums. Chelsea could hear bones that were not really there cracking and rearranging as she morphed back into something recognizable. The process slowed, though, so Chelsea kept going as well as she knew how.

"Yeah, you, uh . . . you need to come up with the song selection for this performance. No one wants to hear any repeats, so go through any arias you know that you didn't do before. Do you know any arias? Can you sing for me right now?" The question technique was supposed to be for wailers, but it was worth a shot. A strange, warbling moan came out of Carmen as her arms snapped and shortened in a half-dozen places at once.

"Okay, okay, good, good. And I need more jokes. You need to help me come up with jokes because . . ." Her voice cracked for just a moment. "Because you know I'm shit at doing this all on my own. I need your help. We all do."

Carmen's knees gave out underneath her and she thumped down to the ground, leaving dents in the pavement. The claws in Chelsea's shoulders dragged down, tearing into her and almost bringing Chelsea down to her knees as well. Carmen looked up with eyes that were still full of fire. Chelsea pushed on.

"And both of us are gonna be in Cyndricka's new routine, okay? She said we can't complain at all. I'm gonna be a—a dog catcher and you're gonna be an actress who's kind of a diva with a big role to play in a new movie, and Charlie is going to have to chase after a ball when Cyndricka throws it to get her attention, and we need to make sure we have all our cues memorized before the show goes on, okay? We don't just need to watch art, we need to make it, okay?"

Carmen's back hunched over and she gasped with her empty lungs. Her figure was shrinking, getting smaller and smaller with each new image. Chelsea had to keep talking until she was all the way back.

"And Cyndricka and I were talking, it's not right to end the show here. We need to go all over the world. There have to be ghosts in London who want to see a great circus, or in Paris, Shanghai, I . . . I don't know, Dubai, Cape Town, anywhere, really. Anywhere there are dead and living people looking for some good entertainment. For some nice laughs. Anyone who needs a distraction from shitty things, just to make them smile, for even a second. Do you think the three of us can do that? Huh, Carmen? What d'you say . . . are you ready to get back on the road?"

The fibers of her dress stretched and reached across the bullet holes to weave themselves back together, like thin vines reaching out in the sun. Her hair flew around her head like ribbons caught in the wind, falling back into a dark braid and tying off to let it fall over her shoulder, just as always. The claws withdrew from Chelsea's flesh and dulled into rounded fingertips. She was there. She was put back together. She was their Carmen once more. She stayed on her knees and let her hands fall to her lap.

"Carmen?"

". . . They thought our neighbors were dealing drugs. Got the wrong address, burst right into the kitchen." She squeezed her dark eyes shut. "I had the radio on. I did not hear them coming. I—at least I was able to push my children out of the way. My beautiful son and daughter. Watching their mama getting killed by the police in her own home."

Chelsea knelt down and wrapped her arms around Carmen. The poltergeist claw marks hurt like hell. She didn't care. Carmen gasped and spoke from a million miles, and forty years, away.

"I am so, so jealous of you. Your love moved on, is able to be happy again. Manuel never did. My children grew up without a mother, because he never moved on. He just mourned me forever . . . obsessed, forever." She turned her face into the curve of Chelsea's shoulder. "I was so . . . so angry. At them. At him. At everyone. So I filled the days as well as I could, knowing that I was never more than a day away from losing myself. I even worked myself into it sometimes . . . Henry St. James never saw a scarier thing in his afterlife than that flash of poltergeist that I showed him . . ."

She held her forehead against and through Chelsea's chest. "When I saw them hurting Cyndricka . . . I care about her so much. I have never felt more whole since my death than I have during this trip. I have to thank you for that, Chelsea. You . . . you and Cyndricka . . . you are more than just distractions. More than ways to stop me from being bored. Please know that."

"I do," Chelsea whispered.

They stayed that way, clutching each other in the darkening park, alongside the stains of blood and the metal spike and above the dents in the pavement from a night that they would never forget.

At dawn they wandered out of the park and into the city just waking up for the morning, through the thin pink-tinged light that shot through their semi-transparent bodies and fell on the ground below them. Once more, both of them moved through the world without leaving a trace behind, through people and objects and animals without a care, two spirits with no more grounding to the physical world. They wrapped their arms around one another's shoulders and called out for Cyndricka as they wandered the streets, passing people trying to go about their days, unaware of the monster that had just inhabited their streets, but probably already very aware of the ones that patrolled them.

They found Cyndricka in a public library with all night hours, curled back behind a shelf in the reference section. Her coat was pulled tight around her to hide her bleeding and Charlie was still clutched to her chest, a trembling ball of fur just like the day they had found her. Cyndricka's eyes went wide when she saw Carmen. Carmen nodded slowly and sat down on the stained carpet next to her.

"I am sorry. That was . . . that is never what I wish to be. And I am sorry that you saw it. Are you seriously hurt?"

Cyndricka winced when she turned to look at Carmen more fully. She shook her head, not taking her eyes off her. Carmen chanced a small smile, tentative and fluttering at the edges.

"Would you like to know what Chelsea reminded me of, to put me back in my proper mind?"

Cyndricka raised her eyebrow and tilted her head in question.

"The thought of performing in the Triple-C Circus again."

. . . *Traveling Triple-C Circus*, Cyndricka corrected, signing around Charlie. Carmen nodded.

"My apologies. The Traveling Triple-C Incorporeal Circus."

The "traveling" part is the important bit.

"I agree . . . we should try to get out of town as soon as possible. Those men will remember what you look like."

Cyndricka's head jerked. *They're still . . . still alive?*

Carmen nodded, but Cyndricka still sought out Chelsea's gaze for confirmation. "Yeah," she said. "Carmen didn't . . . you know, go through with it. I can tell you about it on our way out of town."

Cyndricka hauled herself to her feet with stiff limbs, setting Charlie back to the floor so she could wrap her arms around her core. She hissed out through her teeth and had to catch her breath before she looked ready to even walk out of the building, much less across the state. *How many days do we have left?* she asked.

"Until?" Chelsea knew that she didn't need sleep, but she still felt so very, very tired after that night.

Until the wedding. Dummy.

"Oh. Um, fifteen. Just over two weeks."

Good. It may take me that whole time, in this state . . . if you two want to hurry ahead without me—

Looks from the two ghosts cut her off there, and she couldn't help but smile.

I just thought I would put it out there. But we are a performance troupe, and we do need to stay together.

Charlie meowed by her feet. Cyndricka grinned down at her.

Yeah, all of us. Come on, let's go.

34.

The Conservatory of Flowers was tucked away in Golden Gate Park, a little arc of domed white buildings holding a collection of plants from all over the world. The building had been booked for the day, though most of the action was spread out on the lawn in front of the conservatory, around carefully groomed flowerbeds and centered around the stairway down the hill where Osric and Tamika would take their vows. It was one of the loveliest sights Chelsea had ever seen in her life.

Familiar cars were parked along the crowded park roads, along with a few newer models with bumper stickers and windshield clings that she recognized. Grandma still drove that old sports car. Her cousin Eugene had traded in his sedan for a mini-van full of kids, and there appeared to be some older step-kids mixed in with the baby and toddlers.

It looked like her other cousin Paula, from her mom's side of the family, had finally come out of the closet, and walked away from her car holding her boyfriend's hand on one side, and her girlfriend's hand on the other. Osric and Tamika had not rented a limousine for the day, so Phoebe was bent over in her bridesmaid's dress, tying cans and a sign to the back of their normal old car's bumper.

It hurt more than Chelsea cared to admit to see Phoebe. She had been the family member she had seen the most since her death, the one who visited her grave on the most regular schedule. To think that she had been going to Chelsea's grave without Chelsea there for the past five months made her feel like she had let her sister down somehow, even if it didn't matter to Phoebe, who never knew she was there in the first place. It was all a matter of perspective, of course, but from Chelsea's, it felt like she had committed some betrayal against Phoebe.

Carmen's hand on her shoulder tingled and Cyndricka's hand slipping through hers gave her a surge of sparks and warmth. The Conservatory and lawn were tucked down in a lower area in between a few roads and paths, so Cyndricka had been able to find a vantage point where she wasn't intruding on the event. But while Chelsea's mind was on the topic of leaving people behind, she checked with her friends one more time.

"Are you sure you don't mind wandering the park while I'm here? You could probably stay closer and not be noticed."

I don't have an invitation, Cyndricka pointed out with a wry smile. *Only ghosts can gatecrash this wedding. And they probably don't want a cat in attendance.*

Charlie meowed, either agreeing or defending why she should be allowed to join. Tamika did enjoy fish a lot and it was bound to be on the reception menu, so perhaps the cat would have enjoyed the event. *And there are plenty of places in the park for me to go, to find some shade and take a nap.*

"And I want to give you some time without me hovering over your shoulder," Carmen added. She looked steadily into Chelsea's eyes, trying to convey some deeper meaning. Chelsea smirked.

"You came all this way to watch my back over this, and you're stepping off at the end?"

Carmen nodded. "I think you have proved how well you can keep hold of yourself over the course of this trip." She waved her hand with imperial levels of dignity. "You have my permission to attend on your own."

"Gee, thanks, ma'am."

Carmen slapped her in the head, Chelsea kicked her leg in response, and they both laughed. They hadn't talked much about that night in the park over the last two weeks, but Chelsea had noticed the difference, the way that Carmen had relaxed, changed, become warmer somehow. Chelsea stood up straighter after one last kick and nodded. She looked down at her tattered winter coat, which felt particularly out of place in the bright light of the

California afternoon. "I feel a little under-dressed. Winter clothes over business casual: not exactly wedding gear."

And you've been wearing it for almost three years, Cyndricka teased. *Don't you ever do your laundry?*

"Not in a lifetime." With that incredibly witty line, she turned to walk down the grass slope to her brother's wedding.

Then turned back three steps later to give her friends one more hug each. They responded as well as they could, and Chelsea appreciated it. She was going to need all the strength she could get to make her way through this, and she didn't mind borrowing a little if she had to.

Walking in with the stream of people coming in almost made her feel like a normal guest, filing through ribbons forming rough aisles for the Shu-Jeffers wedding. She could pick out relatives from the crowd, friends, friends of either family, people who looked enough like Tamika that she could connect the dots, and others that she had no idea about. Some local friends with dyed hair and androgynous dress contrasted with the older relatives in suits and dresses.

They all walked through her to trade hugs, cheek kisses, and handshakes. Not a large crowd, but full enough to make the wedding feel busy and inhabited. Many people carried boxes and bags in their arms as they approached the lawn, others had cards peeking out of the pockets of their fancy outfits, and all of them had some degree of smile on their faces as they made their way towards the union of two people who had been waiting a very long time to get there.

Ushers beckoned people down to the lower lawn, but she walked past them and approached the conservatory where the wedding party was milling about, adjusting bow ties and boutonnieres.

There he was. Her little brother. Her Osric. Looking more put together than usual, more groomed, better shaved, and dapper in his tuxedo. A light blue tie with little white polka dots suited him, kept his outfit from looking too stiff. He looked like a grown man, a groom, and her baby brother all at once. If she had still had working tear ducts, she would have found a way to cry. She clutched her good hand over her chest instead, taking in the sight, then left them to finish getting ready.

Soft music played while people made their way down to the seating area, and Osric stood near the stairway having whispered conversations with the rest of the wedding party. Both men and women were represented on both sides, with Phoebe among Osric's side and Tamika's brother Jeremy on hers. Osric leaned over to make some joke, going by the expression on his face, to one of his grooms-women. A lovely woman in a light blue dress, which only clashed a bit with her deep tan skin and chestnut hair. Chelsea still thought she looked absolutely stunning. Heather always did.

She wandered down to the back of the seating area, hoping to see some people before she settled in to watch the ceremony. She scanned the rows of the crowd to find the other person she was looking for. Carmen's words echoed in her mind as she searched, not knowing what she was hoping to see, or how she would feel when she saw it.

Roxanne was seated near the back, far behind the rows of family and close friends of the couple. Her green dress was well fitted and sweet, even if it did remind Chelsea a bit too much of scrubs. She held a program tightly in her hands, and when Chelsea floated close, she could see her painted nails digging into the cardstock, crinkling it and the raised black type on the page.

Her feet moved her through the aisles before she consciously realized what she was doing, phasing through distant relatives and other people's plus one's until she stood in the middle of a row, in front of Roxanne. She was looking out over the wedding, craning her neck to keep an eye on Heather up by the stairs. Chelsea spoke quietly when she talked, as if the moment deserved more decorum.

"I wish you two the best of luck."

Roxanne turned her program over in her hands again, reading and rereading the lists of names and songs.

"I don't really know you, but you seem nice . . . be good to her, or I will haunt the shit out of you. But if you make her happy, well . . . keep it up."

Roxanne kept turning and twisting in her seat. Chelsea smiled and shrugged.

"Yeah, I don't know what else to say. I don't know you that well. But . . . you know, good luck. To both of you."

Roxanne took a deep breath to steady herself and sat still, hands folded in her lap. It probably had absolutely nothing to do with Chelsea's words, but she was glad that she had said them anyway. She nodded before moving out of the row.

She proceeded down the center aisle, looking at all the happy, expectant faces. It had been a long time: there were probably some new people who had not been in Osric and Tamika's lives three years ago, and some people missing from the previous list, drifted apart or divided through conflict, or others who had not survived to see this second date.

But almost everyone there today had been waiting for almost three years for this wedding, and the joy of having it finally here was written on every face. Chelsea could feel herself grinning from ear to ear. She was smiling wide enough to distort the skin and flesh on her bad side, but she didn't care. She didn't even notice.

Their mother was openly crying already, big tears smearing her mascara and dripping into her lovely violet dress. Chelsea's father had his arm wrapped around her. He was misting up too, just doing a better job of hiding it. It was nice to see them crying for a good reason. When they were standing over her grave, there were never those big smiles mixed into their crying. Tamika's parents were sitting on their other side, keeping themselves together far better. Phoebe's on-again, off-again girlfriend Jeong-min sat in the row behind them and reached forward to pat Mrs. Shu's shoulder and pass her another packet of tissues.

Chelsea perched herself on the end of the row and smiled at her parents as she spoke.

"Hey, Mom. Hi, Dad . . . how crazy is it that Osric is the first of us to get married? Though he did just beat me to the punch by a bit." Her mother blew her nose, trying and failing to be delicate. Chelsea laughed. "God, if Phoebe ever gets married, you're gonna be an even bigger mess . . . I miss you guys."

Her mom's hand rested on her knee; she laid her own fingers lightly over it. Mrs. Shu's hand twitched, but she didn't pull it away. Chelsea continued. "I love you, Mom. And you, Dad. Sorry, I'd come over there, I just don't want to sit in Mr. Jeffers during his daughter's wedding, it seems rude. I'm just . . . I'm really happy that I can be here with you guys." She chuckled again. "And it was one long-ass trip. If I get to talk to you guys in fifty years or so, I'll tell you all about it. No hurry, though."

She stood up and looked down at the top of her mother's head, the elegantly arranged hair that was so different from her usual messy bun. And different still from the somber, simple braid she held it back in when she visited Chelsea's grave. Her father wore a suit, but a very different one from what he had worn during the funeral, a lighter shade of grey, a thinner cut that allowed for more fun in his formal appearance.

They looked happy. They looked so happy, and Chelsea was so happy for them. She leaned over and kissed the top of her mother's head. She bent in two, partially phasing through her mother, to kiss her father's cheek.

"I love you guys. Have a nice wedding." Her mother gave a mighty sniff and a watery smile. It was enough.

Chelsea walked the last few feet up to the stairway, looking at her friends and loved ones gathered there, looking out, as if they were focusing on her. She had come close to making this walk herself, so long ago. She stood still for a moment at the bottom of the steps, thinking about what it would have been like. What dress she would have worn, what flowers would have been in her bouquet, how Heather would have looked like standing up there before her. Or maybe she would have gotten up first, and Heather would have walked up to her. Or they would have walked up together. They would have been absolutely lovely together.

Heather was lovely, and she was standing where she would have been, but in a bridesmaid's dress, or grooms-maid, as it were. And Chelsea was in a winter coat, and she wasn't being looked at. Everyone was focusing on the flesh and blood woman arriving at the very end of the aisle, as the music started to crescendo and the crowd stood. Chelsea closed her eyes and listened to it, for just a moment, one brief moment in time to pretend that it was hers.

Then she opened them again, walked up the few steps, and turned outwards. She was supposed to be one of the grooms-maids after all. She was part of the wedding party, and nothing could take that away from her. She held her hands clasped in front of her, mimicking the other members of the wedding party holding their own small bouquets, light blue and white flowers amidst deep green leaves. She didn't have that. Her outfit didn't match anyone else's. But she felt as much a part of them as she possibly could.

Tamika looked gorgeous, walking down the aisle in her dress. They had done away with some wedding trappings, such as having her father walk her down the aisle; he was busy clapping his heart out from his seat in the front row. She and Osric had been together for so long by then that there was no pretense of anyone else giving her away to him, not that she would have appreciated that sort of thing anyway.

Her twisted, shiny black hair was held back and wrapped tightly in a bun, and a small veil was clipped to it, falling forward to cover her eyes. Her soft smirk was still visible underneath it, lips painted a deep red that accentuated the curve, and Chelsea could see Osric beaming like she was the most beautiful thing he had ever seen in his life. His eyes were watering; the Shu's were not a family of stoics by any stretch of the imagination. If she had been able, her face would have been streaming just as much as Phoebe's.

Tamika arrived at the stairway, light blue slippers peeking out from underneath her simple sheath dress as she stepped up. Her bouquet matched those of the wedding party, just bigger, and her accessories were the same tone, standing out against her deep brown skin.

She stood in front of Osric, and he couldn't seem to help reaching out to touch one of the long, beaded earrings hanging down past her hair. She smiled and touched his goofy polka dot tie. They both giggled quietly, and one could practically hear the whole audience cooing from up at the altar. The justice of the peace stood up and started to speak, and they managed to lower their hands to their sides and their flowers, respectively, but their eyes were still stuck firmly on each other, and everyone else's on the two of them.

It was a standard service, from the handful that Chelsea had ever been to. But none of them had ever caught at her heart like this one did, this long-delayed and much fought-for ceremony, that was both a simple formality for a relationship that had already been going on for over half a decade, and a beautiful culmination of everything that they had been through together, and everything that was still ahead of them. They were alive and they were together and they had each other, in the eyes of the law and of everyone. Her baby brother was all right.

A few songs, and a few small speeches from the justice of the peace, nothing huge or elaborate. The ceremony was a big enough deal in and of itself; they didn't need to force anything to make it special. The justice indicated that they had both written their own vows, and stepped back to let the happy couple take center stage. Tamika pulled out a set of cards that had been tucked inside her bouquet and cleared her throat. Then she pushed up her veil.

"Sorry, hon, I know you were supposed to lift it, but I can't read through this thing," she said with a laugh. Osric nodded and grinned.

"It's fine, it's fine. You could put it back down after, but some of the surprise might be lost."

"What did you think you were going to find under here?"

"I don't know, you do enough different stuff with your makeup, I didn't want to take away any wow factor."

"It's a transparent veil, you could already—you know what, stop distracting me, I'm supposed to be telling you how much I love you." She mock-glared at him, drawing a laugh out of the crowd. Osric shrugged to the audience, getting another laugh, and Phoebe stepped out of line to swat her brother's arm.

"Shut up and listen to your fiancée, dork."

Tamika shot a quick smile to Phoebe, then took a deep breath and looked down at her cards. "Osric. I wish I could say that I had loved you from the first day I met you. But I really can't. You and I took a long time to get to know one another, first as acquaintances, then as friends, then as someone that my friends badgered me into going on a date with, then as partners. It was never easy for us to come together. We were very different people when we met, and I don't think those two would even recognize the people we are today."

She glanced up and looked into Osric's eyes. Chelsea could see tears glistening around her mascara and eyeliner. "And I am so, so glad of that. Because if I was still that person, I would have missed out on knowing the absolute love of my life. And I know that the people we will be in another eight years probably won't be able to imagine how they were ever us now. But I'm going to spend those next eight years, and the eighty after that, growing and changing *with* you. And that is going to make it all okay."

Osric gave a laugh half-choked with tears. He held out one hand for hers, and Tamika took it and held on tight, looking into his eyes with her cards forgotten. "We've been through a lot and we are going to go through a lot more. But I always want you by my side and me by yours."

"Me too." It was whispered, probably involuntary, and only the wedding party was close enough to hear the agreement slip out of Osric's mouth. Phoebe wiped away tears, trying to hide it with the bouquet.

"I love you, Osric Shu," Tamika continued. "And I want to be with you for the rest of my life. So . . . yeah. That's it. I love you."

She squeezed his hand tight. Chelsea was briefly hit with a rush of jealousy at her being able to give physical reassurance of her feelings. It was something that Chelsea would have given anything for these last five months. These last three years, really. But the smile on Osric's face took away any thought she had of begrudging him this happiness. He wiped his eyes, glancing at the justice for confirmation.

"It's my turn? It just goes straight into mine after hers? Okay, give me a second. Jesus, Tam, just lay it on, why don't you?"

He took a few deep breaths. Heather passed forward a water bottle that had apparently been stashed for just this occurrence. Osric took a few gulps and rolled his eyes, speaking when his voice was less caught with emotion. "I know, I know, I'm a sap, just give me a second." He passed the bottle back to Heather, who stashed it back behind a vase of lilies, and turned back to his bride.

"Tamika . . . this day was supposed to have happened a long time ago. We should have already celebrated our second anniversary, and been well on our way to our third . . ."

In the audience, Mrs. Shu buried her face into a tissue, Mr. Shu's arm tight around her shoulders. Osric took a breath and continued.

"And this time has been tough, so very, very tough. When I lost my sister, I felt like my world was falling apart." Heather closed her eyes tight and nodded her head over her bouquet for a moment. Tamika grabbed Osric's hand and squeezed.

"But I . . . I always felt like I was going to make it through, as long as I had you," he continued. "But . . . but this marriage isn't going to be about me needing you. It's going to be about me wanting you, forever. You've been with me on my worst days, and I want the chance to show you my best, to share our best together. Because I always want to be the best for you. I love you, and I want to spend the rest of my life making sure that we see plenty of bests."

He looked down at the floor and laughed, a watery chuckle. He glanced back at the justice of the peace. "Can I kiss her now? Is that okay, or do I have to hold off for the end or—"

Tamika cut him off to wrap her arms around his neck and pull him into a kiss. The audience erupted in clapping and whooping, and Osric broke away enough to wave his arm at them wildly, while Tamika laughed and looked away.

"No, don't cheer yet, that wasn't the official one! That wasn't the husband and wife kiss, that was like a mid-wedding pause kiss!" He grinned back up at the justice. Chelsea could see a trace of Tamika's lipstick at the edge of his mouth. "Okay, sorry to interrupt, we can finish the rest of the thing—"

"The wedding?" Tamika provided, pulling off of him to rearrange her dress and raise an eyebrow, even through her wide, wide smile.

"Yeah, that thing, you know what I meant." He cleared his throat and shuffled awkwardly on his fancy shoes. "Sorry for the detour, just needed to do that."

The justice snorted and shook his head at the couple. All of the wedding party looked like they shared the sentiment, including Chelsea. Even on a big day, Osric was still the same guy.

The justice of the peace started into the formal part of the ceremony, the back and forth about sickness and health, richer and poorer, till death do they part. Tamika and Osric agreed along to each question put to them, binding themselves with one another for the rest of their natural lives. Because Chelsea was sure that they were going to last. She had absolutely no doubt in her mind that her brother had found the right person. It would have been a very long trip if she hadn't been so certain.

Heather was now the one to wipe her eyes, smearing a bit of mascara over her cheeks. Phoebe, standing next to her, gripped her hand on her shoulder. The two had never been the closest, always one degree removed. But it warmed Chelsea's heart to see them together, all of them, so many people that she cared about in one place, coming together to celebrate love and life.

"Do you, Osric Huyin Shu, take this woman to be your lawfully wedded wife, to have and to hold, as long as you both may live?" Osric nodded vigorously, not bothering to keep his voice composed for this one.

"I do."

The justice turned to Tamika, gripping her flowers tightly and nodding with each word out of the man's mouth. "And do you, Tamika Rhonda Jeffers, take this man to be your lawfully wedded husband, to have and to hold, as long as you both may live?"

"I do." She almost stepped on the final words in her eagerness to respond. She turned to Osric before the justice finished speaking.

"Then by the power vested in me by the state of California, I now pronounce you husband and wife. You may *now* kiss." The added emphasis got another chuckle out of the audience, before another round of cheering broke out to celebrate the coming together of the newlyweds, in a kiss and in life.

Even if no one heard it, Chelsea cheered the loudest, pumping her fist into the air and whooping for her little brother and his new wife, together at long, long, long last.

The two of them pulled apart and clasped their hands together, raising them above their heads for a moment of long-awaited triumph. The hired photographer dashed forward to get another picture, a great second image after the kiss. The two of them turned to walk up the stairs to the conservatory together, as husband and wife, Mr. and Ms. Jeffers-Shu. They proceeded, followed closely by their wedding party, beaming back and beckoning at their family members as they walked into their new life hand in hand.

Chelsea stayed standing on the staircase as Osric and Tamika, the rest of the wedding party, Phoebe, and Heather all walked away from her. The guests got up from their seats to follow, walking up to the conservatory building to congratulate the happy couple. The park was filled with loud voices, laughter, and cheering, but she whispered to them, a low murmur underneath all the noise of the living.

"Good luck."

35.

Less than an hour later, she walked through the trees of Golden Gate Park into the dimming evening. She had stayed behind to watch the pictures being taken, and to hear the congratulations being given to the happy couple, who couldn't keep their eyes or their lips off of each other.

But she felt no need to follow all of the wedding party and guests to the reception hall, to see all of the decorations and hear all of the toasts. She had come for the ceremony, the milestone of their life. The reception felt like something different already, the first in a new chapter of events that she was not part of.

If she went to that reception, she would be tempted to stay afterwards: to hang around as the party dispersed. To stay in the hotel with her family and lurk over breakfast the next morning, to follow them as they went about the rest of their trip to California. To haunt the family as they tried to peacefully celebrate the wedding of their brother and son. If she went to that reception, she would not be able to stop herself. The wedding had to be the last thing, and so it was.

She found Carmen and Cyndricka in a clearing with a bench and a couple of statues, buried in the forest. It was not a difficult task to find them in the growing lavender haze of evening.

She followed the sound of Carmen's voice, a low, warm song drifting through the paths of San Francisco as she sang in lilting Spanish, while unhearing tourists and runners made their way for the exits.

Chelsea came around a corner and saw them together: Carmen perched on the top of the bench, singing into the night sky, while

Cyndricka laid back and watched the stars, bobbing her head to the melody, Charlie curled in a ball on her chest. Carmen nodded when she saw Chelsea, but did not cut off the song, bringing it to a slow, crooning conclusion, like the end of a lullaby, before falling into silence. Cyndricka glanced over at the end of the song and smiled when she saw Chelsea.

How was it? she signed in the growing darkness. Charlie whimpered in her sleep at the disturbance of being moved. *Was it a good wedding?*

Chelsea nodded. "Yes. Yes, I . . . yeah, it was great."

Carmen watched her closely, her expression purposefully blank. "Are you okay?"

Chelsea nodded again, this time with a hint of a smile. "I think so. I, yeah, I am doing okay. Really good actually."

"That is good to hear . . . I expected you to be gone for most of the night. Did your brother and his new wife choose not to have a reception?"

"No, no, they should be there now," Chelsea said. She tried to gather her thoughts again before she spoke. "I decided not to go. I mean, it's their party, and I would just be lurking around, not really waiting for anything more and . . ."

She laughed and looked up at them guiltily. "Sorry I dragged you guys all this way for a couple hours of stuff. I just felt like . . . like it wasn't somewhere I needed to go. Does that make sense?"

Cyndricka nodded, though she looked a bit skeptical. Carmen, on the other hand, looked approving.

"What?" Chelsea asked.

"Nothing. I am just proud of you. That was a very mature decision to make."

She looked down and lightly kicked her high heel through a patch of grass. "Hey, I can be an adult sometimes. I did die at twenty-seven, you know, not eighteen."

"I know. But as I said, I am proud of you."

". . . Thanks." She came over to hover by the bench as well, looking out across the park. Couples and families strolled by together on the main gravel paths, though they gave their bench a wide berth. "It was a really lovely ceremony. Tamika looked beautiful, and Osric was just totally lovestruck. He's just as head over heels for her as he was three years ago."

"I hope they are able to make it last." She saw Carmen lightly touch the empty spot on her ring finger. "Being married can be a wonderful thing."

"I think it will be, for them."

And they are probably eating some great cake right now, Cyndricka pointed out with a smirk up at the sky. *Going there and stealing some is out of the question, right?*

"Right . . . I want to thank you two for all of this. You didn't need to come all this way, but—"

"But we're glad we did," Carmen said simply. Cyndricka nodded.

They sat in comfortable silence as the park emptied out. Cyndricka sighed and resettled herself on the bench. The sound of crickets took over the night, save for cars driving by on a nearby road. Chelsea found herself watching the stars, and Cyndricka needed to brush her hand through Chelsea's foot to get her attention.

"What, sorry? I was zoning out there, my bad."

I asked, what do you want to do next? Do you have anything else to do in California? Or are we just turning around and going straight back?

Carmen turned to watch her as well, leaning in to catch what she said. It was strange to feel like she had the final say in what happened to them just then.

"I don't . . . I'm not . . ." She paused and thought hard about what she wanted just then. Really, really hard. She'd had plenty of fleeting ideas on the road, things she wanted to see, tasks she still had to accomplish, people she wanted to see again when they passed back through the country.

Imelda and Jose were still back in Utah, but Cyndricka needed that more than she did. Jamie was in the city of wailers, but she had her own life going on and tasks that she was working to accomplish. Tyler and the rest of the ghosts in Cyndricka's circus were back in New York, but that seemed like it was from one hundred years ago. A different time, a different life, all within the span of her death.

What did she want?

Did she want anything?

Did she want?

"I'm not sure," she said. "I don't . . . I don't think I want anything right now. I . . . everything I wanted to do, I did. And I don't know if I need to do anything else."

The other two were silent, watching her. She shifted on her seat on the bench. She felt strange, light-headed, almost. But she kept talking, trying to work through what she was feeling just then.

"I mean, I saw them all. My mom and dad, my sister and brother, my old friends, Heather, everyone who was really important to me. And they're happy. And . . . and it hurts that they're able to be happy without me, it does, but at the same time, I don't want them to hurt anymore. That was always the hardest part, seeing everyone else that was hurt and I couldn't do anything about it . . . and time did it for me, so what else do I need to do? Aside from just . . . let them live their lives? Be happy with them being happy, and just let them live?" She ran both of her hands over her face just to have something to do.

"Chelsea," whispered Carmen.

"Is that wrong? Should I still be sad about it, or I guess sadder, or is it okay? It's not like I don't care about them. I just don't think I can do anything more for them. It's on them now, and it would just be better if I . . . ." She sighed and closed her eyes. "I just need to let them go."

She felt the touch of Carmen's hand on hers, but it felt different this time. Cooler and . . . and more distant somehow.

"Chelsea, open your eyes and look down, please. Please do that for me."

She did not question it, just automatically opened her eyes and looked at her lap, with the two hands resting in it. The two whole hands, connected to full, unbroken arms.

She held them up in front of her face, the digits suddenly healed after three years in the same state. "How—"

But beyond just being facsimiles of full flesh and bone, there was something else about her limbs. A faint glow that clung around the edges of her outline, a light, hazy gold sheen that stood out in the night. She looked at Carmen with her jaw dropped, imploring her for an answer.

"Carmen, what—"

"You're letting go," Carmen said simply, almost flatly. Her eyes were full of something that Chelsea could not begin to place, a potent mix of sadness, joy, and pain. "You are accepting, and as such, moving on. If you go with it . . . I have never witnessed the process, but it is my understanding that if you go with it now, you are done. Out. Gone. Moved on, from them and from life."

"I can't . . . this isn't happening." She felt numb and in shock at the same time, unable to dig through the haze that filled her brain. The gold sheen outlined her whole body, around the curves of her coat, her work suit, her high heels. She could even see a strand of gold-lined hair hanging down her forehead, still in that goddamn pixie cut. She looked back at Carmen. "Can I . . . can I stop it?"

"I believe so, if you want to. If you want to stay here instead." It was up to Chelsea and Chelsea alone.

She heard a sniff just below her. Cyndricka was sitting upright on the bench now, hugging Charlie to her chest and looking up at Chelsea through a coating of tears on her cheeks. Charlie batted at the hem of her glowing skirt, trying to figure out what was different about her already-strange friend. Chelsea met Cyndricka's gaze.

"I'm not going to leave you. I'll stay. I don't want to be one more person to abandon you." The thought of causing her friend any more pain in her life tugged at her heart.

But Cyndricka shook her head hard side to side, dreads flopping over her shoulders.

"What?" Chelsea asked, stunned. "What are you saying, Cyndricka?"

She set Charlie down on the bench before she began to sign, also taking a moment to swipe at her eyes. *You did not abandon me in N-Y-C. You did not abandon me on our trip. And you are not abandoning me here. If you want and need to go, please. Go. I'll be okay.*

"Cyndricka, I . . . I mean, there have been so many bad things on the road already, and how do you—"

There have always been bad things. Her smile was a twisted, wry one. *I think it's my life. But you brought me here, and I have seen so many good things too. I want to go and see more of them. But you don't need to. You can be done, if you want. I understand. It's okay.*

For the first time since she had died, Chelsea felt the sensation of tears on her face, liquid actually moving out of her eyes and down her cheeks.

She touched her fingertips to the smooth flesh that had once been lumpy and smashed. Her fingers came away wet, coated with a shining gold liquid. She looked at Carmen, who shrugged. This was new to all of them. If she went, she went in blind.

She bent down to get on Cyndricka's level. Cyndricka, the truly special person in all of this: special, but not alone. The woman's shoulders were shaking, but she was still smiling. But Chelsea still had to ask.

"Are you absolutely sure? Cyndricka, I can stay if you need me."

"I think I can promise her adequate support for the time being," said Carmen above her on the bench, with a bit of a tease in her voice. "I have done most of the heavy-lifting for protection so far, after all. I will keep her safe and well to the best of my abilities. I can promise you that, Chelsea."

Cyndricka nodded her agreement.

She felt another wave of coolness drift through her, like she was drifting off in the wind, even in the still and quiet night. She nodded, taking in the words. She looked up at Carmen. "And you? You're gonna be okay? You are not . . . you're not going to turn again?"

"I think I managed to get a great deal of that out of my system," she said with a sad little smile. "And I will be traveling with a constant source of entertainment, after all." Her voice dropped low and soft. "If you want to stay, Chelsea, you can stay. But do not feel like you have to for our sakes. You have done enough."

It's not like Curtains or I were going to leave N-Y-C on our own, Cyndricka pointed out. It brought a laugh out of Chelsea.

"I guess so." She felt thinner, somehow, less substantial, less present. Was this what moving on was going to feel like? Just fading away? Like a physical manifestation of being forgotten?

Cyndricka, silent and perceptive Cyndricka, who spent her whole life studying faces and ghosts, climbed off the bench and to her feet, to help.

"What are you doing?" Chelsea asked, and even her voice sounded far away.

You need to see my newest performance, before you go. Like . . . like a grand finale. She stood back and took a spot in the middle of the grass, but stood like she was on a Broadway stage. She closed her eyes, took a breath, and began to move.

It was their story. From the very beginning. With just herself and her own body, her face contorting and jumping as she switched between a dozen characters and even more locations, she told their story.

From humble beginnings, from a cop's bullets in Boston, to two graves in Reno, to a train in New York, the three main characters made their way across the country to meet in one big city, then back across the nation, as a unit now: a traveling circus. Chelsea leaned back on the bench to watch. Carmen sat next to her, resting her hand on top of Chelsea's. Charlie sat between them, for once content to watch her owner rather than jump in. This was Cyndricka's moment to tell their story, and tell it she did. On and on, for hours, she jumped and twisted and acted her heart out as the full dark of night set in and the moon rose.

A few people passed them in the park, gave her strange looks and scurried away, but for once, no one came in to bother or disturb her, the crazy woman apparently putting on a show for her cat. It was not a performance that could be understood by anyone else. No one else would have known what it meant when she dragged her hands over her face like she was melting, or when she pulled the collar of her shirt high to simulate being headless. They wouldn't have understood the importance of pretending to sit at a kitchen table, or petting a cat in a vet's office, or even just sipping a cup of coffee while still flicking rainwater off of her clothes.

But Carmen and Chelsea watched, and laughed, and cheered, and clapped as well as they could. And more and more, Chelsea's form was ringed with gold, a light that shone from the inside out and bright enough in spots to blur where she ended and where the light started. It was beautiful.

And, as all things are wont to do, the show eventually came to an end. A mimed wedding, a kiss, a walk up a staircase hand in hand with a partner, and Cyndricka was back in the park. But she was not playing herself. She was playing Chelsea.

For the whole performance, she had held her arm in a bend to indicate when she was Chelsea. Now it straightened out, but the expressions were still the same, the body language a perfect match. She touched imaginary tears on her face, looked into the dark sky, and ended the show. She looked at them, no longer in performance mode, and took a bow. Tears dripped off of her face, but she couldn't stop smiling.

"Thanks," said Chelsea. She could tell what was happening, knew what would occur the moment she let it, but she needed a few minutes more. Or perhaps just one.

"Thank you. Both of you. Carmen. Cyndricka. I love you." She looked at Cyndricka.

"Stay safe. If I see them, I'll say hello." Cyndricka smiled and nodded. Her tears were flowing freely again, and she made no attempt to stop them.

Only one word left to be said.

Her vision was already gone in a haze of gold, but she still knew she was around long enough for one last word, the one she had never had the chance to say before.

"Goodbye."

And she was gone.

Epilogue

Carmen smiled as the last trace of gold rose and floated off into the night sky. She had always heard about happenings like this, but she had never been able to imagine quite what they looked like. Neither a bang nor a whisper, she supposed, but a sigh. A breath being released after being held for too long, air that was no longer needed being let go back into the world. She probably would not have cried, even if she had the capacity. It was sad, yes, but ultimately the happiest thing she had ever witnessed.

She might find jealousy in herself later. Perhaps. But it was not her time to go yet. Chelsea had completed what she needed to complete and left no loose ends behind. Carmen had a heart still full of conflict and a living woman who still needed her. And she could exist like that, for the time being. She could, for lack of a better way to express it, live with that.

Cyndricka sat down next to her, on the other side of the bench from where Chelsea had just been and now would be no longer. The two women, separated by several decades, drastically different experiences, and a pulse, sat together as companions, a quiet vigil for the first of them to move on.

Cyndricka's hands moved after several minutes.

We'll need to come up with a new name. Double-C Circus doesn't have as good of a ring to it . . . makes it sound like it's about breasts or something.

"We have Charlie. We can still call it the Triple-C Incorporeal Circus. Or we could set about recruiting with some very strict prerequisites."

Or they could have a stage name.

"That too." They fell back into silence and stillness. Charlie curled into a ball on Cyndricka's lap and fell asleep, an animal unburdened by the vastness of her own mortality, content simply to exist and seek pleasure where she could.

Do they talk about where you go when you move on? The other ghosts? I have never heard it discussed, but I didn't know if it was rude to bring up.

"Well, it is a difficult subject. And no one who is still around has any evidence or first-hand knowledge for their claims, obviously. Many hang on to what they believed when they were alive, be it heaven and hell or nirvana or simple nothingness. Others think they are still present, just separated by one more level of reality, unable to be seen by humans or ghosts."

What do you think?

". . . I think that it is a positive state to be in, no matter what the specifics are. And I believe that Chelsea is happy. That is all that really matters, in the end."

I guess so.

The thin sliver of the moon traveled overhead for hours, marking the passage of one more night, one more time to be present and exist in the world for both of them. Cyndricka laid down flat on the bench, her head resting through Carmen's lap. She readjusted Charlie on top of her, and Carmen thought she fell asleep shortly after that. But long after her breathing had gone steady, she raised her hands to sign. She kept her eyes closed, confident that Carmen would speak in words that she could hear: that Carmen was still there.

So I guess I'll ask you. Where are we going next?

Carmen chuckled softly and ran her ghostly hand over Cyndricka's hair.

"On to the next adventure."

‎👣 ‼ 👣

Acknowledgements

This whole journey has been a long time coming, and I would like to take a moment to thank everyone who has helped me along the way. I would like to thank Tanya Oemig, Camille Gooderham Campbell, and Cat Rambo for taking the rough lump I wrote and guiding it into something that I am proud to present. Thanks also to the proofreaders, Maria Judge, Rita Beth Ebert, and Stephanie Hayan. And I am so glad to have Estee Chan's wonderful cover to present this book in. My thanks and gratitude to Emily Bell, Chris Bell, and all of Atthis Arts, for reaching out to me before I had ever considered publishing *Triple-C* and giving me both the chance and the support I needed to get moving.

I would like to thank everyone in the forums of National Novel Writing Month. The original draft of *Triple-C* was written in a mad rush during November 2014, and I want to thank that incredibly supportive community for lighting a fire under me to get it done.

Thank you to everyone at Kinetic Arts Center, the circus theater in Oakland that has served as my home base in California. You all are wonderful and I am glad to have been able to work at an actual circus while editing this book, even if it wasn't a traveling one.

Emily Juneau, I will forever owe you for not only helping out as a beta, but for being my best friend for over ten years and getting me through a lot of hard times. We were roommates during the very rough period of my life when I was writing the first draft of this book, and I know I would not be in the good place I am in now without your friendship and love back then.

To Mom, Dad, and my brother Devron, I send you guys all my thanks and my love, for being some of my best friends and my biggest cheerleaders along the way. I love you all. Dev, you will always be my favorite crappy little green bean.

Andrea Klassen, let me start with the easy one: thank you for beta editing my draft. And thank you for being the love of my life. And thank you for agreeing to marry me. I cannot imagine how different my life would be without you in it, but I know that this book wouldn't exist as it does now. You have loved me through my lowest moments and cheered me on through my highest, and I always want to do the same for you. Here's to us taking on the world as a writing power couple.

And a big thanks to everyone who has helped me out along the way, in big and small ways, to bring this traveling circus to life. Thank you all and I hope to see you again down the road.

About the Author

Alanna McFall is a novelist, short-story writer, and playwright. Originally from Minnesota, she lived in a number of places on either coast before landing in the Bay Area, where she is a resident playwright with PlayGround San Francisco. Alanna is the 2019 winner of the June Anne Baker Prize for female playwrights representing a gifted new comedic or political voice. When not writing, she is a theater administrator, cross-stitcher, and podcast nerd. Follow her work and upcoming projects at alannamcfall.com. *The Traveling Triple-C Incorporeal Circus* is her first novel.

CPSIA information can be obtained
at www.ICGtesting.com
Printed in the USA
LVHW091520210719
624773LV00004B/413/P